THE A

Donald E. Westlake w
raised in Albany, New
many novels, including six John Dortmunder
adventures. Under the pseudonym of Richard
Stark he is the author of the Parker thrillers, many
of which have been filmed.

THE
DONALD WESTLAKE
OMNIBUS

a&b

This edition
first published in Great Britain in 1995 by
Allison & Busby
an imprint of Wilson & Day Ltd
179 King's Cross Road
London WC1X 9BZ

361 © 1962 by Donald E. Westlake
Killy © 1963 Donald E. Westlake

A catalogue record for this book is available from the British Library.

ISBN 0 74900 226 3

Typeset by TW Typesetting, Plymouth, Devon
Printed and bound in Great Britain by
Redwood Books, Trowbridge, Wiltshire.

361

To Fred and Joanne and Nedra

.361 (Destruction of life; violent death.) Killing.
Roget's Thesaurus of Words and Phrases

1

I got off the plane at Maguire, and sent a telegram to my dad from the terminal before they loaded us into buses. Two days later, the Air Force made me a civilian, and I walked toward the gate in my own clothes, a suitcase in each hand.

I was a mess. A twenty-three-year-old bum with mixed-up German and English in his head, two suitcases full of garbage, no plans. It felt fine.

I was at Manhattan Beach Air Force Station. That's in Brooklyn, southeast end, not far from Coney Island. Farther than hell from Manhattan.

I went through the gate and the snowtops didn't look twice, and then I wasn't in Manhattan Beach Air Force Station any more, I was on Oriental Avenue. Ahead to my left there was an asphalt oval by a field, where the buses turned around. There was a bus standing there, green. I went over and got aboard and asked the driver to let me off by a subway stop, I wanted to go to Manhattan. He said he would, and I sat in the sideways seat right behind him.

There were two airman thirds aboard, toward the back, and a Negro nurse, that's all. Then another guy with two suitcases came on, and he and I kind of avoided looking at one another. I'd never seen him before, but he was another new civvy. We acted like we'd both just been circumcised, and if we talked to each other everybody would know.

It was a Tuesday afternoon, and July hot. It was only the twelfth, and my discharge date wasn't till the twenty-third, but the Air Force just gets you back the right month and lets it go at that. Outside, the blacktop was baking. You could see footprints, and in the distance there were rising shimmers. Car chrome gleamed for miles. The field between the bus and the Atlantic Ocean looked like dry brown hair.

After a while, the driver put his *News* away and started the bus. He swung the rest of the way around the oval, his arms moving as he turned the wheel, and his grey shirt was black with perspiration in circles below his shoulders. When he straightened the bus out and headed into the shimmer, a small breeze came in the open part of the window beside his elbow.

At one stop, he said, 'There's your subway, over there,' and pointed at steps going up to an el.

I thanked him, and toted the suitcases off. He called, 'Good luck, soldier.'

I smiled, but I didn't like him. I wasn't a soldier, I was an airman. On that route, by the base and all, he ought to know better.

The hell with it, I wasn't even an airman any more. I was a civilian now. I'd forgotten.

It was the Brighton Beach stop of the Brighton Beach Line. Coney Island was three stops to the left, end of the line. Manhattan was forever to the right. By the time I got the suitcases up the stairs, I was tired. I got two tokens, just in case, and went out on the platform.

There were some kids on the train, maybe fourteen years old, writing on the posters and screaming about it. I kept looking out the window, down at the neighbourhoods. After a while it was all crummy residential – stone buildings, four and five storeys, lots of windows, baby carriages and old kitchen chairs and Baby Ruth wrappers on the sidewalk. Then it went down into an open trench, and there wasn't anything to see. The kids got off at a stop called Newkirk. Then a little later it went underground all the way, and I read the ads above the windows. There was one I couldn't believe: a drawing of a hand with spread fingers, and surprinted over that in green block letters BELCH. Underneath, it said something was three times faster with stomach gas.

The train went over the Manhattan Bridge, with cars and trucks along a roadway right beside us. I felt like in a picture in a kid's geography book, and there'd be a DC-3 flying overhead and a tugboat underneath the bridge, and down at the bottom there'd be three lines of talk about transportation.

2

On the other side, it went underground again, and I took out the paper with the address Bill's wife had given me. I'd thought Bill was coming into town to get me but, when I called to check, his wife told me no, Bill was up at Plattsburg on a fleet sale deal with some trucking company, so Dad was coming down. She gave me the address of the hotel.

That was yesterday I'd called. It felt funny talking to her. My brother's wife. I'd never even met her. He'd met her himself six months after I got sent to Germany, and they got married eight months later. They were almost two years married now, and I'd never even met her.

Three years was a hell of a long time. I knew that now, in my bones.

Her name was Ann.

The paper said the hotel was at the corner of Lexington Avenue and East 52nd Street. The Weatherton. I got up and looked at the map down at the other end of the car. There was a Lexington Avenue Line, and it made a stop at 51st Street. That looked like the one.

I traced things out with my finger, figuring out where I was. I should change at Union Square for the Lexington Avenue Line.

It was the second stop after the bridge. I wandered around, looking at signs, carrying the suitcases, people bumping me. Then I saw a sign that pointed the way out, and I took it. The hell with it. Upstairs on the street, in the sun again, I waved at a cab and told him, 'Lexington Avenue and East 52nd Street.'

It was seventy-five cents on the meter. I gave him a dollar, and a bellhop took my suitcases in. There was a green awning out over the sidewalk, and a doorman in green and gold.

I told the guy at the desk that I'd come to join my father, Willard Kelly, Sr. Two bellboys and half a dollar later I was at the door of his room. 'I'll knock,' I told bellboy number two. 'This is a reunion.'

'Yes, sir.' He pocketed the quarter and went away.

I knocked on the door, and Dad opened it. He grinned at me and said, 'Ray. You son of a gun.'

I grinned back till my cheeks hurt. I went into the room, with

3

the suitcases on the ends of my arms, and he punched my shoulder and said, 'You wrote you were gonna make Staff Sergeant. How come? You goofed up?'

I'd made Airman First with minimum time-in-grade all the way. There'd been time left on the enlistment for me to make Staff. Only I'd made it clear I wouldn't re-enlist. There's no sense wasting a rocker on a short timer. 'I made civilian instead,' I said.

'By God, Ray,' he said, 'you look great. You're taller, aren't you?'

'I don't think so. Wider, maybe.'

'My God, yes. Look at the shoulders on the kid. Listen, wait till you see Betsy, five months old now.' He grinned some more. 'How's it feel, to be an uncle?'

'I don't know yet. I talked to Ann yesterday, on the phone. She sounded okay.'

'She's a good girl. Bill's settled down, she's good for him.' Then he shook his head and blinked, and came over to wrap his arms around me and pat the back of my head with his palm. 'My God, boy,' he said, and his voice broke. I'd been trying to keep it in, but then I couldn't. We cried like a couple of women, and kept punching each other to prove we were men.

Then I wanted to go out for lunch and a beer, and Dad acted reluctant about it. He didn't want to leave the room. He looked okay, so I figured he was just tired from the driving, and the heat. The heat was bad, and the room was air-conditioned.

We ate at a place, and then Dad wanted to go right back to the hotel. I wanted to wander around a little and look at things, but it was three years, so I went back with him. But I kept looking around on the way back. I was born in New York, but Dad and Mum moved out when I wasn't even a year old yet. I didn't remember a thing about the city. Or much about Mum. She died when I was two.

In the afternoon, we sat around the room in our undershirts, with the air-conditioner on. There were two wide beds, wider than singles but not as wide as doubles. I sprawled all over one of them, head propped up by a couple of pillows. Dad wandered around the room, picking up ash trays and glasses and phone

4

books and then putting them down again. I didn't remember him so nervous.

Otherwise, he was the same. It didn't occur to me he should look different. It was as though three years hadn't happened at all. He was a guy, maybe fifty, with red-grey hair and a middle-aged paunch and plastic-framed glasses with old-fashioned round lenses. Same as always. I wore T-shirts, but he still wore the old kind, thin knit undershirts with just narrow shoulder straps, leaving the upper arms and shoulders bare. He had thick meaty shoulders, stooped a little, freckled.

We spent the afternoon filling me in. My big brother Bill was twenty-six now. He had a wife and a kid, and he was working for Carmine Truck Sales, and he got his driver's licence back over a year ago. Uncle Henry was the same as ever. Like everybody, the same as ever.

When we went out for dinner, Dad wanted to go right back to the room again – talked about getting a good night's sleep for the drive tomorrow – but I said, 'Look, it's only seven-thirty. Come on, Dad, this is my only chance to look at this place. We'll get back to the room by midnight, I promise.'

So he shrugged and said okay, and we looked at Times Square and some other places, and I was disappointed. I'd expected something unique. Like Munich, that was unique. When I first got there, I looked at it, and I'd never seen anything that looked like that. But New York was just Binghamton bigger, like a little photograph put through an enlarger. It's all bigger, and you can see the grain and the bad spots better.

We got back to the hotel before midnight, and the next morning we checked out before nine. The breakfast eggs stayed with me, their taste, and made cigarettes taste awful.

Somebody brought the car around from the hotel's garage. It was an Oldsmobile. Dad always bought Oldsmobiles. But I'd never seen this one before. It was last year's, black. When I'd been shipped to Germany, he had a two-tone blue.

The suitcases were loaded into the trunk, and Dad took care of the tipping. Then we got in, and pulled away, heading west crosstown on 53rd Street.

I started to roll the window down, and Dad said, 'No, leave it up. Watch this.'

I watched. He pressed a button on the dash, and I heard a whirring. Then a little chill breeze hit me in the forehead from a vent just above the door.

'Air-conditioner,' Dad said. 'Three hundred dollars extra, and worth every penny of it. Changes the air in the car completely every minute.'

'Lawyering does pretty good,' I said.

'Chased a lot of ambulances lately,' he said. He grinned at me, and slapped my knee. I grinned back. I felt good, to be in the states, to be with my father, to be a civilian. Great.

We went up the Henry Hudson Parkway and over the George Washington Bridge. We took the lower level and Dad said, 'This is new.'

'This part of the bridge? It looks nutty.'

We went up 9 to 17, and then west on 17 toward Binghamton.

Thirty-eight miles outside New York City, when we had the road to ourselves, a tan-and-cream Chrysler pulled up next to us, and the guy on our side stuck his hand out with a gun in it and started shooting.

Dad looked at me, and his eyes were huge and terrified. He opened his mouth and said, 'Cap,' in a high strange voice. Then blood gushed out of his mouth, like red vomit.

He fell staring in my lap, and the car swung off the road into a bridge support.

2

I remember being moved. The doctor said that was impossible, it was a false memory, but I remember it. And a guy saying, 'Look at the leg.'

Then there was a long grey time, and then a time when I knew I was in a hospital bed, but I didn't care. Nurse rustlings, glass clinkings, paper cracklings, they all happened far away in some other world. The same with movement, white against white, people passing the foot of the bed.

Then I realized I wasn't seeing with my right eye. All the layers of fuzzy white were in a plane, I didn't have any depth perspective. When I closed just the left eye, it went away.

I made a sound, and it was awful. Then there was hurried rustling, and a balloon of flesh hung over me, with smudgy eyes. A woman's voice asked, 'Are we awake?'

I didn't say anything. I was afraid to make that sound again. I blinked my left eye. I told my right eye to blink, but the message got lost someplace. I couldn't feel anything around there at all.

The balloon went away. When it came back with a doctor, I was in better shape. Every time I blinked, the left eye worked better. I could make out the wall, and the iron tubing of the foot of the bed, and the high right angle of the door frame. The balloon came in, being a nurse, and then the doctor.

I was just reaching my hand up, slowly, to find out what was wrong with my right eye. The doctor shoved it down under the sheet again. 'Now, now,' he said. 'None of that. Let's not overwork.'

'Eye,' I said. Then I thought he might misunderstand, might think I was talking about me, so I said, 'See.' I was going through the alphabet.

'We'll get to that,' he said. 'How do you feel?'

'See,' I said.

7

'We don't know yet. Are you in pain?'

I was. I hadn't noticed till then, and all of a sudden I noticed. My legs hurt, like fury. Down by the ankles, and spreading up to above the knees. And the right side of my head, a dull ache like ocean waves.

'We'll give you something,' he said.

I guess he did. I went back to sleep.

Every time I woke up, it was a little better. I woke up, went to sleep, five or six times, and then one time Bill came in. They wouldn't let me sit up yet, and I felt like a little kid again, lying flat in the bed, my big brother standing there grinning at me. 'They make us tough, Ray,' he said.

I said, 'Dad?'

He stopped grinning, shook his head. 'Shot,' he said.

But I knew it already. I could still see him, falling sideways toward me, his eyes painted pieces of plaster. He was dead then, before the car even left the road.

'How long've I been here?'

'A month. Five weeks tomorrow.'

'This is August?'

'Tuesday, the sixteenth.' His grin was a little weaker this time. 'You had a rough time, boy. They didn't know if you'd live.'

'Listen,' I said. 'They won't tell me. My eye, the right eye. It's all bandaged.'

He went away, diagonally across the room to a chair with a green back. He brought it over, sat in it beside the bed. Our heads were on the same level. I was getting used to figuring out perspective with only the left eye. Two, three days before, he would have just gotten smaller, and then bigger again. Now, I could think of him going away and coming back.

Three years had changed him. His red hair was bushier, his face paler and the freckles fading, his cheeks jowlier. He looked tougher and more sober. He looked more reliable.

He said, 'They said I could tell you if you asked, but not otherwise. And only if I thought you could take it.'

'It's gone?'

He nodded. 'You went through the windshield. A piece of glass.'

'Good Jesus.' I lay there and thought about it. I was missing an eye, for ever. Never again that eye, never again.

I'd always have to fake perspective.

It might have been both of them. Hell, it might have been the life. I was still around, I could still see.

What the hell did I look like these days?

I asked him. He said, 'Like a turkey's ass, plucked. But better every day. The doctor says you won't have any scars that show. And I've already talked to a guy about a glass eye. He'll fit you for it the minute the doctor says okay.'

'Jesus . . . The feet? They hurt like hell.' I knew they were still there. One time, I'd got my right hand up behind my head – that was before I could move the left hand too well – and pushed my head up so I could look down my length, and the feet were still there. I'd been worried about amputation. I'd heard of people whose legs hurt after they'd been cut off and they didn't have any legs any more. Mine hurt, and I couldn't move them, so I was worried they were gone. But they were there, fat tubular bulges under the sheet, encased in bandaging.

'Your ankles were broken,' Bill said. 'Crushed between the car and the bridge support. They've been doing bone grafts on you.'

'And I'll be okay?'

'Sure.' He grinned one-sided at me. 'You'll live to play the piano again,' he told me. 'With your feet, like always.'

Then I asked him for a cigarette and he said no. So I got one from the cop who came in that evening. His name was Kirk, and he was State Police, CID, in civvies. He had me tell the story, and there wasn't that much to tell. I hadn't recognized either of the men in the Chrysler. I didn't know what 'Cap' meant. I didn't know why two strangers would shoot my father.

When he left, Miss Benson, the thin one, grabbed the cigarette out of my mouth.

Bill came by every day, for about a week. Then one day he didn't come around. I asked Miss Benson. She said, 'He had to go back to Binghamton.'

'Why?'

She got evasive, and I kept asking her. So she told me, and

wouldn't look me in the eye. 'I'm sorry, Mr Kelly. His wife was hit by a car. She was killed.'

'Oh,' I said. 'I never met her.'

3

When I got out of the hospital, three days after Labour Day, I had two eyes, one of them working. With that one, I saw the guy get out of the Plymouth across the street from the hospital and come walking towards me. I slowed down, feeling naked. I still remembered the one who stuck his hand out the side window with a gun in it.

This one was different. Medium height, thin. He'd lost weight recently, and hadn't been able to afford a new wardrobe. His jacket hung on him like a style that had never caught on. His hair was sandy; his scalp was probably sand. His face was sharp of nose and chin and eye and bone, but there was weak pulp behind it, peeking through.

He stopped in front of me, looking at the tie Miss Benson had picked out. She'd had to buy me some clothes. My two suitcases got burned in the car. I'd given her the money, some that Bill had sent me.

He acted as though he wanted to talk to me, but was afraid somebody might notice. I said, 'Okay,' and sidestepped him and walked across the street to the Plymouth. I might have been afraid of him, but he was afraid of me. He came trotting after me, on shorter legs. I could hear him breathing.

I went around the Plymouth and got in the right side. He slid in behind the wheel, next to me. He looked very worried. He got out a pack of Philip Morris Commanders. On him, they were wishful thinking. He pawed one out with two fingers and thumb, and I took the pack away and got one for myself. We lit up in a leaden silence, with him trying to watch the whole outside world at once, and then, jerkily, he said, 'I owe your old man a favour. I come to do it.'

'What sort of favour?'

'A long time back. It don't make no difference now. You're his son. I just want to tell you, you ought to go away. Change your name, clear out for good. Go someplace out west, maybe. But don't go to New York.'

'Why not?'

He lipped his cigarette, made it look terrible. His eyes jerked around in their sockets like ball bearings. At last, he said, 'There's gonna be trouble. You don't want to get mixed in.'

'What kind of trouble?'

'That's the favour,' he said quickly. 'Even-Stephen. If they saw me talkin' to you, they'd gun me. I've done enough, maybe too much.'

'If *who* saw you? The men who killed my father?'

'Go away.' He was getting more and more jittery by the second. 'Interview's over, favour's done. Go away. Get outa the car.'

I laid my left arm across his chest, holding him against the seat. My right hand patted him, didn't find anything that felt like a weapon. He was breathing hard, and looking all over the street like he expected tanks to show up any minute, but he didn't say anything.

I kept my left arm where it was, and thumbed the glove compartment. The door dropped down, and I took out the gun. I don't know guns, this was I guess a .32 calibre. It was a revolver, and stubby-barrelled, all blue-black metal with a plain grip. The drum had places for six bullets. Two showed thin edges on each side, and those four had cartridges in them. I didn't know about the one in line with the barrel or the one underneath. Just above where my thumb naturally rested there was a little catch. It pointed at S. I pushed it to O with my thumb, felt it click.

I took my left arm back, and half-turned in the seat, so I could face him and hold the gun in my lap aimed at him. He gave me a flying millisecond glance, eyed the street some more, and said, 'I come to do a favour, that's all. Nothing else, nothing more. All bets are off. I don't say a word, you might's well get out of the car.'

'Start the engine,' I said.

He couldn't believe it. He wanted to know where I thought I was taking him.

12

'Home,' I told him. 'Binghamton's about a hundred thirty miles down 17. Drive.'

'I won't do it,' he said.

'Self-defence,' I told him. 'I wrestled the gun out of your hands. You were one of the men shot my father.'

He stared at me. But he picked my right eye to stare at, the glass one. He shivered and started the car.

It was a long ride. We didn't talk much, and the highway looked too familiar. It was the same kind of situation, me in the same seat in the car. I kept looking back, and whenever a car passed us I winced, but nothing happened.

We made it in under four hours. We crossed the river on the first bridge, bypassing most of the town, but it was a little after four and rush-hour. It was slow going out to Vestal.

They built it up a lot in three years. The Penn-Can highway was going to bring civilization to the hometown after all. There were even split-level developments now, and ranch-style houses.

Bill lived in a ranch-style out on 26. There was nobody home when we got there, but the garage door was up and the car was out. I had the guy pull the Plymouth into the garage. We got out, and I switched the gun to my left hand again while he pulled the overhead door down. I'd been changing the gun back and forth from hand to hand about every half hour, when the fingers would start to cramp.

The door in the wall between the kitchen and the garage was also open, and the house was full of mosquitoes. The sink was full of dishes. The living-room floor was scattered with beer bottles and newspapers. Both were delivered, I guess. The beer bottles were twelve-ounce stubbies, the little fat ones you never see any-where but at clambakes and sandlot ball games. There were two cases of them out in the garage and maybe a dozen cold in the refrigerator. That was practically all there was in the refrigerator.

The mosquitoes had the house to themselves. There were two bedrooms, and they were both empty. One had a crib and a white dresser and pink walls. The dresser drawers were open, empty. But Bill's clothes were all over the other bedroom and the closet, so he hadn't moved out. He was just boarding his kid with somebody, that's all. Probably Aunt Agatha.

We sat in the dinette and drank Bill's beer, and played gin with a deck of Bill's cards. The blue-black revolver looked strange on the rose-mottled formica of the table. The guy lost consistently. He couldn't keep his mind on the game. Every once in a while, he'd talk to me about letting him go. But he didn't really think he could convince me.

The backyard, just outside the dinette window, gradually became night. In the other direction, through the archway, was the living room and the picture window. It was night out that way, too, with a streetlight off a ways to the side and amber light from the picture window across the way.

Bill came home after ten. By the way he drove, he was drunk. When he was in high school, he owned a Pontiac with no back seat and a Mercury engine, and he shoved it around tracks in stock races. Most of the time he was drunk, and half the time he rode in the money. Sober, he was a good hard driver. Drunk, he shaved his corners.

He came in wide-eyed, blue basketball jacket crooked over T-shirt. He looked at me and shook his head and leaned back against the kitchen wall. 'Don't do that,' he said. His voice trembled. 'Jesus, don't do that. I thought it was Ann.' He held a quaking hand to his chest.

It hadn't even occurred to me. Who but his wife would be waiting home for him, the lights on? I got up, remembering the gun just in time, and said, 'I didn't think, Bill.'

'Jesus,' he said. He shook his head and licked his lips. He pushed off from the wall and opened the refrigerator door, and dropped the bottle he grabbed for. He shut the door and fumbled for the bottle.

I thought he was going to fall over. I waved the gun at my gin-partner. 'Go open it for him,' I said.

He did it. Bill watched him, frowning. He took the bottle and drank from it, and then he said to me, 'Who is this?' He waved the bottle at the guy the way I'd waved the gun.

'He met me outside the hospital,' I said. I told the story, finishing, 'And he won't say any more than that.'

'Oh, he won't.' Bill put the bottle in his left hand, and hit the guy in the mouth.

14

I'd never seen that before, a man knocked out with one punch. The guy just fell down like his strings were cut.

I said, 'That's bright. He'll talk a lot better in that condition.'

'I didn't mean to hit him that hard.' He gulped the beer again, put the bottle on the drainboard, filled a glass with water.

'No,' I said. I put the gun on top of the refrigerator, knelt beside the guy, slapped him awake. Over my shoulder, I said, 'Make yourself some coffee. You're supposed to be three years older than me.'

'I'm sorry,' he said. 'I'm sorry, Ray. I've been feeling sorry for myself.'

'For how long?'

'I know. Two weeks ago today. Ann.' He was on the verge of a crying jag.

'Make coffee,' I said. 'Three cups.'

The guy on the floor twisted his head away from my slap. 'Cut it out,' he whined. 'Cut it out.'

'Get on your feet,' I told him. 'He won't hit you again.'

He didn't believe me, but he got up, shakily. Bill was watching the water not boil. I said to him, 'When you're sensible, come into the living room. Bring coffee with you.' I reached down the gun from the refrigerator.

Bill said, 'I'm sorry, Ray. Jesus God, I'm sorry.'

'If you start crying,' I told him, 'I'll walk out and the hell with you.' I prodded the guy into the living room. We turned on lights and sat looking across the street, where the picture window framed a happy family watching television, just like the ads in the *Saturday Evening Post*. It looked so normal I wanted to cry. Give me back my three years, Air Force. Four years, counting the year before they sent me to Germany. Give it back, I want to be home again, with Dad sometimes good for a game of catch, with Bill a big brother smelling of beer and Pontiac. I don't want to be twenty-three, without a home or an old man. I don't want a brother who's grieving for a wife I never even met. That makes us strangers.

I said to the guy, 'What's your name?'

'Smitty.'

'Crap.'

'Honest to God. I got a library card to prove it.'

That I wanted to see. Not to check the name, but because I wanted to see a library card that this guy would carry.

He showed it to me, and it was a Brooklyn library card. Typewritten, it said: Chester P. Smith, 653 East 99th St Local 36 Apt 2. Then there was a signature that might have been Chester P. Smith and might also have been Napoleon Bonaparte.

So he had a library card. In the same wallet he had forty-three dollars. But no driver's licence, and I'd just been a hundred and thirty miles in a car with him. 'I'll call you Smitty,' I said, tossing the wallet back, 'but I bet Chester P. got mad when he had to go after a new card.'

He put the wallet away. A couple of minutes later, Bill came in with three cups of coffee. Smitty shrank away when he brought the coffee over to him. Bill grinned like a spreading wound, and put the cup on the table beside the chair.

Bill and I sat on the sofa, and Smitty sat in the armchair near the picture window, half-facing us. After a minute, Bill said, 'I'm okay now.'

'Good,' I said.

There was silence, and then Bill cleared his throat and said, 'What are we waiting for?'

'Smitty to start talking,' I said.

Smitty stuck a nervous thumb at the picture window. 'Can't we close these drapes?'

'Do it yourself,' I said.

He did, and sat down again, and looked miserable. He hunched over his knees and sipped coffee. Bill had made all three cups just black. We both drank it that way all the time. Smitty didn't like it, but he drank it.

'It's time to tell us the story, Smitty,' I said.

'I can't,' he said. He looked earnestly over the cup at us. 'I come to do you a favour, pay back your old man. You rough me up. I should of stayed away in the first place.'

I turned my head. 'Bill, can you hit him any softer than the last time? I hate waking him up all the time.'

16

Bill got up, eager, grinning. He wanted to even the slate. 'I've got some beauties in here,' he said, and showed us his right fist. It had red hair and orange freckles all over it. The knuckles were big.

Smitty said, 'Come on. Lay off me, come on.' His voice was higher. He was pushing back down in the chair.

'Tell us an easy part first,' I said. 'What was the favour my father did you?'

His eyes were on Bill's fist. 'It was before you were born,' he said. 'Before repeal. I was driving a truckload in from New Hampshire when the state boys got me.'

'A truckload of what?' Bill asked him.

'Whiskey.' He would have said it with contempt for Bill's ignorance, but he still had respect for Bill's fist. 'The people I worked for threw me away, but your old man was my mouthpiece. For no dough.'

'How did he know you?' I asked.

'We worked for the same people.'

Bill took a step toward him. 'That's a lie.'

'Wait,' I said. 'Okay, Smitty, now the current events.'

'I told you the whole thing. There's gonna be trouble in New York. You don't want any part of it.'

'I want every part of it,' I told him. 'Names and addresses. They killed my father.' I pointed at Bill. 'They killed his wife.'

He looked surprised, for just a second. Then his face closed up again, and he said, 'Okay, right there that tells you.'

'Tells me what?'

'Why you ought to clear out.'

'Because Bill's wife was killed?'

'You don't want to get involved.'

'I *am* involved, whether I like it or not. Tell me about this trouble that's going to happen in New York.'

He hesitated, considering, looking from me to Bill and back. Then he said, 'It's got to do with the Organization. That's all I'll say, that's too much already.'

'What organization?'

'The mob. The outfit. The syndicate, you might call it.'

17

'What do I have to do with the syndicate?'

'On account of your father.'

'What does he have to do with it?'

'He used to work for it.'

Bill went over and hit him twice before I could move. Then I got to him and pulled him away. I said, 'Control yourself, goddamn you to hell, or I take him away and you can screw yourself. You want to cry in your beer, or do you want to help?'

'All right, all *right*.' He pulled away from me and went over and sat on the sofa again.

Smitty had protected himself with his arms. He lowered them now like they ached. His eyes were round. He said, '*I* didn't do it. What's the matter with him? I come to do you a favour. What's the matter with him?'

'He lost a wife.'

'It wasn't *me*. I come to warn you. I should of stayed away in the first place.'

I said, 'Who did it, Smitty? Who killed my father? Who killed Bill's wife?'

He shook his head. 'No. You two are crazy. You'll go after them, and they'll trace it back to me. I just come to do you a friendly gesture. Because of your old man. I don't want to get killed.'

'What are their names, Smitty?'

'They'll trace it back to me. I don't talk any more.'

I said, 'Bill.'

It was a long night. We kept the drapes shut. Bill knocked him out and I woke him up. But there was somebody in the world who could scare Smitty more from a distance than we could close up. The last time, I didn't wake him. We dumped him in a closet and locked the door and went to sleep.

4

In the morning, before we left, Bill wanted to do something nutty like bury him in the cellar or leave him on a side road in his own car and with a bullet in his head from his own gun. 'If we let him live,' he argued, 'he'll go right back and let them know we're coming.'

'No, he won't,' I said. I looked at Smitty and talked to Bill. 'He'll have to tell them he talked to us. They won't believe he didn't give names. So he won't go back to New York at all.'

'No,' he said. 'I won't.' His words were slurred, because of his puffed lips.

'He'll go west some place,' I said, 'and change his name.'

He caught the quote. He said, 'You won't ever hear from me again.'

After a while, Bill took my word for it, and moved his Mercury out of the driveway. Smitty backed his Plymouth out and drove away. He didn't pause to ask directions.

Bill had to go into town and say good-bye to his boss and his kid, and get his money out of the bank. I stayed behind and packed suitcases and locked the windows. When he came back, we loaded the trunk and headed for New York.

I was still shaky in the right-hand seat. I tried driving for a while, but it was too hard. Not only the distance judgement, also the right ankle. They hadn't been able to fix it completely. It wouldn't bend any more, and made me gimp a little. I had to push the accelerator down with my heel and it was awkward. So we switched again, and Bill drove the rest of the way. We went down through Pennsylvania, 11 and Carbondale and 106 and the Delaware Water Gap. It was the same distance, and 17 made us leary.

We went down Jersey and over the bridge to Staten Island and across Staten Island and over the new bridge to Brooklyn. Then

19

we went up the Belt Parkway and through the tunnel into Manhattan.

We'd kept Smitty's revolver. Bill had a Luger that maybe still worked, but no ammunition for it. He'd tried in Binghamton, but neither he nor the clerk was sure what size cartridge it wanted. He was going to try again in New York. Also in the trunk we had two deer rifles.

We got a hotel way up Broadway, 72nd Street, fairly cheap with a garage. Bill had almost four thousand dollars. I had not quite a hundred. The Air Force had sent the second hundred of my mustering-out pay to the hospital. God knew where the third hundred would go. That should be coming soon. Next Monday I'd be out two months. That seemed hard to believe.

It was only a little after two when we checked in. Bill found a bank a couple of blocks down from the hotel. He put three grand in a joint checking account. We both signed cards and got a checkbook. They were unhappy. They wanted to give us one with our names on the checks.

After lunch, we went back to the room and sat on the beds. Bill said, 'Now what?'

I said, 'We go in two directions. The licence plate of Smitty's car is one. But I think that was probably stolen. The other is Dad. He was a lawyer in New York, way back when. He had something to do with the underworld.'

'That's a lie. That punk was lying.'

'No. It's something from that time that killed him. They were looking for him, maybe. He figured it was safe to come to New York, after all these years. But he was nervous about going out of the hotel.'

'But why Ann?'

'Tell me about that.'

'She was in the Civic Theatre. You know, amateur. She spent two, three evenings a week at rehearsals. She'd take the bus in and get somebody to drive her back. I couldn't go get her on account of Betsy. And the bus doesn't run that late. That night, she took the bus in like always. It was three blocks to walk where they rehearsed. She was cross-k-crossing the street. It wasn't

20

even dark, it was only seven-thirty. Early evening. The car came out of the side street, clipped her. She got kno-knocked –'

'Okay,' I said. 'Take it easy. You don't have to tell me now.'

'I'll get it over with,' he said. He lit a cigarette. 'Back onto the sidewalk,' he said. 'The car knocked her back-back –'

'Okay.'

'Jesus.' He breathed loudly, inhale and exhale, staring at the bedspread pattern. He laid his hand on the bedspread, fingers splayed out. He pressed down and said, 'Three people saw it. Nobody saw it clear. The car didn't even slow down.'

I said, 'I wonder if it was the same car.'

He looked at me. 'As went after you?'

'Uh huh.'

'I don't know. I suppose so. Nobody saw it clear.'

He finished his cigarette. I went over to the phone, and looked at the directories. They had the Manhattan and the Brooklyn and the Bronx. I found Chester P. Smith in the Brooklyn book, at 653 East 99th Street. NIghtingale 9-9970.

A woman answered. I asked for Smitty, and she said, 'Who?'

'Chet. Chester.'

'He's at work. Who is this?'

'I think we were in the service together,' I said. 'If this is the right Chester Smith. Medium height, thin-faced.'

She laughed, as though she were mad. 'There's nothing thin about *this* Chester,' she said.

'Can't be the same guy,' I said.

I hung up and looked for the public library in the Manhattan directory. It said there was a Newspaper Division at 521 West 43. I said, 'I'm going out for a while.'

Bill said, 'Where?'

'Library. You could figure out how we check that licence plate.'

'What the hell are you doing at the library?'

'I want to see if Dad ever made the paper.'

'You mean with the underworld? Bootleggers?' He got to his feet, frowning and mad. 'That punk was lying, Ray. What kind of a son are you?'

21

'A son with his last eye open,' I said.

He hung fire, and then turned away. 'Hell,' he said. 'I haven't been getting any sleep.'

'I'll be back after a while.'

He flung himself face down on his bed and I left the room.

5

It was between Tenth and Eleventh Avenue. That whole block was sewing machine wholesalers. The newspaper library was the second floor of a building that looked like a post office. Some papers they had on microfilm, some they had bound in big books.

I looked through the *New York Times Index*. I found it in 1931. Dad was only twenty-seven then. He was married, but he didn't have any kids yet. He'd been a lawyer two years.

There was a guy, he owned a lot of buildings. Most of them were tenements, slum buildings. Almost all of them had speakeasies in them. He was up for allowing liquor to be stored and sold on his property with his knowledge. He got off on a brilliant piece of legal footwork on the part of his lawyer, a member of the firm of McArdle, Lamarck & Krishman. It was so brilliant the *Times* did a profile on the lawyer, whose name was Willard Kelly, and on the firm he worked for.

McArdle, Lamarck & Krishman, 'it was alleged', got virtually all of their business, directly or indirectly, from the liquor syndicate. Willard Kelly had been with the firm less than a year. This was the first time he'd handled a case in court for them. The profile writer was sad that Kelly was selling his brilliance to the underworld.

Your father. You think you know him. You forget he lived a lot of years before he started you. All of a sudden you find out you never knew who the hell he was.

I wrote down all the names. Morris Silber, the landlord. Andrew McArdle and Philip Lamarck and Samuel Krishman, partners in the law firm. George Ellinbridge, the prosecuting attorney. Andrew Shuffleman, the judge.

Willard Kelly didn't show up again. I went back through the *Index*, twenties and thirties, checking the other names. Morris

Silber got a year in jail in 1937 for housing violations in his tenements, mainly rats. His lawyer wasn't named. Philip Lamarck died in bed in 1935, at the age of sixty-seven. Andrew Shuffleman died just as peaceably the same year, at the age of seventy-one. George Ellinbridge was elected State Assemblyman in 1938, but wasn't re-elected.

Andrew McArdle personally defended crime kingpin Anthony Edward 'Eddie' Kapp in his income-tax evasion trial in 1940. The crime kingpin went to jail, with two sentences of ten years and one of five years, to run consecutively and *not* concurrently. Twenty-five years. It wasn't up yet, but there were such things as paroles.

Eddie Kapp. I didn't find any references to him later than 1940. I found a lot of them in the early thirties and late twenties. A friend of Dutch Schultz and Bill Bailey. An important man around that crazy time when Schultz was killed over in Jersey and Bailey became top man for two weeks. Then Bailey walked into a New York City hospital one afternoon and said he didn't feel well. They put him to bed, and two o'clock the following morning he was dead. The death certificate said pneumonia.

Eddie Kapp. Willard Kelly. Connected by a man named Andrew McArdle.

I wasted some time, then, looking in the current year's *Index*. They had monthly indices in a filler book, and July was the most recent. My name was there, for July 14th. I filled out a slip, got the microfilm, and put it in the viewer. I read about the shooting. The *Times* called it 'bizarre'. It only rated a small paragraph on page eight. DRIVER SHOT AT WHEEL.

The woman came over and told me it was five o'clock, closing time. I put the microfilm back in the box, put my pencil and pad in my pocket, and left.

24

6

Back at the room, there was a guy with Bill. He had on a brown suit with the coat open. His white shirt was bunched at the waist. He was thin and his tie was brown and orange and green and he wore a brown hat back on his head indoors.

Bill said, 'This is Ed Johnson. He's a private detective.'

Johnson grinned at me. 'That's right,' he said.

I frowned at Bill. 'What the hell for?'

'We're not going to get anywhere on our own. You got some jerky idea about Dad mixed up with the underworld. We need somebody who knows the ropes.'

I looked at Johnson. 'Get out,' I said.

His grin faded. 'Well, I don't know,' he said. He looked from me to Bill to me. 'I've been given a retainer, to check out a licence plate.'

'We want to do that,' Bill told me.

I sat down and lit a cigarette. 'We don't want to spread our business around,' I told the match. 'We don't want to finger ourselves.'

'I'm trustworthy,' Johnson told me. 'One hundred per cent.'

'Just the licence, Ray,' said Bill. He sounded embarrassed.

Johnson said, 'You couldn't do it, I can.'

I shrugged. 'The hell with it,' I said. 'Go play with the licence plate. It was on a Plymouth.'

He looked from face to face again, and then he said he'd be seeing us, and left.

Bill said, 'That was a hell of a way to talk. He's a nice guy.'

I said, 'He's a stranger.'

'We need somebody dispassionate. You've got this nutty idea –'

I took out the pad and read aloud from it. Then I tossed it on the dresser and said, 'Smarten up.'

Bill pushed words into the silence like a man pushing logs into mud. 'It wasn't Dad. Willard Kelly, that isn't an uncommon name. Hell, it's *my* name, too.'

'Just a coincidence.'

'Sure.'

'Two Willard Kellys. Both the same age. Both in New York. Both lawyers. Both graduates of the same school.'

'Maybe. Why not?'

'You ought to go back to Binghamton, Bill. You're blind in both eyes. You'll get us in a lot of trouble.'

He looked at me, and then he went and sat on the bed. He sat in the middle of the bed, knees folded like a yoga. He looked big and pathetic. His blunt fingers, hairy and freckled, traced the pattern of the spread.

After a while, he said, 'My *father*.'

A while longer and he said, 'He wasn't like that.'

'He changed. Reformed. Quit the syndicate and moved away.'

His eyes had sad, shredded edges. 'That's true?'

'Something like that.'

'That really him, in the paper?'

'You know it.'

He made a fist and pounded the pattern. 'How the hell can I have any *respect* for him?'

I popped the eye out and got to my feet. I put it on the dresser and said, 'Get up, Bill.'

He was puzzled. 'Why?'

'You lose respect too easy.'

'I don't want to fight you, Ray.'

He came off the bed with his hands spread, and I hit him on the side of the jaw.

The third time I hit him, he swung back. I was at a disadvantage, I didn't always judge the distance right. I walked into a few. I kept getting up. He started to cry, and his face was as red as his hair, and he kept knocking me down again. Then he put his hands at his sides and shook his head and whispered, 'No more.' I got up and hit him with my left hand. He didn't dodge or raise his arms or defend himself or fight back. I hit him with the right

26

hand. And the left hand again. He blubbered, 'No more.' I hit him right hand and then left hand. He dropped to his knees, and the vibration knocked the Gideon Bible off the nightstand. I hit him right hand, from the knees coming up, and he went over on his back. He wouldn't get up.

I got the eye from the dresser and went into the head. I washed my face and watched myself put the eye in. It didn't make me want to throw up any more. My knuckles were scraped and there was a ragged cut on the left side of my jaw.

I went back and sat down in the chair again. After a while, Bill sat up. He said, 'All right.'

I said, 'You going back to Binghamton?'

'No. You're right.'

I wasn't sure he knew. I said, 'Why did you think I came here? To play Summer Festival?'

'No,' he said. 'I know that.'

'Do you know what we're doing here?'

'Yes.'

'What?'

'We're looking for the people who killed Dad.'

'For the cops?'

He looked at me. 'Jesus,' he said. He shook his head and looked away. 'No,' he said. 'Not for the cops.'

'For us,' I said. 'Why?'

He looked at me level this time. 'Because he was our father.'

'That's right,' I said.

27

7

We spent the evening in the room, with separate bottles of Old Mr Boston. Johnson woke us on the phone at nine in the morning. I talked to him. He said, 'Those plates are registered to a '54 Buick. Stolen three months ago. Not the car, just the plates. Lots of Plymouths stolen. It's a popular car.'

I said, 'Thanks. The retainer cover it?'

'If that's all you want,' he said.

'Thanks,' I said.

'Listen Mr Kelly, you don't have to dislike me.'

'I don't dislike you.' I hung up and forgot him. I spent a few minutes with the phone directory and a pencil, and then we went out to eat.

It was now McArdle, Krishman, Mellon & McArdle. It was a building on the east side of Fifth Avenue, just down a ways from the cathedral. Friday morning, the early tourists streamed north to look at the cathedral and the Plaza. We pushed across their path from the cab to the doors. The tourist ladies wore green cotton dresses. All the little boys had hats like Daddy's. I gave mine up when I was twelve. It was a Sunday hat, for church. I never wore it in New York. Lots of people don't take their kids to New York. It doesn't mean anything.

The elevator had chrome doors on the first floor. On the twenty-seventh, they were metal doors painted maroon. A clever sign-painter had fitted the whole name of the law firm on the frosted glass of the door. We went in and I asked the girl for Mr McArdle. 'The first one,' I said. She acted snooty, like a whole dancing class at once. She gave us the second one.

He was about forty, with a soft body and a pale round face. His eyes were wet behind black-armoured spectacles. 'Well, boys,' he said. 'What can I do for you?'

'Nothing,' I said. 'We want McArdle number one.'

28

'My father isn't an active part of the firm any more.' He smiled, like a man selling laxative. 'I assure you, I'm almost as good a lawyer as he.'

He was playing us for teenagers. I said, 'Sure. We'll take Krishman. Samuel Krishman. Not a coat-tail relation.'

He frowned, mouth and eyebrows both. 'I'm afraid I'll have to ask you –'

'Tell him Willard Kelly' I said.

It didn't mean anything to him. He looked down at the card on his desk. 'You gave your first name as Raymond.'

'That's my father.'

'Raymond is your father?'

'You're a goddamn imbecile, mister.' I pointed at the phone. 'Pick it up and tell Samuel Krishman Willard Kelly's son is here.'

'I'll do no such thing.'

I went over and picked up the phone. He reached for it and I said, 'Bill.' He looked at Bill, who was coming around the desk, and he sat back, paler than before. 'You won't get away with this,' he said. But he was gabbling. It was just a sentence you say when people push you around and get away with it.

There was a row of buttons on the phone, under the dial. I pushed the one that said, 'Local'. Nothing happened. I dialled zero. Still nothing happened. I dialled some other number, I don't know what. A guy came on and I said, 'What the hell is Samuel's number? I can't remember.'

'Eight,' he said.

I broke the connection and dialled eight. An old man came on. I said, 'I'm Willard Kelly's son. I'm not as dumb as Andrew McArdle's son, but I'm stuck in his office.'

There was a pause, and the dry old voice said, 'What was that name?'

'You heard it right. Willard Kelly.'

'Is Lester there?'

'McArdle two? Yes.'

'Tell him to show you to my office.'

'Tell him yourself. He won't believe me.'

I straight-armed Lester the phone. He took it like it had bitten him once. He listened and agreed and hung up and said to me, 'You could have been more civil.'

'Not to you.'

He showed us down a corridor that was green on one wall, rust on the other. White ceiling, black linoleum. Pastel doors. The one at the end was tan and closed and didn't say anything. He handed us to a girdled brunette with a plaster hairdo. She played electronically and let us in.

When I was a kid I believed in a Business Pope. I thought there was a strict mercantile hierarchy, grocery stores and movie houses down near the bottom, factories and warehouses in the middle, Wall Street up near the top. And a Business Pope running the whole thing. I visualized the Business Pope as a shrivelled ancient white-haired Pluto in a black leather chair. Black-capped chauffeur to the left, white-hipped nurse to the right. Every line on his face would record a decade of evil and cruelty and decay. I knew just what he would look like.

That was Samuel Krishman. No chauffeur and no nurse. Black leather swivel chair. A mahogany desk of wood so warm it glowed. Maroon desk blotter. Two black telephones. Discreet papers, embarrassed to be white.

He said, 'Pardon me for not rising.' Five words he could say without thinking about them, while studying us. He waved a gnarled root of a hand at two maroon leather chairs. His cuff links were round, gold coins with Roman profiles.

He looked at me. 'You say you're Willard Kelly's son?'

'We both are. That's Willard Junior. I'm Raymond.'

The pale eyes flicked to Bill and back to me. 'You're spokesman. You're the one who spoke on the phone.' That was easy. I was looking at him, Bill was looking at me.

I said, 'My father used to work here.'

He smiled. The perfect false teeth couldn't have looked more out of place in a duck's mouth. 'Not here, precisely. Our offices were farther downtown then.'

'He went to work for you in August of 1930.'

'I suppose so. Approximately.'

30

'He made the *Times* once, on the Morris Silber case. They did a profile.'

The smile this time didn't part the lips. It looked healthier. 'I remember that. Willard was embarrassed. A shy young man. Unlike his son.' By him, Bill wasn't even there.

'He made the *Times* again,' I said. 'Two months ago. You didn't see it?'

Thin eyebrows crawled on the rutted forehead. 'Not that I recall. I didn't notice it, perhaps.' The smile was open-mouthed again. 'I read little beyond the obituary page these days.'

I had the system now. When he showed his teeth the smile was phoney. I said, 'This wasn't the obituary page, but it was the same thing. He was killed.'

'Killed?'

'Shot. In a moving car, by a moving car. I was with him.'

'Ah. Did you recognize the attacker?'

'I will.'

'I see.' His hands crept up on the maroon blotter, crawled blindly together, clung. 'That's why you're here,' he said. 'You want vengeance.'

'Second,' I said. 'First, I want understanding. I was away three years. Air Force. Germany. I just came back. No girl yet, no plans yet.' I jabbed a thumb at Bill. 'He was out of it. Married, with a kid. All I had was home, and all that was was Dad. Twenty-three years and they left us alone. When I needed him most, they came in. Arrogant. *Grinning.*' I sat there. We were all quiet. I took my hands off the wooden chair-arms. The palms had the red lines of the wood. 'I want to know why,' I said.

'They killed my wife,' said Bill. It was a truculent apology for being there.

Krishman sighed, and rubbed his face with one dry hand. He wasn't the Business Pope, he was just an old man, afraid to retire because his friends died when they retired. 'That was all so many years ago,' he said. 'That's behind us now. We don't have things like that any more.'

'Anastasia,' I said. 'The Victor Reisel blinding. Arnold Schuster, the twenty-two-year-old witness got killed in 1951.'

31

'This firm,' he said, 'hasn't been involved for nearly twenty years. There were circumstances . . . '

'McArdle number one?'

He shook his head. He looked at me and smiled with closed lips. 'Philip Lamarck,' he said. 'His name came second, but he was the senior partner.'

'He died in '35.'

'It takes a while to break free of connections like that.'

'When did you break free?'

'Shortly before the war. 1940, I suppose.'

'Was Dad still working for you?'

'He left us around then. Left the city, I believe.'

'That was the year of the Eddie Kapp trial, wasn't it?'

'Eddie Kapp? Oh, yes, the income-tax trial. It's been a very long time, you must understand . . . '

'Is he out yet?'

'Kapp? I have no idea. You think there's a connexion between him and your father's death?'

'When he was shot, Dad said his name. "Kapp," that's all.'

'Are you sure that's what he meant?'

'No. But it's likely. Would McArdle know?'

'Know what?'

'If Kapp was out yet.'

'I doubt it. You want to talk to him, I suppose.'

'Yes.'

He nodded. 'I'll call him. I'm sure he'll talk to you. We all liked Willard very much. A brilliant legal mind, for such a young man. And a cheerful red-headed Irishman.' He nodded at Bill. 'You look very much like him.' Back to me. 'You take after Edith more. The fair hair, shape of your face.'

'I suppose so.'

'From what you've said, I take it your mother is dead.'

'Died when I was two. In Binghamton.'

'That's where he went. He should have stayed in New York. His talents would be wasted anywhere else. Corporation law, but with fine courtroom presence.'

32

'He did corporate work in Binghamton. Small-time. You say you've got a different class of client now?'

'Yes. Since before the war. Shipping lines, food packagers. Industrial corporations almost exclusively.'

'McArdle handled the Kapp income-tax case, didn't he?'

'Yes, I believe he did.'

'Did my father have anything to do with that case?'

'I should think so. He had the Kapp file.'

'What?'

'He was the one who normally handled all of Kapp's legal affairs. You see, every regular continuous client has a file, kept by the man in this office who is his immediate contact and who does all or most of his legal work. The income-tax trial, of course, was something else again. Not that Willard Kelly couldn't have handled it as well as anybody. But Kapp was an important client at the time. It was necessary to have one of the firm's partners in charge of the case.'

'Who were Dad's other regular clients?'

'I'm sure I have no idea.'

'What about the files?'

He shook his head. 'Some files,' he said, 'we retain for seven years, some for fifteen years, a few for twenty. We would have no files at all for that far back. Your father left us more than twenty years ago.'

'If you had the same kind of client that you have now, would you have the files?'

Closed-lips smile. 'Most likely.'

'What about Morris Silber?'

'Is that the case when the *Times* wrote the profile?'

'Yes.'

'I'm sorry. He was minor even then. I would have no idea where he is today or if he's still alive.'

'Yes, of course.'

'Can you think of anyone else?'

Parted-lips smile, hands spread out, trembling a bit at the end of his sleeves. 'It's been so long.'

'Sure. You said you'd call McArdle one.'

'Of course.'

He spent a few minutes on the phone. He called McArdle 'Andrew', not Andy or anything like that. He didn't say anything surprising. When he hung up he said, 'Do you have a car?'

Bill spoke for the second time. 'Yes.'

Krishman told him, 'He lives out on the Island. Long Island. Beyond King's Park, on the North Shore. He has an estate out there.' He gave Bill directions, route numbers and so on, and Bill nodded. Then we got up to leave. I thanked him for his answers, he congratulated Dad on producing such fine boys.

At the door, I turned and said, 'Up till 1940, when you made the changeover, about how many professional criminals did you help evade the law?'

'I have no idea.'

'More than a hundred?'

Closed-lips smile. 'Oh, yes. Far more.'

'Aren't you afraid of the retribution of justice?'

'At this late date? Hardly.'

'You will never be punished by the law.'

'Never. I'm sure of it.'

'And you obviously haven't lost your money or your social standing. Do you have ulcers, or anything like that?'

'No. I'm perfectly healthy. My doctor says I'll live past ninety. Do you have a point to make?'

'Yes. To my brother, not to you. He needs an education. He still believes in good guys and bad guys. That they're born that way and stay that way. And that good guys always win and bad guys always lose.'

Closed-lips smile. 'A great number of people believe that. It's comforting to them.'

I said, 'Until the guns come out.'

8

It was forty miles out to McArdle's place. We took the Triborough Bridge and the Expressway. For the first ten or fifteen miles it was all city, slit open by the Expressway. After Floral Park and Mineola it got more suburb. Every once in a while, there was a glimpse of Long Island Sound off to our left. But it still didn't seem any more like an island than Manhattan did.

The last mile and a half was private road, blacktop. McArdle shared it with two other millionaires, and his place was last of the three, where the road made a hangman's knot. There was a bird-bath inside the loop, and a Negro with a power mower. The house was clapboard and brick and masonry. Windows enclosed the porch.

When we got out of the car, the Negro stopped and wiped his face with a white handkerchief. His hat was grey and he held it in his left hand, then put it back on his head. He kept the power mower running, and it sounded loud but far away, the way they do. He never quite looked at us, and he never quite looked away.

We went up the stoop and tried the screen door. It was locked and there wasn't any bell. I rattled the door and shouted. A guy in a white jacket came out, carrying a towel. He looked at us through the screen.

'Kelly,' I said. 'We're expected.'

He pointed to his right. 'Down at the dock,' he said. He went back inside.

The house was backed against a half-moon of forest. A brown path led in among the trees to the left of the house, going grad-ually downhill. We went down it. Behind us, the Negro put his handkerchief away and went back to work.

A voice droned ahead. The path wound downhill. Through the trees, there were blue glimpses of the Sound.

We came out on a narrow strip of shade-mottled lawn. At the

35

lower end, a swath of smooth pebbles led down into the water. A little blonde girl in a ruffled bathing suit stood half-bent in the shallows, filling her green pail with water.

The lawn was flanked by brush and trees, down the sides and overhanging the water's edge. To the right, an unpainted dock jutted out atilt into the water. A white motorboat nodded beside it. A boy and girl of about twenty were on and off a float a ways away. Four people sat in white-fence lawn chairs to the right, three of them watching the little girl.

The woman of about twenty-seven, with the white bathing suit and the ash-blonde hair and the vertical frown lines between her brows, would be the mother of the little girl and the sister of one or both of the people out on the float. The nondescript middle-aged heavy couple in city clothes would be her parents, he the brother of the McArdle I'd met at the law office, this one older and tougher and not a lawyer. The gross ancient bald man wearing young man's sports clothes would be Andrew McArdle.

I stopped and looked at him. The short-sleeved white shirt showed flabby blue-veined white-skinned arms, the muscles so little able to bear weight that the upper slopes of the arms were only skin over narrow frail bone, the fat all hanging in long bags of skin underneath. The shirt was open at the throat, showing grey flesh writhing over a convulsive Adam's apple. There was no chest. The shirt sagged down to a gross belly. Tan slacks covered the stick legs beneath, and the feet were bare, looking like frozen plaster moulds.

His head sagged back, his mouth hung open, the thin-veined lids were stretched over his eyes. The sound of his breathing was very loud.

The voice I'd heard had been the middle-aged man. He stopped and looked at us. The women turned their heads and looked, and then the ash-blonde watched the little girl again. The boy and girl on the float stood still, arms at their sides, gazing in at us. The little girl ignored us. She laughed suddenly and splashed herself with water.

The ancient man gulped and rolled his head around and opened his eyes. He stared at Bill. 'Willard.' His voice was a croak that had once been a ringing bass.

36

I came across the lawn, Bill trailing me. 'Mr Krishman called you,' I said.

The present slowly came into his eyes. He looked at me. 'Yes. Arthur, go up to the house. All of you, up to the house.'

The middle-aged woman smiled like a beautician. 'You shouldn't exert yourself, Papa.' She got up and crouched over him, hoping everyone would think she was solicitous. She was afraid to strangle him. 'Don't you talk too long, now,' she said.

Arthur said to her, 'Come on.'

The ash-blonde called to the little girl, 'Linda. Come here.'

She came out of the water, carrying the green pail. She stopped in front of me, serious, squinting up at me with sun in her eyes. 'Why do you limp?'

'I was in an accident.'

'When?'

'Come along, Linda,' said her mother.

'Two months ago,' I said.

'Where?'

'Your mother wants you.'

They trailed by us, across the lawn toward the path. The middle-aged woman said, 'I'm *coming*, Arthur.'

They trailed diagonally up the lawn. The last thing, the ash-blonde made the little girl empty the water out of her pail. Then they were gone, between the trees.

He told us to sit down, and we did. He kept his head back, twisted at an odd angle on a faded flower-pattern pillow. His voice was just above a whisper, no louder than his breathing. 'Your father is dead,' he said.

I said, 'I want to know about Eddie Kapp.'

'He went to jail. Years ago.' The head shook back and forth, slowly. 'The Federal Government is a different proposition, Eddie.'

'Is he still in jail? Eddie Kapp, is he still in jail?'

'Oh, I suppose so. I don't know. I have taken the final sabbatical, young man. I am no longer chained to the office, I –' His wandering eyes and wandering mind touched Bill again, and he frowned. 'Willard? You shouldn't be here, you know that.'

Bill was scared. He said, 'No, you mean my father.' He broke the mood before McArdle said anything useful.

McArdle's face started to close up. He was in the present again, and he remembered what he'd said. He watched me warily.

I said, 'Why shouldn't he be here?'

'Who? What are you talking about? I am retired, an old man with a bad heart . . . '

'My father shouldn't have come to New York, should he? Why not?'

'I don't know. My memory wanders sometimes, I'm not always responsible for what I say.'

The boy and girl came dripping out of the water. McArdle's head twisted to glare at them. 'Go out there! Stay out there! This is none of your business!'

'We're going up to the house,' said the girl. She was snotty. She'd had money all her life, she didn't care if she inherited or not. 'Come on, Larry.'

They paused to fiddle with towels and cigarettes and sunglasses. I said, 'Better hurry.'

The girl was going to be snotty to me, but then she wasn't. She grabbed her gear and hip-jiggled away. She looked discontented, frustrated. The boy flexed his muscles at me, frowning because he'd been left out, and followed her.

When they were gone, I turned back to McArdle. 'Who would know if Eddie Kapp was out or in?'

'I don't know. So long ago.' The eyes misted again, cleared a little. 'Maybe his sister, Dorothea. She married a chain-market manager.'

'What name?'

'I'm trying to remember. Carter, something like that. Castle, Kimball . . . Campbell! That was it, Robert Campbell.'

I wrote it down. 'That was in New York?'

'He managed a chain market in Brooklyn. A Bohack? I don't remember. A young man. She was young, too, much younger than her brother. A pretty thing, black hair. Glowing.'

He was starting to dream again. I said, 'Who told Willard Kelly to stay out of town?'

'What? What?' His head nearly raised up from the pillow, and then subsided. 'Don't shout so,' he said. His breathing was louder. 'I am an old man, my memory is failing me, I have a bad heart. You cannot rely on what I say. I should have told Samuel no. I should have refused.'

'Samuel Krishman? He doesn't know the answer, does he?'

The belly laughed, shaking him. 'He never knew anything. A fool!'

'But you do.'

He started the old man routine again. I said, 'Tell me who told Willard Kelly to stay out of town.'

'I don't know.'

'Who told Willard Kelly to stay out of town?'

'Go away. I don't know.'

'Who told Willard Kelly to stay out of town?'

'No. No!'

I kept my voice low. 'Tell me or I'll kill you.'

'I'm an old man –'

'You'll die. Here and now.'

'Let me go. Let the past alone!'

I bowed my head, covered my face with my hands. I plucked the glass oval out. I closed my left eye, and then I was blind. I kept the right lid open, but it was a strain with the eye out. It was warm in my palm.

I lowered my hands in my lap. Still blind, I raised my face toward him. I smiled. 'I can see your soul this way,' I said. 'It's black.'

I heard a choking, I opened my eye and he was gaping, staring, choking, his face turning bluish red. I put the glass eye back in.

Bill was already running up the path, shouting for the family.

9

I had meant to frighten him. He was afraid of death, and I think he would have answered me. I had no idea how strongly it would affect him. I hadn't meant him to die.

We had to stay and wait for the doctor. I told them our father had once worked for McArdle, Lamarck & Krishman. I told them he had died recently, but I didn't tell them how. I told them he had told us once to look up his old bosses, they could maybe help us get a start in life.

They believed me. It was believable. Bill listened to me tell it, and then he knew it too. But he wasn't meeting my glance. He thought I'd done it on purpose. I'd have to tell him, once we got away from here.

While we waited, I talked with Karen Thorndike. She was the ash-blonde. She was the daughter of Arthur and the woman with the beautician's smile, as I'd supposed. She was divorced from Jerry Thorndike. She said, 'You don't want to come to New York.'

'Why not?'

'There's nothing here but people clawing each other. Everybody wants to get to the top of the heap, and it's a heap of human beings. A big hill of kicking, struggling human beings, trying to crawl up one another and be at the top.'

'You're thinking of Jerry Thorndike,' I said. 'You got burned. Not all the people in a city are like that.'

'They are in New York.'

Linda, the little girl, came over and started asking stupid questions. She was like her mother, interesting until she opened her mouth. I thought of taking my eye out for her, but not seriously.

The doctor was big and hearty. People paid him to be like him. His name was Heatherton. He wanted to know what we'd been talking about when the old man had had his attack. I said the weather in New York.

Nobody was really upset. He was eighty-two years old. They'd all been hanging around waiting anyway. After a while, I asked Dr Heatherton if there was any reason for Bill and me to stay there any longer. He said no.

As we went out the private road, a grey Cadillac hearse purred by us, going in.

It wasn't yet three. But it was Friday afternoon, so there was quite a bit of traffic headed toward the city, most of it in late-model cars.

We rode in silence for a while, and then I lit a cigarette and handed it out to Bill and he said, 'No, thanks,' without looking away from the road.

I stuck the cigarette back between my lips and said, 'Don't be stupid. I didn't want to kill him.'

'You said you were going to.' He glowered grimly at the road. 'You told him you would and you did. I don't know you any more, the Air Force did something to you. Or Germany.'

'Or being in the car with Dad.'

'All right, maybe that. Whatever caused it, I don't like it. You can have the money in the bank. I'll need the car, I'm going back to Binghamton.'

'You don't care any more.'

'I'll stop off and talk to that state cop, Kirk.'

'And tell him what?'

'I won't tell him anything. Don't worry, I'm not going to inform on you.'

'I'm not worried.'

'I'm going to ask them how they're doing.'

'They aren't doing. Tuesday it'll be two months. They don't have a lead, a clue, a chance, or a hope. If they did, it wouldn't take two months. It's us or nobody.'

'I can't stay with you. I can't be around you, with you pulling things like that.'

'I told you, that was a mistake. I didn't mean for him to die.'

'Sure.'

'You're a cluck, Bill. You're three years older than me, but you're a cluck. He *knew* who chased Dad out of town. Did you hear what he said?'

41

'I heard him.'

'He knew. Do you think I wanted him dead?'

He frowned at the wheel, thinking it over. After a while he glanced at me. I looked innocent. He glowered out at the highway again. 'Then what the hell did you do it for?'

'I was trying to scare him. I didn't know it would hit him that big. It must look pretty bad.'

In some out-of-the-way corner he found a grin. He took it out, dusted it off, put it on his face. It looked good there. 'You don't know how bad, Ray,' he said. 'I about had a heart attack myself. You looked like something out of Hell.' He glanced at me again, back at the traffic. 'A little worse than usual,' he said.

'You want a cigarette?'

'I need one,' he said.

We went back to the hotel and sat around. We went out for dinner and bought some more Old Mr Boston. We drank and smoked and talked and played gin a penny a point. He won.

After a while, we finished the booze and went to bed and turned the lights off. But I saw McArdle's face, bluish red, the eyes bulging bigger and bigger. I got up and told Bill I was going out. He was asleep already, and he just grunted.

I went out and it was one o'clock in the morning. No liquor stores open. I found a bar, but the only thing he'd sell me to go was beer. I had five fast Fleischmann doubles on the rocks, and then I bought two quarts of Rheingold beer and brought them back to the room. I knew they'd make me throw up and they did, but after that I could go to sleep.

10

Johnson was around in the morning again. He wanted to talk. I had a split head, I told him to wait. He sat smoking in a chair while Bill and I hulked around and washed our faces and got dressed. Then the three of us went out for coffee.

We went up Broadway to a Bickford's, and filled our trays. Johnson just had coffee. Bill and I had eggs.

At the table, Johnson stuck a spoon in his coffee and stirred for five minutes without paying any attention, while he talked. 'I want to give you a little background on me,' he said. 'I run a one-man agency. Maybe one or two jobs a month, enough to stay even with the bills. Last year I made thirty-seven hundred dollars. I hate the job, I don't know why I stay in. Same way a little grocer down the block from the A&P won't close up and go get a warehouse job. You keep waiting for something to happen, like in the paperbacks.'

He held the spoon against the side of the cup with his thumb and drank. The spoon handle jabbed into his cheek. He kept watching me while he drank. Then he said, 'Most of the time, it's sitting around waiting for that one or two jobs a month. It's boring as hell. So sometimes I get interested in something. Like you two. Upstate accents, with the broad A, and you're living in a medium-price hotel and you've got medium-price clothes and a whole middle-class feeling to you. You aren't the idle rich. And you're too mad at everybody to be con artists. Besides, you paid me. You're checked into the hotel by the week, for the cheaper rate. You figure to be here longer than a little, but not long enough to sign a lease on an apartment or get a job or anything like that.'

He swallowed coffee again. When the spoon stuck into his cheek, it made him look wolfish. Otherwise, he looked soft.

'You're not salesmen or anything like that,' he said. 'I've been

43

in your hotel room twice, and there's not a thing there to say somebody's employed you. There would be. Display case, envelope from the main office, something. You go out late in the morning, you spend all day away. At night, you drink quietly in the room. One of you hires me to check a licence plate, and the other one gets mad. Doesn't want his business told around. The licence plate turns out to be stolen. I'm told to go away.'

'Why didn't you?' I asked him.

He shrugged. 'I told you. A ratty office in a ratty neighbourhood downtown. It depressed me. You two puzzled me. So I looked you up.' He grinned, bringing the wolf look back. 'You're Willard and Raymond Kelly,' he said. 'Sons of a mob lawyer who pulled out of town way back when. Is it your father you're working for?'

'Not exactly. He's dead.'

'Oh. Sorry.'

'Not at all.' I finished the toast and the last of the coffee.

He sat there chewing a thumbnail. He was stupid, but shrewd. I should have left, but I waited. Bill lit us cigarettes.

Then he stopped chewing the nail and said, 'Oh.' He looked at me, grinning again. 'Do you tell me, or do I go look it up?'

'All right,' I said. 'He was shot.'

'Sure. I knew you were looking for something. I couldn't figure what.' He leaned forward. 'All right I'm a cheap fifth-rate investigator. I can barely scrape up the licence fee every year. But I've been in this business for twelve years. I have contacts, I know how to look and where. I could save you time.'

I said, 'I have one question. Why should we trust you?'

'Because I'm fifth-rate. Poor but honest, that's me. I'd like to do a job because it's interesting.'

I chewed my cheek. 'There isn't anything I can think of for you to do.'

His grin was sour. 'You two talk it over. You probably won't find me in the office, but leave a message with the answering service. If you want me for anything, that is.' He got to his feet, took his coffee check, nodded to us both, and left.

Bill said, 'I trust him, Ray. I think he's all right.'

44

'I want to trust him,' I said, 'but I'm not going to.'

'Maybe we could use his help.'

'We'll worry about that when the time comes.' I lit a new cigarette. We paid our checks and went out to the sidewalk. 'I tell you what,' I said. 'You go on down to the library and look him up in the *New York Times Index*. He said he'd been working twelve years. Maybe he made the paper once. I'd like to be able to check him out.'

I told him how to get to the library, and then I went back to the room.

I was there half an hour when Krishman called. He was mad, but controlling it. 'I read in this morning's paper,' he said, 'that Andrew McArdle was dead.'

'Yes. Heart attack.'

'Did you have anything to do with that? I want the truth. Were you there?'

'We were there.'

'Andrew had nothing to do with your father's death.'

'And I had nothing to do with Andrew's. I didn't want him dead. He knew something. He would have told me, if he'd lived.'

'Knew something? About what? Don't be ridiculous.'

'Somebody told my father to get out of New York. Back in 1940. McArdle knew who.'

'That's nonsense.'

'He said you were a fool. He said you never knew anything.'

'What? That's a lie. Andrew wouldn't say such a thing.'

I said, 'Good-bye.' I hung up.

When Bill called, he said, 'Twice. Once, he was along as witness for divorce evidence. With a husband breaking in on a wife in a hotel room. Somebody'd killed the wife when they went in. Johnson was mentioned as a witness, that's all. There were a couple more stories on the murder, but nothing about him.'

'Okay. Any police names?'

'Detective Winkler. Homicide West. They have two homicide offices here, did you know that? East and West.'

'Winkler,' I said, writing it down. 'What about the other one?'

'His car was blown up. About three years ago. There was a

policeman named Linkovich at the wheel. There wasn't any explanation, and I couldn't find any later stories on it at all.'

'Okay, I'll call Winkler. You come on back. How long ago was this?'

'The divorce evidence thing? Four years ago. April or May, I forget which.'

It took a while to get through to Winkler and then he said, 'Johnson? Private detective? I'm not sure.'

'There was a woman found killed in a hotel room,' I said. 'Four years ago. Her husband and Johnson found her. They were there to get divorce evidence.'

'Yeah, wait a second,' he said. 'I remember that. Edward Johnson. Vaguely. What about him?'

'I'm thinking of hiring him,' I said. 'But I wanted to get a recommendation I could trust first.'

'Did he tell you to call me?'

'No. I found your name in the *Times*. The story on that hotel killing.'

'Oh. Because I barely remember the guy. Hold on a minute.'

I held on. After a while, a man named Clark came on the line. 'You want a recommendation on Edward Johnson, is that it?'

'That's it.'

'Okay. He's honest. He's also stubborn, and a coward. He's efficient, but don't ask him to do anything dangerous because he won't.'

'But he is honest.'

'I think you can count on it, yes.'

I thanked him. Then I looked up Robert Campbell in the Brooklyn phone directory. There were two of them. I dialled the first one and asked for Dorothea and the woman said, 'This is she.'

'Wrong number,' I said, and hung up. Then I copied down the address: 652 East 21st Street. I got out the Brooklyn map and the street guide. I found the address, and pencilled a route to it. Then Bill came back and we got the car out.

11

It was a decayed genteel apartment building, with iron grillwork on the front doors and no elevator. We climbed the stairs to 4A and rang the bell.

Dorothea Campbell was about fifty, tall and stocky and grey-haired. Decayed genteel, like the building. She wore a housecoat and an apron and scuffed slippers. Her face was cold. She had the right and the power to close the door in our faces if she felt like it. She wasn't used to power, she might abuse it.

'Hello,' I said. 'I'm Ray Kelly. This is my brother, Bill. Our father used to be your brother's lawyer.'

'My brother?' Her voice was cold, too. 'What brother?'

'Eddie Kapp.'

She shook her head. 'I don't have any brother.' The door started to close.

'We don't have a father,' I said.

The door stopped midway. 'What do you mean?'

'He's dead. He did wrong things when he was young. But we never turned our backs on him.'

'Eddie Kapp put me through hell,' she said angrily. But she was being defensive about it. I waited, and then she let go of the door and turned away. 'Oh, come in if you have to,' she said. 'Tell me what you want.'

'Thank you.'

We went in, and I was the one who closed the door.

The living room was small, and the furniture was all too big for it. The colours were dull. The metal-cabinet television set looked as though it had been left in that corner by accident.

We sat down on a fat green sofa, and she sat facing us in a matching chair. I said, 'Did you ever know Willard Kelly? Your brother's lawyer. People say Bill here looks a lot like he did.'

'I was eight years younger than my brother,' she said. 'Even if

47

we'd been the same age, we wouldn't have known the same people. I never had anything to do with his cronies at all.'

'This wasn't exactly a crony. It was his lawyer.'

She shook her head stubbornly. She didn't intend to think about 1940.

I shrugged. She probably didn't have a memory to avoid, not one that was useful to me. I said, 'Is Eddie out of jail yet, do you know?'

'September fifteenth.'

'That's when he gets out?'

'He sent me a letter. I threw it away. I don't care what happens to him. Let him rot in prison. I don't care. I don't want his dirty money!'

'He offered you money?'

'I don't need his pity. A man twenty-two years in prison! And he has the gall to pity *me*! 'She remembered she was thinking out loud, and there were strangers present. Her mouth twisted shut like a trick knot.

'He's still in Dannemora?'

'How do I know who you are?' she demanded.

I took out my wallet and tossed it into her lap. She looked suddenly ashamed. 'I don't know,' she said. 'Sometimes, I don't think there's any justice in the world at all. I don't know what to think any more, I don't know what to do.'

'He's in Dannemora?'

'I wish he'd stay there. I wish he wouldn't write me. After twenty-two years of silence.'

'And he's getting out next Thursday, is that right? The fifteenth?'

'So soon?' Desperation flickered in her eyes. 'What am I going to do?'

'He wants to stay here?'

'No, he – He wants me to leave my husband. Brother and sister. He wrote that I was all the family he had. That he had plenty of money. We could live in Florida.' She looked around at what Robert Campbell had given her. 'My daughter works for the phone company,' she said suddenly. She looked at me again. 'I didn't realize it was so soon. Next Thursday. I didn't write him back. I threw his letter away.'

48

She looked at the window. It faced an airshaft running down through the middle of the building.

I got to my feet, walked over, took my wallet back from her lap. 'Thank you,' I said.

'Yes,' she said, distracted. She kept looking out at the airshaft.

Bill and I walked over to the door. I opened it, and then she turned and stared at us as though she'd never seen us before. She said, 'What am I going to do?'

I told her, 'Don't count on Eddie.'

She started to cry.

We went downstairs and walked back to the car. Bill said, 'Now where?'

'Morris Silber,' I said. 'I didn't find any obituary on him, but there's nobody by that name in the phone book.'

'Who is he?'

'The landlord Dad defended when he got the write-up in the *Times*.'

'Hell, kid, that was thirty years ago. He died in Florida long ago.'

I took a cigarette out, but it broke in my fingers. I threw it out the window, and got another one. 'I can't get hold of the story,' I said. 'It was so goddamn long ago. People have died, changed, forgotten, reformed, moved away. Nobody cares any more. Dad had a whole file of regular clients, and most of them came from the underworld. We know two of them. Eddie Kapp and Morris Silber. Kapp's in jail. God knows where Silber is. Nobody knows or cares who the rest of the clients were. We can't even be sure it was Eddie Kapp that Dad meant. Or what exactly he was trying to say. Eddie Kapp did it? Eddie Kapp would know who did it? Maybe he meant Eddie Kapp would be on our side. We don't know enough about anything. And nobody else knows any more, either.'

'Somebody must, or they wouldn't have started killing people.'

'Morris Silber,' I said. 'He might know a couple other clients. They might know some more. With a starting point, after a while we could probably have the whole list.'

'That would take a lot of time, Ray.'

49

'Time's the only thing I've got.' I looked at him, but he didn't say anything. I said, 'I know, it's different for you. You've got the job, and the kid. House and car and the whole thing. I don't have any of that.'

'I'm going to have to go back pretty soon, Ray. I'm sorry.'

'If only we had a starting point.'

He scratched his nose and said, 'What about the guy who did the profile in the *Times*?'

Every once in a while, Bill said something brilliant like that. I said, 'Let's go back to Manhattan.'

12

His name was Arnold Beeworthy. I found him in the Queens directory, on 74th Road. He was the only Arnold Beeworthy in New York City. NEwtown 9-9970. I called from a drugstore, and a sleepy, heavy baritone answered. I said, 'Did you used to work for the *New York Times*?'

'I still do. What the hell time is it?'

'A little after one.'

'Oh. All right, I ought to get up anyway. Hold on a second.'

I heard the click of the lighter, then he came back. 'All right, what is it?'

'You once did a profile of my father, Willard Kelly.'

'I did? When?'

'1931.'

'Holy hell, boy, don't talk like that'

'It wasn't you?' He didn't sound old enough.

'It was me, but you don't have to remind me.'

'Oh. Can I come out and talk to you?'

'Why not? But make it this afternoon, if you can. I have to go to work at eight.'

'All right.'

We had lunch first, but didn't go back to the hotel. Then we went out to Queens. We started on the same route as yesterday, when we went to see McArdle. Then we turned off onto Wood-haven Boulevard.

The cross-streets were all numbered. Some of them were avenues and some of them were roads and some of them were streets. We saw 74th Avenue. The next block was the one we wanted, 74th Road.

Beeworthy lived in a block of brick two-storey houses all attached together at the sides. His was in the middle. There was a white-painted, jagged-edged board on a stick set into the middle of the narrow lawn. Reflector letters were on the board: BEEWORTHY. It looked like one name, and sounded like another.

A woman who hadn't had Eddie Kapp for a brother or Robert Campbell for a husband opened the door, smiling at us, saying we must be Kelly. Both of us? 'That's right. I'm Ray and this is Bill.'

'Come in. Arnie's chewing bones in his den.'

It was the kind of house sea captains are supposed to retire in. Small and airy rooms, with lots of whatnots around.

We went downstairs to the cellar. It had been finished. There was a game room with knotty pine walls. To the right there was a knotty-pine door. A sign on it said, SNARL. It had been hand-lettered, with a ruler.

She knocked, and somebody inside snarled. She opened the door and said, 'Two Kellys. They're here.'

'More coffee,' he said.

'I know.' She turned to us. 'How do you like your coffee?'

'Just black. Both of us.'

'All right, fine.'

She went upstairs, and we went into the den. Arnold Bee-worthy was a big patriarch with a grey bushy moustache. Maybe he'd always looked forty. If he was writing profiles for the *Times* in 1931, he had to be nearly sixty anyway.

The den was small and square. Rubble and paraphernalia and things around the wall and on the tables. A desk to the right, old and beaten, with mismatched drawer handles. Cartoons, and calendars and photographs and match-books and notes were thumbtacked to the wall over the desk. A filing cabinet was to the left of the desk, second drawer open. A manila folder lay open on top of all the other junk on the desk.

His swivel chair squawked. He said, 'It's too early to stand. How are you?' He jabbed a thick hand at us.

After the handshake and the introductions, Bill took the kitchen chair and I found a folding chair where Beeworthy said it would be, behind the drape.

'1931 is a long time ago,' said Beeworthy. He tapped the open folder. 'I didn't remember the piece you meant. Had to look it up.' He swivelled the chair around and smacked his palm against the side of the open file drawer. 'I've got a file here,' he said, 'of

52

every damn thing I've ever written. Some day it'll come in handy. I can't think how.' He grinned at himself. 'Maybe I'll write a book for George Braziller,' he said. 'It's fantastic how things that are exciting in life can be so dull in print. I wonder if the reverse is true. It's a stupid world. And what can I do for you two?' He aimed a thick finger at Bill. 'Do you look like your father?'

'I guess so,' said Bill. 'That's what people say.'

'One thing triggers another. When you called, I didn't know a Kelly from a kilowatt. Then I read that damn thing, and I remembered the look of that son of a bitch Silber in court, and then I remembered the lawyer. Wore a blue suit. I can't remember what colour tie. Anyway, I'm sorry about that piece. I was young and idealistic, then. Went with a girl, a Jewish Communist vegetarian from the Bronx. She gave speeches in bed. That was 1931, a Communist then was somebody who didn't change their shorts every day. I've never been any damn good at interviews, I always do all the talking myself.' The finger shot out at me this time, and he said, 'What the hell are *you* so mad about?'

I realized then how tense my face muscles were. I tried to relax them, and it felt awkward, as though I were staring.

He grinned at me. 'Okay, you've got a problem. It's a little late to be mad at me for what I said about your father thirty years ago. I take it this is something more current.'

I said, 'Two months ago Monday, somebody murdered my father. The cops gave up. It's something from before 1940. We need names.'

He sat still for a few seconds, looking at me, and then he got to his feet and took one step to his right. 'I want to record this. Do you mind?'

'Yes.'

He looked back at me. One hand was on the tape control. 'Why?'

'We don't want anything in the paper. They're after us, too. The whole family. They killed his wife already, three weeks ago.'

Bill said, 'Two weeks and three days.'

'All right, this is off the record. Nothing in the paper unless you say. Unless and until.' He stepped back, pulled open a green

53

metal locker door, pointed at the shelf. Red and black tape boxes. 'I save crap, too,' he said. 'Interviews that go back nine years. Useless. Not a celebrity in the crowd.'

There was a knock at the door. He snarled, and his wife called, 'Open up, my hands are full.'

Bill jumped up and opened the door.

She had a round tray that said Ruppert's Knickerbocker Beer on it. She set the three cups of coffee around on spaces we cleared. She smiled at everybody, but didn't say anything, and went right out again, closing the door after her. Beeworthy said, 'Will you take my word for it?'

I wanted his cooperation. He was a complicated stringsaver. I said, 'All right.'

'Fine.' He clicked it on, and the tape reels started slowly turning. He went back to the desk and sat down and pushed papers out of the way, and there was the microphone.

Then he had me tell the story, in detail. I didn't like spending the time, but I was the one asking the favour.

He was a fake. He knew how to interview. Three or four times he asked questions, and filled in sections I'd blurred. He said, 'You're grabbing for the wrong end of the horse. Find out who's around *now*, and then see which of them knew your father when. I could do that probably easier than you. Some of Eddie Kapp's old cronies, maybe. Let me dig around in the files – not here, at the paper – and I'll give you a call on Monday. Where you staying?'

'I don't think there'll ever be any story in this,' I said. 'Not that I'd want you to print it.'

He laughed and tugged at his moustache. 'Don't believe the reporters you see in the movies,' he said. 'The age of creative journalism is dead. Stories today are things editors point at. I want this for me, strictly for my own distraction and edification.' He got up and switched off the tape recorder. 'What I really ought to be doing,' he said, looking at the tape reels, 'I ought to be editing some small-town paper somewhere. Up in New England somewhere. I never made the move. I should have made the goddamn move.' He turned back. 'I'll look things up,' he said. 'Where can I get in touch with you?'

'Amington Hotel.'

'I'll call you Monday.'

He went upstairs with us. His wife showed up long enough to say good-bye. She smiled and said, 'I hope you didn't sell him a treasure map. I don't think I could take another treasure map.'

Bill grinned. 'No treasure map,' he said.

Beeworthy handed her his cup. 'Coffee,' he said.

He stood in the doorway as we went down the walk to the car. He looked too big for the house. He said, 'I'll call you Monday.'

13

Bill twisted the car around side streets back to Woodhaven Boulevard. 'Where to?'

'Manhattan,' I said.

'Okay.' He made a right turn. 'Any place special?'

'Lafayette Street. Johnson's office.'

'You trust him now?'

'Part of the way. I don't think he'd lie to us. He seems to have the idea he could help. I want to know how.'

'What street was that? You'd better look it up.'

I opened the glove compartment and got out the map and street guide. It wasn't that tough to find. But the nearest parking space was four blocks away. We walked back and took the elevator to the fifth floor. It was a rundown building with green halls. Johnson's office was 508, to the right.

It was one room. Desk, filing cabinet, wastebasket, two chairs, all bought secondhand. Wall the same green as the hall. One window, with a view of a tarred bumpy roof and beyond it a brick building side. The ceiling paint was flaking.

Johnson stood in the corner, wedged between a wallturn and the filing cabinet. His one arm was up resting on top of the cabinet. His face was bloody. He looked as though he'd been standing there a long time.

He turned his head slowly when we came in. 'Hello,' he said. His voice was low and flat, his pronunciation bad. His lips were puffed. 'I was going to call you,' he said carefully.

We went over and took his arms and led him over to his desk. We sat him down and I said, 'Where's the head?'

'Left.'

I went down the hall to the left and found it. The tile floor was filthy. I got a lot of paper towels, some wet and some dry, and went back.

Bill had a bottle and glass out of a drawer. He was pouring into the glass. I said, 'Let me wash the face first.'

He grunted when I touched the towels to his face. Wet first, and then dry. Somebody'd been wearing a ring. He had scrapes on both cheeks and around his mouth. Bill handed him the glass and he said, 'Thanks.'

I wet a couple of towels from the bottle. When he put the glass down, I said, 'Hold still.'

He tried to jump away when I pressed the towels to the scrapes, but I held his head. 'Christ sake!' he shouted. 'Christ sake!'

I finished and stepped back. 'Okay, have another snort.'

He did, and Bill handed him a lit cigarette. His hands were shaking.

I said, 'How long ago?'

'Half an hour? Fifteen minutes? I don't know. I just stood there.'

'Why were you going to call us?'

He motioned vaguely at his face. 'This was because of you. They wanted to know where you were.'

'And you told them.'

He looked down at his hands. 'Not at first.'

'It's all right. We've been looking for them, too. You did right telling them.'

He emptied the glass and reached for the bottle. He drank from the bottle.

I said, 'Where did they connect you with us? They didn't see us together, or they'd know where to find us. You've mentioned our names to somebody.'

He coughed and dragged on the cigarette. 'Half a dozen people. A couple cops I know, a reporter, a guy works for one of the big agencies.'

'It's one of them. You find out which one. You need any money?'

'Not now. Later on, maybe. Unless you could advance me twenty.'

I nodded at Bill. He dragged out his wallet and gave Johnson two tens.

I said, 'Move as quick as you can. And don't be afraid to talk. If they come after you again, tell them anything they want to know. It's okay.'

'Yeah.'

'Call us at the hotel as soon as you've got something. If we're not there, leave a message.'

'You aren't going to move?'

'Why should we? I told you, we want to find them as bad as they want to find us. We'll stay at the same place.'

He shook his head. 'They're mean bastards,' he said.

'You okay now?'

'Yeah, I guess.'

We left and went uptown and checked into a hotel forty blocks north of the Amington. We hung around, and when I called the Amington they said there weren't any messages.

We bought a deck of cards and hung around the room. All we could do was wait.

14

Bill woke me up at nine o'clock in the morning and said it was time to go to Mass. He wasn't kidding. I said, 'No.'

'You need God's help, Ray,' he said earnestly.

I said, 'Go away.'

'You don't think you do?'

'The guys in the Chrysler didn't.'

'Who?'

'The guys who killed Dad. And your wife.'

'Ray, you're still in the Church, aren't you?'

'Do I look it?'

'You've lost your faith?'

'They shot it out from under me.'

'You're one of those, huh? The first tragedy comes into your life, and you blame it on God.'

I rolled over on my side away from him. 'Go on,' I said. 'You'll be late for Mass.'

He did some more talking, but I ignored him, so he got dressed and went out. I fell asleep again.

I was awake when he came back. I was sitting by the window, looking out at the street and thinking about waking up in the hospital.

He put a bag on the dresser. 'I brought you a coffee and a danish,' he said.

'Thanks.'

He had the same for himself. We were quiet and ate for a while, and then we both started to apologize at the same time. We broke off and laughed, shaking our heads. 'Yeah,' I said. 'I was tired, that's all.'

'I should of left you alone.'

'The hell. I don't like this waiting.'

He grinned and shrugged. 'We need to wait, that's all. We've gone this far, now we wait.' His hand was wrapped around the coffee carton. He tilted it, finishing the coffee, and then tossed it into the can. 'All we have to do is to take it easy.'

'Yeah.'

I went over and called the other hotel and asked if there were any messages. There weren't. I went back, and Bill had a rummy hand dealt out on his bed. I scooped up my cards and played standing up, walking around between draws. I went gin on his seventh discard and picked up forty-three points and threw the cards down on the bed and lit a cigarette. Bill told me to take it easy. I walked around some more, and then I came back and shuffled the cards and dealt out the second hand. By the time I went gin I was sitting down.

At quarter to three, I went down and signed for another day and paid. Then I went back up and picked up the hand Bill dealt me and ripped the cards across the middle, so we went out and had hamburgers and bottles of Schlitz. Bill said, 'I think we can go back and get the suitcases now. What do you think?'

I shrugged. 'What the hell? Anything.'

We got the car. Bill drove and I sat beside him and chain-smoked. I looked out at the people. Two months ago less one day I was here with Dad. One of those people out there recognized Dad and went and made a phone call. Or shadowed us back to the hotel first. One of those people on the sidewalk. I wanted to know which one. I wanted to reach out of the car and grab him by the throat, and drag him along beside the door.

We stuck the car in a parking lot and walked uptown and crosstown and came at our hotel from the back, where there was a dry-cleaning store. A little store in the back corner of the hotel, on the side street, open on Sunday for tourists.

We went in. There was a good-looking coloured girl in a green dress behind the counter. I said, 'Hotel maintenance. Survey check. We got to get into the cellar here.'

She shrugged. 'Okay with me.'

I looked around and acted mad. 'Lady, I'm not playing guessing games with you. I don't have the whole damn hotel memorized. Where's the door?'

60

She waved her hand. 'Back there. You'll have to move that rack.'

We went behind the counter, down between the racks of cleaned clothes, and I saw the lines of the door in the linoleum floor. I shoved the rack out of the way, and the girl said, 'Take it easy with the clothes.'

I ignored her. I lifted the door, and it was pitch-black down there. We didn't have any flashlight, and it wouldn't have looked good to back out. I just hoped there was a light switch somewhere.

I just barely saw it as I was going down, tucked away behind a beam next to the door opening. I clicked it on, and continued down, and Bill came after me.

There was a wide, balanced firedoor off to the right. It was filthy dirty. Instead of a lock, there was a latch and hasp, held shut by a twisted piece of thick wire broken off a hanger. By the time I got it untwisted, my hands were coated with dirt. My forehead was wet with perspiration, and I could almost feel the dust settling against it and sticking.

I shoved the door aside on its roller and pawed around on the other side till I found the switch. I turned it on and saw a bigger chunk of basement, just as filthy as this. Up ahead, there was humming. Machinery, not voice.

I went back to the foot of the stairs and shouted up. The girl came over and looked down at me. She stood with her legs pressed together and her palms flat against the front of her thighs, so I couldn't peek up under her skirt. She said, 'I got a customer here. What do you want?'

'We're going on through this way,' I said. 'You can close that door now.'

She started to bitch about it. I turned away and went through to the other part of the cellar. Bill was already over there, waiting for me. The girl kept bitching about how it wasn't her job to close trap doors. I pulled the fire door shut and then I couldn't hear her.

Off this room there was a corridor, low-ceilinged, with concrete walls. The walls were dirt-grey except where fresh concrete had dribbled away and showed flaky white. At the end there was another firedoor. This one wasn't fastened at all. We slid it open and went through to a part that was already lit. The humming was louder ahead of us.

We came to the end of the corridor a little ways after that door, and found a relatively clean part, with an old chunk of linoleum on the floor, and a battered old desk, and a girlie calendar on the wall. There wasn't anybody there except a cat asleep beside the desk. The cat woke up when we got there, and slunk away to the doorway where the humming came from. It was brightly lit in there. I got a glimpse of metal stairs going down and a lot of dirty black machinery and a guy with a white house-painter's cap sitting on a kitchen chair.

On the opposite wall, there was the door of the freight elevator. I pushed the button, and you could hear the loud groaning of the machinery in the bottom of the elevator shaft, even farther down than we were. The elevator came. It wasn't fancy, like the one for the customers. It had wide plank flooring and chest-high sides and only a kind of grillwork on top and a grill gate at the front. We got on and I shut the gate and pressed the button for our floor. The elevator ground up slowly and stopped, and we got off. I pressed the top button and unlocked and closed the door. It went on up.

We came down the hall from the opposite direction that we usually took. There was nobody around. There was a telephone ringing. When we got closer, I could hear it was coming from our room. It rang six times and quit.

I listened at the door of the room. Then I unlocked it and shoved it open fast and ran in crouched, cutting to the right while Bill faded to the left. But I'd heard right, there wasn't anybody there.

We packed what we needed in one bag and left the other one still open on a chair. Then we rumpled the beds. The place had been searched. Quietly, with things put back more or less in the right spot. Nothing had been taken, not even the two guns.

We went out to the hall, and I was just putting the key in the lock when the phone started again. Bill said to forget it but I told

62

him, 'No, we still live here. We don't want them looking some-where else.'

I went back in and picked it up on the fifth ring. A guy's voice said, 'Kelly?'

'That's me,' I said. Behind me, Bill brought the suitcase back in and shut the door.

'Will Kelly? Will Kelly, Junior?'

'No, this is Ray.'

'Let me talk to Will.'

'Who shall I tell him is calling?'

'Never you mind, kid brother. You just put Will on, okay?'

'Yeah, sure. Hold on. I'll get my big brudda for ya.'

'Thanks.' He thought he was the one being sarcastic.

I dropped the phone on the table and said to Bill, 'Some guy. He'll only talk to you. But he says Will instead of Bill.'

'Okay.' He came over and reached for the phone. When his fingers touched it, I saw the stagefright hit him, and I said, 'What the hell? All you have to do is listen.'

'Yeah.' He picked it up and held it to his face and said, 'Bill Kelly here.' He waited and said, 'Why?' Then he waited and said, 'What's your name, friend?' Then he waited some more and said, 'The hell with you.' His eyes swivelled to me and he grim-aced. Into the receiver he said, 'No I'm not hanging up.' He made writing motions with his other hand.

I went over and got the hotel's pen and a piece of the hotel's stationery. Behind me, Bill said, 'For all I know, this is some sort of gag.'

I came back and put the pen and paper on the table and he said, 'What was that name? No, I didn't hear it.' His eyes found me again and he grinned and asked the phone, 'Eddie Kapp? Who the hell is Eddie Kapp?'

I grinned back at him. I lit two cigarettes and held one of them for him. I walked around the room.

'To you maybe it's comedy,' Bill told the guy, 'but to me I've got better things to do. You want to give me a number, go ahead.'

I walked back and stood watching.

'I've got pencil and paper,' Bill said. He was enjoying himself now, acting like he was bored and irritated, all his stagefright gone. He picked up the pen. 'Go ahead,' he said. 'Shoot.' He winked at me, and I nodded and laughed.

'Circle,' he said, writing it down, 'five, nine, nine, seven, oh. Yeah, I've got it.' He read it off again. 'Maybe I'll call it, maybe I won't' he said. He grinned. 'Up y –' Then he looked at me. 'He hung up.'

'You, too. Here's a cigarette.'

He traded the receiver for the cigarette. 'He wouldn't give me his name. He said all he wanted was to give me the phone number. We should stick close to the room until Friday, and then we should call that number. When I asked him why, he said maybe the name Eddie Kapp would tell me.'

'He's getting out Thursday,' I said.

'I know.'

'Hold on a second.' I dialled the number, and after two rings a recorded female voice told me it wasn't a working number. I hung up. 'Okay, let's get out of here. That guy's already calling his buddies in the lobby. The Kellys are home.'

We went out and down the hall to the freight elevator. I'd unlocked the door on the way in. I pushed the button and when it came down we got aboard and I pushed the lock button on the inside of the door. Then I closed the gate and we went down to the cellar.

The cat was sleeping on top of the desk. She raised her head and looked at us. Way down to our right were some whiskey cases. We went down there, and looked around. In a shallow concrete pit there were four tapped beer kegs, the copper coils running up the side wall. So it was all right, it was the bar and not the liquor store. We went over to the stairs and up them. This was a regular door, not a trap like in the cleaners. I opened it and peeked out. I was looking at the corridor between the bar and the kitchen. It was empty. We went through and made a sharp left into the men's room. We washed our faces and hands, and then went down the long length of the bar and out the street door. We turned the corner and walked crosstown and down-

64

town to the West 46th Street parking lot where we'd left the car. There was a sullen veteran in khakis and a fatigue cap on duty, and he walked back to the car with us and stood looking through the windshield at the steering wheel as he said, 'I'm taking a chance on this, but what the hell? I don't do their goddamn dirty work or anybody's.'

He sneaked a quick look at us and glared back at the steering wheel again. 'They screwed me out of two hundred and fifty bucks. What am I going to do, call the goddamn cops on them? They got the goddamn cops in their pocket. *You* know that.'

I said, 'What's the point?'

His cheek twitched, and he kept staring through the windshield into the car. 'I just want you to know, that's all. How come I'll do this. I'm paying the bastards back, that's what, two hundred and fifty bucks worth.' He tugged at his fatigue cap, and turned around quick to look out at the street. Then he turned back. 'A guy came around yesterday afternoon,' he told the car, 'with a sheet of paper and your licence plate on it. He give me, and said I should call in at Alex's if the car shows up. He described the car, red and cream Merc like this one. Only, I wouldn't give them the sweat off my stones. And you've got an out-of-town plate, I figure you're tourists or something and they're trying to give you a bad time. So the hell with them. I didn't call. And I smeared mud on your plates.'

'You did?' I went over and looked at the back of the car. He'd done a good job, realistic, with mud and dirt on the bumper and over the licence plate, so a part of each number was showing. Enough so it didn't look like a covered plate, but it wasn't easy to read the numbers.

I went back and said, 'Thanks. You did a good job.'

'You better go back upstate,' he said.

I dug out my wallet and found a ten. I slid it down the fender to him. 'Here's an instalment on the two-fifty,' I said.

'You didn't have to, but it's okay.' He palmed the ten.

'This guy, what's his name?'

'I don't know. I've heard him called Sal. Or Sol, I don't know which. He comes around sometimes, and sometimes he works here. Every once in a while, he parks some fancy car here. The boss knows him. He's big, with a great big jaw like Mussolini.'

'And Alex's?'

'That's a car rental place, up by the bridge. Up in Washington Heights.' He swiped another quick look at me. 'You don't want to spoil with them, Mister. You better go back upstate.'

'Thanks for the help,' I said.

He shrugged. 'You got to wait out by the sidewalk,' he said. 'I'll bring the car to you.'

'Okay.'

We walked back over the gravel to the sidewalk, and he drove the car out and gave it to us without a word. We went around the block and down to 39th Street and through the Lincoln Tunnel. In Jersey City, we parked the car on a street off Hudson Boulevard and took the tube back to Manhattan, switched to the subway and went uptown to the hotel. We unpacked the suitcase and showered and brushed our teeth.

Bill said, 'Do you want to follow up this car rental place?'

I shook my head. 'That's a Pacific campaign. Fight your way across every useless little island you can find for five thousand miles, before you get to the big island you wanted all along. I want to stay away from the little islands. That's why we switched hotels. Thursday we get to the big island.'

'Fine with me,' he said.

Later on, we went to a movie. I couldn't sit still, so we went down to Brooklyn on the subway and drank a while at a neighbourhood bar. He closed at four and we took the subway back. There wasn't anything to drink in the room. I lay on my back in the dark and stared at the ceiling. 'Bill,' I said, 'I think I know why they fuzzed around on all those little islands.'

But he was asleep already.

15

Monday afternoon I called the other hotel. Beeworthy and Johnson had both called, leaving messages for me to call them back. Since I now knew it was Eddie Kapp I was looking for, at least to begin with, there wasn't any point in calling either of them.

Bill went out for a deck of cards and was gone an hour. When he came back, he had a haircut and he said he didn't know I'd be worried. We played cards and I walked around and the room got smaller. We went out after a while and went to see a movie up in the Bronx. Then we went to a bar.

Tuesday, I called Johnson, just to have something to do. He was frantic. He said, 'Where the hell are you people? I've been going nuts. Did you move out or something?'

'Hell no,' I said. 'We're still here. We aren't around the room much.'

'Jesus Christ, I guess not. I've been over there half a dozen times. I was ready to think those guys got to you.'

'Not a peep,' I said.

'They haven't been around at all?'

'Nope.'

'You son of a bitch, you've moved someplace else.'

I grinned. It was fine just to be talking to somebody. 'We're still registered at the Amington,' I told him, 'and our suitcase is still there. I mean here.'

'All right, you shouldn't trust me with the address, but you don't have to lie to me.'

'We're still at the Amington, Johnson,' I said.

'All right, all right.' He was irritated. 'On that other thing,' he said, 'do you want to hear what I've got to say or not?'

'It's up to you.'

'Oh, crap. You're just trying to get under my skin. I've got it narrowed down to two people. A cop named Fred Maine. And a guy named Dan Christie, he's an investigator works for Northeastern Agency. It's got to be one of those two. I'm pretty sure Maine gets two paychecks every week, one of them from the city. And Christie is a poker buddy of Sal Metusco, he's a numbers collector midtown on the west side.'

'Keep up the good work,' I told him. I didn't say anything about the veteran in the parking lot, because Johnson would have only told the next guy who broke his arm.

We talked a little, about nothing at all, and I said I'd call him back. I didn't say when. Then I looked at Beeworthy's number, but I resisted the impulse. He'd want to do a lot of interviewing, and I wasn't in the mood.

Bill wanted to go to another movie that night, but I couldn't take it. So we sat around the room and drank and after a while I threw a gin hand out the window. A little after midnight, we went down to 42nd Street and saw an important movie that had been made from a Broadway play called *A Sound of Distant Drums*. It was about homosexuality and what a burden it was, but the hero bore the burden girlfully. It didn't convert me.

Wednesday we checked out of the hotel. We also went down and checked out of the Amington. We figured they were looking for us somewhere else by now, so we didn't sneak around. Nobody noticed us particularly. Then we took the tube to Jersey City and got the car and drove up to Plattsburg. I rode in the back seat because I still couldn't face highway driving in the right front. Sitting back there, I read the papers we'd bought in the city. The *Post* had an article about Eddie Kapp getting out of prison tomorrow. They were unhappy about it, and wanted to know if Eddie Kapp had really paid his debt to society. There was a blurred photo of him twenty-five years ago. No other paper referred to him at all.

In Plattsburg, we checked into a hotel on Margaret Street. Bill was bushed, he'd driven three hundred and thirty miles in eight hours. I went out alone and found a bar and traded war stories with a guy who'd been stationed in Japan. If he was telling the truth, he had a better time in Japan than I did in Germany. If I was telling the truth, so did I.

In the morning, we checked out again and drove the fifteen miles to Dannemora.

Dannemora is a little town. In most of it, you wouldn't know there was a penitentiary around at all. The town doesn't look dirty enough, or mean enough. But the penitentiary's there, a high long wall next to the sidewalk along the street. The sidewalk's cracked and frost-heaved over there. On the other side, it's cleaner and there's half a dozen bars with neon signs that say Budweiser and Genesee. National and local beers on tap. Bill had Budweiser and I had Genesee. It tasted like beer.

The bar was dark, but it was done in light wood lightly varnished and it was wider than it should have been for its depth. You got the feeling the bar wasn't dark at all really, you were just slowly going blind. The bartender was a short wide man with a black moustache. There were two other customers, in red-and-black hunting jackets and high leather boots. They were local citizens, and they were drinking bar scotch with Canada Dry ginger ale.

The *Post* had said Eddie Kapp would be a free man at noon, but we didn't know for sure. We got to town shortly before ten and sat on high stools in this bar where we could see the metal door in the wall across the way. I wasn't sure I'd recognize Eddie Kapp. The picture in the Post was blurred and twenty-five years old. But he was sixty-one years of age. And how many people would be getting out all in one day?

We sat there and nursed our beers. I wore my shirt-tail out, and when I sat leaning forward with my elbows on the bar, the butt of Smitty's gun stuck into my lowest rib. Bill had the same problem with the Luger.

At eleven-thirty a tan-and-cream Chrysler slid to the curb in front of the bar. Bill looked at it and turned to me and said, 'Is that them? Is that the ones who killed Dad?'

I didn't say anything. I was looking at the guy in the right front seat. I knew him then.

I started to get down from the stool, flipping the shirt-tail out of the way, but Bill grabbed my elbow and whispered, 'Don't be a jerk. Wait till Kapp comes out.'

I stood there, not moving one way or the other. The gun butt felt funny in my hand. The side that had been against my skin was hot and moist. The other side was cold and dry.

Then I said, 'All right. You're right.' He let me go and I said, 'I'll be right back.' I let go of the gun and smoothed the shirt-tail and walked down the length of the bar past the other two customers, who were talking to the bartender about trout. I went into the head. There was one stall. I went in there and latched the door and took the gun out from my belt so I could lean over. Then I threw up in the toilet. I washed my mouth out at the sink and got back to the stall just in time to throw up again. I waited a minute, and then washed my mouth out again. There was a bubbled dirty mirror over the sink and I saw myself in it. I looked pale and young and unready. The gun barrel was cold against my hairless belly. I was a son of a bitch and a bad son.

I went back out and sat down at the stool and held my glass without drinking. Bill said, 'Nothing new.' I didn't answer him.

After a while, I got fantastically hungry, all of a sudden. I waited, but a little before one I asked the bartender what sandwiches he had and he said he had a machine that made hamburgers in thirty seconds. I ordered two and Bill ordered one. The machine was down at the other end of the bar, a chrome-sided infra-red cooker.

I was halfway through the second hamburger when the door across the street opened and an old man without a hat came out.

His suit, even from across the street, looked expensive and up to the minute. It hadn't been given him by the government. It was grey and flattering. His shoes were black and caught the sunlight. His hair was a very pale grey, not quite white. None of it had fallen out. His face was tough to see from this far away; squarish and thick-browed, that was about all.

As soon as he came out, I spat my mouthful of hamburger onto the plate and got off the stool. Bill said, 'Wait till he reaches the car.'

I said, 'Yeah, sure.'

I walked over by the door. Only Kapp wasn't coming toward the car, he was turning and walking in the other direction. His shadow trailed him aslant along the wall.

He had to be Eddie Kapp. Age and timing. Expensive suit.

The Chrysler slid forward, staying close to the curb. It purred down the block moving at the same rate as Kapp, keeping behind him. He didn't look around at it. Apparently, he hadn't seen it.

Bill said, 'What the hell is that all about?'

I said, 'Go get the car. Stay at least a block behind me.'

He shook his head, baffled. 'Okay,' he said, and went out to the car. The bartender and the other two customers were looking at me. I went out onto the sidewalk and strolled along after the Chrysler.

We went three blocks that way, like some stupid parade. Kapp out in front, on the left-hand side of the street. Then the Chrysler, on the right side, half a block behind him. Then me, also on the right side, another half a block back. And then Bill, a full block behind me on this side, in the Mercury. Kapp was headed for the bus depot, from the direction he was taking. Downtown, anyway.

Then we got to a quiet block, and the Chrysler jolted ahead, angling sharp across the empty street, and it was clear they meant to run him down. I shouted, 'Look out!' and ran out across the street after the Chrysler. The goddamn ankle slowed me down.

Kapp turned when I shouted, saw the Chrysler jumping the curb at him, and dove backwards through a hedge onto a lawn. A dog started yapping. The Chrysler jounced around on a parabola back to the street, up and down the curb. The guy on the right had his head and arm out the window, and was shooting at me, the way he'd shot at Dad. He had a little moustache.

I dragged Smitty's gun out and pointed it down the street and pulled the trigger six times. The guy's head slumped down, and his arm hung down beside the door. The Chrysler made a tight hard right turn, and the guy hanging out the window flapped the way live people don't.

I stood in the middle of the street and grinned. When I was four days in Germany, two guys took me to a Kaiserslauten whorehouse in Amiland, and I was afraid to admit I was virgin and afraid I'd be too afraid to do anything about it. The whore had been so damn indifferent I'd got mad and jumped her trying

71

to attract her attention, I did, and she had an orgasm. She hadn't with the other two. Going back to the base, I broke a bus window for the hell of it. I felt the same way now, standing in the middle of the street and grinning, while the Chrysler took a lump of clay around the corner and out of sight.

The Mercury pulled up beside me, and Kapp came struggling back through the hedge. I could hear the dog going nuts. Kapp looked shaky and wobbly. He'd made a great dive for sixty-one, but now he was acting his age. His left trouser leg was ripped at the knee.

I stopped grinning and opened the back door of the Mercury. I threw the empty gun in there and went over and took Kapp's arm and brought him to the Mercury and shoved him inside. He acted dazed, and didn't fight back or ask questions. I got in after him, and slammed the door. A black-haired woman in a flowered apron came to a break in the hedge and looked at us. Bill tromped the accelerator and we rode away from Dannemora.

72

16

Kapp recovered pretty fast. He pulled Smitty's gun out from under him and looked at it, and then turned to me. 'That was lousy shooting. It took you four shots to find him and then you threw two bullets away.'

'I've only got one eye,' I said. 'I have trouble with distance judgement.'

'Oh. In that case, it was all right.' He looked at the back of Bill's thick neck. 'If this is a heist,' he said, 'you two are crazy. Nobody wants me back money bad.'

'We just want to ask you one or two questions,' I said.

He looked at me again, and grinned. He had white false teeth. They looked better on him than the ones Krishman had worn. 'Were you alive when I went in there, boy?' he asked me.

'Yes.'

'Then you're just lucky you've lived this long.' He hefted the gun, holding it by the barrel. 'What if I were to break your head in with this? What's your partner going to do?'

I looked into his grin and said, 'We're not playing.'

He studied me a while, and then he looked sad and dropped the gun onto the floor between our feet. 'I'm an old man,' he said. 'I'm ready to retire.' He sat back, showing me his profile, gazing up at the ceiling and trying to look sick. 'That hard violent world,' he said, 'that's all behind me now.'

'Not all,' I said.

He quit joking. He turned to me and he kept his lips flat and his voice flat. 'Ask your questions,' he said, 'and go to hell.'

I said, 'Why was Willard Kelly killed?'

He looked surprised, worried, wary, blank, one right after the other. He said, 'Who the hell is Willard Kelly?'

I reached down and picked the gun up and tapped the butt against his knee. 'I hear old men's bones are brittle,' I said.

73

'Naw. I've got a geriatric formula. I take a spoonful of chancre pus twice a day. It's a new thing on the market for senior citizens.'

'They let you read magazines. That's fine, but I'm not playing. How's your kneecap?' I tapped him again with the gun-butt, and he didn't manage to hide the wince. I said, 'Why was Willard Kelly killed?'

'He had B.O.'

I tapped him again. He put his hand down over his knee. His hand was older than his face; it had blue veins ropy against the skin. I tapped the back of his hand, and he said 'Uh,' and took the hand away and held it tight against his chest. I tapped his knee. He said, 'Go on and break it, you clumsy bastard. I could use a good faint around now.'

'You won't faint.' I tapped him again. His face was paler, and there were strain lines around his eyes and mouth. I said, 'Why was Willard Kelly killed?'

He turned his head away and glared out the window. I tapped him again.

He didn't faint. Bill bypassed Plattsburg. A few miles south he took a turnoff that promised cabins by the lake. Lake Champlain. Another sign said, 'Closed after Labour Day.' It was after Labour Day.

There were white cabins with red trim, somewhat faded, fronted by a strip of blacktop. There was no one there, but previous poachers had left their rubber spoor on the blacktop.

Kapp didn't want to get out of the car. Bill came around and pulled him out by the hair and shoved him down between the cabins. He favoured the left leg. We stood him up against the white clapboard back wall of a cabin. Trees screened us from the lake. Bill looked at Kapp and then at me and told me, 'Remember McArdle.'

'I will,' I said. 'I'll be careful.'

Kapp said, 'McArdle?'

'Andrew McArdle,' I said. 'I asked him some questions, but he had a bad heart and died before he could answer them. Bill was telling me to be more careful with you.'

74

He shook his head. 'I don't get it.'

We stood and waited for him to think. He stood slanted against the wall holding his injured hand. The expensive suit looked bad. He was having trouble with the left leg, and the back of his left hand was swelling and turning grey. He had more lines on his face. He was tired and worried and futile. He was being brave when it didn't matter, and he knew it didn't matter, but he didn't know how to stop.

He tried to talk, and he had to take time out to clear phlegm out of his throat and spit it carefully away from us. Then he said, 'I can't figure you two. Those other guys, I know who they were. I can guess, I mean. But not you two. Amateurs, asking the wrong questions . . . ' He shook his head. 'Where'd you get so mean?'

'What's a right question?' I asked him.

He looked up through branches at the sky. 'I was a free man again a little while,' he said.

I said, 'Bill, if he doesn't open his mouth right now I'm going to kill him and to hell with it. We'll go back to the city and go by way of the little islands.'

Bill frowned. 'I don't like it Ray,' he said. 'I don't want to have anything to do with it.'

I said, 'Here, take this gun up to the car and reload it. Better give me the Luger for while you're gone.'

All of a sudden, Kapp laughed. He laughed like a man who's just heard a good joke at a clambake. We looked at him, and he pointed at Bill and cried, 'You silly bastard, you're Will Kelly! You're Junior, you're his son!'

We just looked at him. He pushed himself out from the wall and limped towards us, grinning. 'Why the hell didn't you say you were Will's goddamn kid? I couldn't place you, I couldn't figure you anywhere at all.'

I said, 'Stop. Hold up the reunion a second. There's still the question.'

He looked at me, and his grin calmed down. 'All right,' he said. This time, he acted like he was at the clambake and it was his turn to tell a joke and he had a whopper saved up. 'I didn't

75

know Will'd been killed,' he said. 'But I know why. It was because he was holding something for me. Until I got out of jail. He was supposed to hold it and stay out of the city until I was sprung. He was killed because he was holding it and because I was going to be getting out.'

'What was it he was holding?'

He nodded. 'You.'

'What about me?'

'You look more like your mother than your father,' he said.

Then I got it. 'You're a lying son of a bitch,' I said.

'You look a lot more like her. I know. I see your father in the mirror every morning.'

I laughed at him. 'You're crazy, or you think we are. Or are you just wisecracking again?'

'It's true,' he said.

Bill said, 'What the hell's going on?'

I said to Kapp, 'He didn't get it yet. When he does, he'll take you apart. You better say fast you were lying.'

'I wasn't lying.'

'It was the wrong ploy,' I insisted. 'Bill has a big thing about honour.'

Kapp said, 'We ought to sit down over a bottle of imported and talk. We've got a lot to fill in, the both of us.'

Bill said, 'Goddamn it, for the last time, what's going on?'

'Kapp says we're half-brothers. We shared a mother, only Willard Kelly wasn't my father.'

Bill's eyebrows came down. 'Who does he say is your father?'

'If he's smart, he'll change his story.'

'I say it's me,' said Kapp, 'and it's true.' He was mad at us.

Bill raised his shoulders and took a step and I tripped him. I said to Kapp, 'He's going to kill you now, I swear to God he is. And there isn't a thing I can do about it.'

Bill was struggling to his feet, and Kapp backed away to the wall, talking fast, mad and scared both. 'Your mother was a two-bit whore out of Staten Island, a goddamn rabbit. She sucked Will Kelly into marrying her, with the first kid. The second was mine. I know it, because she was at my cabin on Lake George for six months and she only went back to Kelly because I told her to.'

Bill was on his feet and I was hanging on his arm. Kapp spat words at us like darts. 'Edith got exiled to a burg upstate with Will Kelly and orders to behave and never come back to the city. She couldn't stand it. She was there a year and she stuck razor blades in her wrists.'

Bill threw me away, and I bounced off a tree-trunk. I shouted, 'Tell him you're lying, or you're a dead man!'

Kapp flamed at me. His eyes were on fire. 'And you'll have another dead father to revenge, brat!'

Bill swung a fist like knotted wood. Kapp tried to lean inside it, but he was too slow. It caught him behind the ear and dropped him on his face in the weeds. Bill bent over, reaching to pick him up again.

I came up and clubbed Bill with the Luger. He went down on his knees. Kapp crawled away downslope, and Bill fell on his legs. I rolled him over, freeing Kapp's legs, and Kapp crawled up a tree trunk to a standing position and stood hangdog, his arms around the thick trunk.

I stood in front of him, holding the Luger by the barrel. 'Don't stop talking,' I said.

'Not now, boy, I'm an old man.'

'*Stop playing!*'

He shivered, and leaned his forehead against the bark. His eyes were closed. 'All right,' he said. 'But give me a few seconds. Please.'

I gave him the seconds. When he raised his head, there were fine lines from the bark on his brow. He pushed his lips over in a weakly smile. 'You've got her looks, boy, but you've got my guts. I'm glad of that.' I didn't say anything. He shrugged and let the smile fade out, and said, 'All right. Her name was Edith Stanton. She came out of Rosebank on Staten Island in '34. She went with Tom Gilley a while. He made her pregnant, but he aborted her with some right hands to the stomach. Then she floated around, here and there, with one or another of a bunch that mainly knew each other. This was still just after Repeal, and we were all trying to get organized again. She came across Will Kelly, and he fell for her. He was the only one'd ever held a door for her since Staten Island, and she liked it. Then she got pregnant again, by him this time, and suckered him into marriage. But she didn't like staying home with the kid all the time, and she got to hanging around with the old bunch. Kelly stayed home and changed diapers. I think he's waking up.'

I turned and looked. 'We've still got a few minutes,' I said.

'All right. It's like this, some women come to life with motherhood. I never paid much attention to Edith at all before, but when she started hanging around again she was different. No, she *looked* different. Tougher, maybe. More basic. I don't know what it is, it happens to some women. I took her home. She was a rabbit, but there was something interesting in her besides that. I don't know how to explain it.' He was getting nostalgic.

'I don't even care,' I told him. 'Get on with it.'

That brought him back. He said, 'For a while, in '38, there was some trouble. Baltimore was where heroin and that came into the country. There was a kind of dispute, Chicago and us, as to who was going to run Baltimore. So I went up to a private place on Lake George. I had two boys with me, two I could trust. And Edith. I told her come along and she came. We were there six months, and nobody touched her but me. She came back pregnant. She named the kid Raymond Peter Kelly. That was a private joke between her and me. I owned the cabin as Raymond Peterson.'

Bill moaned. I said to Kapp, 'We'll finish the conversation in the car. Come on.'

'All right.'

He took a step away from the tree and fell down. He looked up at me, shame etched on his face. 'There was a time a workout like this would've meant nothing,' he said. 'Not a thing. Not a thing at all.'

'I believe you.'

I switched the Luger to the other hand and helped him up. He leaned on me and we went back up between the cabins and around to the Mercury. I looked at him. He wouldn't be running anywhere. I said, 'I'll be right back. You won't have to go over this part again.'

He nodded. I opened the back door and he sagged onto the seat, his feet hanging out onto the blacktop, his head leaning sideways against the seatback. I turned away from him and went back and found Bill coming up, one arm straight out beside him holding the cabin. His face was square grey stone.

I stood in front of him. I said, 'Bill, I want you to know something.'

He said, 'Get out of my way.'

'There's an old man up at the car. If you kill him for telling the truth, I'll shoot you down for a mad dog. What did you do when they told you Ann was dead? Punch the guy who brought the news?'

He said, 'Go to hell.'

I stepped aside. 'You can't stamp out facts with fists,' I said. 'Your father was a crook's shyster. My father is sitting in the car up there. Our mother wasn't the kind they have in the *Ladies Home Journal*.'

He let go the cabin and went down on his knees and started to cry with his hands hanging straight down at his sides. I went back to the Mercury and said to Kapp, 'He'll be along pretty soon. He won't do anything any more.'

'Good.' He nodded. His eyes were half-closed, his hands were limp in his lap. The swollen hand looked worse. 'I'm tired,' he said. He pushed his eyelids open more and studied me. He smiled. 'You're my only child, do you know that? The only child I ever fathered. I'm glad to look at you.'

I lit us cigarettes.

17

September is a good time of year way upstate. I stood beside the car and smoked and looked around. The cigarette smoke was thin and blue in the air. The mountains over us in the west were half in the green of summer and half in the browns and reds of fall. The lake, seen down past the cabins and the tree trunks, was blue and deep and cold. I could smell it. Far away over it was Vermont, dark green.

I didn't look at Kapp. I didn't know how to fix my face to look at him. It wasn't as though I'd been an orphan all my life. I already had a father. Kapp had blood claims, but he was a stranger.

After a while, Bill came up into sight from between the cabins. He stood there, not looking our way, and got a cigarette for himself. He fumbled badly with it, as though his fingers had swollen. Then he came over, slow and heavy, and got silently behind the wheel and started the engine.

I didn't know who to sit beside. The front seat still made me geechy, but I didn't want Bill to think he was being cut out. Kapp knew it, and grinned at me. 'Sit up front with your brother. I want to stretch out, I'm tired.'

I got in and slammed the door. Bill gazed out the windshield and mumbled, 'Back to the hotel?'

I said, 'Might as well.'

We drove back to Plattsburg. Kapp said he wanted a drink. Bill went upstairs, walking away with his shoulders hunched, and Kapp and I went across the lobby and into the bar. It was called the Fife & Drum. The glasses were painted red, white and blue to look like drums. Because of the Revolutionary War.

Kapp said, 'I haven't had a drink in fifteen years. What's a good Scotch?'

I shrugged. 'I don't buy good Scotch.'

80

The waiter stooped and murmured, 'House of Lords?'

'Good name,' said Kapp. 'Got a ring to it. Two doubles, on the rocks.'

The waiter went away. I said, 'You were in jail more than twenty years. They let you have liquor the first five?'

He winked. 'I should of gone to Sing Sing, boy, but I had connections. And there was a time when Dannemora was a little easier. Not like a Federal pen.' He made a sour face. 'It is now.'

The waiter came back, went away.

Kapp raised his glass, tasted it, made a face. He coughed. 'I forgot. It's like starting new, it's been so long. Remember how lousy it tasted the first time?'

'You want a mix?'

'A what? Oh, a set-up? Not me, boy. Not Eddie Kapp.' He got out a new cigarette, working one-handed. His left hand looked terrible. I held out my zippo and said, 'I'm sorry what I did to you.'

'Shut your face. Tell me about Kelly. Your brother. He doesn't look like the type to be here.'

'They killed his wife, too.'

'Hah? His wife?' He sat back and nodded at me and grinned. 'That means they're scared,' he said. 'Scared of old Eddie Kapp. That's good.'

'We found a guy said there was some kind of syndicate trouble brewing in New York. That that was why they killed my – my father. Why they killed Kelly.'

'Take it easy. You think of him as your father, call him your father. He was a lot more your father than I was, huh?'

'You were in jail.'

'That's the truth.' He swallowed some more Scotch. 'I'm getting used to it,' he said. Then he watched himself tap ashes into the tray. 'About your mother,' he said. 'I don't want you to get me wrong, what I said before. Edith never worked in a house, nothing like that. She wasn't ever a professional.'

'Let's forget about that.'

He got mad. He glared at me. 'She was a good girl,' he said. 'She gave me a good son.'

I had to grin. 'Okay.'

He grinned back at me. 'Okay it is boy. And I'll tell you something, they're out of their heads. They're panicky. I can look at you two and there's no question which one of you is Will Kelly's boy. No question. But there's always the chance, always the chance. They're panicky, they're afraid of the chance. They'll even go for the kid, you wait and see.'

'Do you think so?'

'You wait and see. Hah!' He sat back again, smoking like a financier, his eyes gleaming in the dim light of the bar. 'We'll give them merry hell, boy! Who wants Florida?'

'The Seminoles.'

'They can have it.' He leaned forward fast. 'You know what I was going to do? I figured I was an old man, washed-up, ready to retire. I wrote my sister – frigid-faced bitch, but I didn't know anybody else in the world – I told her leave that bum she's married to. We'll live in Florida, I've still got plenty stashed away, with an extra twenty years' interest on it. See? Old Eddie Kapp, washed-up, retired to Florida for the sun and the cheap funeral. With my *sister*.'

He ground out the cigarette. 'Family, family, family, that's always the same damn thing.' His voice was low and grim and intense. 'With the mob, with you, with me. Always the same damn thing. I was ready to spend the rest of my life with my sister. Think of it, with my sister. I hate her, she's a hypocrite, she always was.'

'I met her,' I said. 'She's just frustrated.'

He grinned. 'Careful boy, you're talking about your aunt.'

I laughed. 'That's right, isn't it?'

'I tell you, I'd given up. Tony and The French and all the rest, they were writing letters to me. Come on back when they spring you, Eddie, we're ready to roll. We're just waiting on you, Eddie, and we move in. Yeah, the hell with all that. That's the way I figured it, I was an old man, time to retire. And just the one relative in all the world.' He curved a grin of pain. 'It's family, it does it every time. Where's the damn waiter? I'm getting the taste back.'

We re-ordered and it came, and Kapp went on: 'I'll tell you about family. Listen, when I saw you – who knew what you were or what you wanted? Twenty-two years ago it looked easy. When this baby here is in its twenties, I'll be out again, and he'll be at my side. See? But by now, who knew? You were Kelly's kid not mine.' He drank, inhaled cigarette smoke, grinned, winked at me. 'Then I saw you, boy. Raymond Peter Kelly. Keep the Kelly, who cares? I saw you, and I knew you were mine.' He got to his feet, looking around. 'Where's the crapper?'

He had to ask a waiter. I sat and thought about him. I thought, *He copulated with a married woman named Edith Kelly and impregnated her and she produced me*. I could believe and understand that. I thought, *He is my father*. That was something else again.

He came back and sat down. He finished the second drink and we ordered thirds. They came and he went on talking as though he hadn't stopped. 'This thing about family, now,' he said. 'It's an important thing with a lot of people. All kinds of people. And I'll tell you a group of people it's important to, and that's the people make up the mob. Particularly in New York. You don't think so? Hard cold people, you think. No. There wasn't a two-bit gun carrier on the liquor payroll didn't take his first couple grand and buy his old lady a house. Brick. It had to be brick, don't ask me why. It's in the races, national backgrounds, you know what I mean? Wops at the national level, mikes and kikes at the local level. Italians and Irish and Jews. All of them, it's family family family all the time. Am I right?'

I said, 'People get assimilated. Americanized.'

'Yeah, sure, I know that. Believe me, for the last few years, I did nothing but read magazines. I know all about that, when you're Americans you got no roots, you move around, all that stuff. No family homestead, no traditions, nothing. Who gives a shit about cousins, brothers, parents, anybody? Only if they're rich, huh?'

We grinned at each other. I said, 'Okay. So what difference does it make?'

'I'll tell you, boy, there isn't a man in the world doesn't want to be respectable.' He pointed a finger at me, and looked solemn, as though he'd spent long nights in his cell thinking about these things. 'You hear me? Not a man in the world doesn't want to be respectable. As soon as a man *can* be respectable, he is. You got immigrants, they come into this country, how long before they're really Americanized? No roots, no traditions, who cares about family, all that stuff. How long?'

I shrugged. He wanted to answer the question himself, anyway.

'Three generations,' he said. 'The first generation, they don't know what's going on. They got funny accents and there's a lot of words they don't know, and they've got different ways of doing things, different things they like to eat and wear, and all the rest of it. You see? They aren't respectable. I'm not talking about honest and dishonest, I'm talking about *respect*. They're not a part of the respectable world, see? Same with their kids, they're half and half. They've got the whole upbringing in the house, with the old country stuff, and then grade school and high school and the sidewalk outside. See? Half and half. And then the third generation, Americanized. The third generation, they can be respectable. Do you see what I'm getting at?'

I said, 'I don't think respectable's the word you mean.'

'The hell with that.' He was impatient, brushing it away. 'You know what I mean. It takes three generations. And the third generation has practically no crooks in it. I mean organization crooks, the mob. That's almost all first and second generation, you see what I mean? Because every man in the world wants to be respectable, but a lot of guys are going to say, "Okay, if I can't be respectable, I can't. But I still want to make good dough. And only the respectable types like in the *Saturday Evening Post* can get the good jobs with the good dough. But my brother-in-law drives a liquor truck bringing in the stuff from Canada and makes great dough, plus sometimes a bonus for an extra job doing this and that, so what the hell? I can't be respectable, anyway." See what I mean?'

I nodded. 'Yes, and I see what you're driving at. The first and second generations aren't Americanized. So they've got the old feeling for family.'

'Right! And that's where you come in, boy.' He leaned far

84

forward over a table. 'I tell you, family is *all* to these people. You kill a man, his brother kills you. Or his son. Like you, for Christ's sake, going after the guy killed Will Kelly. Or things like this, there's maybe a dispute of some kind, somebody in the mob gets killed by somebody else. And the guy who did it, or ordered it, he sends like a pension around to the other guy's wife. You know what I mean, a few bucks every week, help buy the groceries, get the kids some shoes. You know what I mean. There was a time in Chicago, '27, '28 I think it was, there was almost forty widows getting bootleg pensions all at one time. You see what I mean?'

'You said something about this being where I came in.'

'Damn right.' He stopped and laughed. 'You know, I'm not used to all this talking, all at once like this. It makes me thirsty. And I'm not used to this Kings & Lords, whatever it is.'

'House of Lords.'

'Yeah. I can feel it in my head already, and what is this, my third?'

'Third, yes.'

'Let's make it fourth'

We did, and he said, 'The twenties, those were the years. We organized faster than the law, that was the main thing. We were one jump ahead all the time. Until this income tax thing, and I tell you that was unfair. That was a cheat. I've got no respect for the Federal Government; if you can't get a man fair, you just can't get him, you see what I mean? Now, who in the whole damn country ever filled out a tax form honest? Up till then, I mean.' He shook his head. 'No respect for them at all, they don't go by the rules. Anyway, the point was, we all got organized and we had thirteen good years, and then along came Repeal and we had a tough time getting readjusted, you know? Like the March of Dimes, when this Salk vaccine came along. Shot their disease right out from under them, huh? They had to go quick find some other disease. Same as us. Liquor's legal again, so there isn't any profit in it any more. So we're diversifying, there's dope and there's gambling and there's whores. Gambling's best, it's safest. The other two, dope and whores, the people you have to deal

85

with, by the very nature of the business they're unreliable. You see what I mean?'

I nodded, while he paused and drank.

'Of course,' he said, 'there's also the unions. Lepke led the way in that field, around from strikebreakers to trade associations to pocket unions. But Dewey got him, in '44. Four years after the Federals got me. Frankly, I was one of the people always thought Lepke overdid it. He gave Anastasia more work than you can imagine. Lists of fifteen, twenty people at a time. After a while, it got so that was all he was doing, making up lists of people for Anastasia's group to kill. So the unions are something else again. It's a funny thing, that's the only area with the legitimate base – you know, there's nothing illegal about unions to begin with, like there is with gambling and narcotics and whores – But it's the worst for killing and breaking things up. You know what I mean? The only area where just an innocent citizen who doesn't have anything to do with anything can get beat up or shot, because of where he works or something like that.'

'What's all this got to do with me?'

He laughed, shaking his head. 'I'm goddamned, boy, this House of Lords is going right up into my head. I can feel the fumes going right up into my head. The point was, I was trying to give you some of the background, you know what I mean? '33, Repeal, it all started to fall apart. Everybody's looking for a new way to make a living, fighting it out for territory and what's whose and all. And Dewey came along to make life tough. And then the Federal Government, with this cheating income tax thing. A lot of us got moved out, one way or the other. Died or retired or went to jail or one thing and another. And these new people came in. Businessmen, you know what I mean? Respectable. No more of this blood bath stuff, that's what they wanted. Just a quiet business. Buy your protection and run your business, and let it go at that. I could see it in the papers, all through the forties, everything quieting down. Like a few years ago, the meeting at Appalachin. I could see in the papers and the magazines, everybody was surprised. Like nobody knew there was a mob any more. It called itself the Syndicate now, and people figured it

86

wasn't real, you know what I mean? Here's a guy, he runs a bottling plant for soft drinks, and he's got sixty-five guys out to his house for a meeting, and everybody was surprised.'

'That's right near Binghamton,' I said. 'Appalachin is. I was eighteen then. Some of us rode out in a guy's car to look at Barbara's house. Where the meeting took place.'

That made him laugh again. 'You see what I mean? Sightseers, for Christ's sake. People don't believe it any more. There was a time, in the thirties say, when all the people around a place like that would have stayed miles away, you never know when the shooting's going to start. Now, things've been so nice and quiet for so long, a bunch of kids got out in a car and look at the house.' He shook his head. 'I can't believe it. Why, there was a time, if word got around that somebody like the Genna boys, say, were in town, all the innocent citizens would have gone inside and locked the doors and crawled under the beds. The same as when Anastasia got it in '57. Nobody believed it. There he was on the floor in the barber shop with five bullets in him, and pictures in the *Daily News*, and if you say the word mobster, everybody thinks of the thirties.'

'Not me,' I said. 'One of them shot my fa – father.'

'Just a hired gun. You'll never find him.'

'Wrong. I found him today. He was the guy in the Chrysler.'

'The one you hit, or the driver?'

'The one I hit.'

He grinned and nodded. 'Good boy. You've got a lot of Eddie Kapp in you, I swear to God.'

'Yeah. We were up to '57.'

'Wait.' He ordered another round, took a first sip, and said, 'The last few years, some of the older guys have been coming back. Back from overseas, with the heat off at last, or out of jail, or one thing and another. And these smooth new types say, "Yeah, Pop, but we don't use shotguns any more. We use interoffice memos. Why don't you go write your memoirs for the comic books?" And what can they do? Here's organizations they set up themselves, and now they get the cold shoulder. They try something, and the lawyers and the tame cops come around.

Nobody throws a bomb in the living room any more, they just nag and niggle and slip around. Typical businessmen, see what I mean? Every once in a while, there's an Albert Anastasia, he just won't get reconstructed, and the guns come out. Or like with you. But not so much any more. A good press, isn't that the phrase? Good public relations. Everything nice and quiet.'

'We still haven't got to me.'

'You're the ace in the hole, boy. Family, didn't I tell you? We've got all these old boys, hanging around now, waiting to move in again. But they can't move. There's nobody to set himself up for boss, that's all it takes. They've met, they've written to each other, they've talked it over. And they've decided on somebody they'll all accept to run things. Me.'

He gulped down all of the drink. 'I'm getting the taste back.' His grin was lopsided. 'I wasn't going to do it. I was going to Florida with Dot. Or without her, the hell with her. Because of you. The symbol. In 1940, I was ready to make my move. Not just New York City. Half the Atlantic Seaboard. Everything from Boston to Baltimore, the whole thing. It should have been nine years before, but I'd moved too slow. Only now I had it. I had the support. Hell, I was part of the new look myself! And then these goddamn Federal people came along with this goddamn income tax thing. And I said to some of the boys, "When I come out, this pie is mine." And they said, "Eddie, you'll be sixty-four years of age. Twenty-five years is a long time." And I said, "They'll remember Eddie Kapp. You people will remember Eddie Kapp." They said, "Sure, but you're going to be an old man, Eddie. Who's going to follow you?" And I told them, "Edith Kelly has a kid of mine. When I come out, he'll be grown. And he'll be with me." That's what I told them.' He nodded loosely, eyeing his empty glass. I motioned the waiter. He came and took the glass away.

Kapp watched him go. Softly, he said, 'Don't you think that meant something to them? *Family*. A goddamned symbol, boy, that's what you are. A *symbol*. Eddie Kapp is bringing new blood. Eddie Kapp and his boy. That's why they want me. They got a symbol to come around, something to tie them all together.'

'When my father came into New York to pick me up,' I said, 'somebody must have recognized him.'

'Sure. For twenty-two years, who cared? Before I went in, I told Will to get out of New York and stay out, not to come back as long as he lived. He knew I meant it, and he did it. He didn't know why, but he didn't have to know why.'

'He didn't know I was yours?'

Kapp shook his head, grinning. 'He knew you weren't his. That's all he knew.'

I emptied my glass. All I could see was Dad looking at me, that last second before he vomited blood. 'He didn't know why they were killing him. Jesus, that's sad. Oh, good Christ, that's sad.' When I waved at the waiter, my arm was stiff. I said to Kapp, 'He never once let me know. I was his son. Mum was dead, he brought me up by himself. Bill and me, we were the same, exactly the same.'

I couldn't talk. I waited, and when the waiter brought the glass I emptied it and told him I wanted another.

Kapp said, 'They knew I was getting out soon. They saw Will Kelly in town. They got panicky. They had to get rid of Kelly, and they had to get rid of his sons. They couldn't take the chance on the symbol still meaning something.' He nodded. 'And it still means something,' he said.

I lit a cigarette, gave it to him, lit another for myself. The waiter came with more drinks. Kapp had the cigarette in his right hand. He picked up the glass with his left hand, then grunted and dropped it, and it fell over on the table. His face looked suddenly thinner, bonier. He said, 'Good God, I forgot my hand.'

'Let's see it.'

It was grey. A swollen oval on the back was black. I said, 'The hell with this. We've got to find you a doctor.'

'I didn't feel a thing,' he said. 'Not until I picked that glass up.'

The waiter was there, looking irritated, mopping up with a red-and-white checked cloth. I paid him, and we left, and got the name of a doctor from the desk clerk. And directions, just down the street.

We went there, and the doctor looked him over. He cut the

hand, for drainage, and bandaged it up, and said it would be a couple weeks before Kapp could really use it. In the meantime, keep changing the bandage every day. And stop back in three or four days. Then he checked the left knee, because Kapp was still limping. He said that was nothing to worry about, just bruised. Kapp told him he'd walked into a chair. We both had liquor on our breath, so the doctor didn't question us.

Then we went back to the hotel and up to the room. Bill was lying on his bed. His forehead was bloody around a small hole, and he had the Luger in his right hand.

18

There were three cops I talked to. One was a local plainclothes man, a comic relief clown who chewed cut plug. One was from the county District Attorney's office, a ferret with delusions of grandeur. And the third was State CID, an ice-grey man with no tear ducts.

I told them all about Bill's having lost his wife two months ago in an automobile accident, and his father being killed only a month before that, and how he'd been very depressed ever since, and he'd had the Luger for years but I hadn't known he'd brought it along on this trip with him. And we were just travelling around the state, basically to try to forget our recent losses. But Bill had just got steadily more and more depressed, and now he'd killed himself

The local cop swallowed it whole, with tobacco juice. The DA's man would have liked a hotter story, but he didn't want the work of digging for it. And the CID man didn't believe a word of it, but he didn't care. He was just there to memorize my face.

So it was called suicide. To me, it looked like a lousy job of staging. Aside from the fact that Bill wouldn't have killed himself for anything. It wouldn't have occurred to him.

The local cop had called a local undertaker, who might have been his brother-in-law. He looked at me and rubbed his hands together. We both knew he was going to cheat me down to the skin, and we both knew there wasn't a thing I could do about it.

Thursday night, I went out and got drunk. I bar-hopped out toward the air base. When I started a fight with a Staff Sergeant, the CID man came from out of the smoke and took me away. He drove a grey Ford, and he put me in it and took me back to the hotel. Before I got out, he said, 'Don't do what your brother did.'

I looked at him. 'What did my brother do, smart man?'

'I'm not sure,' he said. 'Whatever it was, you take warning.'

I said, 'Go to hell.' I fumbled the door open and lurched into the hotel. I never saw him again. Whatever had bugged him, he'd either been satisfied or had given up.

In the room, I lay in bed, and for a long while I didn't know what was wrong. Then I figured it out. I couldn't hear the sound of Bill's breathing in the next bed. I listened. He wasn't breathing anywhere in the world. Poor sweet honest Bill.

I once read a book of stories by a man named Fredric Brown. In one of them he quotes the tale of the peasant walking through the haunted wood, saying to himself, *I am a good man and have done no wrong. If devils can harm me, then there isn't any justice*, and a voice behind him says, *There isn't*.

The author didn't say so, but I know. The peasant's name was Bill.

I wished I could go talk to Kapp, but we'd decided it would be best for us to keep away from each other until all the cops went home. It would only complicate things to bring Kapp into it. Just as I said I was alone when I found Bill.

I got up and turned on the light. I went downstairs, but all the bars in Plattsburg were closed. I went back up to the room and turned off the light and sat up in bed smoking. Every time I took a drag the room glowed red and the covers moved on the other bed. After a while I switched the light on and went to sleep.

Friday afternoon, Uncle Henry showed up from Binghamton, and we had a fight. He wanted Bill's body shipped to Binghamton, and I wanted it stuck in the ground here and now. It wasn't Bill, it was just some meat. There wasn't any Bill any more.

I won, because I was willing to pay. Then there was trouble with a priest named Warren because Bill committed suicide, so he couldn't be buried in consecrated ground. I said, 'There are stupid policemen in your town, Father. Bill didn't kill himself.'

He said, 'I'm sorry, but the official view –'

I interrupted him, saying, 'Didn't you hear about the Constitution? They separated church and state.'

I said more than that, and got him mad at me. Uncle Henry was shocked, and told me so when we left: 'The Church has its laws about suicide, and that's –'

'If you say that word suicide once more, I'll shove a crucifix down your throat.'

'If your father were alive –' And so on.

So Saturday six hired pallbearers carried the coffin from the funeral home. There was no stop at a church for the suicide; he went straight out of town to a clipped green hill with a view of Lake Champlain, and into a hole which no priest had blessed with holy water. He would have to make do with God's rain.

Uncle Henry and I were the only ones beside the grave who had known Bill in life. The undertaker came over and wanted to know if we wanted him to say a few words. I had never known till then what a man would look like who had a complete and absolute lack of taste or sensibility. I looked at this wretch and said, 'No. Not ever.'

After the funeral, I arranged for storage of Bill's car. It was mine now, but I couldn't drive it till the registration had been changed, which would take too long. No one can drive a car registered to a dead man.

Uncle Henry came back to the hotel room with me. He said, 'Are you coming back home with me?'

'To Binghamton? I don't have any home there.'

'You do with us, if you want. Your Aunt Agatha would be happy to have you stay with us.'

'I'll be right back.' I went into the bathroom and sat on the floor and cried like a little kid. I wanted to be a little kid. The floor was all small hexagonal tiles. I counted them, and after a while I got up and washed my face and went back outside. Uncle Henry was standing by the window, smoking a cigar. I said, 'I'm sorry. I've been in a bad mood. You were a good guy to come up here.'

'It hasn't been easy for you,' he said.

'I don't think I want to go back to Binghamton. Not yet.'

'It's your life, Ray. But you're always welcome, you know that.'

'Thank you.'

We were silent a minute. He wanted to say something, and he didn't know how. I couldn't help him; I didn't know what it was he wanted to say. Finally he cleared his throat and said, 'About Betsy.'

'Betsy?'

'Bill's girl. We've been caring for her.'

'Oh. I forgot about her.'

'We'd like to keep her. I'd like to adopt her.' He waited, but there wasn't anything for me to say. 'Would that be all right with you?'

'Oh. Well, sure. Why ask me?'

'You're her uncle. You're her next of kin.'

'I don't even know her, I've never seen her. I don't have any kind of home or anything.'

'I'll start the papers then. There may be something you'll have to sign, I don't know. Where can I get in touch with you?'

'I'll write you when I get an address.'

'All right.'

He cleared his throat again. 'I should start back. I don't like to drive at night.'

I went down to the car with him. He said, 'Oh, yes, one other thing. Bill's house –'

'Oh, for God's sake, not now! Some other time, some other year, let me alone!'

'Yes, all right. You're right. Be sure to send me your address. I'll take care of things till then.'

He drove away, and I went to a liquor store and asked for two bottles of Old Mr Boston before I remembered. I took them both anyway, and went back to the hotel room. I sat cross-legged on the bed and smoked and drank and thought. Very gradually, I unwound. Very gradually, I got so I could pay attention to my thoughts again.

It got slowly dark outside, and I treaded heavily through my thoughts to some conclusion I didn't yet know. And Kapp knocked on the door at a little after nine.

I got up and let him in. He said, 'Your uncle gone home?'

'This afternoon,' I said.

'I've been watching. You haven't had any tail. I guess they're satisfied with the suicide idea.'

94

'Aren't you?'

'Crap. Neither are you. If that job was done by a professional, they've got a lot slacker than my day.'

'I know.'

He pointed a stiff finger at his forehead. 'The angle was wrong,' he said. 'You know what I mean? Dead on that way. I saw that right away. Too high.'

'Yeah, I know.'

'What's that you're drinking? I brought some House of Lords.' He had a brown paper bag under one arm. He took the bottle out and showed it to me. 'Want some?'

'I'll stay with this.'

I sat on the bed again, and he sat in the armchair in the corner. He said, 'You feel like talking, Ray?'

'I think so.'

'Before we found Bill dead, I was going to ask you a question. You know the question I mean.'

'I suppose so.'

'I want to make the move, Ray. I want to get a base and call a few people and tell them okay, they can count on me. And the first thing they'll ask me, "You got your son with you?" What am I going to tell them?'

I didn't say anything. I read the label on the Old Mr Boston bottle. What I was drinking was seventy proof.

He waited, and then he spoke rapidly, as though he were trying to catch up. 'I'll tell you the way it stands, Ray. This thing's going to happen, one way or another. People are coming back, people are choosing sides. If you say yes, no, it doesn't make any difference, you see what I mean? It's still going to happen.' He held up a rigid finger, peered over it at me. 'There's only one difference if you say no. Only the one. Eddie Kapp won't be running things. I don't know who will be – maybe there'll be a fight first, I don't know – but it won't be Eddie Kapp. I'll take my sister away from her husband and go down to Florida like I figured.'

'I hear it's nice down there,' I said.

He frowned. 'Is that your answer?'

95

'I don't know. Keep talking.'

'All right. I want you with me. I mean besides everything else, you know what I mean? The hell with it, you're my son. I never thought about it this way. I never knew it'd hit me this way. When I went in, you were just a – you know, just a little *thing* in a crib. I saw you maybe three four times. You weren't anybody at all yet, you know what I mean?'

'And now your heart is full.'

'Okay. And my glass is empty.' He refilled it from the bottle of House of Lords. 'I don't expect you to feel anything like that for me,' he said. 'What the hell? I'm no kind of a father or anything. But it hits me, I swear to Christ it does. You're my *son*, you know what I mean?'

'Yes. I know what you mean. Forget what I said there, I didn't mean to be a smart-aleck.'

'Sure, what the hell? But there's two of the reasons why I want you to stick with me, you see? Because you're my son, and it's as simple as that. And because if you're with me I can make my move. There's a lot of profit in the New York operation, Ray, take it from me. God knows how much these days.'

I held up my hand. 'Wait a second. Let me tell you something. That doesn't matter, it doesn't mean anything to me at all. I don't care about the New York mob. If you take it, I'm not your heir.'

'If you feel that way –'

'I feel that way. Have you got any more reasons?'

'It depends what you want to do,' he said.

'In what way?'

'You still want revenge? Because if you do, you should stick with me. We'll be after the same people.' He drank half a glass. 'It depends whether that's what you want or not,' he said.

'Sure.' I reached over to the nightstand and got the bottle. I didn't need the glass, so I tossed it over onto Bill's bed. I drank from the bottle, and held it, looking at it, while I talked. 'I've been thinking about that,' I said. 'Up here, since my uncle left. Trying to figure out what I'm going to do with myself. You want to hear what I've been thinking?'

'Well, sure. Certainly. I mean, that's just exactly what I want, you see?'

'Yeah. All right, this is what I've been thinking. To begin with, every man has to have either a home or a purpose. Do you see that? Either a place to be or something to do. Without one or the other, a man goes nuts. Or he loses his manhood, like a hobo. Or he drinks or kills himself or something else. It doesn't matter, it's just that everybody has to have one or the other.'

'Okay,' he said. 'I can see that. Like me wanting to live with my sister. So I'd have a home if I didn't have any purpose. I can see that.'

'All right. Now me, I've been a kid, that's all. So what I always had was a home. Even if I was in the Air Force in Germany, I still knew I had a home, and that was on Burbank Avenue in Binghamton, where my father lived. Then they killed him, and I didn't have any home any more. But I had a purpose instead. Vengeance. To kill my father's killer. That's enough of a purpose, isn't it?'

'Sure it is.'

'Sure it is. Only then you came along. And now my father is not my father. Is revenging a foster father just as good? No, it isn't.'

'What about your brother?'

'My half-brother. Wait. Let me tell it to you the way I thought it out. Right now, I'm adrift. I have neither home nor purpose, only bits and pieces of purpose. To continue the vengeance of my father-who-is-not-my-father. To revenge my sister-in-law, whom I never knew. To protect my niece, about whom I care less than nothing. To assist you in your palace revolution, in which I have no stake. To even the score for the loss of my eye, which I can never get back. To save my own life, which isn't worth saving unless I have a purpose. To avenge my half-brother, where at least my own familial blood was spilt.'

'All right, what's wrong with that?'

'Avenging Bill? But I need more than that. It isn't purpose enough.' I raised the bottle and lowered it. While I got out a cigarette, I said, 'In all of it, there still is one purpose worth having. But it dead-ends.'

He shifted in the chair. 'What purpose is that?'

'Somewhere in New York City, there's a man who pointed a finger and said, "Take away Ray Kelly's home." Other men did it, but they were only extensions of the pointing finger. I can cut that finger off. Not because he killed a foster father or a half-brother or a half-brother's wife. But because he killed my home. He left me no choice but purpose. To kill him.'

He laughed nervously, saying, 'It comes around to the same thing, Ray, doesn't it?'

'To kill the man who killed the me who might have been. Not exactly the same thing, Kapp.'

He emptied his glass, refilled it. 'What the hell?' he said. 'However you say it, you're still after the same people as me. The ones running the organization in New York. Same people, different reasons. Why go off by yourself and fight them?'

'Because it's my own purpose.'

'We could double up. I help you, you help me.'

'Fine. What's the name of the man who owns the pointing finger?'

'What?'

'The guy who gave the order to kill Will Kelly. What's his name?'

'How the hell do I know?'

'You want the crown, Kapp. You've got to know who's wearing it now.'

'Hell, yes. But you don't know this kind of organization. It might be any one of half a dozen guys. I don't know which one.'

'A fair trade, Kapp. You give me the name, I'll give you two weeks. You won't need any more than that. The people you want to impress, they want to see me at first, that's all. Once you're organized, they'll be too busy to wonder where the kid is.'

'You mean that? You'll stick around till we're set up?'

'Two weeks. Until – what's the date today? Thursday was the fifteenth, so this is the seventeenth. Thirty days hath September. Okay. Saturday, the first of October, I'm leaving.'

'But you'll play it like you're going to be sticking around, right?'

'Sure.'

'You're my son and heir, right? As far as these guys are concerned, you're set to sit in the throne when I pop off, right?'

'I'll play it that way. All you have to do is give me the name.'

'I will. By the first of October, I'll know which one it was.'

'Not that way, Kapp.'

He jumped to his feet, slamming the empty glass on the dresser. 'Goddamn it, I don't *know* which one! Ray, face it, I know it's got to be one of maybe six or seven men. I could toss out one of their names and you'd swallow it, you know damn well you would. But I don't know for sure which one it is, and I'm trying to play this square. I *want* you to go gunning! That'd work out fine for me, you know what I mean?'

'All right.'

'I'll find out which one it was. I'll have him fingered definite by the time you want to leave. I swear my oath on that.'

'All right.'

'Shake on it!'

I shook his hand. When he left, I finished the other bottle.

19

Monday afternoon we left Plattsburg. The Friday before, Kapp had had a lot of funds transferred to a local bank from a couple of New York and Jersey City banks, and then he'd taken it all out in cash. Monday we walked into the local Cadillac-Oldsmobile-Buick agency, and Kapp bought the showroom Cadillac for cash. I had to drive, because he didn't have a licence. I was getting more and more used to judging perspective with just the left eye, and after a while I found a way to get my right foot comfortable on the accelerator, so it wasn't too bad.

We drove straight south to Lake George, and Kapp rented a place around on the eastern side of the lake. The south and west, he said, were all built up from what he'd known, he didn't like it. Over on the northeast, it wasn't much different from the old days.

The house was big and white, built amid evergreens on a steep slope down to the edge of the lake. There was a dirt road along the top of the slope past the summer houses, and a cleared space beside it for two cars to park. We got out of the Cadillac and walked across the tyre ruts of the road to the hedge that bordered it for this section. There was a gate in the hedge, and a Quonset-hut mailbox on an arm. On the side of the mailbox was written REED. We'd rented from an agency in town who handled the property for the Reeds off-season. The spaced summer houses along the slope between the road and the lake were all empty, except for us.

We opened the gate in the hedge and went down twelve wooden steps to a screen door and a screened-in porch. On this side, the house looked small. One storey high, and just a small screened-in porch with beer and soft drink cases stacked up against the house wall. But this was the top floor of three, the other two sprouting below us down the slope.

Inside, there were three large rooms, all with straw-mat rugs and bamboo or wicker furniture and a lot of dark red cushions. The flooring gleamed rich and well-cared-for in the wide archways between the rooms. There was also a kitchen, white and glittering like an operating room for midgets, with a window overlooking the empty beer cases on the porch. In the middle of it all was a railinged oblong hole in the floor and a staircase with black rubber runners. This led down to the middle floor, where there were four bedrooms, all done in walnut, with little green curtains over the small windows. There were windows at the front and sides, and a side door which led to a path running down the slope from the road to the lake. There was another set of stairs under the first, this one closed off with knotty pine and a varnished door. It led down to the bottom floor, with storage rooms and the boathouse and another screened porch. Off this porch was a square wooden dock beside the boathouse. The whole house was ringed by trees on three sides, and the fourth side was built right down to the water's edge.

We moved in and found the phone wasn't working, but it was too late that day to do anything about it. The next morning, we drove back around the lake to town and got the phone company to activate the phone. Some sort of belated summer had come in during the night, so I bought a bathing suit. Then we went back to the house.

We didn't talk to each other much, going or coming. Kapp was full of his plans. I was already losing my patience. It was the same as doing the tape for Beeworthy, only that hadn't been any more than half an hour, and this was going to be for two weeks. I wasn't sure I'd last two weeks. The only thing that kept me there was the sure knowledge that it would take me longer than two weeks to get the name I wanted if I was just bulling around New York on my own. I'd told Bill I didn't want to do any Pacific campaign. I still felt the same way.

There was a full-length mirror on the closet door in the bedroom I'd picked for myself. That afternoon, when I put the bathing suit on, I looked at myself in it. It was two and a half months since the accident, and this was the first time I'd really looked at myself full length.

Both shins were criss-crossed with white scars down to the ankles. The right ankle looked wrong. A couple of bones were missing from it, and the doctors had had to rebuild it a little. It was too thin and too smooth. It looked more like a pipe joint than a part of a human body. There were more of the white scars above my right knee and across my belly and over my right shoulder.

I opened the closet door all the way, so the mirror was against the wall. I kept it that way from then on. Then I went out and went swimming.

It stayed warm all the rest of the first week. I swam a lot, always by myself. Kapp spent most of his time on the phone. He made a lot of long distance calls to New York and to Miami and to East St Louis and other places. After the first couple of days, he started getting other calls coming back. He did a lot of grinning and winking, whenever he saw me. But we didn't talk much. I didn't know what he was doing, and I didn't care. And he was too busy with his plans for small talk.

We'd stocked up with House of Lords, and he usually had a glass in his hand. He was smoking cigars all the time, and his voice was getting raspy. He seemed pleased with life.

The air was warm, but the water was cold. I liked it. I couldn't swim as well as before, because I couldn't kick with any co-ordination, but I did pretty well.

I developed a swimming routine. Every time I went into the water, I swam straight out into the lake as far as I could go. Then I rolled over on my back and rested there until I had the strength to swim back. Sometimes I thought about diving down and walking the bottom. But not seriously.

They say the Army is hurry up and wait. Air Force, too. When I was in, we used to bitch about that. On an alert, double-time to the truck and climb aboard and then sit and wait for two hours before the truck got moving. I felt now like I used to in the truck except now the Air Force wasn't doing it to me, I was doing it to myself.

I wanted to *act*. But I didn't want it to be finished. Once I acted and it was over with and I'd done what I'd set out to do, then there wouldn't be anything for me at all any more. A walk on the bottom, it didn't matter at all.

I had trouble sleeping nights. I kept some House of Lords by the bed to help. And the light was always on. I spent a lot of time staring at the ceiling. I hadn't wanted any of this. The things I was doing to myself were as bad as the things they'd done to me. But I couldn't go back. July twelfth was back there, the last good day Ray Kelly had ever had, and I couldn't get back to it. I had to keep moving the other way, hoping there was a way out at the other end.

Toward the end of the week, Kapp came to me and said, 'We're going to have to go into town and do some shopping. Some people are coming up. Maybe, Monday, Tuesday of next week. I got the list.'

We bought groceries, and a lot of beer, and more House of Lords. We also got four Army cots and some cheap blankets and pillows. When we got back the phone was ringing. It rang all weekend. Kapp chewed his cigars to shreds. He was smiling all the time now, like a winner. Even when he was just sitting still, he was doing something. I envied him.

The warm spell broke on Saturday. A sudden wind came down out of the north, turning the lake choppy grey. We closed the windows, and turned on the electric heating units in all the rooms. The sun rectangles were gone from the straw rugs. In the sky, the clouds hurried south.

Sunday, I put on a sweater and went for a walk on the dirt road. It was quiet. Under the evergreens the ground was brown. I thought it would be nice to walk among the trees for ever. I'd like to be an Indian, before the white man came.

The phone had been ringing when I left, and it was ringing again when I came back. I carried a folding chair down and sat on the dock and looked out over the lake. That night, the phone stopped ringing.

Monday the first one came. It was in the middle of the afternoon, and I was pouring us fresh drinks in the kitchen. A car horn sounded for just a second. I looked up the slope past the trees and the hedge and saw the side windows of the car and a face under a chauffeur's cap. I said, 'Somebody here.'

Kapp came around the table and stood beside me. He said, 'Go see who it is.'

I hopped up the steps and through the gate and over to the car. It was a pearl grey Cadillac, like McArdle's hearse. Three men were bulky in back. The chauffeur was a black cap and a round large nose. He kept both hands on the wheel, high up, and didn't look at me.

I went past him and bent and looked in the side window. The man in the middle said, 'Let's see Eddie Kapp.'

I said, 'He wants to know who you are.'

'Nick Rovito.'

I went down and told him and he said, 'Okay.' Then he went out, slamming the screen door, and shouted, 'Hey, Nick!'

Up in the car, one of them shouted, 'Is that you, you son of a bitch?' Then car doors slammed, and I saw the chauffeur man-oeuvre the car out of the road.

The three men came down. They all looked alike. In their fifties, barrel-bodied, bull-necked, heavy-headed. Wearing tight topcoats, keeping their hands in their pockets. Smiling with thick lips and thin eyes. Rovito stuck his hand out and Kapp shook it. The other two grinned and nodded at Kapp, and he grinned and nodded back. Then they came in.

Rovito looked at me and said, 'What's your name?'

'Ray Kelly.'

He looked at me and pursed his lips and put his hands back in his topcoat pockets. Then he turned to Kapp and said, 'Mmm.' It seemed to mean, 'I'll let you know.'

Kapp said, 'Come on in and have a drink. House of Lords.'

One of the others said, 'Not for me. Doctor's orders.' He looked embarrassed.

Rovito looked at him. 'Do you still know how to pour?'

'Sure, Nick.'

'Then pour.'

They went into the living room and sat down. I stayed with them. But they talked about old times and the people they used to know. No one paid any attention to me at all. I went down-stairs and out on the dock. They had a window open above me. I could hear the drone of their conversation but not the words.

104

After fifteen or twenty minutes, the one whose doctor wouldn't let him drink came out on the dock and stood leaning against the side of the boathouse. He lit a cigarette and threw the match in the water and looked at nothing across the water for a couple minutes. Then he turned to me and said, 'You're gimpy, aren't you?'

I said, 'Yes.'

'Fall off your scooter?'

I looked at him. He was grinning. I said, 'No.'

'Oh,' he said. 'I see. You don't talk much, do you? You're the strong silent type.'

I hadn't heard any voices from upstairs for the last couple minutes. But I didn't look up. I got to my feet and folded the chair and hit him in the stomach with it. He bent over and I hit him on the back of the head with it. When he fell I rolled him off into the water. Then I looked up at the watching faces and said, 'Satisfied?'

Kapp was grinning. So was the other guy. Rovito nodded. He said, 'So-so.'

I started to go inside. Rovito called, 'Hey, what about Joe?'

I looked up. 'What about him?'

'Aren't you gonna help him out of the water?'

'No. I wasn't playing. I don't play.' Then I went in and up to my room and got the bottle from under the bed.

I heard them go by, on their way down to help Joe out of the water.

20

Two more came Monday night, and the phone rang a few times, announcing more who were staying at motels around on the other side of the lake. By Tuesday afternoon, ten of them had moved into the house. I spent most of the time in my room. Whenever anyone opened the door by mistake, they said, 'Oh, excuse me,' and backed out again. Nobody asked me who I was, and I wasn't introduced to anybody. But they knew.

Appalachin had taught a lesson, though these weren't the same people. But they came in on different highways from different directions. No two cars stopped at the same restaurant or the same motel. They travelled in no convoys.

Wednesday night, eleven o'clock, they had the meeting. Cadillacs clogged the road. Only two of them had New York plates. One had Florida, and one California. Some of the chauffeurs stayed with the cars, some came down to the house.

The two large rooms facing the lake on the top floor had been fixed up for the meeting. All the chairs and tables from all over the house were in those rooms, plus all the ashtrays and wastebaskets. The refrigerator was full of nothing but beer and ice. House of Lords lined the cupboards. The early arrivals played poker while they waited.

Kapp came down to my room at ten-thirty. He was wearing one of the black suits he'd bought in Plattsburg. His shirt was white and his tie was black. Tie and collar were both too wide and too pointed. So were his shoes, which were black. The ring on his left pinky was white gold. His cigar was black. A white handkerchief peeked out of his breast pocket. His grey hair was brushed back till it shone. He didn't exactly look fatter, but he did look sort of heavier, as though he were more solid, more full.

He said, 'The big moment, eh, boy?' He was like an actor, all made up in his starchy costume, ready to go on.

He sat down on the edge of the bed and looked at the empty bottle standing beside the ashtray on the floor. He said, 'You aren't juiced, are you?'

'No.'

'Good. I want to give you a rundown on these people.'

I lit a cigarette and waited. If he felt like talking, I could listen.

He said, 'There's thirty-eight people going to be here, not counting you and me. Nick Rovito and Irving Baumheiler and Little Irving Stein are here because I'm here. There's seven other guys here because those three are. And twelve more here because of the seven. And sixteen because of the twelve. You see?'

I nodded.

'The point is, it's Nick and Irving and Little Irving you got to watch for. Those three. By you, they're the only ones here. Nick Rovito and Irving Baumheiler and Little Irving Stein. You met them, right?'

'Not the last one. Little Irving.'

'Oh. Little guy, baldheaded. You'll recognize him.'

'All right.'

'Fine. Now, all you do is stay with me. You don't have to talk unless you feel like it. The less said the better, maybe. But stick with me, at least till the talking's done. You got to pee, do it now.'

I shook my head.

'You sure?'

'Goddamn it.'

'Okay, okay. Just so you know. You got to stay right with me. Right side, you see? On my right side.'

'All right.'

'You got your brother's Luger?'

'The other one's smaller. The revolver.'

'Where is it?'

I pointed at the dresser. 'Top drawer.'

'Wear it. Where you can reach it, where you can show it. But not where you can't hide it. You know what I mean?'

'In my belt, at the side.'

'Okay, fine.' He stood up, smoothed the wrinkles out of his

jacket and trousers. I reached off the bed for the ashtray and put it on my chest. He said, 'Don't get me wrong. Nobody's going to shoot anybody. But maybe somebody wants to know if you're carrying, you see? And you are.'

'Okay.'

He walked around the room, blowing cigar smoke like a big cattleman. 'There's two kinds of people in this world, Ray,' he said. 'There are leaders, and there are followers. And there's only one kind of follower, but there's all kinds of leaders. There's glorious leaders that take a whole goddamn country over the cliff, and there's ward leaders that wouldn't last a day without the snowshovel patronage. And all kinds of leaders in between, you see what I mean?'

'I see what you mean.' It was a phrase I'd heard him use before. He was talking now because he was nerved up. I didn't even have to make believe I was listening.

'Now most of these guys that are going to be here tonight,' he said, 'they're what you might call middle-ground leaders. They can lead a bunch of followers fine, just so long as somebody else tells them how. Somebody else like Nick and Irving and Little Irving, you know what I mean?'

I looked up at the ceiling and blew cigarette smoke at it. The ashtray rode my chest. Kapp prowled around the room, talking to let off steam. 'Most of these guys,' he said, 'these middle-ground leaders, they've been around straight on through since the thirties. But their top men, like Nick and the Irvings, they've been out of commission for a while. So the rest of these guys have just drifted. Some of them are with the mob now, way down at the bottom of the list, where the crumbs fall. They'll be here, because they want to move up a notch. And they figure Nick or one of the Irvings for their real boss anyway, not one of these thin, slick snotnoses like they have today. So there they are, they've already got a little chunk of the organization in their pocket. When the times comes, they consolidate that chunk and then maybe send a couple arms to help straighten out some other neighbourhood somewhere. See what I mean?'

'Yeah.' I moved the ashtray off my chest and sat up for a while.

108

'And the other kind of guy we'll see,' he said, 'is the independent. New York's a big apple. There's independents working right inside the city limits, not even paying off to the regular organization. A neighbourhood book, a little quiet unionizing, one thing and another. All off in little corners, out in Brooklyn and Queens. Small-time leaders again. They want to be part of the mob, if Nick and the Irvings and me are running it.'

'Yeah.'

'We got half an organization already,' he said. 'All we do is grab the other half. Like plucking a peach.' He laughed. 'You know what I mean? Like plucking a peach.'

Over our heads people were walking back and forth. Kapp looked up at the ceiling. 'I better go up,' he said. 'You come up as soon as you can.'

'Yeah.'

He went to the door and opened it. Then he looked back at me and closed it again and said, 'You sore at something, boy?'

'Nothing special.'

He shook his head and grinned at me. 'You're a surly bastard,' he said.

'I'm the strong silent type.'

He widened his eyes. 'You sore about that little trick on the dock?'

'No.' I swung my legs over the side. 'The hell with it I'm not sore at anything.' I put the ashtray on the dresser and got out Smitty's gun. It was full again. The barrel was cold.

'Get dressed up sharp,' Kapp told me.

'Yeah, yeah.'

'Surly as they come.' He went out, grinning and shaking his head.

I put on a dark grey suit and a light grey tie and black shoes. Square shirt collar. I stuck Smitty's gun inside my belt around on the left side, with the butt forward. So I could reach over with my right hand and get it. Then I went upstairs.

Most of them were there. The archway between the two rooms was wide, almost as wide as the rooms. The chairs were set informally around the two rooms, but so that everybody could see everybody else and nobody had their back to anybody else. The poker players had quit. People in tight suits and fat grins were shaking hands and showing their teeth. Three chauffeurs were doubling as bartenders bringing glasses of beer or House of Lords out from the kitchen. All thirty-eight were talking. Most of them were smoking cigars. The rest were smoking cigarettes. I lit one myself and went around the wall to Kapp. He was with Rovito and a little baldheaded guy with a big nose.

Kapp put his arm around my shoulders and said, 'You remember Nick.'

'Sure.'

We nodded at each other, and Rovito smiled first.

Kapp motioned the cigar hand at the other one. 'And this is –'

'Little Irving Stein,' I said. I nodded at him. 'Nice to meet you.'

'You reckanize me? Sure, why not?' He poked Kapp's elbow. 'Did I tell you? I got a broad works for me, she does nothin' but read books for a mention of Little Oiving. I put the covers on the living-room wall. Mostly paperbacks, you know? Half the wall I got already. You think they forgot? Nobody forgot, don't let 'em kid you. They're still grateful, Ed, they still got a soft spot in their hearts for the selfless bums kept them in booze all those years in the desert. Ain't that right, Nick?'

Nick showed teeth, and didn't quite look down at Little Irving. Kapp said, 'Well, the hell, let's get going.' He turned and put his cigar on the edge of an ashtray and then straightened again and clapped his hands. 'Cell and block!' he shouted. 'Cell and block!'

A lot of people laughed, and then it got quiet.

Kapp said, 'Let's all sit down, what do you say?'

It was the same as any bunch of people at a meeting. Chairs squeaking around, people finishing conversations. Then there was the last cough, and silence.

There were five of us standing, thirty-five of them seated. Kapp leaned against the archway between the rooms, his arms folded and his cigar pointing at the ceiling. I stood to his right and back a little. Nick Rovito stood leaning against the wall near the corner diagonally to my right. Irving Baumheiler, a very fat

110

man in a vest with his thumb in the vest pocket, stood behind a chair facing me, midway between Nick and the opposite side of the arch. Against the far wall in the other room stood Little Irving Stein.

Except for me, there wasn't a man in the room under fifty-five. Most of them were the other side of sixty. Grey hair, dyed hair, and no hair. Half of them in new out-of-date clothes. All of them watching, smoking, waiting.

Kapp motioned to one of the chauffeurs, in the doorway to the kitchen. He came over with a tray and Kapp took a House of Lords. So did I. It was quiet.

Kapp broke the silence. He looked at the full glass in his hand and said, 'There's a lot to tell in this little glass. What's in it made a lot of guys a lot of dough. People who didn't want it said nobody else should have it, and then it made some other people even more dough.' He grinned at the glass. 'Or maybe the same people, who knows? I made my share out of it when they said it wasn't legal. Then they grabbed me for not splitting with them on money they didn't want me to make. And said it was legal after all. And then I went to a place where they didn't serve it, legal or otherwise. Fifteen years without a drop, boys. That's a hell of a long trip to take on a water wagon.'

It was a water-glass, half full. He downed it in three swallows, and tossed it empty, underhand, across the room to the chauffeur in the doorway. Nick Rovito said, low, 'Get on with it, Eddie.'

'That was the ceremony, Nick. The christening. Gents, I want you to meet my boy. My son, goes by the name of Ray Kelly.' Then he pointed the cigar at face after face in a counterclockwise circle around the room, and called off the name of every man there.

I watched for the first seven, my blank face and their blank faces, and then the hell with it. I drank the House of Lords from eight to twenty-one, turned and put down the empty glass on a table from twenty-two to twenty-four, lit a cigarette till thirty-three, and watched the last five. 'And that, Nick,' he finished, 'was the introduction.'

Nick didn't say anything. He didn't move.

111

Kapp inhaled cigar smoke and blew it out again. 'They said liquor was illegal,' he said, talking to the smoke this time, 'and then they said it wasn't. But a lot of money was made while it was. Now, who knows what else they may decide legal? How about Mary Jane? Ray, what do they call it now? Marijuana.'

'Pot,' I said.

'Ugly. All right, what about it? No after-effects, less habit-forming than tobacco or liquor. Maybe we'll wake up one morning and it's legal.'

A guy to the left muttered, 'They better not.' A few others laughed.

Kapp nodded at him. 'Yeah, Sal, I know what you mean. The same with off-track horse betting, huh? Or all of gambling, like Nevada. All over the country. Maybe so, some day. Or whores in ghettos, like they tried in Galveston and some other places.'

Little Irving said, 'What's the point, Eddie?'

'The point? I don't see why we shouldn't figure it all legal right now, that's the point. Retroactive, you know what I mean? Like their stinking income taxes. You see what I mean?'

They grinned and nodded and shifted around in their chairs, relaxing, puffing on their stogies, grinning at one another. Nick grinned, too. He said, 'And that was the joke, huh, Eddie?'

Kapp said, 'Right you are, Nick. And now we get to the pie.'

They quieted again. Kapp said, 'Let's get the size of the pie straight. It isn't the country. It isn't the east. It's New York City. And the stuff around it, Jersey City and Long Island and the rest.'

Somebody said, 'Greater New York.'

'That's the word.'

Somebody else said, 'Why so modest, Eddie?'

Kapp said, 'You tell them, Irving.'

Baumheiler cleared his throat and took his thumb out of his vest pocket. He said, 'I mention to you gentlemen five names. Arnold Greenglass. Salvatore Abbadarindi. Edward Wiley. Sean Auchinachie. Vito Petrone. These gentlemen are old friends of ours, of most of us. They are our contemporaries, more fortunate than we in not having had their careers interrupted in the late thirties or early forties. They would still be considered our friends. They, and others of our friends, are now operative at the national and regional levels. They agree with us that we deserve Greater New York more than the group that now has it, contingent of course on our proving our ability by taking it from the incumbents. National and regional organizations, as well as local organizations from other centres, will not interfere in the struggle. We have their assurances on this point. This is based on our own assurances that we harbour no ambitions beyond Greater New York.'

'For the moment,' said the guy who'd spoken up before.

Baumheiler looked severely at him. 'For ever,' he said. 'We are not, and will not be, a rival organization. We are part of the existent organization, and shall continue to be so.'

Little Irving Stein said to the ambitious one, 'You ought to know better, Kenny.'

Kenny, who was at least as old as Stein and twice the size, shifted uneasily in his chair. 'I just wanted to get it straight,' he said.

Kapp said, 'If we made a move like we wanted a bigger pie, they'd stop us from getting any pie at all. And they could, any time they wanted. Right, Nick?'

Nick nodded heavily. 'That's right,' he said. 'My people understand that already.'

'Mine do, now,' said Little Irving. He glared at Kenny.

Kapp said, 'We know who these punks are, this bunch that Irving called the incumbents. We know them from the old days, right? They shined our shoes in the old days, am I right?'

Somebody said, 'Office boys.'

'That's the word,' said Kapp. 'Office boys. Soft easy-living punks. They ain't in the rackets, they're a bunch of businessmen. You know what I mean? They live quiet, they send each other inter-office memos. They're a bunch of accountants. Am I right?'

Most of them nodded or said, 'You're right.'

'Accountants,' repeated Kapp. 'Office boys. They're afraid of muscle, they're afraid of the noisy hit. A quiet hit is what they like, an old lady's hit. Arsenic in the five o'clock tea, you know what I mean?'

113

They laughed.

'Sure,' said Kapp. He was laughing with them. 'An old lady's hit. They're a bunch of old ladies. They're *soft*. They hear a loud noise, they think it's a backfire. On the payroll they don't have even one good demo man. Huh? Am I right?'

'The only bombs thrown around New York,' said some body, 'are by amateurs.'

'We ought to hire them, that's what I say,' said Kapp. He got a laugh on that one, too. A bunch of old friends, getting set up together, getting along.

Kapp motioned to the chauffeur in the kitchen doorway. 'Time for a round,' he said.

Glasses came around and everybody was noisy for a minute, and then Kapp said, 'As I was saying.' Silence. He smiled into it. 'As I was saying, these pretty people are soft. They're *soft*. Do they know we're coming? Sure they do. Are they scared? So scared, boys, they've been using the noisy hit. I swear to God. They've been trying for Ray, here, my boy. They gunned his foster father, Will Kelly. You boys remember Will Kelly?'

They all agreed, they remembered Will Kelly.

Kapp said, 'They tried to gun me, too, on my way out of D. Ever hear of anybody *try* to gun somebody? They missed! They don't even know how!'

Nick Rovito said, 'We've got the point, Eddie.'

'I want to be sure of that,' Kapp told him. 'We aren't up against people like the Gennas or Lepke or any of Albert A's boys or anybody like that. We're up against a bunch of bush leaguers. We're up against a goddamn P.T.A. Okay.' He became suddenly brisker, more businesslike. 'Okay,' he said. 'They're in, and we're out. And we're not gonna get in *their* way. We're gonna get in *our* way, or not at all.'

Baumheiler said, 'Remember Dewey, Ed. You do not want to stir things up too much.'

'How much does it take, Irving? We want them out. We want us in. How much do we have to stir to get what we want? I promise you, I won't stir any more than that.'

Baumheiler chewed slowly on his cigar. 'I don't like the idea of too much noise, Eddie,' he said. 'Bombs going off, lots of

114

bullets, lots and lots of hits. I don't like such an idea. And I am not an old lady.'

Nick Rovito said, 'What worries you, Irving?'

'Noise, Mr Rovito. I do not –'

'You can call me Nick, Irving.'

'Thank you, Mr Rovito. I do not like –'

Kapp said, 'Irving, are we going to get along here or aren't we?'

'We can discuss the situation, Eddie, surely?'

'On a first-name basis, Irving. When we're back in, you and Nick can hate each other some more. But right now we got to work together.'

'We've always been able to work together in the past,' said Baumheiler, with a side glance at Nick, 'despite our differences.'

'Stick with first names, Irving. We're all old friends.'

Baumheiler shrugged heavy shoulders. 'If you think best, Eddie, then of course. To answer your question – Nick – I do not like noise. I do not like the idea of the State Crime Commission handing me a subpoena. I do not like the idea of being hauled, like Frank Costello, before a televised Congressional investigation. I do not like the idea of Federal accountants interesting themselves overmuch in my affairs. This is a different time, a different world. Our former associates are not used to noise, I agree. However, the citizenry is equally unused to noise. We would find them perhaps less tolerant than was once the case. I recommend circumspection.'

'No citizens, Irving,' said Kapp. 'But hits. Bombs. And you know it. We got no choice.'

'Quiet hits, maybe,' said Nick. 'But not poison in the tea. Lead in the head, huh? Not *too* quiet, huh, Irving? We want them to know maybe we're there, huh?'

'I simply want it made clear that I would not personally appreciate the type of over-enthusiasm which put our lamented friend Lepke in the electric chair.'

The porch door opened. A chauffeur stuck his head in and said, 'There's a car pulled up. A dinge in the back, he says he wants to talk.'

In the silence, I moved out from the wall, saying, 'I'll go see what he wants.'

They watched me go. Nobody talked.

21

It was a black Chrysler Imperial. Amid the Cadillacs, it looked belligerent. There was a white chauffeur and a black rider. He was no more than thirty, dressed out of Brooks Brothers on an expense account. A gold Speidel band was on his watch, a gold wedding band on the third finger of his left hand. He had a chicken moustache and a small satisfied smile and two watchful eyes.

When I got there, he pressed a button and the window slid down. The side and back windows had black venetian blinds. The others were down, the one on this side was up. He looked out at me and said, 'I'm from Ed Ganolese. With a proposition for Anthony Kapp.'

I said, 'All right, messenger. Come on down and say your piece.'

He got gracefully out of the Chrysler. I led the way. Behind me, he said, 'Don't you want to frisk me? What if I were armed?'

'What if you were?'

We went down the steps. At the door I turned and said, 'What name? I'll introduce you.'

'William Cheever.'

'Princeton?'

He smiled. 'Sorry. Tuskegee.'

I didn't smile back. We went in, through the empty room, with chauffeurs showing guns in the kitchen on our right, and on to where the piemen waited. I stopped in the archway and said, 'Mister William Cheever. Of Tuskegee. With a message from Ed Ganolese.' Then I went over and stood beside Kapp.

Cheever's smile was faint and phoney. He nodded at the room, took note of the five standing men, and then looked at the one beside me. 'Anthony Kapp?'

'I'm called Eddie. Not by you.'

117

'Mr Kapp, then. I have been sent, as of course you assume, to discuss terms. My principals –'

'You mean Ed Ganolese, that two-bit bum.'

'Ed Ganolese, yes. He sent me with a proposition concer –'

Kapp said, 'No.'

Nick Rovito said, 'Wait a second, Eddie. Let's hear what he's got to say.'

'I don't care what he's got to say,' said Kapp. 'Ganolese and his sidekicks are in my territory. That's all I have to know.'

'You can't listen to him?'

'No. I can't. Look Nick, they got the pie, am I right? There's only the one pie, and they got it. If we had it, and this bum came in and said his principals wanted some of it, what would we do?'

'We don't have it,' Nick said. 'That's the point.'

'And they won't give us any more than we'd give them.'

Nick spread his hands. 'We can talk, can't we?'

'We can go to the movies, too, Nick. We can scratch our asses. There's lots of ways to waste time.'

'You don't want to ride me, Eddie.'

Little Irving Stein piped up, 'Ganolese couldn't of asked for better. Throw one spade on the table and watch everybody fold.'

Nick said, 'Oh, the hell with it. All right, Eddie, you're right.'

'Okay, fine.' Kapp looked at Cheever. 'What the hell you still doing here? You got your answer. No deal.'

Little Irving said, 'Why don't we send this buck back with pennies on his eyes? So they'll know we mean it.'

Baumheiler said, 'No. They already know it.'

Little Irving said, 'Come on. We got ourselves here a little Fort Sumter.'

Baumheiler said, 'It's just such noisiness as this that I have in mind. I consider it dangerous.'

Nick said to Cheever, 'Go on, little man, you better go home.'

Cheever opened his mouth. Kapp said, 'Move!' He shrugged and nodded and went out, gathering the sheepskin folds of his dignity about him as he went. He closed the door and somebody said, disgustedly, 'A deuce.'

'Like I said,' Kapp told them, 'they're all deuces. I believe we

118

were splitting the pie, boys, before the dark cloud blew in.' Sometime, he'd started a new cigar. He clenched it, and talked through it. 'I figure to do this democratic,' he said. 'What we're going to need at the outset is enforcers. Lots of them. And trustworthy. Not deuces like that one, that'll go running back to Ganolese all of a sudden. And the boys that bring in the most arms get the most gravy. You see what I mean?'

'You mean a redistribution, Eddie?' asked Nick.

'Not at our level, Nick. We work the same as always. You've got Long Island and Brooklyn and Queens, Irving has Jersey and Staten Island, and little Irving has the Bronx and Westchester. And the four of us operate Manhattan together. Same as we discussed, right?'

'Then what's this talk about gravy?'

'Down in the neighbourhoods, Nick. There's gonna have to be a redistribution in the neighbourhoods. There's a lot of disloyal types we've got to replace, you know what I mean?'

Nick nodded. 'All right,' he said. 'That sounds like an incentive for the rest of you guys, huh?'

There was scattered agreement, and Kapp said, 'Okay, so let's talk about arms. How many and where. And how much capital do we need to get rolling?'

Two or three of them started talking at once, telling about athletic clubs and veteran's organizations and other things, and Kapp smoked while the three top men argued with their assistants.

I didn't care how they sliced their pie. I walked through them to the kitchen and got a bottle of House of Lords and went downstairs and got my folding chair out of my bedroom and brought it down to the dock.

There was a cold wind ruffling the sea and blowing away the words of the peasant kings upstairs. But the wall of the boathouse protected me from most of it. The sky was dark and the lake darker. I sat and smoked and held the bottle till it was warm and wet in my fingers. Then I drank from it and set it down on the warped white wood beside the chair.

After a while, the door opened behind me and Kapp came out.

119

I could still hear the voices upstairs. Kapp came over, grinning, trailing grey cigar smoke, and said, 'It's coming along, huh, Ray?'

'I guess it is,' I said.

'And all on account of you. Now, we all got together, we got a firm base here, you know what I mean?'

'Is Ganolese the one?'

'You figured that, huh? I thought you did. Yeah, if he's the one making the propositions, then he's the one ordered the guns.'

'That's what I thought.'

He walked out to the end of the dock, looked out into the darkness a minute, and then turned and winked at me, grinning. He glanced up at the lighted windows on the top floor, where his staff was readying his army, and then he walked back to me and said, 'You bring me luck, Ray. I didn't figure it to run this smooth. Only a little trouble between Nick and Irving, everybody else coming along nice. We can't miss, boy.'

'Nick and Irving don't like each other, huh?'

'They hate each other's guts. Always have. But they work together. It's the way of the world, you know what I mean?'

'I know.'

He walked around the dock some more, and then said, 'You figure to go after Ganolese, huh?'

'Uh huh.'

'But there's no hurry, right? You're better off, you wait a while. You see what I mean?'

'No, I don't.'

'Pretty soon, Ganolese is gonna have full hands. We're gonna hit his bunch of bastards so hard and so often he won't know which way is Aqueduct. That's the time for you to slip in at him, right? When he's too busy to see you coming.'

'I guess so.'

'Take it from me. I know the way these things work.'

'Maybe you're right.'

'Sure. One more thing. What did you think of the spade?'

'Cheever? Nothing at all. What should I think?'

'I wondered if you picked that up,' he said. 'But maybe you wouldn't. You don't have the background for it.'

120

'Pick what up?'

He stood there and unwrapped a cigar. 'It's this way,' he said, 'A mob, an organization like this, it's in some ways like a business, you know what I mean? Lots of details, lots of executives and vice-presidents, people in charge of this and that and the other thing, you see? No one man running the whole thing.'

I nodded. 'All right.'

'Now Ganolese,' he said, 'he's the one pointed the finger at you, and Will Kelly, and your brother, and your sister-in-law. But he wouldn't have thought it up all by himself. The word would come in, Eddie Kapp's planning a move and thus and so, and somebody would go up to Ganolese and tell him the situation and make a suggestion. Do this or that, boss, and the whole thing is clear.'

'Cheever?'

He paused, looking out at the lake while he lit his cigar. Still looking out that way, he said, 'And when an operation falls apart, it's the guy who suggested that operation in the first place who gets any dirty jobs that might come up because of the failure. Like carrying messages to the enemy. Things like that.'

'I see.'

'I thought you might want to know,' he said. 'I thought maybe you wouldn't pick it up.'

'I didn't.'

He chewed on the cigar, looking at me out of the corner of his eye. After a minute, he said, 'You remember what we were talking about in Plattsburg, family and respectability?'

'I remember.'

'This is about Cheever again. The Negro. He wants to be respectable, too, same as everybody else. But he can't be, and it don't matter how many generations he's been here, you see what I mean? So he's liable to wind up in the organization. If he's smart and he's got a good education and he's tough, he's liable to get himself a good position in the organization. Better than he could get outside.'

'Us minorities got to stick together,' I said.

He laughed. 'Yeah, boy, like you say. But I was making a

121

point. About family. The Negro, see, he's got the respectability itch, same as the Italian or the Jew or the Irishman or the Greek, but he don't have the same itch about family, you know what I mean? He's had that part sold out of him. Brought over here as slaves, Papa sold here, Mama sold there, kids sold up and down the river. And it wasn't so long ago the selling stopped.'

'A hundred years,' I said.

'That ain't long. He still ain't gonna get dewy-eyed over somebody else's family. That's another point to consider.'

'Yeah, I see that.'

'It's nice up here,' he said suddenly. He inhaled noisily, blew breath out at the lake. 'I figure to stick around a while, a week or so, till things get moving. You ought to wait till then, anyway. Why not stay here?'

'I hadn't thought about it,' I said.

'We get to know each other,' he said. 'Father and son. What do you say?'

I shrugged. 'I don't know. I'll think about it.'

He patted my shoulder. 'You do that. We can talk about it tomorrow. You coming up?'

'You need me?'

'Not unless you want to come. This is just the business meeting now.'

'I'll stay here a while.'

'Okay. See you in the morning.'

'Sure.'

He went inside. I heard him going up the stairs. I sat a while longer, looking out at the lake. After a while, I tossed the bottle off the end of the dock and went back up to my room. I packed the suitcase and went out the side door and up the slope toward the road. They were all still talking back there in the throne room.

I told the chauffeur, 'You're supposed to drive me into town.'

He did, and I found the Greyhound station. I waited in the diner across the street until the New York bus came. Then I got aboard and went to sleep.

122

22

I awoke at Hudson, with the dim grey of pre-dawn on the bus windows. It was sprinkling, and the long wipers smacked back and forth across the windshield. I sat midway down the aisle, on the right side. There were only about four other passengers. I had both seats all the way back and I was sprawled at an angle on them, head against the windowpane and shoeless feet in the aisle. I was cramped and muggy. I'd been in that position too long. I felt like wet wool.

What woke me up, the bus had stopped. A man came running across the sidewalk from the store-front bus depot. He had a slick black raincoat draped over his head. The driver pushed the door open and the other man stood in the gutter, and they shouted back and forth over the sound of the rain. Then the man turned and ran back in, and the driver closed the door, and we started out of Hudson. They always do that, whenever it rains. I don't know what they say to one another.

I couldn't get back to sleep. I was sitting on the wrong side to see the dawn, so I looked out at the darkness and wished the bus were going to Binghamton.

It got lighter and lighter outside the window. The towns passed by. Red Hook and Rhineland and back across the river to Kingston. Then West Park and Highland and across the river again to Poughkeepsie. Then Wappingers Falls and Fishkill and Beacon, Peekskill and Ossining and Tarrytown, White Plains and Yonkers and New York.

I got off at 50th Street. I walked a ways and went into the Cuttington Hotel on 52nd Street.

They would all be looking for me now, so I'd have to register under a phoney name. Walking up from the bus terminal, I chose Matthew Allen. A reasonable but forgettable name, and it didn't use my initials.

Stupid things happen. I got terrified when the register was turned toward me. I'd never given a false name before. My hand shook as I wrote the name, so bad it wasn't my writing at all. And I couldn't look the woman desk clerk in the eye. She spent a long time explaining to me that I was signing in at an unusual hour and she would have to charge me for last night, because the day ended at three p.m. I told her it was all right, and got away from her as soon as I could, following the bellboy.

Once in the room, alone, it struck me funny. After all that had happened, practically to faint when I had to write a phoney name. I lay down on the bed and laughed, and the laughter got out of control. Down in the corner of my mind the laughing frightened me. Then the laughter got mixed around and turned upside down and I was crying. Then I laughed because it was funny to be crying, and cried because it was sad to be laughing. When I was empty, I fell asleep.

I woke up at one with smarting feet. I hadn't taken my shoes off. I stripped and showered, and walked around the room naked while the last of the stiffness went away. Then I got dressed, and sat down at the writing table, and wrote a little letter to my Uncle Henry, telling him to write me as Matthew Allen at this hotel. Not in care of Matthew Allen, but as Matthew Allen. Then I left the room.

I made it to the bank on time, where a little more than half of Bill's three thousand dollars still waited in our joint account to be spent. I took out two hundred, and went to a luncheonette and had breakfast, surrounded by people eating a late lunch. And then I had nothing in the world to do. I bought four paperback books and a deck of cards and went back to the room.

I knew that Kapp was right, that I should wait before going after Ganolese. If I were to get to him, without myself being killed, it would be better to wait till his attention was distracted. Kapp and his junta would make a fine distraction. Once they had made their move, I could make mine.

The thing was, it wouldn't be sufficient for me to be killed attempting my revenge. I wasn't trying to sacrifice myself. I wanted to come out alive on the other side. So it was best to wait.

But I'm not good at waiting. The first afternoon, I read a while and then I ripped up all four of the books. They were action mysteries, and they were supposed to help me stop thinking about myself. But all they managed to do was keep prodding the open wound I'd been trying to ignore. All they did was remind me that, if all went well, I *would* be alive when this was over. That was the part, most of all, that I didn't want to think about.

Life uses people up. When I was finished with what I had to do, I could hardly be the same person I'd been the day the Air Force had made me a civilian and I had re-met Dad. Who I would be, what use or purpose I might find – I didn't know, and I didn't want to ask. Yet I had to live, or it would be their triumph after all, and my defeat, even if I were to kill them all and then be killed myself, by my hand or theirs.

It was simpler for the lead characters in the books. They suffered, they involved themselves with tense and driven people, they handled sudden death like a commodity in a secondary market. But when it was all finished, they were unchanged. What they had walked through had left no mark at all on them.

It would be nice to believe that. But the writers were blandly lying. They weren't using up their lead character, because they needed him in the next book in the series.

So I went out and bought a bottle of Old Mr Boston, and on Friday I went to the newspaper library and wasted the day reading about Ed Ganolese. Every once in a while, it seemed, he was served a subpoena and he answered questions before an investigating body of some sort or another. The investigators were always after someone else and usually they asked Ganolese about his relationship with that someone else as of twenty years before. His answers were never informative, but he always managed to be just barely cooperative enough to avoid the legal wrath of the investigators.

Once, there was a photograph. It showed a man somewhat older than fifty, well fed but still strong-looking. He had a kind of brutal handsomeness, softened by time and weight, and the waist-up dignity of the *nouveau riche*. He sat before a microphone shaped like a hooded snake, and he brooded at his inquisitors.

Another time, a reporter explained that the name was pronounced

'Jan-o-lease', and was originally spelled Gianolliese, but the family had shortened and somewhat Anglicized it.

No one had ever done a profile on him.

Friday night, I saw two science-fiction horror movies on 42nd Street. The weekend inched by. Sunday morning, I awoke with a bitter headache at eight o'clock, with less than four hours sleep. But I couldn't drop off again, and it took me an hour to understand why. Then, feeling like a fool, I got up and dressed and found a Catholic church, and prayed for Bill, who wasn't here. It wasn't that I attended Mass. Bill's stand-in came to Mass, and he was me. When Mass was over, I left with no more interest in the place, my duty done. I went back to the hotel, and to bed, and to sleep.

Starting Monday, I read the papers, all of them. It was five days since the meeting at Lake George. The *coup d'état* should begin soon.

It began on Wednesday night. Reading Thursday morning's papers, I nearly missed it. I took a cab back to the hotel from the *Daily News* building on East 42nd Street, where I had bought the Brooklyn and Queens and Bronx editions of that paper. I bought the other morning papers in the hotel lobby and went upstairs and worked my way through them. I sat cross-legged on the bed, turning pages with my left hand, holding the Old Mr Boston bottle in my right.

I went all the way through, and something was bothering me. Something in the *News*. I took the Queens edition and went through it again, and this time when I came to the candy store explosion I stopped.

It was a small candy store in a bad section of Queens. At ten-thirty last night, a gas heater in the back of the store exploded, killing the proprietor. It was the proprietor's brother, a man named Gus Porophorus, who told the firemen about the gas heater.

There was a photograph of the burned and jumbled back part of the store. The photograph showed a blackboard along one wall.

I got up from the bed and lit a cigarette and walked around

126

the room, laughing. I'd seen posters in subway stations, advertising the *Daily News*. The poster would have a big blowup of an unusual photograph, and the caption, 'No one says it like the *News*.'

A blackboard in the back room of a candy store! No one says it like the *News*. The horseplayers wouldn't have anywhere to place their bets in that neighbourhood for a few days.

I'd been expecting something like the movies. Banner headlines screaming, GANGLAND SLAYING. I'd forgotten what Kapp had said to Irving Baumheiler: 'Quiet hits. Hits, but quiet hits.'

I went through all the papers again, and this time I knew what to look for. A stationery store fire in the Bronx, owner killed in the blaze. And a man named Anthony Manizetsky, 36, unemployed, killed when his car rammed into a steel support under the West Side Drive at 22nd Street. There was a photo of the car, last year's Buick. And an import firm's warehouse burned down on Third Avenue in Brooklyn.

I got yesterday's papers out of the closet, wondering if I'd missed the opening gun. But I hadn't. It had started last night.

I felt twenty pounds lighter. I had been hating the hotel room. I put the top on the Old Mr Boston bottle and called Ed Johnson. When I told him who it was he said, 'I wondered what happened to you. It's been almost a month now.'

I said, 'Have they been asking you questions about me any more?'

'No, thank God. Just the one time. I had a tail for about three days after that. He was lousy, but I figured it would be a bad move to lose him. Since he left, nothing at all.'

'Good. I've got a job for you, if you want it. Can I trust you?'

'If you think you can trust my answer to that,' he said, 'you think you can trust me.'

'All right. I want a man's address. I want to know where I can find him for sure.'

'Is this number one, or are you still poking around?'

'If I don't tell you, you can't tell anybody else.'

'All right, I'm not very brave. I don't get paid enough to be brave. What's the name?'

'Ed Ganolese.' I spelled it for him. 'I'm not sure what the Ed is short for.'

'All right. He's in New York, for sure?'

'Somewhere around here. Maybe he commutes.'

'Wait a second, I've seen this name somewhere.'

'He's one of the people who run the local syndicate.'

'Oh. Well – I'm not sure. I can't guarantee anything.'

'I know that.'

'I'll have to be careful who I ask.'

'More than last time.'

'I know who it was that time. I wish I had the guts to do something about it. Where do I call you?'

'I'll call you Saturday. Three in the afternoon. At your office.'

'I don't blame you,' he said. 'This isn't my league.'

'Then don't kick yourself for it. I'll call you Saturday.'

Then I went out and bought a pair of scissors. I came back and clipped the war news.

23

The afternoon papers carried more of it. A boiler explosion in a residence hotel off Eighth Avenue, in the middle of Whore Row. A liquor-store owner shot to death in what the papers called a hold-up attempt, though the 'bandit' had stolen nothing – it was suggested that he had been scared off after firing the four shots that had killed the owner. Another fatal automobile accident, this one in Jackson Heights, in which the driver, who had been alone in his year old Bonneville Pontiac, was listed in the paper as 'unemployed'.

The *coup* was less than twenty-four hours old. I had seven clippings. Each separate item was explainable in some manner less dramatic than the truth. No outsider, reading these separate and minor reports from the front, would guess that a revolution was taking place.

Most of the action wouldn't be hitting the papers at all. There were surely men who had disappeared in the last twenty-four hours, and who would never be heard from again, but no one would be calling the police to find them. Other men, insisting that they had fallen downstairs, would be entering hospitals with no more public fanfare than is given any obscure accident victim. Store owners would be gazing gloomily at wrecked showcases and merchandise, about which they would not be calling the police or the insurance company.

Thursday night I walked around Manhattan steadily for five hours. I avoided midtown and Central Park, so most of my time was spent between 50th and 100th Streets, on and near Broadway. I had no goal. I simply had to burn the energy off. I saw no signs of the struggle.

Friday morning, I added three more clippings. Friday afternoon, I added another five. Among them was a resident of the Riverdale section of the Bronx, who broke his neck when he fell down a flight of stairs in his house. I recognized the name. He was one of the men who'd been at the meeting in Lake George. So the incumbents were fighting back.

The police must know what was going on. But they wouldn't be anxious to advertise it. Like Irving Baumheiler, they would want it all very quiet. No sense upsetting the citizenry.

Saturday morning the papers reported, without knowing it, the results of a major battle the night before. The *News*, the *Mirror* and the *Herald Tribune* all reported the Athletic Club blaze in Brooklyn. The *Herald Tribune* and the *Times* reported the boiler explosion in the East Side night club half an hour after closing. Two more of the Lake George insurgents had run into fatal accidents, one in his home and one in his car. All in all, I had clippings on eleven incidents in the battle, not one of them found sufficiently newsworthy to be mentioned by all four of the morning papers.

When I called Johnson at three, he sounded nervous. 'What the hell were you setting me up for, Kelly?'

'Why? What happened?'

'Nothing. I stuck my nose in and pulled it right back out again. Something's going on.'

'I know.'

'You could've warned me.'

'I did. I told you to be careful.'

'Listen, just do me one favour. Don't call me any more, okay?'

'All right.'

'Whatever the hell it is, I don't want any part of it. I don't even want to know about it.'

'All right, Johnson, I understand you. I won't bother you again.'

'I'd like to help you out,' he said, and now he sounded apologetic. 'But this just isn't my league.'

'You said that before.'

'It's still true. I'm great on divorce.'

'In other words, you don't know where Ganolese is.'

'I got both his addresses. An apartment in town here, and a house out on the Island. But he isn't at either one of them. And

130

whatever's going on, this doesn't look like a good time to ask where else he might be.'

'All right.'

'I'm sorry. I did my best.'

'I know. Don't worry about it. This shouldn't be anybody's league.'

We hung up, and I lit a cigarette and decided I'd have to do it the other way around. I looked in the phone book and found William Cheever's law office listed, but no home phone. He wouldn't be there on Saturday afternoon.

It was a long weekend.

24

Cheever's office was on West 111th Street, the edge of Harlem. Monday morning I took the subway uptown.

I got off at 110th Street, the northwest tip of Central Park, and walked north into the ghetto. I wore my raincoat over my suit, bulky enough so Smitty's gun made no bulge under my belt. It was daytime, so no one looked at me twice.

The building was eight storeys tall. A large record store chromed the first floor. The rest of the building, ancient brick and dusty windows, stuck up out of all that chrome and glass and gaiety like a wart.

The door I wanted was off to the left, stuck under the record store's armpit. I went up narrow-canted stairs for three flights, each time looking up toward a bare twenty-five watt bulb.

William Cheever's name was fourth of four on the frosted glass panel of the door. It wasn't a law firm, it was one of those set-ups where a number of unsuccessful professional men get together to share the rent and the receptionist and the futility.

The receptionist was as light as a Negro can be and still have Negroid features. She had relentlessly straightened her hair and then recurled it in neo-Grecian twists. She wore a high-necked and lace-fringed blouse designed for the bustless girls of midtown, and she was far too ample for it. Looking at her dressed in it, the first word that came to mind was 'unsanforized'.

She smiled at me and closed a slim volume of Langston Hughes, one finger marking the place. 'May I help you?' Her accent was softly British, so she was probably Jamaican.

'William Cheever,' I said. I hoped the attorneys at least had separate offices.

'He isn't in this morning.'

'Oh.' I frowned as worriedly as I could. 'I wanted to get in touch with him. As soon as possible. Would you have any idea when he'd be back?'

'Mister Cheever? Oh, no. He very seldom comes to the office.' She withdrew the finger from the Langston Hughes book. 'In fact, to tell you the honest truth, I sometimes wonder why he has an office here at all.'

'Doesn't he meet his clients here?'

'Not so's you'd notice it.' She'd been dying to talk about Cheever for days, maybe weeks. 'The only clients of Mr Cheever's that *I've* ever seen,' she said archly, 'are those gamblers and bookmakers and numbers sellers that he sends here for Mr Partridge to represent.' She leaned confidentially forward, her bosom bracketing Langston Hughes. 'Personally, I think Mr Cheever is *using* Mr Partridge, giving him business like that. I think it can do terrible harm to Mr Partridge's reputation as a courtroom lawyer if he becomes linked in the public mind with hoodlums and gamblers.'

I smiled at her earnestness and the well-memorized sentence, phrased and rephrased in countless imaginary dialogues. 'Once you marry Mr Partridge,' I told her, 'you'll be able to overcome Mr Cheever's influence, I'm sure.'

She blushed. She was light enough to do it beautifully. Her fingers fussed with the papers on her desk.

I was sorry to embarrass her, she was a pleasant girl. But she would sooner answer my question if distracted. I said, 'Could you give me Mr Cheever's home address? I do have to talk to him today.'

'Yes, of course!' She was overwhelmingly grateful at something else to think about. She scooped up a small notebook and leafed through it. I borrowed pencil and paper and copied down the address. It was only a few blocks away, on 110th Street, a building facing the park on the north side.

It was a sprawling old stone apartment building, dating back to Harlem's days of eminence, when all four sides of the park were limited to the white well-to-do. It had fallen since. Plaster peeled in the huge foyer. The same drab obscenity was scratched seven times in the elevator walls. The eighth floor corridor was

133

marred by bubbled, cracked, dry and eroded paint crumbling from the walls. I went through a grey door marked SERVICE E-H. I was in a small pentagonal grey room. Bags of rubbish leaned against the walls. The concrete floor was a darker grey. The four doors curving around me in Cinemascope each had a letter scrawled on it in white paint, far less professionally than on the front apartment entrances out along the corridor.

The door marked G was locked. I stopped when I realized how relieved that made me.

I had killed one man without meaning to. I had killed another man in the midst of rapid action, without having a chance to think about it. I had no idea whether I could kill a man coldly and intentionally.

What if I couldn't? To talk of revenge is one thing, but what if I couldn't do it?

I forced into my mind my last picture of Dad, dying in terror, spewing blood. I thought of Bill, and the wife I hadn't met. I remembered how I had looked in the full-length mirror at Lake George. I felt the dead seed in my head where a small glass football could not replace an eye. I looked at the jagged hole that had been clawed into my life.

But it did no good. I didn't hate Cheever. I didn't hate any of them. I felt a sad lonely pity for myself, and that was all.

Wasted, it was all wasted. I was frail and ineffectual, I'd come all this way for nothing.

I leaned back against the entrance door and slid down it till I was sitting on the floor, knees high before my chest, raincoat bunched around my hips. I crossed my forearms on my knees and rested my brow on my arms. Weak, and wasted, and meaningless. Lost, and broken, and impotent.

Until I got mad, at myself. I raised my head and glowered at the white-painted G and whispered stupid insults at myself in idiotic fury. And then after a while that dulled too, and I just sat there, legs stretched out now, and looked at the bags of rubbish, and let my head do whatever it wanted.

I sat there about two hours. When I got up my back was stiff, but I had my role straightened out. I had jerrybuilt a justification for my existence. I was a weak and unworthy vessel, but I would take the life from William Cheever and the other one. If I had been strong and capable, I could kill them out of a cold fury, a dispassionate rage. Instead, I would kill them cheaply, I would kill them only because that was what I was supposed to do.

Back doors get cheap locks. A nail file between door and jamb worked as well as a key in the lock. I pushed the door open silently, and entered the kitchen. Some rooms ahead, I could hear the murmur of talking.

I went left through an empty bedroom. The door was closed, but didn't set snug. Through the crack, I saw him in the living room, talking on the phone. I could only see a narrow strip of the room, so I couldn't tell if he were alone.

He was abusing the receptionist for having given away the secret of his address. His face was naked and jagged and grey. I was glad he was afraid of me.

It hurt him that he couldn't let the girl know just how strongly he was upset. He was having trouble restraining himself, keeping his voice down. He was making do as best he could with heavy sarcasm and cruel caricature of her accent. At last he said, 'No, he hasn't come here. How long ago was he there? – It's over two hours. You should have called me, sweetheart, and not wait around till I called you. – Honey, none of my clients are okay, you know that. When was the last time you saw a white man in that office? Oh, the hell, why waste time talking to you? Besides, it's time for you and Benny Partridge to have lunch together on his sofa, isn't it? – What do you *suppose* I mean, dumplin'?'

He listened a few seconds more, then slammed the receiver down and glared desperately around the room. The way his eyes moved, I could tell he was alone. I reached in under the raincoat and jacket and dragged out Smitty's gun.

Cheever reached for the phone again. He dialled jerkily. I counted ten numbers, so he was calling someone out of town. He told the operator his number, and then he waited, fumbling a Viceroy out of the pack one-handed. All at once he dropped the pack and said quickly into the phone, 'Let me talk to Ed. Willy Cheever. – Yeah, sure, I'll hold on.'

He managed to get the cigarette out and lit before he had to talk again. Then he said, 'Ed? Willy Cheever. Somebody came around to my office this morning, asking for me. – Well, the thing is, the stupid girl at the office gave him my address. – I'm home now. I want to come up, Ed. If I could stay at the farm just a couple days – Just a couple days, Ed, until – Ed, for God's sake, she told him where I live! – There isn't anyplace else. – Ed, I've never asked you for any special favour before. I – Ed! Ed!'

He jiggled the receiver and I stepped into the living room and said, 'He hung up on you, Willy.'

His head swivelled around and he stared at me. He didn't move. I had Smitty's gun in my right hand. I went over and took the phone out of his hand and cradled it. Then I backed off from him and said, 'You better pick up your cigarette. It's burning the rug.'

He picked it up, moving like a robot, and put it in the ashtray beside the phone. It smouldered there, and he stared at the gun.

I said, 'Ganolese threw you away. He's got too much to worry about, and you're just a cheap Harlem shyster. He can replace you with a nod of his head.'

'No.' The word jolted out of him. His hands started to twitch together in his lap. 'Ed listens to me. Ed respects my advice.'

'He threw you away.'

'Oh, God!' His hands snapped up and covered his face.

I crossed the room and sat down opposite him and waited for him to finish. When he finally took his hands down, his eyes were red and puffed, his flat cheeks gleamed wet. The little moustache was only silly, like a little girl wearing her mother's shoes. He said, 'He called me boy. Like the kid who shines his shoes.'

'Eddie Kapp is taking over,' I said. 'Ganolese doesn't have time for shoe-shine boys. Not even if they went to college.'

'He's a son of a bitch. Goddamn him, I treated him right.'

'Drive me up there. I'll put in a good word for you with Eddie Kapp.'

He stared at me a second, then shook his head. 'Not a chance. Not a chance.'

'Ganolese is losing. If he was winning, he'd have the time to kid you along like always.'

136

'Oh, *damn*!' His eyes squeezed shut and he pounded the chair arms with clenched fists. 'I never tommed!' he cried. 'I never sucked! He treated me like a white man, he never made me play the colour!'

'That was when he needed you.' I got to my feet. 'Take me up there.'

He was calming again. He brooded at the wall. 'He shouldn't have hung up on me,' he whispered. 'He shouldn't have called me boy. He's a slick wop, he's nothing but.'

'Come along,' I said.

He looked at me, and started to calculate. 'You'll put in a good word for me with Kapp?'

It was easy to lie to him. 'I will,' I said. 'You've got no reason not to trust me.'

'All right,' he said. And bought himself an hour or two more of life.

25

His car was this year's Buick, cream and blue, half a block away in a tow-away zone. He had a special permit in the windshield that let him park there.

He drove across 110th westward and turned north and boarded the Henry Hudson Parkway. I sat beside him, Smitty's gun in my lap. We didn't talk.

He took the George Washington Bridge into Jersey, and 17 a while. General Motors cars are all very much alike. The last time I rode this way was with Dad in an Oldsmobile one year older than this Buick. I was sitting in the same seat. I felt the nervousness creeping up from my stomach.

He left 17 and crossed the Jersey border back into New York State, still heading north. I said the first words spoken by either of us in the car: 'How much farther?'

He looked quick at me, and then out at the highway again. 'A little ways beyond Monsey,' he said. 'Up in Rockland County.'

'What's this Monsey? A town?'

'Yes. Small town, built up in the last few years.'

'Then they'll have a shopping centre. Stop at a sporting goods store.'

'All right.'

After a while, he turned off the highway on a curving exit that took us under the road we'd just been on and, a little farther, over the Thruway. Then we were on 59, which was lined with newish stores fronted by blacktop parking spaces. Cheever braked nose in before a sports shop with shotguns and hip boots displayed in the window.

I took the key out of the ignition. I'd already checked the glove compartment and it was clean. I said, 'You wait here.'

'Don't worry,' he said. He had some of his bounce back. 'All I can count on now is you and Eddie Kapp. I won't try to run away from you.'

'Glad to hear it,' I said. The fact that, under other circumstances, I might have liked this smooth and quiet collegian only irritated me.

I bought, in the store, a .30-.30 rifle and a box of cartridges. It cost me a hundred eighty dollars, almost all I had with me.

Back in the car, Cheever drove again while I read the instruction booklet and practised loading the rifle. Then Cheever said, 'About a mile more up this way.'

We were passing an intersection. There was undeveloped land around us, and a general store called Willow Tree Corner. I said, 'Is the house right out on the road?'

'No. It's set back about half a mile. All uphill from the road. There's a dirt road in.'

'Will there – slow down a minute – will there be people watching out at this end of the dirt road?'

'Yeah, there will. That's why I had to get permission to come up. I wouldn't want to turn in there without permission.'

'All right. Then go on by. But point it out to me.'

'All right.'

'You can drive faster again now.'

A couple of minutes later he said, 'That's it. On the right.'

I saw a dirt road that jolted down a bank and curved into the trees. There was a thick wood along here, climbing a steep slope away from the road toward the Ramapo Mountains. I caught just a glimpse of an automobile parked in the road under the trees.

Cheever said, 'Now what?'

'Make the first right you can.'

About a mile farther on we turned right. It was a smaller road, asphalt, climbing steeply upward. Incongruously, there was suddenly, to our left, a small gravel parking area and a fireplace and picnic table and mesh rubbish basket. I said, 'U-turn, and stop over there.'

The car was too big and the road too small. He had to back and fill. No other cars came along. It was Monday, the tenth of October, the wrong time of the year for traffic on this road.

Cheever stopped on the gravel and pulled on the emergency brake. I got the keys out of the ignition and climbed out of the car. I carried the rifle and Smitty's revolver over and set them on the picnic table.

Cheever came over after me. I said, 'Sit down here.'

Something in my face or voice tipped him off. He stopped, across the table from me, and looked at my face, warily. His hands were out in front of him, the fingers splayed wide apart. He said, 'What is it? What's the matter?'

I said, 'Do you know who I am?'

'You were with Kapp. Up at Lake George. You were the one came up to the car.'

'But do you know my name?'

He shook his head.

I said, 'Ray Kelly. Will Kelly's son.'

He kept shaking his head. 'It doesn't mean a thing to me. I don't know what you think, but you're wrong.'

'Kill the Kellys,' I said. 'That's what I'm thinking. Somebody whispered that in Ed Ganolese's ear. Kill the Kellys, kill them all. The old man and both sons and the daughter-in-law. The whole tribe, because Eddie Kapp is coming out of Dannemora, and we can't be sure –'

He cried, 'No! You got it all wrong! It wasn't me!'

'Because we can't be sure,' I finished, 'which boy is Eddie Kapp's son and, even if we get the right one, some other member of the family might stand in for him, and Ed you know how sentimental those old wops can get. Isn't that right, Cheever? Somebody whispered that to Ed Ganolese, and then he pointed the finger.'

His head was shaking again, and he was backing away from me, away from the table. 'Not me!' he was crying. 'You got it all wrong, Kelly, you got to believe me! It wasn't like that, it wasn't *like* that!'

'You set the whole thing in motion, Cheever,' I said. I picked up Smitty's gun.

He turned and went running off into the woods, away from the road. In just a second, he was out of sight, and I could hear the sounds of his thrashing getting farther away.

I should have killed him. I could have. When he took his first running step, I had the revolver on him. There was one fraction of a second there when I was sighting down the top of the revolver barrel right into his left side, under his arm, his arm up in the running motion, and my brain told my finger to squeeze the trigger. And it didn't.

I lowered my arm, and listened to him tumbling away through the woods, ripping his trouser legs, catching his shoelaces in the tough weeds, falling and scrabbling and running scared.

I couldn't kill him. I told myself it was because I wasn't sure of him, because there was still a chance it was somebody else who'd done the whispering in Ganolese's ear. There were other reasons why he might have been the one picked to go up to Lake George.

It was true. But it wasn't the reason. I hadn't killed him because I couldn't kill him.

He was gone. The woods were silent. Right doesn't make might.

I went over and tossed the keys on the front seat of the car. I picked up the rifle and the revolver, and went across the road and into the woods on the other side, heading toward where the farm hideout should be.

I had to kill Ed Ganolese. I *had* to.

141

26

It was late afternoon, the sun was orange-red low in the sky behind me. It was evening dark there under the trees. I kept my direction by following the slant of the long red sunbeams.

I came to the dirt road first. I stepped out on it before I knew it was there, and then I pulled back into the trees again. I stood still and listened. Off to my right I could hear faint sounds of men talking. That would be the guards, down near the road. I turned left and moved slowly uphill through the trees, keeping close to the road.

The farmhouse was painted yellow. It was two storeys high and sprawling. Three cars were parked in front of it, a black Cadillac and a tan-and-cream Chrysler and a green Buick. Four men sat on the stoop, talking together in monotones.

The house was shabby. Stretching away to the right, along a levelling of the ground, was what had once been cleared land. Behind and to the right of the main house was the barn.

Keeping to the woods, I circled to the left around the house. Once past it, the ground sloped more sharply uphill. I climbed until I could come around directly behind the house, and then I moved slowly back down to the nearest safe point. Then I sat down with my back to a tree, and watched the rear windows, and waited.

It got dark almost as suddenly as turning off a light. Then it got colder. The jacket and raincoat weren't enough to keep the cold out. I stood and walked back and forth, flapping my arms.

From time to time, a light went on in one of the back rooms. Whenever that happened I stopped my prowling around to study the room and the people in it. I saw the kitchen, and a number of bedrooms. There were a lot of people in the house, men and women both. But it was almost ten o'clock before I finally saw Ed Ganolese.

He came into the kitchen and got a glass from the cupboard and ice cubes from the refrigerator. There were bottles on the drainboard. He stood with his back to me and made himself a drink.

I'd been out there nearly five hours. My hands were cold and I hadn't chanced smoking a cigarette. Now I was afraid my aim wouldn't be any good. I'd always done well with the carbine in the Air Force, but this was a different weapon and I was shivering and I was nervous for need of a cigarette.

So I let him go the first time. I hunched over with my back to the house and lit a cigarette, and stood behind a tree smoking it, my hands under my jacket pressed against my sides. When the cigarette was gone, I checked through the scope again. The kitchen was empty.

This wasn't any good. I hadn't been able to kill Cheever. Now I'd seen Ganolese in the sights, the chiefest devil, and I'd found another reason not to pull the trigger.

I couldn't let that weakness come over me again, the way it had with Cheever. I had to do this, and get it over with.

The sky was overcast, with no moon. I moved down the slope closer to the house, until I was nearly down to the level of the kitchen windows. I was in the open now, but I couldn't be seen from the house. I was beyond the rectangles of light from the windows.

I crouched, the rifle leaning against my shoulder, my hands kept warm against my sides beneath my jacket. And when Ganolese came back to the kitchen, the empty glass in his hand, I refused to think of excuses.

I was so close now that his white-shirted back filled the scope. I got into kneeling position, as I'd been taught in the service. Right knee on the ground, left knee up, left elbow over left knee. I sighted down to his left shoulder blade in the white expanse of his shirt, and when I fired, the barrel kicked up and for a second I couldn't find the kitchen window through the sight. I didn't hear the sound of the shot at all.

When I found the window again, Ganolese was slowly folding forward over the drainboard, bottles skittering away down the

143

slope into the sink. A tiny dot of darkish red had stained the back of his shirt, low and to the right of where I'd aimed.

I fired again, a bit high and to the left, and this time I was ready for the recoil, and I kept the target in the sight, and saw the bullet kick him forward, and the second red dot form, and then he slid down out of sight and I got to my feet, the rifle slack in my right hand.

Then sound came back to the world. I hadn't heard either shot, or anything else between them, but now all at once, as though a radio volume knob had been turned up, I heard men calling and shouting to one another, and even the sound of heavy feet running on wooden floors inside the house.

I turned and went back up into the woods and over to the right, moving slowly in the blackness. I kept moving for half an hour or more, only the slope of the land keeping me going in a straight line. When I stopped, I was alone in silence. There was no pursuit.

I sank down against a tree to wait for dawn. It got deadly cold. I slept fitfully, dreaming of ogres and childish things. Every time I awoke again, I smoked a bitter cigarette, cupping my hands around it for warmth.

With dawn, I stood and moved around, trying to get warmth back into my body. But I kept near the same tree until the sun was up. Then I walked back through the damp woods to the house, leaving Smitty's gun and the rifle against the tree.

It was deserted. All the cars were gone. I walked down the dirt road to the asphalt two-laner and turned left. A woman in a station wagon with two young kids and a Doberman pinscher gave me a lift to Suffern. I got a bus there for New York. I went back to the hotel room and took a long hot shower and went to bed. I slept fourteen hours, without dreams, and woke up drugged, to find there was mail for me.

It was a letter from Uncle Henry, a thick envelope fat with papers. There was a note from him, telling me to be careful, telling me I should come home to Binghamton. There were documents to be signed, about Bill's house and Bill's car and Bill's kid. And there was a clipping from the *Binghamton Press*.

In the note, Uncle Henry said about the clipping, 'This ought to relieve your mind.' The clipping showed a photograph of a scared balding man in a dark suit, his elbow held by a sunglassed policeman. The story with the photograph told how methodical police laboratory work had finally cracked the hit-run accident of August 29th, in which Mrs Ann Kelly, mother of one, had been killed. The driver of the death car was an electrical appliance salesman from Scranton, named Drugay.

He had nothing to do with the organization at all.

27

Eddie Kapp lied to me. He lied to me.

The organization didn't kill my sister-in-law.

He lied to me. In some ways, in every way, in how many ways I didn't know.

Why did he lie to me? So I would stay with him.

But if he wanted me to stay with him, then his lies should have been the truth. His lies made sense, or there was no sense in his wanting me to stay with him.

He said I was a symbol, around which his cronies would gather. Was that a lie? If so, it had no purpose. His cronies *had* gathered around him. Nick Rovito had tested me. No one had asked what I was doing there. So how could that have been a lie?

He said Ed Ganolese knew about the symbol, and was trying to destroy it. Was that a lie? But a tan-and-cream Chrysler had killed my father, and had tried to kill me. And the same tan-and-cream Chrysler had tried to kill Eddie Kapp. And the same tan-and-cream Chrysler had been parked at the farm where Ed Ganolese was hiding out. So how could that have been a lie?

Or was it only half a lie?

I was alive. *I* was alive.

The tan-and-cream Chrysler had pulled up beside us, thirty-eight miles from New York, and the man on the right-hand side had reached out his arm and shot my father. That was all.

They must have known my father was dead. They must have seen their bullets hit. And they had driven on. They hadn't stopped to be sure that *I* was dead. They hadn't even fired a shot at me.

They hadn't been *trying* to kill me. They had killed the man Ed Ganolese had pointed at. Will Kelly.

He was the symbol. The trusted lawyer, the right-hand man from the old days. The others might have objected that Eddie

Kapp was too old, that he couldn't handle the whole operation by himself, or that he might die very soon after they'd made their *coup*, and then there'd only be another power fight, and they wouldn't want two fights like that so close together. So there was a second man, a younger man, the trusted lawyer, who knew the operation and who could handle its administration, a man they could all agree on to succeed Eddie Kapp. Will Kelly.

Without Will Kelly, Kapp couldn't rally the others around him. So Ganolese had Kelly murdered.

And Eddie Kapp had given up. He'd written his sister, he'd planned his retirement. And then I came along.

He hadn't been sure it would work. He'd had to talk and argue and reason and explain for a week on the telephone at Lake George, before the others would go along with it.

I could almost hear the way he'd put it: 'Here's my son, Ray Kelly. Will Kelly took care of him for me while I was out of circulation. Will trained him, gave him the background, explained the set-up to him. The boy's young, but he knows what's going on, and he learns fast. He'll take over when I'm gone, and he won't be greedy, he'll be content with New York. And there'll be forty, fifty years in him.'

It took him a week, and probably a lot more arguments than that, but he talked them into it. And he gave me that song-and-dance about me as a symbol because he knew I didn't want to have anything to do with his mob. Once he was in the driver's seat, after the *coup*, he didn't care how many of his cronies knew the truth.

I'd told him about Bill's wife being killed. That gave him the idea to sell me that family-purge story. Because then all he had to do was point me. I was a loaded gun, held by Eddie Kapp.

Bill. My brother Bill.

When I'd left Lake George, I thought I was ridding myself of Eddie Kapp for ever. I wasn't. I had to find him again. Now.

28

That afternoon, I went up to Riverdale. It was just a week to the day since the revolution had started. Five days ago, the first sign of the counter-attack had appeared in the papers, when Patros Kanzantkos fell down the stairs in his Riverdale home and broke his neck. The address was given in the newspaper story.

I took the subway as far as it would go, looking out at the big-shouldered, dull brick apartment buildings when the train became an elevated in the Bronx. At the last stop, I got a cab. I had three hundred more in my pocket from Bill's dwindling bank account. Bill's Luger was huge and bulky against my side, tucked under my belt. The raincoat was supposed to cover it.

The house was colonial-style, two storeys, white, in a very good section, all curving roads and trees and backyard wading pools. There was a black wreath still on the door.

The obituary notice had said that Kanzantkos was survived by a wife, Emilie, and a son, Robert. It was the son who answered the doorbell, an angry black-haired boy of my chronological age, his face marred by a petulant mouth, his black suit oddly awkward on his frame.

I said, 'I'd like to talk to your mother, please.'

He said, insolently, 'What about?'

'Tell her Eddie Kapp's son is here.'

'Why should she care?'

'If she wants you to know, she'll tell you.'

That struck a nerve. He paled, and when he said, 'Wait there,' his voice was harsher, more strained.

He closed the door, and I lit a cigarette and looked at the careful rock garden fronting the pretty house across the way. And then he came back and said, 'All right. Come on in.' He was still angry.

I followed him upstairs to a small room furnished with two sofas and a stereophonic record player. The walls were ranked with bookcases holding record albums. Mrs Kanzantkos, a small and brittle woman with a narrow nose, said, 'Thank you, Bobby. I'll want to talk to Mr Kapp alone.'

He went away, glowering reluctantly closing the door. I said, 'He doesn't know what his father did for a living?'

She said, 'No. And he never will.'

'A boy should always know who and what his father is,' I said.

Coldly, she said, 'I'll be the judge of that, Mr Kapp.'

'Kelly,' I corrected her. 'Ray Kelly.'

Instantly she was on her feet. 'You said you were Eddie Kapp's son.'

'I am. I was brought up by a man named Kelly.'

The distrust didn't all leave her eyes. 'And what do you want from me?'

'I was with my father when he got out of Dannemora,' I said, 'and at the meeting at Lake George. I met your husband there. He mentioned me, didn't he?'

'Mr Kanzantkos rarely discussed business with me,' she said.

'All right. The point is, my father and I were separated after Lake George. I had another job to do. Now it's done, and I want to get in touch with him again.'

'I would have no idea where you could find him.'

'I know that. But you must know at least one or two of the other people who were at Lake George. I wish you'd call one of them and tell him I'm here.'

'Why?'

'I want to get together with my father again. Isn't that natural?'

'And he didn't tell you where you could get in touch with him?'

'We parted hastily. I had this other thing to do.'

'What other thing?'

'I had to kill a man named Ed Ganolese.'

She blinked. The silence was like wool. Then she got to her feet. 'Wait here,' she said. 'I – I'll call someone.'

'Thank you.'

She seemed glad to leave the room. She closed the door softly after her.

149

Ten minutes later, the door opened again, and the son came slipping in. He shut the door after him and leaned against it and said, his voice low, 'I want to know what's going on.'

'Nothing's going on,' I said.

'She's keeping something from me,' he insisted. 'You know what it is. You tell me.'

I shook my head.

'Why are you here?'

'It has nothing to do with you.'

'My father?'

'No.'

'That's a lie. Who's my mother calling?'

'I have no idea.'

He came away from the door, arms high. 'I'll twist it out of you –'

Before I could do anything to him, the door opened and his mother was standing there. She ordered him from the room, and he refused to go until he found out what all the mystery was. They screamed at each other for five minutes or more. I spent the time looking at the record collection. Classical music and stringed dinner music. One small section of Dixieland jazz.

When at last Robert left, his mother said to me, 'I'm sorry. He should have known better.'

'As you say, it's your business.'

'Yes. I phoned a friend of my husband's. He promised to call back as soon as possible. Would you like to come down to the kitchen for coffee?'

'Thank you.'

The kitchen was white and chintz. Through the window, I could see a well-tended back lawn and a flagstone patio. Rose bushes lined the fence at the back of the property. From the cellar came the drumming rhythm of someone at a punching bag. That would be Robert, forcing me to talk.

We waited in silence. She didn't ask me any questions. We sat there twenty minutes before the phone rang in another room on the ground floor. She excused herself and went away, coming back a minute later to say, 'He wants to talk to you.'

It was Kapp. He said, 'Ray? Is that you?'

'Yes, Kapp, it's me.'

'You recognized my voice?'

'Why not?'

'That was you got Ganolese Monday night?'

'That was me.'

'I'll be a son of a bitch.' He sounded happy, and half-drunk. 'You lovely little bastard, you're a chip off the old block. You're done now, huh?'

'I'm done. It's squared away. And there's nothing else for me to do. I'd like to stick with you.'

'Goddamn it, Ray, you don't know how that makes me feel. Oh, goddamn it, boy, that's great. I hoped to God you'd decide that.'

'I'm glad,' I said. 'I came looking for you right away, as soon as I was done with the other.'

'Do you want me to send a car?'

'Are you in the city? If you are, it'd be quicker for me to take the subway.'

'Sure thing. We've got ourselves a suite at the Weatherton. That's at Lexington and 52nd.'

'I know where it is.'

'It's under the name Peterson. Raymond Peterson. You remember?'

'I remember. I'll be right there.'

I hung up, and the woman said, 'I'll drive you to the subway, if you want.'

'Thank you.'

We went out to the garage. From the cellar came the drumming of the punching bag.

29

I walked the block from the subway stop to the Weatherton Hotel. I remembered it. It was the one where Dad had stayed, where we'd both stayed the night before they killed him. Kapp wouldn't know that.

I asked for Mr Peterson's suite, and they sent my name up, then told me the fifteenth floor. I rode up in the elevator. 1512 was to the left. I could hear party sounds.

I knocked on the door and a smiling man with a broken nose opened it and said, 'You're Kapp's kid, huh?'

'That's right.'

'Put her there! He keeps tellin' us how great you are!'

His hand was huge, but soft. I shook it, and went inside.

The suite went on and on, room after room. A nervous little man took over from the first one and showed me my bedroom. I left the Luger on the bed, under the raincoat. Then I followed the nervous man through more rooms to the party.

It was a huge parlour, with French doors leading to the terrace. A radio played bad music in one corner, competing with a television set across the way. Sectional sofas and coffee tables were scattered all around. Two portable bars stood full and handy.

There were about thirty people in the room, maybe ten of them women. The women all had high breasts and professional smiles. The men were laughing and shouting at one another.

Kapp had one of the women in a corner. He was talking steadily to her, and his right hand kneaded her breast. She kept smiling.

Somebody saw me and shouted, 'Hey, Kapp! Here's your kid!'

He looked around and then came running over. Behind him, the woman smoothed out the wrinkles with a little contemptuous shrug, but kept smiling.

Kapp punched my arm and hugged me and shouted at me how

great I was. Then he pranced me all around the room, introducing me to all the men and telling them all how great I was. He didn't introduce me to any of the women, but they all kept watching me.

For fifteen minutes, it all whirled around. Half a dozen people told me the reason for the celebration. The national committee had given the nod. They were in. *Coup* successful. And they all had me to thank, because bumping Ganolese had done the trick. That was what had clinched it. There was only a little reorganizing left to do, and from there on life was gravy.

Kapp finally calmed down a bit, and people stopped shouting in my ear. I took his arm and said, 'Kapp, I want to talk to you. I want to tell you about it.'

'Goddamn it, boy,' he said, grinning at me. 'Let's get away from this mob.'

I led the way toward the bedroom where I'd left the raincoat. On the way we came across the nervous man, hurrying somewhere. I grabbed his elbow and said, 'Come along with us for a minute.'

Kapp said, 'What the hell for?'

I said, 'You'll see.'

We went into the bedroom and Kapp said, 'What the hell do you want Mouse here for?'

'He's my messenger,' I said. I reached under the raincoat and took out the Luger and held it on them as I closed and locked the bedroom door.

Kapp stared at the gun, and sobriety washed down his face like lye. He said, 'What the hell are you up to?'

I said, 'Mouse, you listen close. My name is Ray Kelly. Eddie Kapp is my natural father, my father by blood. Isn't that right, Kapp?'

'Sure that's right. Why the hell –?'

'Hold on. You got that part, Mouse?'

He nodded jerkily, his eyes on the gun.

'All right. I also had a mother and a foster father and a half-brother and a sister-in-law. My mother killed herself because of Eddie Kapp here. Isn't that right, Kapp?'

Relief hit him so hard he sat down heavily on the edge of the

153

bed. 'Oh, for God's sake, Ray, that was twenty-one years ago. And who knew she was going to do something like that? You pull a gun on me for something twenty-one years old?'

'I'll get more current in a minute. Just hold on. About my mother, and Will Kelly. He was your sideman, he worked with you every step of the way. You were just about to make the move, take control of the New York organization, and Will Kelly was an active part in it, working right next to you all the way. Then somebody sicked the Federal Government on you because –'

'Ganolese,' he said. 'That filthy bastard, Ganolese.'

'– because of your taxes. The government put you out of the way, so Ganolese could take over instead of you. And Will Kelly had to get out of town. His wife couldn't stand the small town life, but she didn't dare come back to New York. She killed herself.'

'Twenty-one years ago, Ray. For God's sake –'

'Shut up. I told you I'd get more current. You knew you were getting out September 15th. You got word to Will Kelly, one way or another, that you were going to make the move again. And you started lining people up, telling them Kelly was going to be with you. The word got to Ganolese. He had Kelly killed.'

'You're a sharp boy, Ray,' he said. 'You figured that out all by yourself.' He wasn't really worried at all yet.

'I figured more than that,' I told him. 'Those people out there at the party wouldn't buy you without Will Kelly. Without somebody reasonably young as the heir-apparent. They figured you were too old.'

'Not Eddie Kapp. I'll live to a hundred.'

'No, you won't. I'm not done yet. My sister-in-law got killed in a hit-run accident. They caught the guy.'

'Good for them,' he said.

'Up till I showed up, you thought you were through. You wrote your sister, you figured to retire. Then you saw me, and it was worth a try, see if you could get the boys to accept me rather than my father.'

'*I'm* your father, Ray.'

154

'You sired me. It isn't the same thing. You knew I wasn't interested in your empire, so you gave me that song and dance about family and symbols, to talk me into sticking with you. When I told you my sister-in-law had been killed, that gave you the idea. If she hadn't died, you wouldn't have been able to pull it.'

'I would of thought of something else.' He grinned like a banker. 'Aren't you proud of your old man, boy? I think on my feet.'

'Not for much longer. There's one more. My brother Bill. He was killed, too. He was my half-brother by blood, just as you're my father by blood. And you've always got to avenge blood.' I turned to Mouse. 'You've always got to avenge blood, Mouse? Isn't that right?'

He swallowed noisily, and bobbed his head.

'Now, Mouse, Eddie Kapp here killed my brother Bill.'

Kapp jumped up from the bed, howling, 'What the goddamn hell are you talking about? For Christ's sake, why would I do a stupid thing like that?'

'You wanted me with you, or you wouldn't be leading the revolt. You were afraid, once I found out Will Kelly wasn't my father, I'd stop, I'd lose heart and give the thing up. Same as if I found out he was still part of the mob, all this time. And then I wouldn't stick with you for a second. So you murdered Bill. I was supposed to think Ganolese did that one, too, and you could offer the partnership. "We both want the same people, only for different reasons." That's exactly what you said.'

He shook his head. 'You got it wrong, Ray. I was with you from the time Bill went upstairs to the time we found him dead.'

'No. You were gone ten minutes, to the head. And nobody else could have gotten their hands on Bill's gun. He would have put it on the dresser. Any stranger came in, the gun would have been in Bill's hand. You could go in and talk to him, tell him you want to be friends, and walk around the room until you angle over to the dresser, and there you are.'

When he moved, it was dirty. He jumped for Mouse, trying to shove him into me. I ran back and to the side, jumping up onto

155

the bed and down on the floor on the other side, turning to face the door. He had his hand on the key when I shot him. I emptied the Luger into him before he could hit the floor.

Mouse lay quivering on his stomach on the floor, arms over his head in stupid protectiveness. I wiped my prints from the Luger and dropped it on the floor and went around to poke Mouse in the side with my toe. I said, 'Get up I'm not finished talking to you.'

It took him a while to get his limbs working right. I waited till he was standing, then I said, 'You wait till I leave here. You give me a good five minutes. Then you go back to the party and tell them what happened. And tell them why it happened. You got that?'

He nodded. There was white all around the pupils of his eyes.

'This was a blood matter,' I told him, 'not a mob matter. Blood revenging blood. There's no need for them to come after me, to avenge Eddie Kapp. I'm his son, and I say there's no need for it. And I don't remember a single name or a single face that I saw here today or at Lake George two weeks ago. You got that?'

He nodded again.

'Five minutes,' I said.

I went out to the hall. The party was raging to my left, too loud for them to have heard the shots in that closed and bulkily furnished bedroom. I walked down to the right. The big man with the broken nose was sitting in a fragile chair by the door. He said, 'What they doing? Shooting guns off the terrace? They'll get cops up here if they don't look out.'

'I hope it's over pretty soon,' I said. 'I need my sleep.'

'You moving in?'

'Just going to get my luggage.'

'You won't get much sleep here.' He laughed. 'This'll go on for a couple days yet.'

I left, and took the elevator down, and went out to the street.

30

I went into the first bar I came to on Lexington Avenue, but it was lunchtime and full of bland smooth people. I stayed only long enough for one shot of bar whiskey on the rocks and one long session emptying my stomach into the toilet in the men's room. Then I headed west.

It was all bland and arid till Sixth Avenue. My stomach was empty, but from time to time I had to lean against light standards and wait through an attack of dry heaves. On Sixth Avenue I found a White Rose, where the drinks were ample and cheap.

I couldn't stay in one place. I spent about an hour in that first place, and then moved downtown, stopping for a while in each bar I came to. At four in the morning, another guy and I were thrown out of a place somewhere downtown and the other guy said he knew a great place to sleep out of the wind, behind a theatre. We went there, and someone was sleeping there, with a half-full bottle of wine. We took it away from him and found another place, and went to sleep. But before we did, I tried to tell him all my troubles. I couldn't enunciate very well, and he couldn't concentrate at all, so he never found out that I was trying to tell him that I had killed my father.

In the morning, I woke up first, freezing cold and with a bitter grinding headache. I finished the wine and felt better, somewhat warmer, and the headache fuzzier.

From there, it all blended together. I got in a couple of fights, and once I went to a place in New Jersey late at night where the bars opened at five. I threw up in the H & M tubes.

Until one morning I woke up in a great grey metal box. The sides of the box were all incredibly far away. The top of the box kept coming closer and then receding. Other human beings were in the metal box with me, making small and ghastly noises.

I don't know how long I lay on the floor before I realized I was in a room and not a box, nor how much longer before I realized I was in a jail. In the drunk tank.

First time crept, and then it leaped up and flew a while on wide black wings. I tried to count to sixty, to get in my mind how long a minute should be, but when I started to count my brain scraped against the inside of my skull and I cried out because I thought I was going to die. A lot of people grumbled and shouted at me to be quiet. I rolled over on my stomach and pressed my forehead against the cold floor and waited.

It did finally lessen, and I could sit up. And then I could stand, and take stock of myself.

My shoes were gone. So was my wallet. So were my raincoat and my suitcoat and my tie. So were my watch and belt and high school ring. So was my glass eye.

I found an empty bit of wall to sit and lean against, and dozed and wept and by the time a jailer came and opened the clanging door and called my name, the worst was over. I was empty, in every way.

I followed him to a small narrow room with a wooden table and four wooden chairs. Johnson stood up from one of the chairs, and the jailer went away.

We looked at each other. Johnson said, 'You get it all out of your system?'

'Yes.'

'I've been looking for you. I thought you might wind up here. I've had a friend of mine here keeping an eye out for you.'

'What day is it?'

'Tuesday.'

'What date?'

'The twenty-fifth. Of October.'

One day less than two weeks. 'It took me a while, didn't it?'

'I guess you had a lot to get over.'

'I guess I did.'

'You feel strong enough to go for a walk?'

'Where to?'

'My place first. Get you cleaned up.'

'They stole my eye, Johnson.'

'We'll get you another one.'

He shepherded me like a strayed child. He lived in a ratty apartment on West 46th Street, west of 9th Avenue. I told him the hotel and the name where he could find my suitcase. While he was gone, I showered and shaved. Looking at myself in the mirror, when I started to shave, I got a shock. My face was gaunt and filthy, hair and beard shaggy, the empty eye socket a grim dull red.

When Johnson came back, I was wearing his robe. He brought me an eye patch, till I could get another eye. I dressed out of the suitcase, and then he came over with a bottle of Gordon's gin, only two or three shots gone from it. 'Do you want some?'

I shook my head. 'Not now. Try me in a couple of weeks. I'll be ready for social drinking then.'

'It's all over, then.'

'Yes, it really is.'

'All right. I've got something for you.' He returned the gin bottle to his dresser drawer, under the shirts, and came back with a small envelope. 'Two hard types came to the office Friday before last. They said this was for you. If I ran across you anywhere, I should give it to you. I got the feeling I should make an effort to run across you.'

I took the envelope and ripped it open. Inside, there were five one hundred dollar bills. And a note: 'No hard feelings, L.G.'

Johnson watched my face. 'Well?'

'I don't get it.' I showed it to him.

'You don't know anybody named L.G.?'

Then I got it. Lake George. 'I know now,' I said. 'Never mind.'

'They're telling you they won't bother you, is that it?'

'Let's flush the note down the toilet or something.'

'Shall I burn it, like Secret Agent X7?'

'I think you ought to.'

He did. Watching it burn in the ashtray, he said, 'Do you remember your talk with Winkler?'

'Who?'

'Detective Winkler, of New York's finest.'

'I talked to him?'

'You wanted to confess to half the killings in the United States. A couple of racketeers named Ganolese and Kapp, and some old lawyer out on Long Island, and I don't know who all.'

'I did?'

'Winkler says it was a real wild story, except you refused to give any names except of the people you killed.'

I looked around the room. 'Then why am I here? Why didn't he lock me up?'

'Officially, Ganolese and Kapp aren't even missing. No bodies, no murder weapons, no witnesses. Officially, the lawyer died of a heart attack. It said so on the certificate. Winkler says I should tell you not to come bothering him with any more wild stories.' He grinned at me.

'They don't care.'

'Not about people like Kapp and Ganolese. Not even a little bit.'

I stood up and walked around the room and stretched. This was the other side. I came through, and this was the other side.

Johnson emptied the ashtray. 'One thing more,' he said. 'I was looking for you anyway, even before those hard types showed up. Two days after you called me the last time a guy hired me to find you. Arnold Beeworthy, his name is. You mentioned me to him. He said you were supposed to call him back about six weeks ago.'

'I forgot about him.'

'Tomorrow, why don't you take a run out there and say hello?'

'Okay.'

I slept on his sofa. In the morning, I spent two hours being fitted for a new eye. I paid for that out of the five hundred, and gave the rest to Johnson. He didn't want to take it, but I told him he was being paid by the guys who beat him up.

In the afternoon, I took the subway out to Queens. Beeworthy grabbed me the minute he saw me and stuck me in front of the tape recorder. We stopped for dinner and went back at it and didn't quit till midnight, I slept in the guest room. The next morning, he drove me into Manhattan to get my suitcase from Johnson. When we got back, Sara was listening to the tape and crying. Arnie told her to cut it out and make us some coffee.

160

KILLY

To Dave and Sandy and Nedra

1

I first met Walter Killy in Washington, D.C., on a very hot sunny day in late June. The city was as muggy as a swamp that day, as though the Potomac River and Chesapeake Bay had both evaporated off into the breezeless air, but Walter Killy's office in the AAMST Building was air-conditioned, and when the slim blonde secretary showed me in I could feel the chill of drying perspiration on the back of my neck.

Walter came bounding around the desk to greet me, his big clean hand outstretched. 'I'm Walter Killy,' he told me, 'and I wish I could tell you to call me Wally, but Wally Killy sounds like a suburb of Baltimore.' He grabbed my hand and pumped it.

He was a big man, with yellow hair cut very short in a crew-cut as stiff as a military brush. Dr Reedman, in the placement office back at school, had told me Walter was thirty-eight, but he looked no more than a boyish thirty. And though I was twenty-four, he made me feel more like seventeen.

He let go of my hand and clapped my shoulder. 'And how's the old Alma Mater, Paul? It's Paul, isn't it?'

'Oh, I'm sorry. That's right, Paul. Paul Standish.'

'Glad to know you, Paul. And how's good old Monequois U?'

'Still there,' I said. Walter had overpowered me; it was the best I could think of to say.

'That damn place will go on for ever,' he said, grinning at me. His teeth were even and white. 'Just so long as there's an alumni to gouge. Sit down, Paul, take a load off. What do you think of this *weather*, huh?'

'A little damp,' I said. There was a modernistic chair, mainly of dark blue leather but with discreet glimpses of chrome, positioned in front of the steel and formica desk. I settled into it, glad of the chance to sit down after having walked from the bus depot through the outside heat, and while Walter leaped back behind the desk I looked around at the office.

Walter Killy, in the hierarchy of the union, the American Alliance of Machinists and Skilled Trades, was actually little above junior-executive level, so his office was no more than ten feet square and boasted only the one window. But there was such a determined modernity to the room – the chair I sat in, the hard sweep of the pale blue desk, the bareness of the dull powder-blue walls, the air-conditioner hunching in the window like the control panel of a jet bomber, the colourless grey carpet, the functional frameless casement-type window, the lack of mouldings – that it all exuded a kind of opulent austerity, as though no expense had been spared in making this office look clean and simple.

The one single touch of Grand Rapids in the room was the mahogany trophy case against the right-hand wall, with the gold-plated cups and frozen figures visible behind the glass. Walter Killy, in his four years at Monequois, had been a star athlete in football and basketball and baseball and gymnastics, and the record of it all was in that trophy case. After college, he had spent three years playing professional football in the Midwest before coming to work for the Machinists, and the record of those years was in the trophy case, too.

'Well, now,' said Walter suddenly, and I realized I'd been gawping around like Cousin Elmer in Bigtown. I gave my attention back to Walter, and saw him now sitting at the desk, poised on his noiseless swivel chair, elbows on the desk and fingertips together to make a church steeple, over the top of which he studied me. Behind him, the air-conditioner hummed quietly to itself. Because the window was closed, the traffic sounds from the street were muted to near-silence, to the barest threshold of audibility.

There are many natural businessman types who can turn charm on and off at will, but Walter was the only man I've ever met or heard of who was naturally charming and could turn business-like brevity and dispassion on and off at will. I saw it happen for the first time when I looked across the desk at him, saw the

166

smiling mouth now a straight impersonal line, saw the laugh crinkles gone from around his eyes, saw the stiffness that had come into his spine and shoulders.

When he spoke, it was as though he were reading a clipped and abbreviated report. 'As you know, Paul,' he said, making my name simply another word in the sentence, 'this is the first time the Machinists has taken on a student-trainee under the Monequois system. Or any other system, for that matter.' He smiled, briefly and falsely. 'So all of this is as new to us as it is to you.'

It was fantastic to watch him. When he wore the businessman's mask, even the charm was false, the smile too mechanical and the first-name basis too obvious a stratagem. I think that's what made it possible for me to like Walter so much. The brawny crew-cut football-hero club-car ideal usually grates on me, but in Walter's case it wasn't a pose. Walter couldn't be a successful phoney, and when he tried he was irresistibly likeable simply because of his failure.

Breaking the church steeple, Walter reached out and pulled a pale manila folder toward him. 'Dr Reedman sent me your record,' he said, opening the folder, 'and it's a good one. Economics major, junior year, over-all B minus average. You worked for Hamsbro Surveys last year, didn't you?'

I nodded. 'I rang doorbells for six months. I never knew what any of the surveys were about, really, so I don't think I learned much about economics.'

'You'll learn with us,' he promised me. 'It may not be economics, but you'll learn.' He closed the folder and made the church steeple again. 'The Monequois system is a good one,' he said. 'I'm a product of it myself, you know, and I couldn't be more grateful. Six months in a class room, six months working in the field in a job connected with your major.' The false businessman's smile flickered on his face again. 'More or less connected,' he amended.

I smiled back, because it was expected.

'Your job with us,' he went on, 'will mainly be to tag along and keep me out of trouble.' The smile came and went. 'In other words, you'll be my assistant for the next six months. That being the case, it'll be easier to tell you what I do than what you'll do.'

He paused to take a pack of Newports from the handkerchief pocket of his grey suit jacket. He made a flipping motion with his wrist, and a single cigarette popped halfway out of the pack, a trick I've never been able to figure out. Extending the pack towards me, he said, 'Do you smoke, Paul?'

'Thanks,' I said, 'I'll stick to Luckies.' I got my own pack of cigarettes from my shirt pocket, and fumbled one out the old way. Then Walter was half-standing, leaning across the desk, a gas lighter hissing flame in his outstretched hand. I took the light, thanked him, and he settled back to get the cigarette started.

Once the lighter was put away, he said, 'My job here is organizer. Now, in the bad old days, a union organizer was a fellow who came into town and gave all the workers baseball bats to hit the scabs and deputies with. Happily, that isn't the way we work it any more. These days we use speeches, throwaways, parlour diplomacy with the spokesmen for management and the local working force, plant surveys, and the ultimate decision is usually made by the local workers all getting together and voting whether to stick with their company union or local independent or what-not, or come in with the national union. The organizer these days is the man in the field, the representative of the national union on the spot to answer questions and get the ball rolling.'

He paused, as though for question or comment, but I had nothing to say, so I just nodded. He took the nod to mean something or other, and went on. 'Another difference,' he said, 'is that these days we make sure we're not barging in where we're not wanted. We keep a steady flow of propaganda going through the mail to workers' groups eligible to join the national organization, but an organizer doesn't actually go into the field unless he's asked for.' The business smile flickered on his face. 'Which means,' he said, 'that we spend most of our time sitting on our duffs here in Washington, answering correspondence.' He motioned the cigarette at his full in-basket. The out-basket beneath it was about half as full.

'Is that what my job's going to be?' I asked him. 'Answering correspondence?'

'Not yet. To tell you the truth, I had a sort of training campaign more or less mapped out in my mind, what you'd be doing
the first few weeks here.' He tapped a small bundle of printed
matter on the corner of his desk. 'I was going to have you read
all this stuff first,' he said. 'Every blessed pamphlet and brochure
and throwaway we throw away. I wanted you to know the union,
where and how and why it started, and what it's done since, and
what it's doing now, and what it plans to do in the future, as told
by its own advertising.'

'That ought to be interesting,' I said politely.

He grinned again, more naturally this time. The businessman
was gradually fading away, and Walter's own personality was
coming to the surface again. He could never keep the façade up
for very long. 'A lot more interesting than you'd think,' he said.
'The history of this union makes pretty exciting reading sometimes. Anyway, after that I was going to give you a selected tour
of the files, correspondence that's come in in the past and what
we did with it and what happened next, and so on.' He leaned
back in the swivel chair, smiling. 'I had it all worked out,' he said.
'Within a month, you'd have taken over my job completely, and
I could spend my days loafing at the beach.'

I returned his smile, wondering what had made this plan of his
conditional. He answered the question without my asking it, by
picking up another manila folder and holding it out to me across
the desk. 'I got this deal tossed in my lap yesterday,' he said.

I took the folder and opened it. Inside, stapled together at the
upper left-hand corner, were three sheets of paper. The first and
third were cheap white stationery, medium-size, written on both
sides in ink in a sprawling hand that made huge loops in the l's
and d's and b's. The second was business-letter-size, flimsy white
onion skin, with the carbon of a typed letter on it. I read the three
sheets in order:

25th May

Dear Sirs,

I am writing to you in reference to a little booklet of yours which
I saw from a friend of mine. This was a booklet about joining the

169

American Alliance of Machinists and Skilled Trades, and how dissatisfied workers which are saddled with company unions or such could write to you a letter and you would send a representative to help the workers form a Local of your union.

Well, I want to tell you that this is exactly the sort of situation there is here in Wittburg. There is a growing number of us workers at the McIntyre Shoe Co. plant which are dissatisfied with conditions here and know we are not going to have anything better unless we become a Local of a national union such as yours. If you keep a record of things like that, you will see that nine years ago there was an attempt made to organize this plant in favour of your union and that it failed when the workers at the election decided to stick with the company union. I was working at the Co. at that time, having been an employee here for the last fourteen years, and I voted against joining the national union then just like anybody else, but times have changed a lot around here since that time. In the first place, old William 'Bill' McIntyre is dead now, and a lot of nephews and nieces own the Co. and are leaving it in the hands of managers that don't care about the workers. In Bill McIntyre's time, any worker with a grievance could go up to his office on Friday afternoon any Friday, because that was the day his door was always open, and you wouldn't get fired, you'd get listened to. And he was the one built the hospital, and the stadium, and the low-in-cost houses for the workers such as the one I bought and financed through the Co. and am living in right now.

But ever since the old man died four years ago things have been going to Hell around here, with managers that don't care anything about the workers, and the Co. owned by nephews and nieces that aren't even living in this town but are off somewhere living off the sweat of our brows. You don't catch any office door open on Friday afternoon, and the Co. union is now in the pocket of the manager, whose name is Fleisch. If you were going to send a representative up here today to make another try at getting started with that Local, you'd find it was a different story. I would vote all in favour of it now, and just about everybody I know says the same thing. So that's why I'm writing to you, such as you suggested in that booklet which I mentioned, which was called, *Why A National Union?*

> Very sincerely yours,
> Charles R. Hamilton
> 426 4th Street
> Wittburg, N.Y.

Charles R. Hamilton   June 4, 1962
426 4th Street
Wittburg, N.Y.

Dear Mr Hamilton:

Your letter of May 25th has been received, and we thank you for your interest in AAMST. I've looked it up in our records, and I see that we did attempt to organize a local in the McIntyre Shoe Company nine years ago, and that we wound up with seventeen per cent of the vote, while eighty-three per cent of the workers voted to stay with the company union. To be perfectly frank, Mr Hamilton, I hadn't known we'd *ever* lost an election by that wide a margin. 'Bill' McIntyre must have been quite a man, to get that much loyalty from his workers.

If it hadn't been for that previous unsuccessful attempt, there would be no question of our sending a representative to Wittburg in response to your letter, Mr Hamilton. But you'll have to admit that our showing was just a bit disheartening that first time out. Therefore, I'd appreciate it if you could give me some sort of concrete suggestion as to the strength of the desire for a national union among your fellow workers at the present time. A letter signed by a group of your co-workers, for instance, or local newspaper clippings of recent labour disturbances in the shoe company plant, would help to give us more solid footing for constructive planning.

Hoping to hear from you soon again, and thanking you once again for your interest, I remain

                              Sincerely,
                              Everett Freeman
                              Executive Assistant

EF:jl
Enc.

                                                               June 12th
Dear Mr Freeman,

I guess I can understand why you people don't want to come running in where you got your nose broken for you once before, and I appreciate your answering my letter as quick and pleasant as you did, and sending along that other literature about your union. I showed your letter and the literature around to friends of mine and people I know at the Co., and a bunch of them agreed to sign a letter to you, as there hasn't been any kind of labour disturbance here of the kind that would get into the

171

newspapers. They are all going to sign on the back of this letter, and if there is anything else you want me to do I'll do it.

Thank you very much for your interest in our problems here.

Very sincerely yours,
Charles R. Hamilton

After I finished reading the third letter, I turned it over and looked on the back at the signatures. Most of them were in pen, but a few were in pencil. I counted them, and there were twenty-five.

'Doesn't seem like many, does it?' Walter asked me. 'Twenty-five signatures, and that plant employs thirty-five hundred people.' He was leaning back in the chair, one hand resting casually palm-down on the desk. 'They used to have a rule of thumb round here,' he said. 'Before my time, before the war. For every man who says he's with you and is willing to sign his name on the dotted line, there are five more that are with you but afraid to sign their name to anything. What with one thing and another, that ratio's gone up since the war. Today it's closer to fifteen-to-one.' He pointed to the folder in my hand. 'Those twenty-five signatures stand for closer to four hundred workers who are with us, ready and willing, if the statistics are right. Which would give us a percentage even lower than the seventeen per cent we had nine years ago.'

He leaned forward over the desk suddenly, and said, 'But this is one of the times when the statistics are wrong. Did this fellow Hamilton talk to everybody in the plant? No. He talked to a bunch of his friends and co-workers. If you follow the statistics, he had to talk to three hundred and seventy-five people who were on our side before he could find twenty-five willing to sign. But he didn't talk to any three hundred and seventy-five people. He more likely talked to fifty, and even that's probably too big a number. But if he talked to as many as fifty people, and half of them felt so strongly that they were willing to sign that letter, we've got a situation to drive the statistics crazy. We'll walk into that town and the workers will strew roses at our feet.'

'We're going there? What about this Mr Freeman?'

172

'He started his vacation last week. Ordinarily, the job would have waited for him, but I knew about it and asked for it. Because of you, Paul. You've got a golden opportunity here to see union organizing at its best and sweetest, and it'll be your very first job with us. I told the boss I wanted this one, to take you along and show you the ropes in an ideal situation, and he said fine.'

'So do I.' I smiled, feeling an excitement for this job totally unlike anything I'd felt for my other in-the-field semesters. 'When do we start?'

'Tomorrow. You haven't got yourself a place yet, have you?'

'No, I just came in on the bus, I left my stuff in a locker. I figured I'd come here first, and then, you know, look around after that.'

'Good. There's no sense looking for an apartment yet, we might be up in this town a month or more. I'd be glad to have you stay over with us, but it's just my wife and I, we've got one of these efficiency apartments, and there really isn't any room.' He chuckled in embarrassment. 'There's isn't even enough room for us,' he said.

'Oh, that's all right. Really. I'll get a hotel room tonight.'

'Let me call for you,' he said, reaching for the phone. 'Get you a couple dollars off. There's a hotel we book our visiting firemen into, won't take a minute.' He was honestly embarrassed at his inability to offer me shelter for the night, and felt he had to do something to make up for it.

He made the call, and gave me the address of the hotel. Then he gave me the pile of pamphlets he had on his desk, and told me to read them over and we could talk about them tomorrow. 'I'll pick you up around ten,' he said. 'We'll be driving up.'

'All right. Fine.'

He jumped up and came around the desk again, and I switched the pamphlets to my left hand to accept his handshake. 'I think you'll enjoy the job, Paul,' he said.

'I think I will, too.'

Outside, in the small tan reception room, I had to ask the blonde secretary which way I should go to find the elevators. She

173

told me, with a smile, and I left. I thought briefly of asking her for a date – she was a good-looking girl, Washington-thin, and probably no more than twenty-two – but then I reminded myself I had all those pamphlets to read tonight, and the bus trip in had worn me out more than a little, anyway. But going down in the elevator I had to admit to myself that I'd simply been bashful, that I'd been feeling as though somehow she was too old for me. Walter was partly to blame for that, making me feel so young and awkward, but he had simply intensified an attitude that had already been there before I'd met him. When you go to college too late – drift around for a year after high school and then go into the Army for three years, so you start college as a twenty-one-year-old freshman – a kind of regression takes place. You're in an environment constructed for people in their late teens, you're surrounded by people in their late teens, and gradually you begin to adapt yourself, until you've lost two or three years from your maturity. I remember in the Army, in basic training, there was a man I met, twenty-five years old. He'd managed to avoid the draft long enough to get a master's degree in American history. He told me one time that Army basic training was engineered for a seventeen-year-old boy with two years of high school, and that the training programme was far less flexible than the human mind. 'Every day in every way,' he told me, 'I'm getting younger and younger.' I'd been too close to the norm myself then really to understand him, though I did recognize the fact that he acted an awful lot like a kid, and not like a man in his mid-twenties with a master's degree. Once I got to college, I could finally understand what he was talking about, and I sometimes wonder if you can ever get back those two or three years that are wiped away.

At any rate, I left the AAMST Building and walked back toward the bus depot. After the air-conditioning in Walter's office, the heavy mugginess of the air amid the white marble buildings was even stronger and more unreal. As I walked along, moving slowly because of the heat, I suddenly realized another result of my childishness. I hadn't talked to Walter about salary. I knew that I was to get fifty-three dollars and sixty-seven cents a week,

174

but I had no idea when the first payment was due, and I only had thirty-four dollars to my name. I would have to ask about money the first thing tomorrow morning.

If worst came to worst, though, I knew I'd be able to borrow some money from Walter. He was that kind of man.

2

We travelled northwards at a steady sixty-five miles an hour on Route 111. Walter drove the company car – a pale grey Ford with less than six thousand miles on it – with practised ease and nonchalance. Sitting behind the wheel, his bristled yellow hair bright in the sun, he looked big and competent and sure of himself. He held the steering wheel high in his right hand, his left elbow out the window, and watched the hard stripe of road unreel before us. On the back seat were his tan leather briefcase and the cartons full of pamphlets and posters and throwaways. In the trunk were our suitcases, his matched set and my lonely orphan.

As we drove, we talked about what I'd read the night before. The literature had been of two types, one aimed at convincing independent workers it was to their advantage to join the union, and the other at explaining to interested union members the history and objectives of the organization. The latter type had been more informative to me, though the former – because of the Gung Ho style of the writing – had been more interesting.

The AAMST was rather large, as unions go, boasting nearly two hundred thousand dues-paying members in thirty-seven states. Its objectives, to oversimplify slightly, were to gain for its workers increasingly shorter hours of labour for increasingly higher rates of pay. This policy was kept from reaching its illogical conclusion – no work at all and a millionaire's income – by a combination of government control, managerial stubbornness at the bargaining table, and a number of realists among the union executives. The history of the union since 1940 was relatively free of strikes, and totally free of such long bitter strikes as the one at the Moehler furniture plant.

Since all of the large unions overlap into each other's territory tremendously, there wasn't a single member of the Machinists who wouldn't have been eligible to join one or more of the other national unions instead. And as with so many of those others, the Machinists was an amalgamation of a number of earlier unions, two or three of them having vague connections with the Wobblies of the twenties. Whatever the philosophical or theoretical antecedents might have been, however, the Machinists was today strongly in favour of capitalism, stating unequivocally in its literature that industry belonged in the hands of private enterprise rather than with government, possibly because a plant owner, no matter how rich or influential, was still less awesome an opponent across a bargaining table than the United States government would be.

The union did practise socialism – having its own welfare fund and retirement fund, and being in favour of Social Security and Workmen's Compensation – but it was no more socialistic than the rest of the national economy. As for Communism, the last Red in this part of the labour movement had been demobbed a generation ago. 'One of the strongest weapons against Communism in all the arsenal of liberty,' one of the pamphlets had said, 'is a strong patriotic *pro-American* labour movement.'

On other fronts, the union favoured high tariffs and low immigration quotas, tax relief for the small wage earner, an end to government restrictions in labour disputes, industry-wide adoption of the guaranteed annual wage and the totally closed shop, and state bonuses for Korean War veterans. In political campaigns, support was usually but not always thrown to the Democratic candidate.

For the last three years, I had been a college student, majoring in economics. This meant, of course, that I'd taken a lot of courses in English, maths, history, the natural sciences, a foreign language (French), and other social sciences, in order to fulfil the requirements for a degree, but it also meant that every once in a while I'd been able to squeeze in a course in economics. Now, full of what the books had told me, I studied this union's pronouncements about itself, and gradually a number of facts and theories and ideas I'd memorized in class began all at once to make sense to me. This union – any large national union – was a potent economic force. Its major arena was the economy itself,

177

but since our society is so infinitely interconnective, the influence and interest of the Machinists spread wide into other areas, into federal and state and municipal politics, into governmental theory, into international relations. And the attitudes and beliefs of the union, in every case, were based solely on what has been called enlightened self-interest. High tariffs, for instance. Whether high tariffs were good or bad for the nation – or for the entire world – was not the union's concern; high tariffs were good for the members of the union, since they cut foreign industrial competition and therefore made more jobs available in American industry. A department-store chain, on the other hand, might favour low tariffs because they allowed the department store to buy comparable goods cheaper, sell them cheaper, and therefore sell more of them, therefore keeping more money active in the economy. In an ideal world, all the human beings would get together and decide what was best for all of them, but in the practical world *groups* of human beings get together and squabble to get as much as possible of what is best for each of them. With so many groups, fired by so much conflicting self-interest, push- ing and pulling in so many directions at once, a kind of shaky balance is usually maintained.

All of this I had heard about, often and in different ways, in the classroom, but none of it had ever truly been real for me. Now I was inside one of the pushing groups, seeing the relation- ships and the effects from the angle of its point of view, and all at once the dogma and dictum of the textbooks began to take on flesh and blood. It was all true, I realized, it was just exactly the way the books said, and I began to pity the poor maths major, who could never see the laws of his persuasion acted out upon the stage of life.

Riding northward, Walter and I discussed what the pamphlets had said, and I found that he was passionately interested in his job and in the entire field, that if the term vocation can be used in reference to a profane occupation, then Walter had a vocation. I asked him questions, not because I couldn't figure out the answers for myself but because I wanted him to believe that I was interest- ed, too, and he answered them with pleasure, and in great detail.

We stopped in Harrisburg for hamburgers and coffee, and to stretch our legs. Walter flirted with the waitress, a leggy redhead with green make-up on her eyelids, and I was annoyed to find that now I felt about twelve years old, that it was a surprise my feet reached the floor under the table. After Harrisburg, we took Route 22 to Allentown and picked up the Turnpike Extension, northbound. Route 11 took us across the line into New York State, at Binghamton, and that's where we stopped for dinner.

It was dark when we left the restaurant and went back to the car, but Walter said, 'I think we can make it tonight. Only about a hundred and fifty miles to go.' We'd travelled nearly three hundred and fifty already.

The last stretch, up through Syracuse, I dozed off. Eight hours sitting in the car, talking for long times and then being silent and watching the green-black countryside go by for long times, had drugged me. I felt thick and muggy, like Washington, but without the white marble, and just above Binghamton I fell asleep.

When Walter woke me up, I had no idea who he was or where I'd come to. Through the windshield I looked at a flat blue wall with a pink door in it and a casement window backed by a yellow shade, the whole lit by a spotlight shining full on it from somewhere behind me. And a large grinning man was shaking my shoulder and saying, 'Here we are, this is our unit.'

I was out of phase for only a few seconds, and then it was the dashboard of the Ford I recognized first. That led to the recognition of Walter, and the further recognition of the fact that the structure in front of me must be a motel. 'Dozed off,' I said, my mouth dry and thick-tongued, and sat up. My back and shoulders ached, and I crawled out of the Ford like a cripple. I stood there blinking in the light – the spotlight was at the base of the roadside sign, and shone directly at the motel – while Walter unlocked the trunk. He had to call me to come get my bag.

We had a double unit, which meant twin beds in a single room, separated by a bowlegged night table with chipped mahogany finish and bearing a lamp with a pleated shade. Walter shucked out of his clothes and went away to take a shower, but I felt so beaten down all I wanted to do was go back to sleep so

179

I wouldn't know what condition I was in. I crawled into the nearest bed, and fell asleep with the sound of rushing water in my ears.

3

I got my first real look at Wittburg the next morning, when we went out for breakfast. Walter had given me the vital statistics, that the town had a population of not quite nine thousand, thirty-five hundred of whom worked in the McIntyre Shoe Company plant. The other fifty-five hundred served as the plumbers, doctors, carpenters, grocers, wives, teachers, and delivery boys for the first thirty-five hundred. The shoe factory, therefore, was the only possible reason for the town's existence.

It was situated about ten or twelve miles from Watertown, along the Black River. The river, which actually was black, split the town in two, and at one point – being more a creek than a river – was straddled by one of the shoe company buildings. But though the river formed a natural division of the town, it was not along this boundary that the social tracks were laid. The river ran east and west, and midway through town was crossed by Harpur Boulevard, running north and south. The factory buildings and the lower-class homes were to the west of Harpur Boulevard, and the more expensive part of town was to the east. Harpur Boulevard itself – which was actually a part of the unnumbered spur road leading into the town from Route 3 – was the entire downtown section, and boasted two movie houses and a Woolworth, but no Kresge.

The Wittburg Motel was just south of town, on the road that became Harpur Boulevard an eighth of a mile farther north. After my shower in the morning, Walter and I got into the Ford and drove that eighth of a mile and stopped for breakfast at the City Line Diner. The Ford had no union markings on it, so no one paid more than casual attention to us. The people I saw on the street and in the green upholstered diner looked grimy and hard-working, wearing clothing of dull colours. It was a hot day, but far less humid than Washington had been, and ten hours' sleep had left me feeling chipper and my rightful age. Sitting at the booth in the diner, I looked out the window and saw an elderly man go by, mopping the back of his neck with a red handkerchief. Finishing my eggs and sausage, I tried to remember when I had last seen a red handkerchief.

While on the road, Walter and I were on an expense account, the details of which Walter was handling, so he paid the check for both of us and left the tip. We went outside to the morning sunlight again, and stood on the sidewalk, squinting in the light and looking up and down the street. It was nine-thirty in the morning, very bright, with a kind of silent buzz in the air. A few women pushed children in strollers, and some Chevvys and Plymouths were angle-parked on both sides of the street. The stores mostly had their awnings down, and as I watched I saw a short man in rolled-up shirt sleeves come out of a shoe store with a metal rod and crank the awning down there.

I lit a cigarette, pleased to be alive, and turned to Walter. 'What do we do now?'

'Take our time,' he said. 'I want to talk to this fellow Hamilton, but first let's just look the place over a little. Get the feel of it.'

I grinned, saying, 'I feel like the advance scout of an invading army.'

'You are,' Walter told me. He punched my arm, grinning, and we went over to the Ford.

We drove here and there for a while, back and forth, every once in a while crossing Harpur Boulevard again. To the east, we found one block of rolling tended lawn and well-separated brick homes, half of which showed doctors' shingles. Other blocks on that side of town were middle-class clapboard, two storeys high, less separation between houses, with lengths of hose curled on the grass at the side of the house and with a porch containing a tricycle or a glider or both. Trees lined most of these streets, and along some blocks the trees were so old and huge they roofed the street in greenery, making a cool shadowed waterless grotto of an entire block. Through screen doors came television laughter, and here and there I caught a glimpse of an infant in a playpen in a back yard.

To the west was a different town, dominated by the ancient brick piles of the factory buildings. There were six or seven of these buildings, all close to the river on one side or the other – the town had ten bridges, all of them short and most of them white-washed concrete – and all the factory buildings were Midlands grim in style. Four or five storeys high, squared off and topped by black metal bulks, the old brick grimed by smoke and grease and time, rows of dusty unshaded windows, and small green doors at the corners. This was not a plant; a *plant* is one of those modern one-storey prefab shells that look like one of those modern one-storey prefab grammar schools. This was, without question, a *factory*.

In among the buildings of the factory was the slum. If a town has three buildings, one of them will immediately decay so the town can have a slum. It seems to be a rule. Outside staircases with rotted risers, broken windows patched with cardboard, frayed and faded cotton curtains flapping from open windows where mattresses were humped to air, lumpy lots with their quotas of old tyres and rusted cans, board fences unpainted and crumbling, three junkyards, a bar in a sleazy tilting corner building and calling itself the Crystal Palace. The residents over here seemed to be about half and half white and black, and a few that seemed to be truly half and half.

'All these towns look alike,' said Walter at one point. 'In fourteen years, I've seen a lot of them. And they all look pretty much like this. Except the cement towns, the towns where the cement factories are. There, everything looks dusty white all the time, like the towns in northern Italy.' He glanced at me. 'You ever been to Italy?'

I shook my head. 'I never got out of the States. The Army had me in Montana for a while, and then Texas, and then St Louis.'

'I played football in Italy one time,' he said. 'Believe it or not.' Then he went on to explain, the professional team he was with went to Italy, and it had something to do with the State Department.

That somehow led to my telling him a story about a girl I met at the USO in St Louis, one of the few cities in the world that still has a USO and then he told me about a girl who got into the locker room when his team was playing at Detroit one time, and I told a story about somebody else in Mexico, which I heard from a friend of mine and which was probably false, but which made a good story. And as we told our half-truths to one another, we drove back and forth across the town, looking at it and getting used to its existence.

After a while, we found 1st Street. Hamilton lived on 4th Street, so Walker decided to go looking for him.

This, we discovered, was still another section of town. 1st Street ran east and west, about ten blocks north of the river, and the numbered streets marched away northward beyond that, and beyond what should have been the city line but wasn't any more. This was the low-in-cost housing 'Bill' McIntyre had built for his loyal subjects, little square boxes with peaked roofs and brick doorsteps and storm fencing around the tiny yards. At 1st Street, Harpur Boulevard started to climb, and the slope rapidly became very steep as the street surfacing switched from concrete to blacktop. The blocks here were square, absolutely square, forming a grid on the steep slope, the numbered streets going across the slope up to the number twelve, and the slope-climbing streets designated by first names. There was Sarah Street, and William Street, and Frederick Street, and Marilyn Street, and it didn't take much imagination to guess that they were the first names of members of the McIntyre family.

By 4th Street, the incline was so steep that the people living on the uphill side could look out their living-room windows across the tops of the houses on the downhill side and have a panoramic view of the city. The people on the downhill side could have their panoramic view from their kitchen windows.

An aluminium-awning salesman had visited the four-hundred block of 4th Street, between George and Catherine Streets, and the awnings he'd sold had mostly been pink. 426 sported the complete set of two, one over the door and one over the living-room window. Being on the downhill side, I guessed a third awning shaded their kitchen-window view of town.

Walter parked in front of the house, and we went down the six

184

concrete steps from the sidewalk to the level of the front door. Between the storm fencing and the front of the house, the lawn slanted steeply downward, and either Hamilton or his wife had carefully constructed a rock garden of it. A slate walk led around to the side of the house. Like all the rest of the houses up here, there was neither a garage nor room for one to be added.

Walter had brought along his briefcase, and as he rang the doorbell I suddenly felt like a travelling salesman. A real one, not the one in the jokes. I noted the fact that most of the front doors up in this section were closed, as this one was, whereas most of them had been open in the middle-class section of town.

After a minute, the door opened and released the thunder of airplane motors onto the air. A short, tired woman in a flower-print dress and a mismatched flower-print apron stood peering mistrustfully at us through the screen door. There was a metal H in the middle of the screen. She said, 'What is it?'

'Good morning, Mrs Hamilton,' said Walter. 'Is your husband home?' His business face was up, and I was suddenly embarrassed at the obvious phoniness of it.

'He's at work,' she said. She glanced down at Walter's briefcase, and said, 'What do you want with him?'

'We're from the Machinists, Mrs Hamilton. Your husband sent us a letter some –'

'Come in!' A startled look on her face – almost a terrified look – she peered past us upward at the empty sidewalk, and pushed open the screen door. 'Come in! Come in! Hurry!'

Walter stepped across the threshold, his business smile looking puzzled, and I followed him. Inside, a carpet-covered staircase pushed down into a narrow crowded hallway. The hallway was dark, with dark wallpaper and a dark rug and a dark-framed mirror on one wall. Down at the farther end was a glimpse of sunlight from the kitchen. At the head of the stairs was a landing, and beyond that a wall with cream-coloured paper on it and a closed pale-varnished door.

The woman led us to the right, through a draperied archway, as a sudden burst of machine-gun fire lanced across the continuing roar of the fighter planes. We entered the living room, which

185

was small and square and full of dark bulky furniture. There was an old small-screen television set in one corner, with a rose in a glass bowl atop it. From the television set came the roaring and the shooting, as some unidentifiable picture flicked upward in an unending series across the screen. On the wall above the sofa was a painting in sepia: *The Return from Calvary*.

The woman crossed the room and switched off the television set, and the silence seemed to bulge toward me. She turned around, more in control of herself now than when she'd told us to come in, and said, 'I want you to leave my husband alone.' Anger and alarm were mixed in her voice, and in her expression. She looked at Walter when she spoke, correctly picking him as the leader, me the follower.

I don't think Walter expected a reaction like this; I know I didn't. I looked at him to see how he'd handle it.

Like a businessman. 'Mrs Hamilton, your husband did write to us, asking –'

'He shouldn't have, I told him not to.'

'But he did, that's the point.' Walter shrugged, and smiled politely. 'And we really should talk to him, rather than you.'

'I'm telling you to leave him alone! He doesn't know what he's –' She stared helplessly around the room, as though wanting to explain something to us and not knowing how. 'Chuck is forty-three years old,' she said. 'He lost the little finger from his left hand in the war. No, that isn't it.' She ran a hand through her hair, distraught. 'He's a bitter man, Mr –'

'Killy.'

'Chuck thinks the world was unfair with him. Nothing he has is as good as he planned. The finger, his job, this house. Me. Not that I blame –' She turned away in distraction, looking helplessly around the room. 'Here,' she said, 'I want to show you –' She went over to the small drum table to the right of the lumpy sofa. A table lamp, a white porcelain rabbit with a green plant growing out of its back, a white ragged doily, and a framed photograph, all were crowded together on its top. She picked up the photograph – a glossy black-and-white eight-by-ten behind glass – and handed it to Walter. 'Do you see him? Can you see what he's like?'

I looked over Walter's shoulder. In the foreground was a man in Army uniform, standing on greensward, and in the background was a castle. His mouth was fixed in a tight confident grin. His hands were in his pockets, and his feet were slightly spread, and the Army hat was canted jauntily atop his head. A youngish man, happy and self-confident. From what I could see of his face, it was handsome, with a kind of rough strong charm.

'That was taken in England,' Mrs Hamilton said. 'More than twenty years ago. Before he lost his finger, before he knew that all his plans – before it all went sour for him. Wait, I want to show you – wait, please.' She started to the doorway, then paused, not quite stopping, to say, 'I want to make you understand.'

She left the room, and I looked at Walker. He shook his head and shrugged, and put the framed photograph back on the drum table. As he straightened, Mrs Hamilton came in again, this time carrying a small snapshot. 'He doesn't know I have this,' she said. 'He doesn't like pictures of himself now. Only that one there.' She handed the small snapshot to Walter and said, 'This is Chuck now. My brother took that picture last year.'

Once again I looked over Walter's shoulder. This time, I saw Charles Hamilton's profile. The scene was an outing of some sort, people sitting at picnic tables in the background, against a deeper stand of trees. In the foreground, Charles Hamilton sat at one of the picnic tables, a soiled paper plate in front of him. His elbow was on the table, his other arm around a giggling girl with large breasts and a young empty face. Hamilton wore a short-sleeved polo shirt, and was leaning forward slightly, smiling at something to the left of the photo, partially blocking the girl. His bare arms were thin and wiry, as though he would be strong, and there was some sort of tattoo on the upper arm, impossible to make out. A cigarette dangled from the corner of his mouth, and the one eye visible in this picture was squinted against the rising smoke.

It was the same man, now forty-three instead of twenty-three. The self-confidence was still there, in the position of the head and shoulders, in the same tight hard grin, but there was no denying it had soured with the years. I looked at his face and knew he had never given up the dreams and self-image that had shone in the earlier photograph, that he was still a *young* man and always would be.

'Can you see?' Mrs Hamilton asked us. 'Can you see what he's like?'

'I'd have to talk to any man to know him,' said Walter. He handed back the snapshot.

Mrs Hamilton took it. 'He's still very handsome,' she said. 'And he's very strong. But nothing's gone right for him.' She lowered the hand holding the snapshot, and said, 'We own a De Soto. He hates it, he says, "They don't even make the damn things any more." And before that we had a Hudson. Never new, always third- or fourth-hand, and he has to park it out by the kerb, he – It isn't the *union*, don't you understand? It's everything in his life. Don't take advantage of him, Mr Killy, please.'

She'd come as close as she could to telling us her husband was unfaithful to her, showing us the snapshot, and telling us Hamilton was dissatisfied with *all* of his life, but still she pleaded with us and wanted to help him. Or at least thought she was helping him.

I said, 'Why did he write to us, Mrs Hamilton?' The man she had been describing, I thought, wouldn't be the one to write that letter.

'McIntyre,' she said, 'the old man, he made promises to Chuck. They got along together, I think he liked Chuck more than almost anyone else he knew. But he made promises, or at least Chuck thought he heard promises, and then he died. And this new man, this Mr Fleisch, he doesn't even know Chuck's alive. Chuck would go up on Fridays, and I think he saw himself getting a job in the office some day. But now there isn't any chance of that any more.'

Walter said, 'Mrs Hamilton, I don't think you understand what Paul and I –'

'You don't think I understand? He's a bitter man, Mr Killy, a bitter angry man, and he doesn't care how much he risks because he doesn't have anything he values at all. Can't you have the decency not to – to – *use* him?'

188

'Twenty-five people signed the letter,' Walter said gently. 'It wouldn't be fair to them –'

'It wouldn't be fair to Chuck! Do you think – don't you realize –?' She stopped, gasping for breath, fighting to control herself. 'Do you think you can win? Do you think you can take anything away from the people who run these things? All you're going to do is make trouble, for Chuck and all the others, and especially for Chuck. I've told him and I've told him, I begged him not to send you that first letter, and then when he got the answer, it was worse. But it won't do any *good*, don't you know that?'

'I'm sorry,' said Walter. But the words sounded faint; I knew he was thinking about something else. This was supposed to be the ideal situation here, where the workers would strew roses in our path. That's why I'd been brought along. But Mrs Hamilton didn't belong within the framework we'd been expecting.

Walter hefted his briefcase, and said, 'I'm sorry, but I don't have any choice. I'm an employee too, Mrs Hamilton. I have to at least talk to your husband, and to some of the other men who signed the letter. If it looks as though this area isn't ready for a national union yet, we'll go back to Washington and say so. Is that fair?'

'If they see you talking with him –'

'Who, Mrs Hamilton? If who see us talking with him?'

Her brow furrowed, and she glanced at the curtained window. 'I don't know. Anybody. Anybody at all.'

Walter sighed. He himself made sure that he was always in the best possible shape, physically and mentally and emotionally. People who were run-down and flabby in any of those ways sooner or later got on his nerves, making him impatient and bored, and Mrs Hamilton, with her photographs and her vague fears, was run-down emotionally, her feelings loose and undefined. Walter said to her, his voice sterner than before, 'What time does he come home?'

She held the snapshot so hard it creased. 'Then you won't leave us alone?'

'We can't.' Walter sighed and shook his head. 'I've already

explained why. What time does your husband come home, Mrs Hamilton?'

'What if I don't tell you?'

'Then we'll wait outside, in the car.'

'No! Please!'

Embarrassment forced me to speak up again: 'What if he came to us instead? Then your neighbours wouldn't know.' Anything to end this uncomfortable and useless interview.

Walter glanced over at me, smiling, and nodded. 'That's an idea,' he said. To Mrs Hamilton he said, 'We're in the Wittburg Motel, on Harpur Boulevard. Until seven. We'll talk to your husband there if you want.'

'But I don't want you to talk to him at all.'

'We have to.' Walter half-turned to the archway, then paused to say, 'If he isn't there by seven, we'll come back and talk to him here.' He glanced at me. 'Come on, Paul.'

She was stony-faced. Her head lowered, and she watched her fingers try to smooth out the crease she'd made in the snapshot. I hesitated, and mumbled, 'Nice to meet you.' And then, hearing the inanity of it, I hurried out after Walter.

We got into the car, and Walter drove back down into town. He was silent, and he gazed bleakly out through the windshield at the street. After a block or so, I said, 'What do you think, Walter?'

He shook his head. 'I don't know. I hope she's just a nagging wife, one of these women who sees disaster every time her husband takes a deep breath, but I don't know.'

'She seemed almost terrified, you know it?'

'I know.' A traffic light stopped us at the base of the slope, and he looked over at me and grinned. 'If this really is one of the sewed-up towns, we'll be back in Washington before you can say Taft-Hartley. We're not up here to be heroes, Paul, or martyrs either.'

'Do you think that's what this is? A sewed-up town?'

'I don't know. That's the way she talked, but it doesn't figure. I've seen towns like that. The factory keeps the town alive, the way it does here, the way it does in half the towns in the country.

190

But you get a real son of a bitch running the factory, and he decides to run the town, too. He owns the newspaper and the radio station, the police chief and the most prominent minister, the bank and the supermarket and the hospital and most of the private homes. When you run into a town like that, you just turn around and go home again, and give the name and forget it.'

'Give the name?'

'Oh. I forgot to tell you about that.' The light turned green, and Walter accelerated across the intersection. 'We have an office,' he said, 'keeps an eye on really tight plants. Subscribes to the local papers, and stuff like that. You see, a sewed-up town is a powder keg, and sooner or later it blows up. All of a sudden the workers have had enough. Until that happens, there's nothing we can do, but the minute it does happen we send a flying squad in armed to the teeth with leaflets, and before that town knows it, it's organized.' He grinned at me, and winked. 'You ought to see a job like that sometime,' he said.

'Maybe I will, right here.'

'Not on your life. I don't think this is a bad town, that was just a bad wife. But if it is, we clear out. For now, let's go back to the motel and wait for Hamilton.'

4

At quarter after six, a knock sounded at the door. Walter was sitting in the room's one armchair, reading a paperback book, while I was sprawled on my bed and reading a pamphlet entitled 'What is an AMERICAN Union?' We both looked up at the sound of the knock, and I bounced from the bed, wanting to be useful, saying, 'I'll get it.'

'Right,' said Walter. He tucked the paperback away in the drawer of the night table, and I went over and opened the door.

Two men with drawn guns bundled into the room, shoving me backward, and one of them shouted at Walter, over by the night table, 'Hold it right there! Just stop right where you are!'

No one had ever pointed a gun at me before. I stared at it, the one in the hand of the man nearest me, and my stomach seemed to shrink in on itself, as though trying to make a smaller target, while a trembling started in the back of my legs. My mouth was suddenly dry, and cold dampness lined my forehead.

I saw Walter, his face expressionless, slowly raise his hands over his head, and I did the same. My forearms were trembling, and I wasn't sure I was going to be able to keep standing. I made no guesses in my mind as to who these men might be or what they might want; I didn't think at all, but simply stood and hoped I could keep on standing.

A third man came into the room. He was fiftyish, very tall and still muscular. His head was square, with a seamed tough-skinned face, and he wore a hat pushed back to show a high widow's peak of grey hair. Like the other two men, who were younger and slightly smaller versions of himself, he wore a wrinkled suit and a white shirt and a dark plain tie. He came into the room, looked at me and then at Walter, and reached into his hip-pocket. He pulled out a cracked alligator-skin wallet and flipped it open with a gesture that somehow reminded me of

Walter's trick of popping just one cigarette halfway out of the pack. A badge was pinned to the inside of the wallet, and behind a square of clear plastic there was some sort of an identification card with a photo on it. He showed us this for just a second, then flipped the wallet shut again and put it back in his pocket, saying, 'Police. Frisk them, Jerry.'

One of the other two men put his gun away, in a small black holster up under his coat tail, and came over to me. 'Spread your legs,' he said.

I stood spraddle-legged. Jerry went around behind me and patted my chest, my sides, my back, my belly, my hips, and my legs. Then he went over and did the same with Walter, while his partner still held the gun on us, and the older man shut the unit door and stood leaning against it, arms folded, watching us.

The man named Jerry came back into my line of vision, saying to the older man, 'They're clean.'

'All right.' The older man looked around the room. Aside from what had been already in it when we'd arrived, there were now the three suitcases along the back wall, a blue laundry bag next to the bathroom door, Walter's portable Smith-Corona type-writer on the writing table, our suit jackets lying on our beds, and some leaflets and pamphlets on the night table where I'd left them.

The older man looked at all this, and then at Walter again. No one looked at me, not even the man with the gun. The older man said to Walter, 'When did you two get to town?'

'Last night.'

'What are you doing here?'

'We're representatives – Can we put our arms down?'

He made an impatient gesture. 'Put them down. But don't do any walking around.'

I lowered my arms, gratefully, and felt a tingling in the tips of my fingers as the blood rushed back. I turned my head and watched Walter's carefully expressionless face as he said, 'We're representatives of the American Alliance of Machinists and Skilled Trades.'

The older man frowned. 'What's that, a union?'

'That's right.'

'What are you doing here?'

'Looking into the possibility of organizing the workers in the shoe factory here.'

The three of them glanced at one another, and the older man raised and lowered his eyebrows. Then he said to the man with the gun, 'Keep an eye on them.' He pulled open the door and went outside and closed the door again.

There was silence. The two policemen and I looked at Walter, and Walter looked at the door. He smiled just a little, and then he wiped it off.

I tried to say excuse me, but all that came out was a sort of hacking cough. Everybody looked at me, and I tried again, with a little more success. 'Excuse me.'

They were all looking at me already, and waiting. I licked my dry lips with my dry tongue and said, 'Is it all right if I sit down?'

The policemen were both grinning at me. The one with the gun said, 'I think it would be all right,' with mockery in his voice.

I didn't care. I needed to sit down. I backed up to the armchair and dropped into it, and immediately felt even weaker. I put one hand up and wiped the clamminess from my forehead.

We waited three or four minutes, and then the older man stuck his head in and said, 'Jerry.' Jerry went outside with him, and closed the door. Another minute, and they both came back in. The older man looked at me sitting down, raised and lowered his eyebrows, and then said to Walter, 'We got to search the room for the gun. Any objections?'

'I always abide by a search warrant,' Walter told him.

'That's good,' said the older man. He motioned, and Jerry started towards our suitcases.

Walter cleared his throat. 'You forgot to show me the warrant,' he said.

'I forgot to bring it with me. You want me to make an extra trip. You wouldn't want to make things tough for me, would you? I could so easy make them tough for you.'

Walter shrugged, and the small smile licked at his lips again.

Jerry went on over to the suitcases. He opened them one at a

194

time and dumped everything onto the floor. In moving around, he stepped on the clothing, and he held my suitcase too far open, so I heard something rip. Then he went over to the writing table, and in opening the drawer he knocked the typewriter onto the floor. He looked at Walter and grinned. 'Sorry about that,' he said.

'That's all right,' Walter told him.

Jerry searched the writing-table drawer, dumping the stationery onto the floor, and in going over to the bathroom he stepped on the typewriter keyboard. He paused to empty the socks and underwear out of the laundry bag, and then he went on into the bathroom.

Walter looked over at me and said, conversationally, 'What do you bet he finds it taped to the inside of the top of the water closet?'

I didn't know what he meant, so I didn't say anything. The way they were breaking things, I wouldn't have said anything anyway, not wanting to draw attention to myself.

The older man said, 'What do you mean by that crack?' I looked over at him and saw his face flushed dark with anger. He was glaring at Walter.

Walter shook his head, and the smile came and went again, a tantalizing superior sort of smile, and I had the feeling he was going out of his way to antagonize these people. 'Not a thing,' he said.

'Are you trying to imply I'd plant evidence on you?'

'Not a bit,' Walter told him. 'And I wouldn't imply your man would do anything like break up my typewriter on purpose, either. Or rip my friend's suitcase.'

'You want to register a complaint, is that it?' He was very angry now, his hands balled into fists at his sides.

'Definitely not,' said Walter. 'I think you deserve a commendation, to tell you the truth, for the way you do the job you swore to do.'

Before the older man could say anything, Jerry came back from the bathroom. 'Not yet,' he said.

'Keep looking.'

'Right.'

He took the beds next, stripping off the covers and knocking everything to the floor, and managing to walk on both of our coats. He looked under the beds, and searched the night table. 'Careful with the lamp,' Walter told him quietly. 'That doesn't belong to us.'

Jerry just grinned at him and went on searching.

The door opened and a man came partway in, wearing the first police uniform I'd seen. He said to the older man, in a stage whisper, 'Mr Fleisch is here.'

'Shut up!' The older man spun on the new one, his rage getting even worse. 'Get the hell out of here, you damn fool!'

'Yes, sir. Yes, sir.' The policeman backed away from the doorway, blinking rapidly, and the older man followed him out and closed the door.

I looked over at Walter, but of course he'd caught it, too. Fleisch was the name of the man who managed the McIntyre Shoe Company for the relatives who owned it. Walter smiled sweetly at me, and went back to watching Jerry wreck our room.

By the time Jerry couldn't find anything more to take apart, the older man was back in the room. Jerry told him he hadn't found it, and the older man said to us, 'Put on your coats.'

I got up from the chair and picked up my coat from the floor. I brushed off Jerry's footprints, shrugged into the coat, and Walter and I went out into the late afternoon sun. The sky was red, far away to the west, and the sun was red-gold and close to the horizon. A black Lincoln Continental was parked on the gravel, near the motel sign, with a chauffeur at the wheel and a figure vaguely distinguishable in the back seat.

There were two police cars there, bracketing our Ford. They put Walter in one of them, with Jerry and the other man, and I rode in the other with the older man and the uniformed one. As we drove out onto the street, I craned for a look at whoever was in the back seat of the Lincoln, but he was in shadow and I could make out no features.

196

5

The police station was one block west of Harpur Boulevard, on the wrong side of town. This close to the main street, the neighbourhood hadn't quite deteriorated into the slum it would become two or three blocks farther west. Here on Clinton Street were the secondary shops, housing plumbers and cobblers and television repairmen and automobile-body shops. Amid them was a brick building, three storeys tall, lined with blank windows and looking like a smaller version of one of the plant buildings, and this was the police station. Four slate steps led up from the sidewalk to double arched doors flanked by ancient green light globes with black lettering POLICE curved across their street sides. Beside the building was a blacktop driveway, which the two cars went down to a gravel parking lot at the back. There was a fire escape rusting on the back wall, garbage cans rusting next to the three cars already parked there.

There had been no talk on the trip in, and when the car stopped, there was still no talk. The grey-haired man simply got out of the car and motioned for me to do the same. I saw Walter get out of the other car. They marched us through a black metal back door and up a flight of steps and down a long green corridor. The floor was old and oil-soaked, the boards shrunken away from one another and the dust of years black in the cracks.

They stopped us at a door, wooden and unmarked, midway down the corridor. The older man took out a batch of keys, selected one, and unlocked the door. Then he motioned to Walter, saying, 'Inside.'

Walter went on into the room. I started to follow, but the older man grabbed my arm and said, 'Not you. This way.' So I followed him to the next door, while Jerry and the other man went into the room with Walter. The older man unlocked the other door, told me to go inside, and I did. He closed it, and I heard him lock it again, and then I was alone.

197

It was a small grey room, with drab blue linoleum on the floor. The one window, overlooking the driveway at the side of the building, was covered by a heavy mesh screen on the outside and crossed metal bars on the inside. There was a hanging light globe, unlit, in the middle of the ceiling, directly over the smallish battered wood desk which was the room's main piece of furniture. Behind the desk was a wooden chair with wooden arms. An olive-drab round metal wastebasket was on one side of the desk, and a wooden chair without arms on the other side. A brass ashtray stand stood in one corner, a third chair – armless – in another. An empty coat rack filled the corner by the door.

For a minute or so, I just stood there, waiting, wondering what was going to happen next. But nothing happened next. Either the walls were thick, or the station was unusually silent; I heard nothing but muffled street noises filtered through the dusty window. I looked around at the room, and felt my heart pounding, and what finally broke the spell was my thinking, *I wonder what Dr Reedman would think about this*. The idea of that bent, gentle man assigning one of the students to this room in this police station struck me so funny I laughed aloud, though the thought wasn't really funny, nor was it even very clear in my mind. I just needed something to get my brain started again, and the thought of Dr Reedman was what did it.

I took out my cigarettes, lit one, and started to put the pack away again. Then I hesitated, because I didn't know how long I was going to be kept in here, and counted the cigarettes I had left. Including the one I'd just lit, eight. At two an hour, I could survive four hours in here. After that, I wasn't sure what I'd do.

I put the cigarettes away and looked again at the desk. Curiosity prompted me to go around and open the drawers, just to see what this room was usually used for. The drawers were all empty, except for the ubiquitous blue and red stains that seem to grow of their own accord on the bottom of every old desk drawer in the world. So the room, therefore, was usually used for nothing. They'd been saving it for years, just for me.

Just what was I doing here, anyway? With the shock and the excitement – and the abject fear inspired by the show of guns –

I hadn't really asked myself that question before. Policemen had come into my room and searched my person and ripped my suitcase and walked around on my clothing. Then they had taken me to police headquarters and locked me away in an unused room. But I hadn't *done* anything. What had I done? Nothing illegal, nothing at all. So none of this could possibly have happened. So what was I doing here?

There was the door. All I had to do was go over and knock on it, and when somebody came I would explain that I had done nothing, and ask that somebody to tell me just what they thought I had done, and straighten everything out with no trouble at all, and then Walter and I could go back to the motel, with apologies from the policemen, and they would pay Walter for the broken typewriter. And if they refused to listen to logic and truth and common sense, I knew that I was supposed to be allowed one phone call, and I would call a lawyer.

I thought back, into everything I'd ever heard in a classroom, into everything I'd ever read in any textbook, to see if anywhere in my education I had been given any sort of reason for not following that plan, for not going over and knocking on the door. There was none. My entire education, all fifteen years of it, whenever it had touched on law and police matters at all – which had, in fact, been rather seldom – had either stated or implied that knocking on that door was the only thing I should even think of doing.

Yet, somehow, I didn't do it. Somehow, I understood instinctively that all I had been taught about the law had been a sort of complicated Piltdown man; a hoax. A well-intentioned hoax, perhaps, an attempt on the part of sympathetic educators to keep me from the harsher realities of life, but a hoax nevertheless. I was helpless. The Constitution and the Bill of Rights and all the Wars Fought for Democracy existed every one of them in the land next door to the one occupied by Peter Pan; for in the world containing this grey room with its blue linoleum floor, I was as helpless and defenceless and doomed as a baby sharing a crib with a hungry rat. But why talk to the baby about justice? If you can't talk the truth, Dr Reedman, why don't you shut your toothless mouth for ever?

Anger was churning in my belly, the anger of the natural victim, the anger of the serf whose wife has been taken away to the castle, the anger of the slave whose child has been auctioned to a different buyer, helpless muted anger which I knew I dared not show. I sat at the desk and smoked my cigarette, and despised myself for not being numbered among the fittest in this pretty jungle in which we live.

I don't know how long I waited. I was on my third cigarette when they came in, but I think I'd been smoking more than two an hour. I hadn't worn a watch since the mainspring had broken on my old one a year and a half before.

The older man came in, and Jerry, and the third man from the motel, plus another man in mufti whom I hadn't met before. This man, carrying a stenographer's pad and a pencil, went immediately to the chair in the corner. The older man looked at me behind the desk and said, 'On your feet.'

I stood up.

'Put out that cigarette,' he said. 'Over there,' motioning at the ashtray stand in the corner. 'And pick those butts off the floor. You wouldn't throw butts on the floor in your own home.'

Retorts sprang to my mind, but not to my lips. I did as I was told. When I turned back, the older man was seated at the desk. He looked sour and grim. He said, 'Put your wallet on the desk here, and sit down.' He motioned at the chair beside the desk.

Once again, I did as I was told. Sitting there, with Jerry and the other man leaning against the wall to my right, I watched the older man finger my wallet. 'Paul Standish,' he said. In the corner, the stenographer started writing. 'Here's an activity card from Monequois University. That where you went to school?'

'I still do,' I said.

'Then what are you doing here?'

'At Monequois, we study for six months and then work at a job connected with our major for six months.'

'What's your major?'

'Economics.'

'Mmm. Where's your draft card?'

'I've been in the Army already. Three years.'

200

'You volunteered?'

'That's right.'

'Maybe you volunteer too often.' He closed the wallet and tossed it to me. It fell on the floor and I stooped and picked it up and put it back in my pocket. He said, 'You ever been in trouble before?'

'No, sir,' I said. I hadn't meant to say sir; it just slipped out. I promised myself it wouldn't slip out again.

'All right.' He hitched around in the chair and said, 'Tell us your movements today. All day long.'

'I got up about eight o'clock. We went to the City Line Diner for breakfast around nine-thirty. Then we drove around town till maybe one-thirty or two o'clock this afternoon. Then we went to see Mr Charles Hamilton, but he wasn't home. We talked to his wife, and Mr Hamilton was supposed to come see us at the motel by seven o'clock, so we went back to the motel and waited for him.'

'What time did you get to the motel?'

'I'm not sure. Maybe two-thirty, maybe earlier than that.'

'And you stayed there all the time?'

'Around five I went out and got us hamburgers and coffee to go at the diner.'

'You did. How long were you gone?'

'Maybe fifteen minutes.'

'And your partner, this Killy character, he was there when you got back?'

'Yes.'

'Did he leave at any time during the afternoon?'

'No, because he wanted to be there when Mr Hamilton showed up.'

'Where do you know Hamilton from?'

'I don't know him.'

'Where does Killy know him from?'

'He doesn't know him either. We just –'

'How do you know he doesn't know him?'

'Well, we were just –'

'How long you known Killy?'

201

'Just a few days.'

'So he could have known Hamilton for years, and you'd never know it.'

'He would have said something about it.'

'Are you sure?'

'Well, of course I'm sure.'

'Mmm. What'd you want to talk to Hamilton about?'

I hesitated. The hostility we'd met could only be in reference to our roles with the Machinists. These people didn't know me as a student, as a veteran, as a son, as a human being; they only knew me as an employee of the Machinists. I didn't know how much to tell them, therefore, about the business of the Machinists. 'About union business,' I said.

'What union business?'

'Listen,' I said. I glanced at the other two, leaning against the wall, but they were acting bored, and neither of them was even looking at me. To the older man, I said, 'Listen, why are you asking me all these questions? What am I supposed –?'

'I ask the questions,' he said. 'You give the answers.'

'No,' I said.

He looked at me, and his eyebrows went up and down. 'What do you mean, no?'

'You people can go to hell,' I told him. Not because of what the teachers and the textbooks had said, but just because even a baby can stick his finger in the rat's eye. What worse can the rat do than what he intended anyway?

He flushed, the quick anger rising in him. 'You better watch your tongue, boy,' he said.

I folded my arms and stared at the window.

'Now, look here,' he said. 'I've been taking it easy with you, but if you want to make things tough for yourself it's up to you.'

'*Easy?* That moron of yours rips my suitcase and walks all over my clothes and breaks my friend's typewriter, and you call it *easy?* You arrest me for no reason at all and lock me away –'

'I didn't arrest you,' he said.

'Good. I'm going home.' I got to my feet.

'Sit down,' he said. 'You were brought in for questioning.'

I stood there glaring at him. 'About what?'

'Just sit down,' he said.

'The hell I will! I –'

Then a hand had a painful grip on my shoulder, and I was shoved back into the chair. I looked up, and saw Jerry smiling down at me, and I clenched my fist, but he said, 'You don't want to try it, buddy.'

'Get your hand off me.'

The older man said, 'It's all right, Jerry.'

Jerry let me go and went back to lean against the wall again.

The older man said to me, 'You want to watch that temper, boy. It could get you into a lot of trouble some day.'

'I'm sorry,' I said. 'I'm just not used to this. In the town where I was brought up, the policemen were decent human beings.'

His palm hit the desk. 'You watch that mouth. Nobody asked you and that smart-ass friend of yours to come into this town, stirring up trouble –'

'*What* trouble? We drove around for a while and we talked to one woman, whose husband had asked us to come here. So what trouble are you talking about?'

But he had control of himself again. 'About that time when you went out for the hamburgers and coffee,' he said. 'What time was it you said you went?'

'I don't know for sure. Around five o'clock.'

'And what time did you get back?'

'Around quarter after, I guess. It took about fifteen minutes.'

'You don't know for sure.'

'No.'

'But you do know for sure it took fifteen minutes.'

'*About* fifteen minutes.'

'Twenty minutes?'

I shrugged, not seeing any point to all this, just more irritation. 'Maybe.'

'Half an hour, maybe?'

'No, not that long. I told you already, about fifteen minutes.'

'You walked?'

'No, I drove the car.'

203

'And it was five o'clock when you left.'

'Yes.'

'On the dot?'

'How do I know? Around five o'clock, that's all I know.'

'For all you know,' he said, 'you could have left there at five-thirty instead of five o'clock, and not got back till six. Isn't that right?'

'No. It was around five o'clock when I left and around quarter after five when I got back.'

'Mmm. What kind of gun has this Killy character got?'

'I didn't know he had a gun at all.'

'You never saw it, huh?'

'No.'

'He just told you about it.'

'He never said anything about it.'

'Then what gave you the idea he had one?'

I was about to answer, but then I stopped, and forced myself to grin at him. 'You took a correspondence course in psychology, is that it? *You* gave me the idea he had a gun. You think I'm one of your local simpletons?'

'The people around here are all simpletons, is that it?'

'All I've met so far.'

This time he didn't get mad. Instead, he smiled and said, 'You're a smart boy, well educated. Tell me, do you know why they call a jail the cooler?'

'No, Mister Interlocutor, why do they call a jail the cooler?'

But that didn't make him mad either. 'Because it cools wise guys off,' he said. 'And you could use some cooling.' He glanced at Jerry. 'Better put him away upstairs for a while,' he said.

'I get a phone call!' I shouted.

'Oh, I know it. But our phone's out of order.'

Jerry was standing next to me again, reaching out for that grip on my shoulder. I knocked his hand away and stood up. He was an inch or so taller than I, and maybe thirty pounds heavier and ten years older. He was also a fighter and a brawler, from the look of him, which I'm not and never will be, but I meant it sincerely when I told him, 'You lay a hand on me, and your friend will have to pull me off you.'

204

Jerry laughed at that, looking past me at the older man. 'Hotter'n pistol, isn't he?'

'I noticed that.'

He nodded and grinned and backed away from me toward the door. 'All righty, your highness,' he said. 'You just come along nice, and I won't have any call to touch your lily-white skin.' He opened the door, and made a mock bow as he ushered me out to the corridor. 'This way,' he said. 'Pretty please.'

6

It's hard to describe the third floor of that building. You take an old building like that, and on one floor you scoop out all of the interior walls and partitions, leaving just a big empty rectangle bounded by the outer walls. Inside that rectangle you build a metal box, the bottom and top flush against the floor and ceiling, – the sides about three feet smaller than the dimensions of the building, leaving a kind of areaway corridor all around the box. One side of the box you make of vertical iron bars, so air can get in, and at one end you cut a space for a door and put in a metal door with double safety glass in a small window in it at eye-level. Inside this metal box you make new partitions, of slabs of metal and rows of vertical iron bars, and then you daub the whole thing thickly and sloppily with grey enamel paint. Then you have a jail.

Just outside the door to the box there was a desk, and a man in uniform sitting at it. Jerry said something cute to him about me, and he took a large manila envelope out of a drawer of the desk and told me to put my valuables in it, and my belt, and my shoelaces. The only valuable I had was my wallet. I handed the envelope back, and then Jerry said, 'His glasses, too. We wouldn't want him to break them and cut himself.'

'That's right,' said the uniformed man.

'I need my glasses,' I said. I held them on with my right hand, feeling something very close to panic.

'Not here,' Jerry told me. 'There's nothing to see up here.'

'Come on, come on,' said the uniformed man impatiently. He rattled the envelope.

I took off my glasses and gave them to him. He put them in the envelope. Then he asked me my name, and wrote it on the flap, and then he and Jerry escorted me into the box. They put me in the second cell on the right, and left me there.

I have very bad eyes, 20-150 in the left and 20-200 in the right.

206

I stood squinting and blinking by the bars for a little while, trying to make out my surroundings. The cell I was in was bounded on three sides by metal walls, and contained a metal cot suspended from the wall by chains, a small dirty sink, and a small dirty toilet. On the fourth side was the barred door, facing out onto the central open area running the length of the box. There were six cells on each side of this area, and I could look across through the bars of my cell and through the bars of the cell across the way – which was empty – and through the bars at the back of that cell, and catch a small corner glimpse of a window in the original outer wall. Without my glasses, the glimpse was a vague one.

After a while, when I got used to the idea that they had gone away and left me, I turned away from the bars and went over to sit down on the metal cot. There was a thin Army blanket stretched out on it, and I rubbed the palm of my hand against the rough surface.

I have never been in trouble with the Law, not at home and not in the Army and not at college. I have stayed out of trouble, I think, not out of fear of consequences but simply out of disinclination. Negative morality, you might call it. The sort of thing that leads to arrest and imprisonment had never been the sort of thing that I wanted to do. I hadn't changed, not in my attitudes nor in my actions, and yet here I was in a jail cell, robbed of most of my sight, bullied and taunted.

Could this really happen? Could malignance behind a badge suddenly pounce on *anybody*, anybody at all? What a terribly dangerous world I'd been living in, all along, not knowing it.

Being without my glasses for some reason made me feel drowsy and sluggish. My nerves were jumpy, from what had happened and from not knowing what would happen next, but the drowsiness overcame that and after a little while I stretched out on the metal cot and closed my eyes.

I hadn't intended to fall asleep, but I did anyway, and woke up when the uniformed man was in the cell, shaking me. I came out of it fuzzily, and from a great distance heard Jerry saying, 'Look out there, Clarence, he don't like people to touch him.'

'That's too bad. Come on, you, on your feet.'

I got up from the cot, stiff and sore, blinking in yellow light. Jerry, standing just outside the cell, said, 'Come on along, Little Lord Fauntleroy. Captain Willick wants to talk to you again.'

I stumbled out of the cell, and followed him obediently, Clarence trailing along behind me. I had slept humidly and heavily; perspiration glued my clothes to my body, and my head was a hive of buzzings.

We went back downstairs again, and down the same corridor, and into the room with the blue linoleum floor. The older man – he must be Captain Willick – was seated at the desk again, and the hanging globe was now lit, filling the room with bright shadowless light. There were other men in the room, but because I didn't have my glasses I couldn't see them very well, they were only shapes around the walls.

Captain Willick said, 'Come in here, Standish. Sit down.'

I went over to the desk, but misjudged and knocked my knee against the chair as I went around it to sit down. I sat down and rubbed the knee, and Willick said, 'Where's his glasses?'

Jerry answered. 'With his other valuables.'

'Get them.' Just two words, but in a tone and manner that surprised me. They were said heavily, and reluctantly, and with a kind of dull anger that seemed to be directed inward rather than at – me or Jerry or anyone else. For the first time, the idea came to me that Captain Willick didn't like what he and his minions were doing to me, and the idea surprised me. I squinted at him, trying to see his face clearly enough to read his expression but I couldn't, and I knew it didn't matter. His face wouldn't betray him. If I'd had my glasses, if my sight had been working as well as my hearing, if I hadn't been in the position of having to depend so much on my ears, I might not have caught the inflection in his voice either.

But if he didn't like what he was doing, then why didn't he stop? It didn't make any sense, there wasn't any answer in the world I could think of, and so I asked him, 'Why do you do this if you don't like to do it?'

He answered quickly, and angrily. 'You shut your mouth! I had enough smart-aleck cracks out of you the last time!'

208

'But I didn't mean –'

A calm voice from the side said, 'Better keep it in, boy,' as though in friendly warning. I didn't recognize the voice, and I couldn't make out the speaker, but I took his word for it. This Captain Willick was very touchy, maybe because of that dislike for what he was doing, and the best thing for me to do was keep my mouth shut. They'd been right; a spell in the cooler had cooled me off. I still felt that I was being treated unjustly, but I no longer believed I was capable of righting wrongs simply by shouting for a specified length of time. This, too, will fade; the evil ones will eventually tire of me, release me, and go prowling for fresher prey.

We waited in silence till Jerry returned and gave me back my glasses. I put them on, and blinked a few times as the world came back into focus. I saw now that there were three men standing along the wall, the one who had been with Jerry and Captain Willick earlier, plus two more built from the same model. They all had their suit coats open and their hands in their pockets, and their ties hung askew on their shirt fronts.

Captain Willick had a thin stack of papers on his desk, stapled together at the corner and covered with typewriting. He was studying the top sheet gloomily, but now he looked over at me and said, 'You feel like answering questions now?'

I hesitated, pushing down the angry answers, and said, 'Yes.'

'Good. Now, tell me about the first time you met Charles Hamilton.'

'I thought I told you – I never met him.'

'Never at all.'

'No.'

'Mmm. And when did Killy first meet him, do you know that?'

He seemed to want to antagonize me all over again, but I refused to let him get to me. I said, 'He'd never met him either.'

'You're sure of that, are you?'

'Yes.'

'He told you he never met Charles Hamilton.'

'He told me we would both be meeting him for the first time.'

'In so many words?'

'I don't remember his exact words.'

'When you got back to the motel at six o'clock, you say Killy was there?'

'I got back at quarter after five, and he was there.'

'Did he leave before you went to the diner, or after?'

'It must have been after,' I said, surprised. I hadn't known Walter had gone out at all. Then, too late, I realized that had been another of the twist questions, that Walter hadn't gone out and wouldn't have gone out, because he'd been waiting for Hamilton.

But Willick didn't seem to take any notice of the answer. All he said was, 'And neither of you went out from the time you got back till the time we showed up, is that right?'

'That's right.'

'And when you were with Killy earlier in the day, he hadn't visited anybody but Mrs Hamilton, is that right?'

'Yes.'

'Who did he visit while you went to the diner?'

'Nobody.'

Willick glanced at me, affecting a sluggish surprise. 'Then where'd he go?'

'Nowhere.'

'You said he went out while you were gone.'

'No.'

'You didn't say that?'

'No.'

'I could have sworn you said that.' He looked over at the men leaning against the wall. 'Isn't that what it sounded like to you boys?'

They all agreed that was what it had sounded like to them. I pointed at the male stenographer, at work again in his corner, and said, 'Why don't you ask him?'

Willick studied me as though I'd just asked to marry his daughter. Slowly, he said, 'Are you trying to tell me how to do my job?'

'No,' I said.

'You're just trying to irritate me,' he said. He got to his feet

210

and said to the men against the wall, 'I'll be back in a little while. See if you can get a straight story out of him.'

'You betcha,' said Jerry. He came over and sat behind the desk, grinning to himself, while Willick left the room. The other three men came over and stood around me, looking down at me.

Jerry said, 'You were gonna tell the Captain about Killy's gun. You can tell me instead.'

'He doesn't have a gun,' I said.

One of the other men said, 'He just keeps contradicting himself, doesn't he?'

'I know it,' said Jerry. 'Take off your glasses.'

'What?'

'The specs,' said one of the other men. He reached out and took them off me. 'We want them off.'

I sat blinking, suddenly as afraid as when I'd first seen the guns. I sat lower in the chair, and my shoulders hunched.

Jerry said, 'Now, did Killy tell you where he went while you were at the diner?'

'He didn't go anywhere.'

One of them slapped my face, open-handed and not very hard, and a voice said, 'Just answer yes or no, boy.'

'I'll repeat the question,' said Jerry. 'Did Killy tell you where he went while you were at the diner?'

I said, 'No.'

'Do you *know* where he went?'

'No.'

'Do you know what he did with the gun?'

'He didn't – No.' I heard a chuckle.

'All right,' said Jerry. 'Now, why did Killy threaten Mrs Hamilton?'

I said, 'No.'

There was a baffled silence, and then Jerry said, 'What?'

'No.'

'What do you mean, no?'

'You told me to answer yes or no.'

One of the others said, approvingly, 'Oh, he's a cute one,' and the hand slapped my face again, a little harder.

211

'Now, Paul,' said Jerry, 'why make things so difficult for yourself? This is a serious business here, don't you realize that?'

'No.' The hand slapped me again, and I said, 'I'm beginning to realize it.'

'That's good, Paul.' Jerry rested his hand on my knee and said, 'You know, boy, I like you. You've got guts.'

'I hate your guts,' I told him.

This time the hand swung hard, and I nearly lost my balance and fell off the chair.

Jerry said, 'Easy there, Ben, you bumped into the witness that time. Now, Paul, I want to ask that last question again. Why did Killy threaten Mrs Hamilton?'

'Ben's going to hit me again,' I said. 'Killy didn't threaten her.'

I didn't get hit, which surprised me. Paper rustled, and Jerry said, 'This I don't understand. Listen to this, Paul. Mrs Hamilton told us Killy said to her, and this is a quote, quote, if your husband doesn't show up at the motel by seven, you'll be sorry. He better show up or else, unquote. Now, Paul, do you mean Killy never said that?'

'Not in those words,' I said, 'and not with that kind of meaning.'

'Paul, you aren't trying to play word-games with me, are you? Killy's admitted those are his words.'

'But they aren't. Mrs Hamilton didn't want the neighbours to see her husband talking to union people, so we said we'd talk to him at the motel instead, but if he didn't show up by seven we'd go back to the house and talk to him there, that's all there was to it.'

'That may be,' said Jerry. 'You may be telling the absolute truth, Paul, and I'd like to think you are. But you should've explained it all that nice and clear to Mrs Hamilton. You had that poor lady worried, don't you realize that? Why didn't you *tell* her you were just a couple of boys working for a union?'

'We did tell her.'

'Oh, come on now, Paul. She told us you two forced your way into the house and –'

'She's a liar!'

The hand stung my face again, and a voice said, 'Don't interrupt.'

'Now, listen, Paul,' said Jerry. 'Mrs Hamilton signed a sworn statement that you two knocked on the door, forced your way into the house, looked through it for Mr Hamilton, and then demanded to know when he got home from work. She refused to tell you, and then you told her you were staying at the motel and Hamilton had ought to come there by seven or you'd be back for him. And that's *all* you told her.'

'She's lying,' I said. 'We told her we were from the union first thing, and she knew about the letter her husband had written us –'

'She says she never heard of such a letter. And you know we didn't find it when we looked through your place.'

'It was right in the briefcase.'

'*I* didn't see it.'

I remained silent, because there was nothing I could have said that wouldn't have resulted in my being hit again. But I was hit anyway, and a voice said, 'Answer the question.'

'There *wasn't* any question!'

Slap. 'Don't raise your voice.'

'Now, Ben,' said Jerry. 'Paul, why do you want to protect this Killy fellow? We know *you're* in the clear, so why don't you get smart and tell us the truth?'

'I don't know what truth you want,' I said. The side of my face was aching, like an undefined toothache.

'Well, there's only one kind of truth, Paul, isn't there?'

'That's what I always thought.'

'All right, now. You don't want to call Mrs Hamilton a liar, do you?'

'I have to.'

'No, you don't. Listen, there's no reason to make yourself trouble. You explained what Killy meant, and I believe it, but why tell a lot of lies? He said what Mrs Hamilton told us, and she just misunderstood it, that's all. Isn't that possible?'

'We didn't force our way into the house.'

'I'm not talking about that, Paul. I'm talking about what was

213

said. That quote I read you. Now, was that an accurate quote or wasn't it?'

'No, it wasn't.'

'Now, wait a second.' He read the quote to me again, and said, 'Isn't that just about what Killy said? Not word for word, maybe, but pretty close.'

'But that isn't *all* he said!'

'That isn't what I'm asking you, Paul. I'm asking you if Killy said that there that I just read you, or something very close to it.'

'Yes or no,' said a warning voice.

I spread my hands, helplessly, but they were waiting. 'Yes,' I said.

'All right, then,' said Jerry. 'I'm glad to hear you say that, Paul. I'm glad to know you're going to come clean now. I know you didn't really *want* to call Mrs Hamilton a liar.'

'But she *is* a liar.'

'Oh, now, Paul, there you go again. You just *admitted* –'

'*We didn't force our way into the house.*'

Slap! 'Don't interrupt.' Slap! 'And don't raise your voice.'

'You son of a bitch –' I jumped up out of the chair, swinging wild at the vague shapes in front of me. My fists hit nothing but air, and then I was hit solidly in the stomach, just under the belt. I doubled, unable to breathe, feeling the blood rush to my head, and somebody pushed me back into the chair. My mouth stretched wide open of its own accord, trying to find air, and my arms were folded across my stomach.

Jerry said, 'Now, Paul, you weren't trying to strike an officer, were you?'

I tried again, even though I couldn't breathe, and this time I tried to get my hands on Jerry. But the hands shoved me back into the chair before I was fully out of it, and then the door slammed behind me and Captain Willick shouted, 'What the hell is going on around here?'

Jerry, sounding suddenly sheepish, said, 'He was gettin' awful unruly, Captain.'

'I thought I told you to give him back his glasses.'

'Yes, sir.' My glasses were shoved into my hand, but I didn't

214

try to put them on. The breath was scraping back down my throat into my lungs at last, burning all the way, and I despised myself because I knew I was going to cry any second.

'You people ought to be ashamed of yourselves,' Captain Willick was saying. 'Get the hell out of here and leave this boy alone.'

'Yes, sir.' There was a shuffling of feet, an embarrassed silence, and then the door closed again and Captain Willick and I were alone.

He came around and sat at the desk and said, 'Put your glasses on, son.' His voice was kindly and compassionate.

And the tears came, burning salty tears of rage and frustration and humiliation. I bent my head and covered my face with my hands and pounded my feet on the floor, *willing* the tears to stop. But they wouldn't.

Willick laid a fatherly hand on my head, and said, 'Take it easy, son, it isn't as bad as all that.'

I jerked away from his hand and glared at him, and with the idiotic tears still streaming down my face I screamed at him, 'Get your hands off me! Do you think I'm a moron, do you think I don't know what you're doing? Hard and soft and hard and soft, don't you think I know that? First they slap me around, and if that doesn't do it then you come in and play father-confessor for a while. Don't you think I *know* you were listening at the door all the while?'

'If that's what you think of me, son, I'm sorry.'

'You hypocrite. Hypocrite hypocrite *hypocrite*!'

'Now, you just settle down, you hear me?'

'Hypocrite, hypocrite, hypocrite, hypocrite, hypo –'

And I got slapped again.

I stopped then, and regained partial control of myself. I wiped my face and put my glasses on, and said, 'All right, so it has to be hard and hard. When your hands are tired, *they'll* come back. You can all go to hell.'

'All right,' he said. 'All right. We can all go to hell. But on the way there, boy, we're going to make some hell for you. This is a serious situation, and if you think your punk wisecracks and snotnose –'

'*What's* a serious situation? If you people think you've got a *reason* for all this bullshit, why don't you spit it out and quit treating me like Humphrey Bogart's stand-in?'

He stopped; his mouth twisted around as he glowered at me from under lowered brows. Then he nodded and said, 'All right, boy, I'll spit it out. You and that fellow Killy come into town here, come into a nice peaceful town where nobody's causing you any trouble and nobody wants any trouble. You come into town and threaten Mrs Charles Hamilton, and four hours later *Mister* Charles Hamilton is shot to death in the parking lot out beside the Work Boot building of the shoe company. Now, what do you think about that?'

7

Think? I couldn't think. I could only gape, slack-jawed, frozen in that breathless instant between the crash of lightning and the sound of the thunder.

Shot to death. The phrase rebounded in my mind. Shot to death. Shot to death. Shottodeathshottodeathshottodeath . . .

A phrase repeated often enough ceases to have any meaning. I once said *piano* to myself, over and over and over again, and after a while it actually did work. There was the object, this large musical instrument, and over here was this sound pattern, piano, and they didn't go together any more. It only lasted for a few minutes, but it was kind of frightening; in those few minutes I went around half-convinced that *piano* was a nonsense word I'd made up and that there was actually an entirely different word to describe that musical instrument.

I think my mind was trying to do something like that with *shot to death*. The phrase just kept bouncing back and forth, back and forth, a hard quick syllable first, and then a small, barely present syllable, and finally a long fading syllable leading to silence and the briefest of pauses and the repetition of the first hard quick syllable again. Shot   to   death

But it doesn't always work. Scenes of war movies: a running soldier suddenly falls, and the camera pans on, a soldier in a foxhole throws up his hands and falls backward. Scenes of crime movies: the killer in the black suit lurches, and falls off the fire escape, the bank guard, crouching, drops all at once to the sidewalk. Scenes of western movies: the Indian rears back, and falls from his rushing horse, and rolls in the dust, the cavalryman in the Conestoga wagon slumps.

I had never seen a man shot to death; I had only these simulations to pictorialize the phrase in my mind. The phrase bounced back and forth, the remembered fictitious images flashed and flashed, crowding together, and I hung still in the empty space between the lightning and the thunder. And Willick waited with me, watching my face.

My mind was full of leaping images, and sentence fragments. *Shot to death.* And then: *Murder in the first degree.* 'We find the defendant guilty.' 'And there to be hanged by the neck until you are dead.'

Me? *Me?*

As the thunder rolled over me, I focused again slowly on Willick's waiting face, and whispered, 'You're going to frame me.'

He stared at me. 'What?'

'Mr Fleisch told you to frame us. He told you to.'

'Why, you rotten little punk.' His face was mottled with rage again. 'Who's trying to frame you? Nobody charged you with anything, did they? Nobody even *accused* you!'

My mouth flapped open, driven by panic. 'No, no, and nobody slapped me around or locked me in a cell or ripped my suitcase or broke Walter's typewriter or tried to get me to say Walter was out of the motel while that man, that – that, he – *Hamilton*, was being killed. And, and, nobody faked up a lying affidavit from Mrs Hamilton or tried to get me to say Walter had a gun and used to know Mr Hamilton or –'

'Shut up!'

'A – and nobody took my glasses away or punched me in the stomach –'

He leaped toward me out of the chair, grabbing my shirt front and hauling me up to my feet. Our faces were only inches apart, and his breath smelled of cavities. 'You keep your face shut,' he whispered. 'You push me too far, and I will pin a rap on you. I'll get you for assaulting an officer, and don't think I can't do it. If you don't want two fast years in a cell, you better wise up right this minute.'

I was shuddering all over. I squeezed shut my mouth and my eyes and my fists, and I held my breath, and I waited. I waited for Willick to tell me there was no hope, that I was enmired in this terrible jungle for ever; and the instant I knew that for sure, that he intended to do the very worst to me that he possibly could, I would open again just long enough to kill him.

218

I *am* capable of it, Willick, you see? I hadn't known that till then, that I was capable of thinking the thought, *I will kill him*, and meaning it utterly. What a teacher you were, Willick!

But the silence lengthened, and he didn't say any more, the die was not yet cast, and I continued to hang shuddering from his hands, until at last he let go of my shirt and stepped back from me. I opened my eyes then, and saw him sitting down again at the desk, his face stiff and dark. He glanced at me and said gruffly, 'Sit down.'

I sat down. The shuddering was receding.

'I'm sorry I lost my temper,' he said. 'You don't want to ride me like that.'

What a knack he had for being the injured party!

'One thing you said,' he muttered. He flipped open the sheaf of papers. 'About Mrs Hamilton's statement. She dictated it, and she swore to it, and she signed it. I want to believe you on most counts, but we keep coming back to this. Now this time I want the truth. I don't want to play around with you any more, I want the simple truth, and then we can be finished with each other.'

I waited. He still might say the word of finality. I waited.

'All I want to know,' he said, 'is why you two didn't tell Mrs Hamilton you were from the union.'

So there it was. I actually felt myself relax, felt relief spreading out through my limbs. The point had been reached at last. I would tell him the truth this one last time, and then he would tell me that hope was gone, and then I would reach across the desk and close my hands around his throat and no power in this world would release my hands till he stopped breathing.

My voice surprised me, calm and low. It said, 'The first thing Walter told Mrs Hamilton was that we were representatives of the Machinists.'

'God *damn* it!' He shoved the papers at me. 'Here, *read it*!

Why should I read his inventions? I left the papers where they were and said, 'The first thing Walter told Mrs Hamilton was that we were representatives of the Machinists.' And now?

He leaned back in his chair and gazed at me, his eyebrows up. After a minute he said, 'You know, I'd almost believe you, I

219

really would. Except your partner already admitted it, and explained it away by saying he didn't think it was any of her business who he was or where he was from.'

I hesitated before answering. I could change my story now, to agree with Walter's. It might even be the best thing to do. But without having foreplanned it, I had reached a position from which all retreat was impossible. I *couldn't* go back now, even if I wanted to.

'Well?' he said.

'Walter's smarter than I am,' I said. 'He probably didn't want to be hit by Jerry.'

He thought that over, twisting his mouth around again, his eyebrows going down low over his eyes. He fiddled with a corner of the papers, and after a while he said, 'But why should she lie? What possible reason would she have?'

Was he sincere? I watched him, trying to understand him, and slowly the calm of panic faded away, and it was possible for me to think again. Had Mrs Hamilton *really* made that statement? But why?

After a minute of silence, he got heavily to his feet. He seemed older now, and more troubled. Watching him, I thought, *He's just a guilt-ridden hypocrite, after all, no more.* And what would his defence be, how would he forgive himself?

If I didn't do it, somebody else would. And a man's got to make a living.

Is that all there was to him? I nearly laughed, remembering that only a minute ago I'd thought him real enough to kill.

He looked down at me for a second, and then said, 'You wait here. I'll be right back.'

I looked away from him.

He went out, moving heavily, and closed the door behind him. I lit a cigarette, and it tasted foul. I had been asleep for I didn't know how long, and hadn't had anything to eat since waking up. I made a face, but I kept smoking, managing without difficulty to avoid all thought. And when I finished the cigarette I put it out in the ashtray in the corner.

As I was straightening from the ashtray, the door opened and

Willick came back in. He stood with his hand on the knob and said, 'You're free to go. They've got your stuff at the desk. There's a reporter wants to talk to you.'

I looked up, interested. 'Oh, is there?'

'I wouldn't go shooting off my mouth to her, if I were you.'

'Her?'

'She's waiting in an office downstairs, if you want to talk to her.'

'I'd love to talk to her.' I was free, the ultimate had been avoided. A kind of wild joy now filled me. The longer I spent in this building, under this cloud, the more my emotions fluctuated, and the greater the fluctuations.

Willick grunted, and led the way out to the corridor. I followed him out and down the stairs to the first floor. He pointed at a door and said, 'In there.'

I started thinking about what I would say to her, the girl reporter, and my emotions shifted heavily again, and I found myself feeling angry, feeling more and more enraged: I'd planned a smart remark with which to part from Willick, but now I swept it out of my mind and left Willick without a word.

8

The minute I saw her I remembered her, though I couldn't figure out from where. She was about nineteen or twenty, very trim and slim, with assured and rather sharp good looks. Her black hair was modishly short, and softly waved to curve around and frame her face. She wore eye make-up, and managed not to look too young for it. She was wearing a dark blue suit with a tight long tubular skirt and a brief ineffectual jacket over a white blouse. Her legs were nyloned, and she stood in black heels.

She had been standing looking out the window, on the other side of the long table flanked by wooden chairs, which were the room's only furniture, and when I came in she turned and came toward me, an impersonal professional smile forming on her lips. She came around the table and extended a slender pale hand toward me the way Audrey Hepburn might, and said, 'How do you do? I'm Sondra Fleisch, of the *Beacon*.'

My hand stopped halfway to her. 'Fleisch?'

The smile widened. 'Yes, that's my daddy. But I don't work for him, I work for the *Beacon*.'

Then I remembered. I said, 'Well, for God's sake.'

Pencilled eyebrows rose, and she said, 'I beg your pardon?' Her hand still hung out there between us.

'You go to Monequois,' I said.

The poised professional smile turned a trifle puzzled. 'Yes, I do.'

'So do I!'

The smile wilted, and total bafflement showed through. 'You do?'

'Well, sure I do. Here, wait, let me show you my activity card.' I pawed at my hip pocket, then remembered they'd taken my wallet. 'Wait a second, let me get my wallet back; they're supposed to have it at the desk.'

'No, no,' she said. 'I'll take your word for it.'

'Well, for Pete's sake,' I said. I stared at her, and grinned like a fool, and sat down at the table.

I hadn't connected the name before, primarily because I didn't really know Sondra Fleisch. But she had a column in the *Indian*, the college paper, so I'd noticed the name more than once, and I'd seen her on the campus now and again. We'd never met because she travelled with the rich crowd and I travelled with the grizzled vets, and never never never will that twain meet.

But now, under rather odd circumstances, we had met after all, and I looked upon Miss Sondra Fleisch as though she were an old friend. A familiar face – no matter how vaguely familiar – a reminder of the more normal and sensible and sane world in which I'd always lived; she was worth more to me than diamonds. I just sat and stared at her.

She enjoyed my staring, I think. She smiled again, with obvious pleasure, and went around to sit across the table from me. 'You surprise me,' she said. 'I never thought to find a schoolmate in our local bastille.'

'I never thought to find me here,' I said. 'But what the – what in the name of all that's holy are you doing here?'

'I'm on my six months,' she said. 'Daddy wants me to be home at least part of the time, so here I am. I'm a journalism major, so my six months in the field are spent on the *Beacon*.' She shrugged, smiling. 'It isn't the *New York Times*,' she said, 'but I guess that can wait till I graduate.'

'Boy,' I said. I really and truly said 'boy.' 'After all the cr— all the, the nonsense I've been through, you're a sight for sore eyes, I mean it. And sore jaws,' I added, and stroked my face where the generalized toothache was still slowly receding.

She frowned at that. 'You mean they hit you?'

'That isn't the half of it.'

'Well, now.' From a large black shoulder bag she withdrew pencil and steno pad. 'You tell me all about it,' she said.

I did. I told her about my job, and the letter from Charles Hamilton, and everything that had happened since we'd come to Wittburg. She took notes in a rapid shorthand, and asked questions to fill in details, and listened all the while with a serious disturbed expression on her face. When at last I'd finished, she sat for a minute, gazing at her notes, and then she said, 'This is terrible, Paul. I never thought the police in this town could be so vicious, and I can't believe my father would ever have ordered them to act like this. They must have done this on their own, and if they thought my father would be pleased they were wrong. I'm going to tell him about it, believe me, and I'm going to talk my editor into putting this story on the first page. You wait till you see the paper this afternoon. They won't get away with this, Paul, believe me.'

'I'd love to think they won't,' I said.

'They won't.' She got to her feet, very young and very determined and very good-looking. 'You just wait and see. Are you still staying at that motel?'

'I guess so.'

'I'll give you a call there,' she promised. 'We'll get to the bottom of this.' As she spoke, she was coming around the table. When she came close to me, she held out her hand again, and this time I took it. 'This is what a reporter is for,' she said. 'To see that the people get the facts.'

I smiled at her earnestness. 'We'll give them hell,' I said.

'You bet we will.' She gripped my hand hard, and released it. 'I've got to get back to the office, make sure this story gets into today's paper.'

'Right you are.'

'I'll call you, Paul.'

'Right.'

We went out to the hall together, and I walked her as far as the front desk, where a man in uniform, with stripes on his sleeves, sat high on a raised platform behind a massive oak desk. There we shook hands again, and she promised again to call. She walked out of the building, and I went over to the desk. 'I'm Paul Standish,' I said. 'You have my wallet.'

'That's right.' He reached under the desk and came up with the envelope. 'Check the contents,' he said, as though by rote, 'and sign this form if everything is intact.'

Everything was intact. I signed the form, and then put my belt and shoelaces back on, and stuffed my wallet into my hip pocket. Then I went back to the desk and said, 'I want to talk to my friend. Walter Killy.'

'Visiting hours,' he said, in the same memorized manner, 'are from two to three.'

'Visiting hours? Is he under arrest?'

'You can talk to him at any time between two and three.'

'Well, but – why aren't they letting him go? They let me go.'

'I wouldn't know,' he said. 'Visiting hours are from two to three.'

'I'll wait for him,' I said.

He shrugged. 'Suit yourself.'

There was a bench along the opposite wall. I went over and sat down. A large clock on the wall behind the man at the desk read six-twenty. It was morning already, and I'd spent twelve hours in this building. I lit a cigarette and hitched around to a comfortable position on the bench, ready to spend twelve more. I had to talk to Walter, find out what was going on and what I was supposed to do about it all. I was an amateur at this game, lost without Walter.

At twenty-five minutes to seven, Jerry came wandering into the room from deeper in the building. He came over to me, and grinned and said, 'Do you know what the sentence for loitering is?'

'I'm waiting for Mr Killy,' I told him.

He glanced at the clock. 'See the second hand? There it goes, past nine. The next time it goes past nine, you'll be loitering. And I'll take you over to the desk there and book you for loitering. And then you'll spend thirty days in here. Do you think you'll like that?'

Leave Walter? But I'd be lost without him, I wouldn't know what to do. I watched the second hand go round, past twelve to one and two and three, and wondered if it was worth trying to out bluff him. I couldn't go alone into this town. The second hand went past four and five and six, and I looked up at him and knew he wasn't bluffing, that he would like nothing more than for me to still be sitting on that bench when the second hand reached nine again, so he could have an excuse for bringing me back inside again. As the second hand swept past seven I got to my feet, and as it was reaching out for nine I was pushing open the front door.

The sky was dirty with dawn, and the street looked old and abandoned. I went down the steps to the grey sidewalk, feeling the chill of early morning, and stood there on the sidewalk looking back at the building, until Jerry came out to the top step and stood grinning down at me. Then I moved, heading away to the left.

Where could I go? What could I do? They still had Walter; I had to rescue Walter. I had to save us both, break us both free of this town. But how could I do it?

I should call someone. Passing a closed drugstore, I noticed the metal blue telephone bell sign beneath the window, and I thought to myself, *I should call someone.*

Who? Should I call Washington? But I didn't *know* anybody in Washington, I'd never really met anyone at the Machinists building except Walter. I didn't know them and they didn't know me, and so far as they knew, Walter was working in a town where there were no problems at all.

Who then? Dr Reedman? The thought came to me, and I stared at it, offended. What the hell could *he* do?

I came to Harpur Boulevard and turned, and ahead of me I saw a diner open. I tried to keep concentrating on the problem – Walter was still in jail! – but that lit neon confounded me. I was starving. I hadn't really noticed the fact before; there'd been too much else to think about.

I tried to walk past the diner, feeling it was unfair to Walter for me to think of food at a time like this, but I couldn't. Shame-faced, I went in, and put away two orders of bacon and eggs, an order of wheatcakes and sausage, and three cups of coffee. After-ward I felt better both physically and mentally. Smoking as I took my time with the last cup of coffee, I relaxed somewhat and started to think.

Most of my thoughts, it seemed, ended with question marks.

What was happening to Walter at this very minute? What was going to happen to me? How were the two of us going to get ourselves away from this terrible town? And who had in reality killed Charles Hamilton, and did his death have anything to do with the presence in town of two representatives of the Machinists?

Up to a point, I could begin to make sense out of the sequence of events. First, Hamilton had been killed. Shot to death. The police had gone to his wife, and she had told them about us, but for some reason she had distorted our visit and said she hadn't known why we wanted to talk to her husband. Then they had come to us, coming in with drawn guns because we were mysterious strangers who had threatened a woman and then quite possibly murdered her husband. As soon as they found out we were from the Machinists, Willick went out to the car and phoned the news in and got his instructions from Fleisch; give the boys from the union a bad time. Fleisch had even hopped into his limousine and hurried down to get a look at us.

From the moment they knew who we were, I don't suppose Willick and the others had really thought of us as murder suspects any more, but they'd been busy following Fleisch's orders. They'd given us a bad time. They were still giving Walter a bad time. I could only assume they had eventually let me go because they realized I was too naïve to understand the bad time and was liable to get self-righteous on the long-distance phone after a while.

That much I could reason out for myself. But why Mrs Hamilton had lied I couldn't begin to understand. Why her husband had been killed, and by whom, I couldn't understand. How I could have lived for twenty-four years without knowing that any of this was possible I couldn't understand.

I glanced up at the clock, as I put my cigarette out in my saucer, and was baffled to see it read five minutes past eight. That couldn't be; it hadn't even been seven o'clock when I'd left police headquarters.

Time was slipping by me, time and time, and all I had was time. No knowledge, no power, no influence, no nearby friends, nothing but time; and even that was limited.

A sudden feeling of urgency came over me, as I realized how much time I'd let slip away since being released, and I hadn't yet done a thing, not a thing. I had to *do* something, I had to get to work somehow.

I thought again of making a phone call to somebody or other, but once again rejected it. Aside from the fact that I couldn't think of anyone worth telephoning at such an hour, the making of a phone call to ask for help was essentially a passive move, and I wanted to be active. I'd been released; now I had to make the most of it.

Well, what was there to do?

There was Mrs Hamilton, damn her. I could go find out just what she thought she was pulling.

I paid the check, left the diner, and started walking southward toward the motel. Full day had arrived by now, still damp with birth. Traffic got steadily heavier on Harpur Boulevard, all heading northward, deeper into the city. I walked along, feeling the casual glances of the people in the cars as they went by, wanting to turn and scream at them, 'Do you know what your town has *done* to me? Do you know, do you know?' I lit my last cigarette, and continued to walk.

The emotional jag brought on by my hours in jail hadn't really worn off yet. A whole host of emotions were all quivering close to the surface, popping out one after the other, swaying this way and that. Rage and fear and self-pity and confident joy and the calm of panic all ebbed and flowed within me, so that from one minute to the next I was never exactly the same person. But from one minute to the next I continued to walk southward toward the motel, stopping off to buy more cigarettes, and continued to be sure that what I was going to do was confront the Widow Hamilton.

I finally reached the motel. Going past the office, I glanced in and saw by the clock on the back wall that it was now nearly quarter to nine. I went on and tried the door of our unit, and it was unlocked.

Nothing was changed. The mess was still as it had been when Walter and I had been taken out of here. Even the keys to the

228

Ford were still on the writing table, next to where the typewriter had been before Jerry broke it.

I picked the typewriter up and put it back on the writing table and looked it over. Jerry had done a good job on it. The keys were bent far out of alignment, there was a gouge out of the platen, and the whole carriage was sprung. The typewriter, I knew, belonged to the union rather than to Walter, but the senseless vicious destruction was still sickening. I left the typewriter and went on about the room, straightening things up the best I could. I'm not sure why I took time to do that, rather than go straight out and head for the Hamilton house, but I was working under a kind of neatness compulsion or something.

My suitcase, an antique to begin with, was now beyond hope. The top had been half ripped off, and Jerry had managed somehow to pull one side of the handle out. I put the poor thing down and gathered up the spilled clothing. Shoe marks were on our white shirts, on our underwear and socks. There was a squat bureau in the room and I stowed everything into it, Walter's clothes intermingled with mine. Then I put the dirty clothes back into the laundry bag, the scattered stationery back into the drawer of the writing desk, and the sheets and blankets back onto the beds. When I got to Walter's briefcase, some impulse made me look through the papers in it. The letters from Charles Hamilton were gone, and somehow I had known they would be. So now Willick – and Fleisch – had the names of the twenty-five men who had signed the second letter.

They had to be warned. I sat down on the edge of my bed, and tried to remember at least one of the names; if I could warn one, he could warn the others. But I'd never really paid any attention to the names, and now I couldn't find one of them in my memory.

Well, Mrs Hamilton might know some of the men who'd signed, and she could tell me. She damn well had better tell me, that and also why she'd lied to Willick.

I left the motel unit at last, locked the door behind me, and climbed into the Ford. I backed out away from the parking space, and headed northward on Harpur Boulevard.

9

On 4th Street, it was yesterday again, hot and sunny, with a clear blue sky. The same unmoving quiet hung over the block today, with the impression of housewives watching television in darkened living rooms while their children were all out somewhere playing or swimming or taking hikes. I parked the Ford in front of the Hamilton house, went down the steps to the front door, and rang the bell.

There was no answer at first. I rang again, and waited, and then simply held my finger pressed to the button. At last, the door was yanked open, and she stared out at me with a kind of feral fear in her eyes. 'Go away! Don't come back here! Leave me alone!'

'I want to talk to you,' I said. I was calmer than I'd thought I'd be; her excess of emotion had served to settle mine somewhat.

'Go away!' She hissed the words, harsher than a whisper but not loud enough to be a normal speaking voice.

'Because of you, I spent the night in jail,' I told her, my voice rising. 'My friend is still there, and it's your fault. You lied to the police, and I want to know why.'

Her eyes flickered, and her face became troubled. 'I don't want any of this,' she said, speaking softly, more to herself than to me. 'I don't want any part of this.' Then, looking at me again: 'My husband is dead. Don't you understand? I have to be to the funeral parlour this afternoon.'

'I want to know why you lied.'

The screen door separated us, and she peered through it, begging me to go away, but I was too angry to feel compassion. Finally, she slumped against the door frame. Gazing dully at my tie, she said, 'I was frightened. I didn't want to say anything about the union, about Chuck's letter, I didn't want them to know. I was frightened and I didn't think, and then it was too late, I'd already said one thing and I couldn't change it.'

'You can change it now,' I said. 'My friend is still in jail. You can call down to police headquarters and tell them –'

'No, I can't, I –' She looked up at my face, and then beyond me, and her face suddenly changed. 'Leave me alone!' she shouted. 'I don't want to talk to you!' And she slammed the door.

I turned and looked up, and saw Jerry coming down the steps toward me, smiling and shaking his head. One of the others was standing up on the sidewalk. Jerry said, 'You just don't have a brain in your head, do you?'

'Did you hear her?'

He nodded, slowly and mockingly. 'I heard her. She told you to go away. I think that's just a great idea.' He reached out for my elbow. 'You come on along, sonny. That's twice now you've upset that lady.'

I pulled away from his reaching hand. 'But she told me why! She told me why she was lying, why she lied to you. She was afraid to mention the union, that's all. Ask her, she –'

This time he got the grip on the elbow, and squeezed down hard. 'Haven't you got any natural feelings? That woman's just been widowed, don't you know that? Now, you leave her alone.'

'But she was *lying* to you.'

He was pulling my arm one way, and I was pulling it the other. Now we both stopped, and he looked at me and sighed, and said, 'Do I have to tell Ben to come down here and help me with you?'

I looked up at the other man. 'Oh, is that Ben?'

'That's right,' said Jerry.

'He's the one that was slapping me, isn't he?'

Jerry grinned. 'I do believe he bumped into you a couple of times, yes.'

I peered up at the other man, remembering the helpless fear and anger I'd felt when he was slapping me. 'I had my glasses off then,' I said, 'so I couldn't see very well which one of them was doing it.'

Jerry tugged at my arm again. 'Why don't you come on up for a closer look?' he asked me.

There was a trembling in my stomach, as though I was going to do something rash and was preventing myself from knowing what it was. 'I'd like that,' I said.

We went up to the sidewalk and I looked at Ben. He was big and slightly sloppy, like all of them, like ex-Marines who'd gotten way out of condition, and his eyes were too tiny for his heavy jowly face. I looked at him, and he looked back at me with no expression at all on his face. But he expected me to do what my stomach was afraid of; he *wanted* me to do it. He wanted me to take a poke at him, or try to kick him, or jump at him.

So I didn't do any of that. I looked at him, carefully, and said, 'You're big to be a coward.'

Jerry laughed uproariously, and pounded my shoulder. 'Now, that's what I call spirit!' he shouted. 'Wouldn't you say so, Ben?'

'A punk,' said Ben. He turned his head slightly, and spat phlegm.

'Naw, Ben,' said Jerry. 'He's a college boy. Isn't that right, Paul?'

'That's right.'

'There, see? I like you, Paul,' Jerry admitted. 'I like you just fine. Don't you like him, Ben?'

'A punk,' said Ben again.

Jerry shrugged, and then turned serious. 'Well, now, Paul,' he said, 'I tell you what. You give your car keys to Ben, here, and then you ride along with me, how's about that?'

'What for?'

'Why, to see Captain Willick,' he said, as though that explained everything.

'Now, wait a second,' I said.

Ben hitched his pants up, and said, 'That's it. Resist arrest.'

'Aw, naw, Ben,' said Jerry. 'Paul's going to be a good boy.'

I said, 'I suppose you'll try to strip the gears.' I handed him the keys.

Ben took them without a word, and went away to the Ford. There was a pale blue Plymouth behind it, unmarked, and Jerry led me to it. We got in, and followed the Ford back down into town.

After a while I said, 'How'd you know I was up there, anyway?'

He turned to grin at me. 'Why, we followed you, Paul. Watched you eat your breakfast and everything. We take an *interest* in you, boy.'

'Oh.'

I turned away and looked out the window. How had I come to this? I wasn't the kind of person – I didn't lead the kind of life – where I would be followed, where the police would be constantly dragging me down to headquarters, where mindless pragmatists like Ben could slap me around to their heart's content. I was a student, and an employee, and an honest man. How had I come to this?

We went back to the familiar ugly building and around to the parking lot in back. Ben wordlessly gave me back the keys to the Ford, and the three of us went inside. This time, we stayed on the first floor and went to a long narrow room with a bench along one wall. 'You just have a seat,' Jerry told me. 'I'll be right back.'

I had a seat. Ben leaned against the wall by the door and smoked a cigarette, looking at nothing.

After a minute Jerry came back through the other door and motioned to me. 'The Captain wants to talk to you,' he said.

I went on in, followed by Ben. This was apparently the Captain's office, and was a smallish room dominated by his large wooden desk. Papers were littered all over the desk, and there were two filing cabinets to one side. A window looked out at the street.

Captain Willick was sitting at the desk, looking sour and angry. 'All right,' he said. 'What's your explanation?'

There was nothing to do but tell him the truth. I wasn't adept enough in this world to try evasions and cunning. So I said, 'Mrs Hamilton lied to you. I went up to ask her why.'

'You did, huh?'

'Yes. And she told me why. She was afraid to mention the union, and the letter her husband wrote. She didn't want anybody to know about her husband's connection with the union. Later on, when she realized it didn't mean anything any more, she thought it was too late, and she was afraid to admit she'd lied.'

233

Jerry shook his head in mock admiration. 'Ain't he a talker?'

'Shut up, Jerry.' Willick said it in a monotone, without raising his voice or turning his head. In the same voice, he said to me, 'I happen to run the police force around here, young man. I have the badge and the authority. When the time comes to question witnesses, I do it, or order somebody to have it done.' He pointed a rough finger at me. 'You have no authority, and no standing. You're just a smart-aleck youngster from Washington who thinks he can get away with a lot of lip. Now, we're still holding that gangster friend of yours, until he decides to co-operate, and by all rights we should still be holding you. But you're young and you don't seem to know any better, so I was easy with you, I let you go. But if I hear of you so much as opening your mouth to anyone in this town, anyone at all, sticking your nose in where you've got no business, you'll be back in the cooler so fast it'll make your head swim. Do I make myself clear?'

I nodded.

'All right, then,' he said. 'Get on out of here.'

I should have gone, and I wanted to go, but I stayed a little while longer. Willick had reminded me of Walter, still imprisoned here, and I was the only one who could possibly help Walter. And by now it seemed as though the only way I could get Willick to let Walter go was to let Willick know I could *prove* who had really killed Charles Hamilton. And to do that I needed information.

So I took my courage in both hands, braced myself, and said, 'I'd like to ask you a question.'

He looked at me, and his lips compressed. 'I think you're getting closer to that cell,' he said. 'But go right ahead and ask.'

'I'm not trying to be a smart aleck, I simply want to know. If you don't want to answer the question, just say so and I'll leave.'

'Cut the preamble.'

I took a deep breath, feeling that I *was* getting closer to that cell, but driven by Walter's dependence on me to ask the question anyway. 'Do you care at all who killed Charles Hamilton?'

The question seemed to surprise him. He didn't get mad, and he didn't answer right away. He gazed at me, frowning, and after a minute he said, 'What do you think?'

234

'You've assigned two men to follow me. You've got other men tied up giving Walter a bad time. But Walter and I didn't have anything to do with Hamilton's death, and I think you know it.'

Willick gnawed on his cheek and studied the mess of papers on his desk for a minute, and then he said, 'I'm going to answer your question. At five o'clock yesterday afternoon, Hamilton left the Work Boot building along with all the rest of the employees, and went into the parking lot next door. As he neared his car, four shots sounded, and he dropped down dead. There were about a hundred and fifty people in the parking lot at the time he was killed. More than half of them didn't even know it happened, and a lot of them just got into their cars and drove away. But every last one of those employees has been questioned, and believe me that was a lot of work. It added up to nothing, because none of them saw anything. There was a crowd walking through the lot, and anybody at all could have taken a gun out of his lunch bucket, plugged Hamilton, put the gun away in the lunch bucket and kept on going. All he had to do was be dressed like everybody else.'

He sighed, glanced at Jerry and Ben, then looked down at the desk again and went on: 'The slugs have been retrieved from Hamilton's body, all four of them, and have been sent to Albany. Hamilton's locker at the plant has been searched, and so has his car, and so has his home. All of his cronies have been questioned, including the bartender at the bar where he usually hung out. His girl friends have been questioned, and his wife has been questioned. As a result of questioning Mrs Hamilton, we learned about you two. You'd been acting suspiciously, so we brought you in. When we learned your partner was union muscle, you looked very promising, so we leaned on you a little bit to see what would happen. At the same time, we have been continuing the investigation on all other fronts. As for yourself, I'm pretty well satisfied now you're in the clear. But you were away from your partner at the time Hamilton was being killed. I tried to make you change your timing on that, to see how sure you were, and you were dead sure. So you're in the clear, but Killy isn't. Nevertheless, you feel a loyalty to him and an antagonism toward us,

235

so you're harping on Mrs Hamilton's story, even though what she told us won't break the case one way or the other. In the meantime, we haven't charged Killy with the crime, and won't, until and unless we have a case we can give the district attorney. But Killy isn't going to leave here until I'm sure in my mind about him.' He looked up at me at last. 'You satisfied now?'

I was, though not in the way he meant. I was satisfied that I knew as much about the murder as I was likely to learn from the police. As for his meaning, I wasn't completely satisfied. There were things he'd left out. Mr Fleisch, for instance, being at the motel in his Lincoln. Jerry breaking up our possessions. And he hadn't said whether he believed Mrs Hamilton was telling the truth or not. But to go into any of that would be to question his motives, to needle him in the soft spot, and I knew how quickly that could enrage him, so I said, 'I guess I'm satisfied. Thank you.'

'Sure. Get out of here.'

I got out of there, and climbed into the Ford, and drove back to the motel. On the way, I looked in the rear-view mirror and saw the blue Plymouth a block behind me. I clenched my teeth and stared through the windshield at the street.

Back at the motel, I paced and paced, this way and that across the room, around the furniture and back again, like an animal in a cage, like one of the big cats in the zoo. The urgency was on me stronger than ever, and I was so full of nervous energy I wanted to jump up and down. But there was nothing to do. I had hoped Willick would tell me something I could use for a lead, but he hadn't. Time inched by, hulking painfully past me, and I prowled the room, alive to dangers I could barely name. There was nothing to do, nothing to do. I wanted to race down Harpur Boulevard, roaring, bearing a burning torch. I wanted to leap and scream and hit out with my fists. But there was nothing to do, nothing to do. The Plymouth waited outside, and I waited for two o'clock.

Walter would tell me what to do. He had to, he had to give me direction. I walked and prowled, I jumped up on the bed and down on the floor again, but I built up the nervous energy faster than I could dispel it, and the sense of urgency grew stronger and stronger. I did sailor jumps in the middle of the room, I did push-ups, I got to my feet again and walked and walked, and I waited for two o'clock. Walter would give me direction.

10

I talked to Walter in the same room where I'd met Sondra Fleisch. Captain Willick had managed to get me about half-convinced that he possessed a sort of rough integrity, despite everything, but one look at Walter cured me of that idea.

Ben, or somebody else, had leaned a lot harder on Walter than they had on me. One eye was puffed and discoloured, encircled by bluish-grey flesh. He had small raw nicks along both sides of his jaw, as though he'd been hit more than once by someone wearing a ring, and his left thumb was swollen and red. His tie was gone, three buttons had been ripped from his shirt, and the handkerchief pocket of his jacket, where he kept his cigarettes, had been ripped half off and now dangled forlornly.

He was pushed in, not gently, by a pinch-faced man in uniform. The pinch-faced man went over to stand by the window and watch us, and Walter came up to the table, where I was sitting. When he smiled, I saw that one side of his mouth was puffy, too. He said, 'Hello, there. Welcome to the worker's Utopia.'

'What happened to your thumb?' That was all I could think about, for the moment; I didn't even bother to say hello first.

He looked at it, in mild surprise. 'Somebody stepped on it,' he said. He smiled, and added, 'By accident.'

'You should see what you look like,' I told him.

'I know.' He sat down, moving gingerly. 'Although I came out of a few football games in worse shape than this. But they aren't very bright around here. In a bigger town, they'd know enough not to leave any marks on me.'

'What do you want me to do, Walter? They let me go.'

'They told me. I'm glad of that. I'm sorry I got you into this.'

'That's all right.'

'I thought this was going to be a piece of cake, you know it?'

238

The unbruised side of his mouth smiled. 'It turned out to be a piece of shit instead.'

The uniformed man by the window said, 'Watch your language, you.' His voice was high and nasal, and he glared at us around his narrow nose.

Walter grinned at him, and said to me, 'If we converse in polysyllables, he won't comprehend.'

'Fine,' I said.

'Tell me the causation of the distress.'

'You don't know?'

He shook his head. 'The inquisition has been unidirectional thus far.'

'Oh. Well, our correspondent,' I told him, looking around for the right long words, 'is a decedent.'

His eyebrows raised. 'Was he assisted on the journey?'

'Via a quatrain of metallic ovoids, rapidly propelled.'

'And the decedent's espoused? There was something about a statement.'

'A prevarication resulting from panic. Additional panic ensued, fortifying the original prevarication.'

He nodded. 'Communication with our point of origin seems indicated. You remember Mr Fletcher?'

I'd never met any Mr Fletcher, but I knew what he meant. 'Of course,' I said.

He smiled again, and seemed to relax. 'The only thing we can do is wait,' he said. 'I'm not guilty of any crime, so they'll have to let me go sooner or later.'

'I know.' The long word game was over. There hadn't been any real need for it, but we had both enjoyed it, and both needed it in a way. We, Walter more than I, had been ground beneath an impersonal heel, and some dignity and self-respect are bound to be scraped off in the process. This small meaningless victory, using our superior vocabulary over the guard as a kind of code, helped, in a childish way, to restore some of the self-respect.

'How long have you been out?' he asked me.

'Since this morning. By the way, we may get some help in town here.'

239

'How's that?'

'I talked to a girl this morning, she works for the local paper.'

He frowned, studying me. 'I hope you were careful,' he said.

'She's a schoolmate of mine. She's on her six months too, at the local paper.'

'So what did you tell her?'

'Everything.'

He shook his head. 'I don't like that,' he said. 'It could boomerang.'

'She's on our side, Walter, she really is. She was shocked when I told her what had been done to us. By the way, she's Fleisch's daughter.'

He started, and said, 'By the way! For God's sake, Paul!'

'Now, wait a second. Don't prejudge her, will you?'

'And you gave her the whole story.'

'Why not?'

'I can hardly wait to see the paper,' he said.

'Maybe they can carry your picture in tomorrow's edition,' I told him.

'Just call Fletcher, will you? Reverse the charges.'

'Okay, I will.'

There was a pause, and then he said, 'You wouldn't have a cigarette on you, would you?' He flapped his dangling coat pocket and said, 'They took mine away from me.'

'Yeah, sure.' I reached for my cigarettes.

'No smoking in here,' said the guard. So he had his small meaningless victory, too.

Walter shrugged, and smiled at me. 'No imagination,' he said.

'They'll have to let you go eventually.'

'It's the occupational risk,' he said. 'Union organizers aren't always welcome. I should have checked this place out better before bringing you up here.'

'I don't mind,' I told him, and oddly enough at that moment it was true. Just being able to talk to Walter had done a lot to calm me and bring back my self-confidence. I said, 'Is there anything I should be doing? I've been walking around in circles.'

'Just call Fletcher,' he said. 'And then sit tight.'

'I went to see Mrs Hamilton,' I told him, 'but after that I couldn't think of anything else to do.'

Walter smiled at me, and reached out to pat my arm. 'You're a good friend, Paul,' he said.

I was embarrassed, and didn't say anything.

The guard said, 'Time to go.' He sounded pleased that it was so.

We stood up, and Walter said, 'Be sure to call Fletcher first thing.'

'Right.'

We shook hands, and I left the building as Walter was taken back upstairs. I'd left the Ford a block away. I walked over to it, lighting a cigarette on the way, got in, and drove back to Harpur Boulevard. After two blocks, I found an angled parking space near a drugstore. Leaving the car there, I went on into the store and got two dollars' worth of change, then closeted myself in a phone booth to make the call.

It took a while to get through, since I didn't know the number, but finally a cigar-smoker's voice said, 'Fletcher here.'

'My name's Standish, Mr Fletcher,' I said. 'I'm in Wittburg, New York, with Walter Killy.'

'Uh huh.' He sounded as though he was writing everything down as I said it.

'Our contact up here was murdered, Mr Fletcher, and they're holding Walter in jail.'

'Uh huh. Charged him?'

'No, they're holding him for questioning. They had me in there for twelve hours. Walter calls this a sewed-up town.'

'Uh huh. Where you staying?'

'The Wittburg Motel.'

'Uh huh. What's the nearest city to you?'

'Watertown, I think.'

'Never heard of it. Something bigger.'

'Syracuse.'

'Uh huh. Make me a reservation in that motel for tonight. Can you get in to talk with Walter?'

'Not till tomorrow. Visiting hours are from two to three.'

241

'Uh huh. All right, I'll be up tonight. Better reserve two double units.'

'All right, I will.'

'Good.' Click. He was gone.

I came out of the phone booth feeling at least two hundred per cent better. There had been something about the dry dispatch with which Mr Fletcher had handled the call that had instilled total confidence in me. Walter was a good man, but his field was union organizing, not legal shenanigans. I felt assured that when Mr Fletcher arrived Captain Willick and his bully boys would suddenly find the tables turned. Mr Fletcher would stand for no nonsense.

On the way out of the drugstore, I saw that the afternoon paper was already in the rack by the door. I grabbed a copy, paid the seven cents for it, and went out to the car. I had time left on the meter, so I sat there and looked for the story.

I found it on page three:

UNION TOUGHS QUESTIONED
IN HAMILTON SLAYING

by Sondra Fleisch

The investigation into the brutal slaying of McIntyre worker Charles (Chuck) Hamilton (Work Boot) took a dramatic turn late yesterday when it was learned that two men, said to be 'organizers' for the American Alliance of Machinists and Skilled Trades (see Ralph Kinney's column, page 6), had been apprehended at a motel just outside the city and taken to police headquarters for questioning. The two men, Walter Killy (38) and Paul Standish (24), both of Washington, D.C., were taken into custody after police, under the direction of Captain Edward Willick, learned from Charles Hamilton's widow, Mrs Ellen Hamilton, that they had visited the Hamilton home at 426 4th Street shortly before the fatal shooting, demanding to see Mr Hamilton. Learning that Mr Hamilton was still at work, in Building Three (Work Boot), they allegedly made threatening statements and then left.

'The two incidents,' Captain Willick said in an interview, 'may be no more than a coincidence. I am holding this man [Killy] until I know for sure that's all it is.'

The other union 'organizer', Standish, upon his release early this morning, stated, 'Those simpletons [the local police force] can't hold Walter. I'm calling Washington.' This and other vague threats were his only answer to the charges being considered against himself and his partner.

When asked why the sneering, defiant Standish had been released, Captain Willick stated, 'We believe the other man [Killy] is the brains of the pair. Standish is a recent recruit for this (cont. page 11, col. 4)

QUESTION TOUGHS
IN SLAYING
(fr. page 3)

union, and probably doesn't know the full story himself. At any rate, he's being watched.' Captain Willick added that if Standish were to try to leave the city 'he won't get far'.

The slaying of Charles Hamilton, the most vicious in the city's history, occurred yesterday afternoon in the East Parking Lot at Building Three. Mr Hamilton, a McIntyre employee for fourteen years and a veteran of the Second World War, was a local citizen who had lived his entire life, except for his Army tour, in Wittburg. 'Chuck was one of the best guys at the plant,' stated Robert Lincoln, a friend and co-worker of the murdered man, 'and if those two union guys killed him they deserve to be hung.' Henry Barton, a foreman at the Work Boot Section, stated that Mr Hamilton had always been 'a willing worker' and 'a real good friend'. 'He will be missed,' said another of the murdered man's friends, Stanley Macki, also of Work Boot.

The slaying reminded local citizens of the attempt made nine years ago by this same union to organize a local at the McIntyre plant. Citizens recalled that threats and intimidation had been the main tactics employed by the union in the earlier unsuccessful attempt. 'It didn't work the last time,' stated one worker, 'and it sure won't work this time.'

Leonard Fleisch, general manager of the McIntyre plant, has announced that the entire plant will be closed a half-day tomorrow morning so that the many friends and co-workers of Charles Hamilton may attend his funeral at nine-thirty A.M. in the Bertoletti Funeral Parlours at 500 Sarah Street.

11

Yes, it was red.

That old saying about seeing red when you're full of anger is true. I crumpled the newspaper and threw it to the floor of the car and stared out through the windshield, wanting to kick something, and the whole sunny world had turned a bruised red, as though thousands of blood vessels had broken beneath the skin of the day. Windows and doors and moving people were edged in trembling red, and red motes danced at the corners of my vision.

I saw Sondra Fleisch scream and wave her arms as I hurled her from a cliff. I bayoneted her, I hit her with furniture, I smashed my heel against her face. Beneath my clenching hands, her throat felt like leather, and her face was old and vicious.

I clung to the steering wheel with both hands. It was as though winds were shaking me, shaking the car. I stared out at the reddened day, betrayed, monstrously betrayed.

When I could, I caught hold of the rage and contained it, forcing it down inside me where it wouldn't show. Reaching up, I turned the rear-view mirror till I could see my own reflection in it, to see if what I felt was successfully concealed. My face looked a little strained, my eyes somewhat unusually intense, but that was all. Satisfied, I climbed out of the Ford.

A woman was walking toward me, pushing a stroller. I went up to her, saying, 'Excuse me.'

She stopped and looked at me blankly. 'Yes?'

'Do you know how I can get to Leonard Fleisch's house?' I gestured at the Ford. 'I've got those samples he wanted, but I can't find his house.'

'Oh,' she said. 'It's the big yellow house on the hill.' She pointed toward the workers' village section. 'You go right up McIntyre Road,' she told me, 'right to the top. Just beyond 12th

244

Street, you can't miss it. The big yellow house. Used to be the McIntyre place.'

'Thanks,' I said. 'Thanks a lot.'

'You're very welcome.'

I got back behind the wheel and pulled out of the parking space. I was facing the wrong way, so I decided to go around the block. As I was making the turn of Harpur Boulevard, I remembered that Jerry and Ben were still following me, and as I made the second right to the next block parallel to Harpur I saw their pale-blue Plymouth make the turn a block behind me.

They'd never let me get to Fleisch's house. But I had to go, I had to get my hands on Sondra Fleisch.

They were following me casually, unworriedly. I was an amateur, and they didn't really expect me to try to evade them. But an amateur fed by rage is something else again. I drove straight for two blocks, going very slowly, so that I hadn't even gone halfway down the first block when they made the turn behind me and came into sight. As I'd expected, they slowed down to match my pace.

At the second intersection, I came to a complete stop and looked in both directions. Then I crawled around the corner. They had dropped to a block back again, and were barely moving themselves. The instant I was out of their sight, I tromped hard on the accelerator. I swung hard right into Harpur Boulevard, cutting off a Dodge that yapped at me, and raced back southward a block and made another hard right turn. Then I slowed to a more sensible speed, and when I turned back into the street where I'd last seen them, they were out of sight. Nor had they appeared at all in my rear-view mirror.

I turned left and drove deeper westward, into the local slum, and crossed the Black River at the last possible bridge. Then I angled gradually back toward the section I wanted, eventually coming down 7th Street to McIntyre Road. I drove up McIntyre Road to the top and saw the big yellow house off to my right, with curving blacktop leading through a stand of fir trees between it and the road. It was a huge house, bulging with bay windows, built in turn-of-the-century style and constructed of

245

neat clapboard. A wooden sign on a post to the left of the black-top turn-off read:

Private Road
No Thoroughfare

Behind it, another wooden sign, this one nailed to a tree, read:

No Trespassing

I made the turn, spurred on by the two signs, and followed the curve through the fir trees to the house. The black Lincoln and a cream Thunderbird were already parked in front of it. I stopped the Ford next to them, gathered up the newspaper from the floor, folded it up carelessly, and climbed out of the car.

The mechanical work of driving, and the passing of time, had served to calm me down just a little. I was no longer feeling quite so unreasoning and total a rage. I burned now with a steadier fire, and so when I went up the steps to the broad front porch I didn't bull on into the house, but stopped and rang the bell.

I'd expected a maid or butler to answer the ring, but the middle-aged woman who came to the door was too expensively dressed to be either. She looked out at me, vague and distracted, frowning slightly through the screen door at me, and said, 'Yes? What is it?'

I had to gain entry. There was no sense shouting till I'd found the girl. As calmly as possible, I said, 'Is Sondra at home?'

'Who's calling, please?'

Sondra and I had a dual relationship. I used the more innocent one. 'I'm a classmate of hers.' But then I couldn't help adding, 'Paul Standish.'

The name, surprisingly, meant nothing to her. Perhaps she didn't read her daughter's journalistic efforts, if this was actually Mrs Leonard Fleisch, Sondra's mother, and I thought it probably was. She smiled cordially, and pushed open the screen door, and said, 'Come in. Sondra's just home from work.'

'Thank you.' I stepped across the threshold, and showed the newspaper. 'I've been reading something she wrote.'

'She's very good, isn't she?' Sondra's mother, surely.

246

'Very good,' I said.

'If you'll wait in the living room –? I'll tell Sondra you're here. Right through there. Paul, was it?'

'That's right. Paul Standish. Thank you.'

I went into the living room, an outsize room with bay windows in two walls. The walls were all complicated by mouldings and bric-a-brac, and sliding doors were closed in the wall to the right. Heavy maroon ceiling-to-floor draperies flanked the windows, and the carpet was busy dark Persian. But the furniture was foam-rubber modern, in shades of tan, with plain black iron legs. Whatever furnishings had originally been in this room, complementing the room's style, had been gutted out, and this sleek fragile plain styleless junk put in its place. There wasn't a stick of it that wouldn't have looked perfect in Walter's office, just as his trophy case would have looked perfect here, in the corner between the bay windows.

I didn't sit down. I stood in the middle of the room, facing the entranceway through which I'd come and in which I expected to see Sondra any minute.

But she came in from the other direction, through the sliding doors. They rumbled apart and there she was, smiling there, like an elfin female Orson Welles. If I had expected guilty embarrassment or hot denials or fevered explanations or sullen defiance or icy aloofness – if I had expected anything expectable – I was wrong. She stood posed for a second, slender well-groomed vixen's body framed between the doors which her hands still held, her head ducked just slightly as she smirked at me, her eyes glittering at me through lowered lashes. Then in a voice hardly able to control its exultation, she half-whispered, 'What did you think of it?'

Now I could explode, now. 'You vicious little slut! You lying conscienceless –'

'Shush shush shush shush.' She fluttered her hands at me and came gliding the rest of the way into the room. 'Don't shout so, you'll bring Daddy down on us.' She slid the doors closed.

I inhaled, and started again. 'You egotistical snob! You two-faced brat! You illiterate incompetent idi –'

247

'Now, wait! Now, wait just a minute!' Something in my tirade had finally hit home. 'What do you mean, incompetent? You take that back!'

I waved the newspaper in her face. 'You stupid nonsensical little bitch, don't you realize you could be *sued* for something like this?'

'Oh, but that's where you're wrong! I *can't*!' She chortled in her joy. 'That's the best part of it, don't you see?'

The wall of my rage was breaking down, battered by a baffling indifference. I stared at her and said, 'What in God's name are you talking about?'

'Give me that paper.' She pulled it out of my hand, scattered the pages around on the floor, and retained only the sheet containing on one quarter page three and on another quarter page eleven. 'Look at it,' she said: 'Show me one word that's libellous or slanderous or any other kind of ous you can think of. Look for instance. "Sneering, defiant Standish." You *were* sneering, darling, at all those awful clods of policemen. And you were certainly defiant. You still are. And you did call the police simpletons and say they couldn't hold your friend.'

'I didn't say anything about calling Washington.' From belligerent rage, I had somehow been turned to a sullen defensiveness.

'I bet you did, though.' She looked up at my face, and laughed when she saw she'd been right. 'You see? Now, admit it, isn't that a first-class piece of writing?'

She was proud of it, actually proud of it, and she wanted me, her victim, to compliment her on her skill. She gazed up at me like a cross between a well-fed cat and a well-petted puppy, and she asked me to tell her how deftly and skilfully she had slipped the knife into my back.

I had come to this house boiling with rage, wanting only to shout at Sondra Fleisch till I felt better, and if I had been met by either guilt or defiance, in any of their forms, I could have accomplished my mission with no trouble at all. But this praise-demanding pride of hers, like one of those megalomaniac scientists pleased with his 'clean' bomb, had thrown me com-

248

pletely off the track. I think there must be many people like that in our world today, people who are not at all concerned with any moral judgement about the work they do but are interested only in how skilfully the work is done. And if the victim objects – particularly if he objects on some sort of quaint and antiquated grounds of morality – they are simply baffled by his bad form in not saying, instead, 'Touché!'

The realization that Sondra was one of these conscienceless moderns – and that my rage could never do more than baffle her – jolted through my mind, and for a second I was all at sea. I didn't want justice in this house – I knew better than that, at least – but I did want revenge. I had wanted to make Sondra Fleisch understand just how heinously she had acted, so I could leave with the satisfying knowledge that she would now be gnawed by a bad conscience. But that goal, now that I had seen her, was obviously unattainable. Still, I wanted revenge, and suddenly I saw how to get it. Only one of my invectives had really stung her, only one.

All right. There's more than one way to get even with a cat. 'As a matter of fact,' I said, 'that *wasn't* a first-class piece of writing. I'd say it was a little closer to fourth-class.'

Her smile flickered and faded, and she stepped backward a pace from me. A shadow crossed her eyes as she studied me, trying to see if I really meant it. Then the shadow left, and she said, 'Oh, you're just miffed.'

'No, really,' I said, now all calm and helpful, no longer the indignant moralist. 'Here, let me show you.' I took the paper back from her, scanned the article, and pointed. 'Here, for instance. Look at this. "This, and other threats, were . . ." You see? You got the person wrong. It should be this *was*, not this *were*.'

She frowned at it, trapped, and then shook her head impatiently. 'It reads better the other way,' she said.

'No, it doesn't. It caught my eye right away. Oh, and another part.' I adjusted the paper. 'Here in the first paragraph, where you meant to say that Walter and I threatened Mrs Hamilton, but where you really say the *police* threatened her.'

She read that paragraph over and over, and now vertical lines had appeared between her brows, and all at once her cheekbones seemed more prominent. She slapped at the paper with her hand, finally, and turned away from me, saying, 'That's just being picky. You can see what I *meant*.'

'It's sloppy writing,' I told her. 'It doesn't matter if people can figure out what you were trying to say or not, the important thing is it's sloppy writing.' I turned the paper around, to page eleven. 'And the same over here, where you say, "The slaying of Charles Hamilton, the most vicious in the city's history . . ." Vicious what?'

She turned back, frowning more deeply, not knowing what I was talking about.

'You say that Charles Hamilton is a vicious *something*.' I told her, 'but you don't say *what*.'

All of her pleasure had been wiped away by now. 'What are you, some sort of language purist?'

'Well, if you're going to write, you really ought to get your sentence structure straightened out.' I could risk a smile now. 'I guess it doesn't matter much on a little paper like the *Beacon*,' I said, 'but you wouldn't want to try for the big time yet. In fact, maybe you shouldn't paste this story in your scrapbook.'

I had hit home. She yanked the paper out of my hand and threw it to the floor. 'You better get out of here,' she said. 'If I told Daddy who you were –'

'Maybe you ought to do a second draft from now on,' I said.

'I did *three* drafts on that,' she said angrily, and then caught herself. 'I'm going for my father,' she said.

'I'll leave.' I glanced at the paper scattered all over the floor. 'You can have that copy,' I told her. 'I'm all done with it.'

I turned away and started out of the living room, almost bumping into a man on the way in. He was perhaps in his late forties, a stout jovial man with pale kindly eyes. He looked at me, smiling in polite surprise, and said over my shoulder to Sondra, 'Well, now. Who's this?'

'Daddy,' she said, and her voice was acid, 'I'd love you to meet Paul Standish.'

The name didn't connect for just a second, and in that second I stuck my hand out and smiled and said, 'I'm very glad to meet you, sir. I'm a classmate of Sondra's.'

'Well, well,' he said, smiling more broadly, and took my hand. Then the smile started to falter, and he looked at me more closely.

'That's right, sir,' I said. 'I'm sneering, defiant Paul Standish, the union tough your daughter's been writing about. Did you read the article?'

'Yes,' he said doubtfully. His eyes were harder and colder now; he was wondering what I was doing here.

'Not very well written, of course,' I said, 'but it does show promise. By the time she graduates, I bet she'll be ready for a full-time job with the *Beacon*.'

'I'm afraid,' he said carefully, 'I don't under –'

'He was mad,' his daughter told him. 'He came up here to holler at me for betraying him.'

He stepped backward from the entranceway. 'I think you'd better leave,' he said.

'Of course, sir.' I stepped past him, then turned around to say, 'I'm sorry, but when I get back to school I'll have to tell Dr Reedman what happened to me here.' I looked past him. 'I'm sorry, Sondra, but you wouldn't expect me to lie for you.' I turned toward the door.

He said, 'Just a minute,' and I turned back to face him. He was studying me as though puzzled. 'Are you really a student at Monequois?'

'Of course. Didn't Sondra tell you?'

He looked at his daughter, and she said, 'I guess he is. I've seen him around the halls sometimes.'

'I confess,' he said to me, 'I don't understand. Are you a graduate, is that it?'

'No, I'm on my six months, the same as Sondra.'

'With that – that union?'

'It's a legitimate job, Mr Fleisch. We don't sell dope in schoolyards. It's a far more honest and moral job than the job your daughter did on me, or the job your police department did on me.'

251

'I think we should talk,' he said. 'Do you have time?'

'Yes, I do.'

'Come into the living room. No, Sondra, you'd best stay.'

'I have other things to do,' she said angrily.

'I want you to hear this, too,' he told her. To me, he said, 'Sit down in the living room. I'll be right back. There's something I want to show you.'

'All right.'

We waited in hostile silence in the living room, not looking at one another. At one point, I picked up the section of newspaper with the story in it, and folded it up. 'I'll need it after all,' I said. 'For Dr Reedman.' I tucked it away in my pocket.

She looked at me with angry contempt. 'Why don't you go to hell?' Then she stared out the window again.

When Mr Fleisch came back into the room, he carried a maroon cardboard case with him, tied with its own string. 'I don't think you know very much about that union you work for, young man,' he said. 'When I came to this position here, I was aware of the fact that the Machinists had tried to organize a local in this area once before. I had the feeling, now the plant was under new management, they might try again, so I've been keeping a file of newspaper clippings, all about the Machinists. I think you ought to look at them.' He untied the string, opened the flap of the case, and handed it to me, 'They're all jumbled up in there,' he said. 'There isn't any real order to them.'

I took the case from him. 'Thank you.' As he sat down across from me, his hands folded in his lap, I started to read.

Most of the clippings had to do with various Congressional committee investigations into labour unions. Men like Jimmy Hoffa and Dave Beck had captured most of the headline space in those investigations, but a number of other unions had come under the Congressional surveillance as well, including the Machinists. Machinist officials were charged, in the halls protected by Congressional immunity, with misappropriating welfare funds and dues receipts. Several locals in larger cities like New York and Chicago had been shown to be largely staffed by men with criminal records. Elections in many of the same locals

252

had turned out to be rigged and fraudulent. At least three local executives in as many parts of the country had continued to draw their union salaries while serving jail terms, two for gambling and one – in Detroit – for smuggling. All three cases were in the late forties, the most recent being 1949. An editorial clipped from a Southern newspaper – about half the clippings were from the eight Deep South states – stated: 'The Machinists is, in its way, more dangerous than any Hoffa or any Torio, for it is faceless. There is no evil genius of the Beck-Hoffa-Torio type at the helm of this union, who can be readily exposed and stripped of his powers. The Machinists is run by a faceless committee of per- haps a dozen men, each as corrupt and venal as anyone in organized labour. Their number gives them a kind of anonymity, which means protection from the wrath of Public Opinion. There is no one name or one face to put before the Public as the archi- tect of evil. Before the labour movement can truly be purged, this unholy combine which now holds the Machinists in its grip must be broken and scattered.'

I read through all the clippings, and then I looked over at Mr Fleisch. 'This is selective, isn't it?'

'Oh, of course. The union can do a good job of telling its own good points. That in your hand is my rebuttal.'

'I see two kinds of crimes here,' I said, tapping the case. 'The proved, and the charged. Proved crimes in every case occurred five to ten years before the committee hearing. Charged crimes, with no proof, were supposed to be current. But I don't see any clippings about indictments or trials or verdicts. Just charges, in Congressional hearings.'

He smiled palely. 'They are a clever group, the Machinists,' he said. 'They've covered their tracks very well.'

'I see here,' I went on, 'where the Machinists insisted they'd already purged themselves, gotten rid of the criminal elements, and so on. But I don't see any proof they were lying.'

'As I said,' he told me, 'they've covered their tracks very well.'

I shook my head. 'I'm sorry, but I don't see that you've proved your case. You've selected the best you could find for your point of view from the hostile press, and you still haven't proved your case. There isn't a union in the country that hasn't had to have a house-cleaning every once in a while.'

'I believe,' he said, 'that it would not be in the best interests of the workers here to join the Machinists.'

'Why not let them decide for themselves? That's a method called Democracy.'

'Frankly,' he said, 'I'd rather not chance it. I'm still a relatively new broom here. My name isn't McIntyre. In fact, to some the name Fleisch sounds positively Jewish, though I'm German. The point is that I haven't yet managed to obtain the loyalty of the workers the way it was given to the McIntyres.'

I remembered Hamilton's letter, and the signatures, and Walter's statistics. 'I can well believe that,' I said.

He spread his hands, an affable gesture. 'Now, see here,' he said. 'I'm going out of my way to explain the situation to you. You're young, you're inexperienced, you've been thrust into this mess without knowing what was going on. I want you to see my side of it – and Sondra's side, too – and I want to try to make you understand that perhaps you aren't on the side of the angels after all.'

I tapped the case again. 'Even granting everything in here is true,' I said, 'which I don't grant, but even so, what's the alternative? What's your side of it? Your side of it is that you have corrupted the local police force to do your bidding –'

'Now, just a minute!'

'You came down to the motel in that Lincoln parked out there, and told your cops to rough the union boys up a little. They smashed a typewriter and ripped my suitcase and generally wrecked the place.'

'I'm honestly sorry to hear that,' he said.

'Why? You ordered it. I went to jail and got slapped around – You should see *Walter*. They blackened his eye and cut his face and stepped on his hand. And you ordered all of that, too.'

'I most certainly did not. If your friend Walter tried to resist –'

'Come off it.' I got to my feet. 'It doesn't matter to you whether the union is good or bad. The union wants to take a part of your power away from you, and it's as simple as that.'

He smiled benignly. 'Then why am I troubling to justify myself to you?'

'Because I'm a babe in the woods. And you're a civilized wolf, so you feel compassion. But your compassion is cheap stuff, and it can't buy my loyalty.'

'I'm not trying to buy your loyalty,' he said. The smooth surface was beginning to be ruffled just a bit. 'I was trying to make you understand the facts. If all you want is to be stubborn and bullheaded, you're welcome to it.'

'Do you care who killed Charles Hamilton?'

His head shook slightly. 'What?'

'I asked you if you cared that Charles Hamilton was murdered. Do you care who killed him?'

'It's the job of the police department to find out who killed that man,' he said indignantly. 'What on earth are you talking about?'

'A man was alive. Now he's dead. You've used the fact of his death to give Walter and me a bad time, but does his death mean anything else at all to you? Don't you care that he's dead?'

The hands spread out again, and he said, 'But I didn't even *know* the man.'

'You've got to *care*. Somebody's got to *care*.'

'Well, I imagine his wife cares. And his children, if he has any?'

'He didn't have any,' said Sondra. Her tone was blank, noncommittal.

'I don't see the point,' admitted Fleisch.

'Don't you remember Donne? "No man is an island, entire of itself; every man is a piece of the continent, a part of the main; if a clod be washed away by the sea, Europe is the less, as well as if a promontory were, as well as if a manor of thy friends or of thine own were; any man's death diminishes me, because I am involved in mankind; and therefore never send to know for whom the bell tolls; it tolls for thee."'

'Oh yes,' he said, 'Hemingway used that.'

'Is that all that means to you? A parlour game. Guess who used this famous quote. Next we'll try The Song of Solomon: Lillian Hellman, Peter de Vries, John van Druten –'

'I think I've heard enough,' he said. He was no longer at all genial.

'Yes,' I said. 'I think we all have.'

I went back out to the Ford, having accomplished next to nothing. I'd met the chiefest enemy in his own den, but if I'd bearded him there, neither of us had noticed it.

I turned the Ford around and drove back into town and through to the other side and the motel. First I went into the office to make the reservations for Mr Fletcher and his party, and then I went into the unit.

There was nothing more to do, nothing at all, not until Mr Fletcher arrived. I moped around the unit a little while, and then got out the paperback Walter had been reading. It was a private-eye mystery, and as I read it I realized that the world in this book was the one I'd suddenly been thrust into. The difference was that the private eye in the book *knew* he was living in that world, knew what it expected and how to react. Whenever a knock came at his door, he reached for his trusty .45 instead of the knob, because in his world it wasn't ever the Fuller Brush man or a neighbour on the other side of that door, it was always Trouble.

But that wasn't *my* world. In *my* world, when somebody knocked on the door I opened it, and it was somebody wondering what tomorrow's assignment in French was, or it was somebody selling magazine subscriptions, or it was somebody bringing a six-pack for a quiet evening's bull session.

I read for about twenty minutes, and then a knock sounded at the door. I was startled by it, and dropped the book. But then I felt like an idiot, too caught up in the fictional world of the book and in my own dramatizing of the situation in a town more sordid than dangerous. I got up from the bed and opened the door.

Jerry came in, moving fast, pushing me back out of the way. Ben came in after him, and another man, the one who'd been along on the first police trip here. They shut the door and Jerry looked at me with mock-sadness and said, 'You know something, Paul? You're the slowest learner I have ever come across, do you know that? First you ditch Ben and me, and then you go up and bother Mr Fleisch. Now, when are you going to start getting some sense?'

'What's this, another trip to Captain Willick?'

'Oh, no. No, indeed. You *got* your last warning.'

The third man had come around to my left as Jerry was talking, and now he suddenly jumped at me and grabbed my arms. He stood behind me, holding my arms bent back, cupped inside the crook of his arms, and Jerry said to me, 'You know where we are right now, Paul? We're in the basement at head-quarters, playing poker.'

Then he stepped aside, and Ben started hitting me.

12

A cold wet cloth stung my face. I twisted away from it, jabbing my arms around, and a thick hempen knot turned in my guts, scraping the walls of my stomach with sharp pain. I stopped moving, tensed in an awkward half-turned position, my arms angled up into the air, afraid to move again because of the pain. A gravelled voice said, low. 'Take it easy, mister.'

Then I opened my eyes, and looked into a face I'd never seen before, and beyond it a ceiling. The face was very close, looking down on me, and I saw it with such bright clarity that every single stiff spike of grey beard stubble on his leather-wrinkled cheek stood out plain as a pyramid on a desert, making its own shadow. The nose, I saw, was knobby and twisted as a shillelagh, with great oval nostrils clogged with black hairs. The eyes were huge and watery and brown, like the eyes of an old dog, and though he wore no glasses I clearly saw the spectacle-dents on either side of his nose, way up close to the eyes. The forehead was seamed and cracked a thousand times, like the instep of an old boot, and was high and broad, with prominent temples and wispy straggles of grey hair lying limp down across it. Farther back were jug-handle ears, with centre holes sprouting more hair. A broad mouth with cracked dusky lips was stretched in a reassuring smile, showing uneven yellow-stained teeth in a ragged line along the top, too-even bright white teeth in a straight line along the bottom.

I looked at this face, and my first thought, before all else, was that it was a lonely face, the lonely face of a lonely man who had led a lonely life for more time than I had existed. After that came the thought that it was an old face, and the thought that it was a friendly face, and the thought that it was, in its way, a magnificently ugly face.

The broad lips moved, the teeth clacked together, and the

gravelly voice said, 'You shouldn't ought to move, mister. Just take it easy.'

Warily, afraid of the knot in my stomach, I relaxed again onto my back. I was lying on the floor in the motel room, near the foot of the two beds. I remembered Ben, his face blank with concentration, his fists slamming into my stomach, left and right and left and right, and how he'd seemed to know just when to back out of the way so the stream of my vomit would miss him and land on the floor. And after that the fists had crisscrossed my face, working more delicately because he hadn't wanted me unconscious yet. And when he had wanted me unconscious, how he had taken the full swing, and how the fist had grown larger and larger in my red vision, making me think of freight trains, and run over me and smashed me into nothingness until the rough texture of the cold wet cloth had stung my face.

The cloth came into my view now, held in the old man's gnarled hand. It was a white washcloth, stained brownish-red in places. 'I'll try not to hurt you,' he said, and the cloth came down and touched my face again. It stung, as before, but I held against it, refusing to pull my head away.

After a while, he went away to rinse the cloth out, and I lay breathing slowly, because when I breathed too deeply the knot twisted and scraped all over again. He came back, and stroked my face some more with the cloth, and then he said, 'Do you think you can get up on the bed?'

'I don't know.' My throat ached, too, as though I'd been breathing through my mouth for an incredibly long time, so when I spoke the best I could do was a hoarse whisper.

'I'll help you,' he said, and came around to grasp me under the arms. He was a lot stronger than I'd have supposed. Getting to a sitting position was terrible, because of the hempen knot, but after that it was easier. We didn't try to get me to my feet; I crawled on my knees around to the side of the bed while he stayed with me, his arms in my armpits holding me up. Then he lifted me, as I clung to the bed covers, and rolled me onto the bed. I wound up on my back, gasping, salt tears stinging my eyes from the pain in my stomach, and he stood back and nodded in

259

approval. 'That's good,' he said. 'Some of Fleisch's bully boys done this to you, I guess.'

'Police,' I croaked. 'Ben. Jerry. Another man.'

He shook his head. 'Don't know the police,' he said. 'Don't care to. Had a brother on the force, once. Shot by a bootlegger out of Canada. Different men down there now, different *kind* of men. Where's it hurt?'

'Stomach.'

'Excuse the imposition.' He smiled as he said the unlikely word, and then he unbuttoned my shirt, unzipped my trousers, and pushed the clothing out of the way so he could see my stomach. His wide mouth frowned and he shook his head. 'All bruised up,' he said. He touched me, and I shrank away from fire. 'Hurts,' he commented. He stuck a big knuckle in his mouth and gnawed on it, looking down at me. 'Expect we'd better get a doctor,' he decided at last. He glanced around and said, 'No phone? No. Well, don't you go anywhere.' He nodded at me, smiling that slow wide smile of encouragement, and went away from my line of vision. I heard the door open and close, and then I closed my eyes and decided not to be conscious any more. It was too much struggle to be awake.

Probing hands, burning the inside of my stomach with lit cigarettes, drove me back awake. I opened my mouth and screamed, a higher, louder sound than I'd known I was capable of, until a hand with a taste and smell and consistency of leather clamped down on my mouth. I stared up past it, goggle-eyed, and saw the old man again, shushing me. 'We don't want no attention, mister,' he said. 'You just got to keep it in.'

I kept it in. In and out of my vision bobbed a small round bald head wearing wire spectacles, while fire and ice coursed through my stomach. The old man kept his hand on my mouth, just to be on the safe side, and the smell and taste of leather filled my senses.

After a while, the round bald head bobbed up again, and said to the old man, 'Not a thing broken, would you believe it?'

'Some of them are experts,' said the old man. 'I remember my brother telling me about that kind of thing. Bootleggers working each other over, and hardly leaving a mark.'

'Well, these men left plenty of marks, I'll say that much for them.' His bright small eyes looked down at me, and he said, 'I'll tape you up around the middle, make it easier for you to get around. Bandage up that face a little bit. You won't look like new, but you'll run pretty good.'

He did as he'd said he would do. In the taping he had to move me around a lot, and I came close to passing out a few times, but I never did. I wished I could. Then he touched a little wet brush to various spots on my face, put patches of bandage on me, and nodded in satisfaction at his work. He and the old man went over by the door and murmured, and then the doctor left and the old man came back to the bed, dragging the armchair over with him. 'You owe me six bucks,' he said.

I tried to reach for my wallet. 'I've got it right –'

'Oh, now cut that out.' He pushed my arm down again. 'We got other things to talk about. Pay me tomorrow.'

'All right.' My voice was still a whisper, still hoarse, but less painful. Saliva was returning to my mouth, and now the major pain there was when I tried to swallow.

'My name's Jeffers,' he told me. 'Gar Jeffers. I guess your name must be Standish.'

I nodded.

'In that piece in the paper,' he said, 'they give where you was staying. I took a chance on them getting at least one thing right in that story, and come on down to talk to you. The door was open a little bit, and I seen you laying there. That's how that part happened.'

I nodded again. It was easier than trying to talk.

'Now, I want to talk to you about Chuck,' he went on. 'They killed him, and he was one of the better young men working around the world today. Chuck Hamilton was my good friend, and I was proud to work beside him. And you know and I know they ain't going to do anything about the one that did it to him. But I'll be damned to hell fire eternal if I'm going to just sit back and twiddle my thumbs and say tch, tch, what a shame. Do you know what I'm talking about?'

Another nod.

'That's good. Now, I know this isn't really any concern of yours, you never knew Chuck or anything about him. It's up to me, and I know it. But I don't think this is the kind of job I know very much about, so I come around to you to ask for some help.'

'It matters,' I whispered. I shook my hands in the air. 'Nobody *cared*. It wasn't right that nobody cared.'

He smiled in gratification. 'I was hoping that's the way you'd be,' he said, 'but there's so little of that left in the world any more. Everybody thinks like bootleggers nowadays, and I figured anybody who'd go up against the devils around here like the way you and Mr Killy done, you had to have a lot of good in you.'

'I can't help,' I whispered, embarrassed by what he'd said. 'I can't even help myself.'

'I figure you're young and smart,' he said, 'and that's maybe half the battle right there. And I know the people and some things about what's been going on, and maybe that's the other half. Maybe we could team up and whup them.'

We could team up, and Ben could whup us both with one hand tied behind his back, but I felt an irrational pleasure at the idea of siding with Gar Jeffers. He had such a simple clear straightforward view of things. I had been wallowing ever deeper in emotional confusion, but I had the feeling confusion couldn't survive very long in the presence of this old man.

'Now,' he said. 'You remember that letter we all sent you, with our names on it.'

'I remember. But I think they got it. If it isn't in Walter's briefcase –'

'That thing over there? Hold on.' He went over and looked through the briefcase. 'Nope. Gone.'

'So they've got your names.'

He winked, and the wide mouth stretched wider in a sly grin. 'I retire in three weeks,' he said. 'What do you suppose they can do to me?'

'Look what they did to me.'

'You're a stranger in town, no kin or friends to protect you.'

'What about Mr Hamilton?'

'Well, now.' He came back and sat down beside the bed again.

262

'That's right, isn't it? Well, I've lived pretty near sixty-five years already. That's quite a bunch.'

'Yes.'

'All right, then. They've got the letter. I'll have to let the word around tomorrow. But for tonight, let me just tell you what I know. You remember in that letter, the one you people sent up, you all asked for newspaper stories or things like that. Well, there wasn't any newspaper stories, and there wouldn't be, and I guess now you know why.'

I nodded.

'So Chuck figured maybe he could look around here and there, turn over some rocks, and maybe get some facts for you people. And yesterday, on the job, he was talking like he had something. You know how a man will do, he'd tip me the wink and grin a bit and say he had some news for everybody, soon as the boys from the union came. I told him to keep it low until then, no sense looking for trouble, and he said he surely would.'

I chewed that over, but I didn't like the implications. There was an easy conclusion to jump to, but I didn't care for that conclusion. I tried to explain why to Jeffers. 'I met Mr Fleisch,' I whispered. 'I don't like him, he's smooth and bland and he doesn't have any conscience. But I can't see him killing Hamilton or ordering him killed. He has a big envelope full of bad press about the union, and a line of patter to go with it. He's ready for the public fight, with both hands full of mud. I don't think he'd be set up that way if he was afraid of the kind of mud that could be thrown back at him.'

'Well, maybe what Chuck found out was a great big blob of mud he would be afraid of.'

'But it's too extreme. He's a precise, cautious man, he really is. He wouldn't *kill* somebody just to keep his job. Hamilton would have had to know something that would put Fleisch in jail, at the very least.'

'It wouldn't surprise me a bit,' he said.

'But he doesn't *act* that way, like a man with something that terrible to worry about.' I shook my head back and forth, angry at my inexperience in this sort of thing. 'I don't know, I don't know, maybe I'm wrong, but it just doesn't make sense.'

'Now, take it easy, Mr Standish,' he said, and laid a gentling hand on my arm. 'Just take it slow and easy for a little while.'

The use of the formal name got to me. He was forty years older than me, and he called me *Mister* Standish. I felt even more like an imposter, playing detective, playing grown-up. 'I just don't know,' I whispered. 'I just don't know.'

'Now, just relax there a minute and don't get het up, and let me talk at you for a minute. I've been thinking about what happened, and what maybe I could do about it, and this is what I come up with: Chuck learned something, found something out. I know that as well as I know my own name. Now, see if this don't make sense. If he found out something, that means there's something there to find. And if *he* could find it, that means *we* can find it. And once we do find it, why, then we'll know who killed Chuck. Does that make sense to you?'

'I suppose so.'

'You're tired,' he said. 'Why don't I come back tomorrow morning, and we can –'

'No. Please, I'm sorry,' I closed my eyes, and shook my head back and forth. 'You're right, we've got to think this out. There's so many of them, and they're so much better at this than we are – we probably don't have much time.'

'You're most likely right about that,' he said. 'So what do you think we ought to do first?'

'I just wish I could think straight.' I covered my eyes with my right hand, and tried to force my brain to work. I could see through Hegel, for God's sake, so why couldn't I do some constructive thinking on this problem? After a minute, I whispered, 'There's one more thing we ought to say. Besides that there's something there to find, and it's possible to find it. We also know that the killer *knew* Hamilton had found it. Right?'

'Absolutely,' he said.

'All right. Then there were two ways the killer could have learned that. Either Hamilton tipped his hand in his snooping around, asking questions of the wrong person or something like that, or one of the people he talked to yesterday afternoon passed the word on to the killer.'

'1 don't see how that could be,' he said. 'I don't know of anybody he talked to except to me, and I told him right off to keep mum.'

'Are you sure he didn't talk to anybody else? Maybe before he talked to you.'

He frowned, doubling the creases and lines of his face. 'I can't be sure,' he admitted. 'But even if he did, it would have been just to some of the other boys what signed that letter, and it wouldn't have been any of them, carrying tales up to the management.'

'Maybe one of them mentioned it to somebody else.'

'No, sir, Mr Standish, I'll stake my life on it, they'd know better.'

'Well, you know them, Mr Jeffers, I don't.'

'Oh, come on now, forget that Mr Jeffers stuff. An old lag like me. Call me Gar if you don't want me to get all choked up.'

I glanced at his smiling ugly face, and winced in embarrassment. He had called me Mr Standish twice. I should have been the one to say, 'Call me by my first name,' but politeness and protocol and the social graces have never been my strong suit. Even coming in second, I still felt awkward when I said, 'Then you ought to call me Paul.'

'That I will, Paul,' he said, and nodded hugely, and smiled at me in comradeship. 'And pardon me for interrupting your train of thought.'

'No train. Barely a handcar. But what I was going to say, you know those other workers and I don't, so I'll go along with you, at least for now. That means we can concentrate on the other possibility, that Hamilton exposed himself in his snooping around. Do you have any idea where he did that snooping, who he talked to or where he searched?'

He shook his head slowly, staring past me at the far wall. 'No, sir, I don't. I didn't even know he was up to anything, not until yesterday.'

'Then we'll have to go it blind. Try to figure out how Hamilton thought, where he would have gone and who he would have talked to.'

'Well, sir,' he said, 'that's where I need help. I couldn't even begin to make a guess about a suggestion of a perhaps.'

'If I worked for a company,' I whispered, 'and I was looking for dirt about that company, to give to a national union, where would I look?' I thought it over, staring at the ceiling, and then I said, 'I know two places *I'd* look. First, I'd look at the company union. Second, I'd look at the bookkeeping department.'

'Well, sir, you're absolutely right!' He slapped my forearm and beamed at me. 'See if the company union's doing anything it shouldn't, and then see if anybody's playing ring around the rosy with the company money. Yes, sir!' He leaned forward, old eyes aglitter. 'And I tell you, Mr – I tell you, Paul, I can help you a little bit. I got me a granddaughter works in the bookkeeping department. What do you think about that?'

'I think that's great,' I told him.

'Right you are! And you just let me think about it, and talk to one or two people, and see if I can come up with somebody we can talk to in the company union, how's about that?'

'Now, it doesn't have to be in either of those two places,' I warned him. 'It might be something in the shipping department, or in the department that buys the raw materials, whatever it's called. Or it could be in administration, or almost anywhere. Those are just the first two places *I'd* look, and I'm trying to guess they'd be the first two places Hamilton would look.'

'Well, of course they are, I can see the sense of that.' He got to his feet, spry and eager. 'Now, I tell you what you're going to do, Paul,' he said. 'You're going to get yourself a good night's sleep, and then in the morning I'll bring you home and you can talk to my granddaughter. She's lived with me the last nine years, since her folks got killed in an auto crash.'

'I don't think we have time –' I started, rising up on the bed.

'I know just what you're going to tell me,' he interrupted, 'but a man can always make time to get a decent rest. You can't do your best work when you're behind on your sleep. So you just get yourself rested up, and I'll come around in –'

The door jolted open, and we both twisted around, staring at it, as Sondra Fleisch came striding into the room

13

'Don't think I want to be here,' she said. There was sullenness in her, but there was a lot more, too. She had the cold angry sorrowful bitter determined urgency of a Greek queen deciding to kill some relatives. Her gaze flicked at Gar, and she said, 'Who the hell is that?'

Gar, looking worried and apologetic, started for the door, saying, 'I guess I'd better be –'

I raised my hand and shook it at him, whispering, 'Don't go.'

'Don't worry,' she said to me. Her voice was icy with contempt. 'I'm not going to beat you up.'

'I'll see you in the morning, Paul,' said Gar.

'Tell her to get out of here.'

'Nobody tells me anything.' She flounced into the armchair. 'I can wait,' she said.

Gar looked from her to me, puzzled. I think he'd originally thought she was my girl friend or something, but now he wasn't so sure. He said to me, 'Do you want me to stay, Paul?'

She was so blasted angry. And if she didn't want to be here, why was she here? 'No,' I said. 'It's all right. She does her fighting with one of the few pens around that isn't mightier than the sword.' Gar looked more puzzled than ever, so I said, 'This is Sondra Fleisch. She's the one did the article in the paper.'

'Oh.'

'It's all right,' I whispered. 'I'll see you in the morning.'

'Fine.' He glanced again dubiously at Sondra, and then left.

Lying flat on my back, I felt at a disadvantage, so I hitched myself to a half-sitting position, my back propped against the pillow and the headboard. It hurt my stomach, but not badly, and I felt in a psychologically better position. 'All right,' I whispered. 'What do you want?'

She grimaced. 'Cut it out,' she said.

'Cut what out?'

'That idiotic whispering. And all the grunting and making faces when you sit up.'

'I'm sorry,' I told her, 'but I have to whisper. My voice is gone. And my stomach is taped up; it hurts when I move. I'm sorry if it bothers you, but I didn't ask you here.'

'Who taped your stomach? The old geezer?'

'A doctor.'

A little doubt had crept into her expression. 'They really beat you up that bad?'

'Badly,' I said.

She flushed, and half-rose from the chair, but then settled back onto it. 'I don't really blame them,' she said. 'If anybody ever went around looking for a beating, it was you.'

I closed my eyes. 'Why don't you go home?'

'I came here because my father asked me to,' she said. 'He sent me with a message for you.'

I kept my eyes closed. I hated all these people, all of them. Even Charles Hamilton, the one whose letter had brought me here, had turned out to be a cheap adulterer, according to what his wife and Captain Willick had said. And Mrs Hamilton was a moronic frightened fool. Captain Willick and his bully boys, Leonard Fleisch and his daughter – what a scurvy collection of jackals they all were. I wanted nothing from Sondra Fleisch but her absence. I kept my eyes closed, and waited for her to go away.

She didn't go away. Instead, she said, 'My father wanted you to know he didn't order your beating, and he doesn't condone it. Jerry Mosca called a little while after you left, looking for you, and we told him you'd been at the house. He got those other two and came here of his own accord. He wasn't following orders from anybody. My father was very angry, and so was Captain Willick.'

'And will I please forget the whole thing when I go back to school. Is that it?'

'I don't care what you do,' she said. 'I told you my father sent me. And I'll tell you something else, too. It wasn't my father in

268

the Lincoln yesterday, when you were arrested. It was me. I wanted to see what union tough guys looked like. You didn't look so tough.'

I opened my eyes at that, and gazed at her. She was trying to look very scornful, but she was failing. At last, at long last, she was troubled. 'I'm not tough,' I told her. 'I never claimed to be tough.'

'Why don't you get away from here?' she asked me, as though she meant it. 'Why not just pack up and go away? You can only get hurt here.'

'From what you said in the paper, I shouldn't try to leave town.'

She brushed it aside with an impatient gesture. 'Never mind that. You can go, if you want. I think Captain Willick's ashamed about what happened to you. I know my father is.'

'And you?'

'I don't know,' she said, and for once she was trying to be honest. 'You have a talent for making me mad, but I don't think you're really mean. I think you're just in over your head.'

'Sure.'

'Why don't you go? It would be better for you, Paul.'

'And what about Walter?'

'Who? Oh, the other man.'

'Yeah, the other man.'

'What about him? He can take care of himself.'

'He's my friend.'

She shook her head. 'You pick strange friends.'

'You should know.'

'All right, Standish,' she said, bristling. 'Let's get something straight. I had a job to do, and that's all there was to it. What if I'd come to you and said, "Listen, buddy, I'm a member of the loyal opposition, and I want to do a smear piece on you. Give me something quotable, will you?" What if I'd said something like that?'

'Why do you have to do a smear piece at all?'

'It's my job.'

'Nice job.'

269

'You should talk. What about the people you work for?'

'Don't believe everything your father reads.'

She started to say something, then hesitated, then said, 'You really do see yourself as pure, don't you?'

'That's an exaggeration. I don't see myself writing smear pieces, if that's what you mean.'

'You'd be perfectly willing to smear my father with his employees, wouldn't you?'

'Only with the truth.'

'You wouldn't say very much, then, would you?'

'What's that supposed to mean?'

'It's supposed to mean you haven't got the corner on truth, Sir Galahad.'

'You're missing the point,' I whispered. 'We didn't come up here to start a war. We got a letter. Some of the workers wanted to start a local of the Machinists, so we came up to set up an election, and if the majority wanted a local, fine. And if the majority wanted to stick with the company union, that was fine, too.'

'And the majority is always right.'

'Isn't it?'

'You're such a moron!' She got to her feet, agitated. 'Why do I bother about you? I told you what my father said, and that's all. He didn't order you beaten up, and he didn't want you beaten up. And if you have any sense you'll go away from here. But you don't have any sense, do you?'

'Not much, I guess.'

'A moron,' she repeated, angrily. She strode to the door and flung it open, then glared back at me. 'Say what you want to Dr Reedman,' she said. 'It doesn't matter to me. If I'm trying to help you, it's not because I'm scared you'll talk.'

'Then why is it?'

'Because you're such a moron, that's why. Because everybody feels sorry for a yearling.' She stormed out, and slammed the door.

As soon as she left, I lay prone on the bed again, easing my stomach. Even talking in a whisper, I'd done too much, and now

270

my throat ached more than ever. I breathed carefully through my nose, and stared at the ceiling, and tried to understand why she'd really come here. Her father had sent her, she'd said. Had he? Thinking about it, I had to suppose he had; she'd been so sullen and reluctant at first, I had to accept her statement that she hadn't come of her own free will.

But later. Advice, and irritation, and the news that she felt sorry for me. Because I was a moron and a yearling. A pretty portrait, that; I hoped it wasn't a good likeness.

Although I ached all over, and although it had been too long since I'd last slept – and that sleep, in fact, on a metal cell cot – I suddenly found myself restless. No, restless is too weak a word. The way a horse champs and stamps in its stall during a thunderstorm, that's the way I felt. I wanted to raise my head and stamp my feet; I wanted to be out in the clean air, and running.

Finally, I couldn't keep it in any longer. I pushed myself off the bed, grunting at the sharp twinges in my stomach, and moved shakily – like a drunk or a paralytic – to the door. For some reason, I switched the lights off first, and then pulled the door open. It had nothing to do with caution, not wanting to outline myself against the light or anything like that; I just didn't want to spoil the outer night with an overflow of yellow.

Outside, everything was crisp and clear, and it somehow seemed easier to walk, though I still couldn't straighten completely. But it was a cool night, with a far black sky full of minute stars, and with a silence accented by the calls of peepers in the woods behind the motel. There was moonlight, too, grotto-pale.

Either my senses were heightened, or there was an aural clarity about the air. When I walked out from the shade of the building onto the moonlit gravel, the soft crush of it beneath my feet was the clearest sound I'd ever heard. I walked straight out, to the modernistic sign by the highway, standing on gracefully arched metal posts, and then just stood there for a while, looking at the pale cement of the road.

A car came by, coming from the south and heading toward town. I stepped closer to the sign, and waited as it whished by, throwing headlight beams out to either side. Then I turned and walked the other way, along the dirt shoulder beside the road, southward, away from Wittburg.

I walked and walked, and only two more cars passed me, both heading north. For the rest of the time, the road was mine. My steps sounded clear on the ground, the roadway was faintly luminous, and trees formed a solid black bulk on my left. I felt like running, but when I tried it my stomach knife-twinged badly, and I had to stop. So I kept walking instead, not thinking, paying attention only to my senses, to the sight of the road and the sound of my footsteps and the smell of the clean country night.

After a while I had to stop, because my legs were getting shaky. And only then did I remember Walter, and realize what I had actually been doing. I'd been running away. But I hadn't even admitted it to myself; I'd distracted myself with sensory impressions.

There were white concrete posts spaced along the side of the road at this point, and I sat on one of them and lit a cigarette, my first since leaving the motel. My first, in fact, since Ben had beaten me up. I took one puff on it, choked and coughed as it burned my throat, and then threw it away.

You're a coward, Paul. Yes, you're a yearling, and yes, you're a moron, but those are only the secondary characteristics. The primary fact about you, Paul, is that you are a coward. You are trying to run away from Walter Killy. You are trying to run away from Everyman's responsibility at least to try to avenge himself of personal injustices. You are trying to run away from a life more complicated than you'd expected. You're a coward, Paul.

Knowing this, I also knew I was doomed to stay here till the end. Knowing I was a coward, I also knew I was too much of a coward to let myself run away. My cowardice in the face of the brutality of Ben and Jerry, the hypocrisy of Captain Willick, the power of Leonard Fleisch, and the bland amorality of Sondra Fleisch, was pale before my cowardice in the face of my own self-revulsion. I was more afraid of losing my own high opinion of myself than of anything else on earth. So I got to my feet again, and retraced my steps.

It seemed longer, going back. The motel loomed finally, squat and primitive in the darkness, like a long low Indian mudhut. I went into my cubicle, but didn't turn on the light. I undressed, moving slowly because now I was stiffer and more fragile than ever, and crawled into bed. A car went by on the road, northward, angles of lightbeam sweeping backwards past the windows, and then there was silence.

In the silence, there were buzzings. A drone of low bed conversation from far away, the passing of another car, a frail distant murmur of night insects. In my throat there was a dim buzzing of hoarse ache, and the white taping held my stomach taut. I closed my eyes, and drifted into the deeper buzzings of sleep.

14

Pounding woke me. My eyes opened to pitch darkness, and I moved, hampered by the unexpected restriction around my middle. The pounding stopped, and then the doorknob rattled, and then the pounding started again.

I was afraid. Before the beating, I would have been angry, but now I was afraid. I cowered on the bed in the dark, thinking of the walls as fragile. The pounding stopped again, and a voice called, 'Wake up in there!'

'Who is it?' But I whispered it, to myself.

The voice muttered, just barely loud enough for me to hear, 'God damn it to hell.' There was irritation in the voice, not menace. The doorknob rattled angrily.

I got up slowly from the bed, as though afraid to make a sound, put on my glasses, and crept across the dark room to the door. The rattling had stopped, again, and now an aggravated silence awaited without. I leaned against the door, the side of my face pressed to the panel, and heard low murmurings in the wood. 'Who is it?' With a great effort, I could make the hoarse whisper loud. But it dried my throat again, and made me cough.

'At last,' said the voice. 'It's Fletcher. Open the door.'

'Oh. Oh! Just a minute.' I'd forgotten all about Fletcher. I pawed the wall beside the door, felt the light switch, clicked it on, and blinked in the sudden glare. Then I unlocked the door. As I opened it, I realized I was still in shorts and T-shirt. But Fletcher was already coming into the room.

He was of medium height, around fifty years of age, stocky of body, well dressed and full-faced. He looked like a very busy and successful lawyer. He came in, looked around the room, and said, 'Killy's not released yet.'

'No, sir.'

274

Then he glanced at me. 'You didn't say anything about all that,' he said, and gestured at my face.

I touched my cheek, felt the bandages. 'That happened since.'

'Local toughs?'

'Police.'

He grimaced. 'Bad. That the reason for the voice?'

'I – I guess so.'

'Better close the door.'

'Yes, sir.' I closed it quickly, made sure the snap-lock was on. When I turned back to the room, Fletcher was seated in the armchair, opening his suit coat. 'You'd better sit down,' he told me. 'You look pale.'

'Yes, sir.'

'What's that? You're taped up?'

'Yes. Around my stomach.'

'Anything broken?'

'No, sir.'

'Good.'

I lay down on the bed again, feeling weak. Then a sudden temporal panic struck me, and I sat up to say, 'What time is it, do you know?'

He glanced at his watch. 'Quarter past two. Would have been here earlier, but the car-rental people fouled up in Syracuse.' The way he said it, it was plain he considered incompetence the greatest sin, total competence the only worthwhile goal. Such an attitude instilled confidence, and I lay back down pleased that my earlier confidence in him had been justified.

He brought out a flat silver cigarette case, and snapped it open. 'I don't suppose you feel like smoking right now.'

I shook my head. 'No, thank you.'

'Thought not.' The cigarette case contained a lighter. He used it, slipped the case back in his pocket, and said, 'I don't want you to use your voice too much. But I need to know what's been going on around here. Just give me the highlights.'

'There was correspondence with a man named Hamilton, a worker at the shoe factory here. Walter and I came up to see him.

We talked to his wife, but he was still at work. Then we got arrested, here, and they kept me all night, and they've still got Walter. They didn't tell me till morning what it was all about. Hamilton had been killed. Shot.'

'And they haven't charged Walter?'

'I don't think so. They've been holding him for questioning. They've beat him up some, too.'

'What about you? What did you do to get all that?'

'I – well, there's a girl working for the paper here, she goes to the same college I do. She's the daughter of the factory manager, but I thought – well, I talked to her. And then, in the paper, she twisted everything around and called me a tough and sneering, defiant Standish, and I went up to tell her off.'

'At the paper?'

I felt myself blushing. 'No, at her father's house. And I talked with her father there.'

'Argue with him?'

'No – not really. He tried to tell me the Machinists was a bad union.'

Fletcher made a brief sour smile. 'Told you all about Hoffa,' he said.

'Yes, sir.'

'They always do. Men like Hoffa do more good for management than NAM. Say the word union to a management man, and the first thing he says is Jimmy Hoffa. But they won't tell you the clean unions wish Hoffa'd never been born.' He shrugged, showing again his irritation for sloppiness. 'So you won't be won over, and when you left he turned the dogs on you.'

'Something like that,' I said.

'You're too new at this,' he told me. 'I'll have you driven down to Syracuse in the morning. You can take a plane to Washington.'

Again it was offered, the nearly honourable out, but I said, 'I don't think I'm supposed to leave town.' That wasn't true, but the truth would have sounded sentimental and simple-minded to this pragmatic, clear-headed man.

'Mm. In that case, stay here. Don't move from this room. I'll have food brought in for you. Don't go anywhere, and don't talk to anybody.'

'Well, there's –'

He gazed bleakly at me. 'There's already somebody else?'

Embarrassed confusion came over me, and I nodded.

He sighed, and shook his head. Now I was the one who was sloppy and incompetent. 'Tell me about it,' he said.

'When I came to, after they beat me up, there was an old man here. He got a doctor for me, and paid for it himself. He was a friend of the dead man, Hamilton, and he told me Hamilton'd learned something.'

'What?'

'I don't know. He was trying to – Hamilton was trying to dig up any dirt he could that would help the union. And he found something out, but he wouldn't say what it was. This old man – Jeffers, his name is – he wanted me to help him, to – well, to go over Hamilton's trail.' As I said it, it sounded ridiculous.

Fletcher gazed at me, his mouth thin, and said, 'And you see yourself in the role of Philo Vance, is that it?'

'Mr Fletcher, nobody *cares*! Hamilton is dead, and the police won't do anything about it, and nobody else is doing anything about it, and this man Jeffers asked me to help him, and I *want* to help him.'

'You won't do any good,' he told me. 'You'll do only harm. Harm to yourself, harm to this old man, harm to Killy and the union, harm all the way round. Keep out of it. You should know by now that you don't know enough to participate in this kind of battle.'

'I don't care. I want to do it.'

He sat back, studying me. Finally, he said, 'This isn't your fight. There's no reason to get yourself embroiled.'

'A man is *dead*, Mr Fletcher.'

'You didn't know him, you had no part in his death, you don't owe him anything.'

'But –'

He raised a hand. 'One moment. I am not saying that his death doesn't matter, or that there's no point in striving for justice.' He

277

smiled thinly. 'I wouldn't be in the work I'm in if I thought that. But there's a best way to go about anything, and a worst way, and many mediocre ways in the middle. The way you're choosing strikes me as being one of the very worst. All I'm asking is that you give us a chance to try the *best* way first.'

'What way?'

'This city is controlled by a tight small clique, with its power based in the shoe factory. But that power is very delicately balanced, ready to totter. The murder proves that, and so does the treatment given to you and to Killy. If they were secure in their power, they could ignore you. In other words, with the impetus of the last two days, and given the proper knowledgeable direction, that power can be made to collapse utterly. The key is in the union, in the workers. I will predict that a local of the Machinists will be the bargaining agent for the workers here within a month. Now, I've seen this happen before. Once the workers have a source of power of their own, a general clean-up of the city follows in very short order. A union local, particularly when it represents such a high percentage of a city's population, is a potent political tool. Within two years, this will be a clean city. And the local, you can be sure of it, will not rest until the Hamilton murder is reopened and solved. *That* is the best way.'

He made sense. And he was right, I *had* been casting myself as a sort of Philo Vance in the rough. But Philo Vance didn't seem like a very successful survival type – in the rough.

Still, I was part of this. Too much had happened to me, too much had been done to me, for me to be able to accept the good sense of my further non-involvement. I *was* involved, good sense or not. Fletcher could do a better job than me of freeing Walter. A local of the Machinists could do a better job of forcing the police to find and punish the murderer of Charles Hamilton than I could ever hope to do. These were true, and good sense, but they couldn't get around the fact that I was involved, that I had been hurled into the middle of this thing and I had to get myself out of it, self-respect more or less intact. And it would take more than baiting a nasal guard with my superior vocabulary.

Nevertheless, a degree of caution had been pounded into me.

Innocence had failed rather abysmally, and anger had failed in an even more spectacular manner. The only other method I could think of was guile. I had no idea how good I'd be at guile, but it was the last tool in that weapons chest. And, of necessity, I used it first on Fletcher.

'I guess you're right,' I said. 'Will you talk to the old man tomorrow?'

'I'll be glad to. He may be able to help.' He got to his feet. 'I'll have to see about releasing Killy first thing tomorrow. If your friend gets here before I come back, ask him to wait.'

'I will.' I wanted to talk to Gar before he met Fletcher, anyway.

He paused, glancing at the other bed. 'Shall I have someone stay here tonight? Do you think the police might be back?'

'I don't think so.'

'All right, then. You can meet the others in the morning. Sorry I had to wake you.'

'It's all right.'

15

In the morning, I met the others. They were an accountant, a public relations man, and a protector, and I met them in the room next door to mine, one of the two double units I had reserved for Fletcher.

The accountant, here to study the company union's books if he ever got a chance at them, was a small dry man with wire-rimmed spectacles and a narrow apologetic handshake. He was dry all over, as though he'd been left out in the sand and wind, except for his eyes, which behind the spectacles were watery and very weak. His name was Mr Clement, and he murmured briefly when I was introduced to him by Fletcher, and then retired at once to the fringe of the group.

The public relations man, here to counter anti-union slander if he could, was also small, but wiry, with a long thin nose and eyes as sharp as knives. His name was Phil Katz, and his handshake was hard and bony. He said, without smiling, 'Non illegitimus carborundum, guy.'

I smiled, and said, 'I'll try not to.' My voice was better this morning, but still hoarse.

The protector, here to keep the rest of us from being quite such easy prey for the Jerrys and the Bens, was introduced to me as George; I never did learn his last name. He was huge, barrel-chested and barrel-gutted, triple-chinned and possessing arms that looked too heavy to lift. His face was so heavily padded by roughened flesh that eyes and mouth and nose seemed insignificant afterthoughts. He grinned, showing crooked broken teeth, and said, 'Just point 'em out, little friend.'

I hoped I would get the chance.

After the introductions, Fletcher said, 'Paul, you stay here with Phil and George. I'll be back as soon as I can; I want to see about getting Killy released. You come along with me, Albert.'

Albert was Mr Clement. He bobbed his head in our general direction, and followed Mr Fletcher from the room.

George stretched, spreading his arms out like a transport plane, and said, 'I don't know about them two, but I'm hungry.'

'Ditto,' said Phil Katz. To me, he said, 'Where do we eat around here?'

'There's a diner not far. I'll drive us.'

In case Gar should arrive before our return, I thumbtacked a note to my unit door. *Be right back. Wait for me.* Unaddressed and unsigned, just to be on the safe side. Then I joined the other two in the Ford.

We went to the City Line Diner. We didn't talk much during breakfast, just comments on the weather and so forth, but on the way back Phil said, 'I hear they got the paper sewed up.'

'They sure do. You should see the article they did about Walter and me being arrested.'

'It's a girl reporter or something, isn't it? You talked to her.'

'I didn't know any better.'

'Yeah, well, live and learn. You got a copy?'

'Back at the motel.'

'Show it to me.'

When we got back to the motel, I saw my note still tacked to the door, so Gar hadn't arrived yet. Phil Katz checked next door, saw that Fletcher wasn't back, and the three of us went into my unit. George immediately stretched out on Walter's bed. 'You ought to lay down after every meal,' he told us seriously. 'It's good for the digestion.' He lay on his back like a felled tree, his legs together and his arms down against his sides. His chest and stomach bulged up into the air. He kept his eyes open and breathed shallowly through his mouth.

I got the paper with Sondra's article in it, and handed it to Phil. He read it, his lips pursing and relaxing, his head nodding every once in a while, and when he was finished he said, 'Awkward here and there, but she's got the feel of it.' It was the impersonal comment of a fellow professional.

And it irked me. 'I thought it stunk,' I said.

He shrugged, and grinned at me. 'Well, it figures. It was your back she stuck it in. Any chance of buying her?'

'You mean, convince her the union's right after all? Not much, she's the boss's daughter.'

'Well, it was an idea. Here, for your scrapbook.' He gave me back the paper.

I said, 'What happens here now?'

'Phone calls. Everybody calls Washington, and Washington says do this, do that. Then we do this and we do that. In the meantime, we just sit. You got a deck of cards?'

'No, I don't.'

'Play gin?'

'Some.'

'Good. This George here, you got to tell him what the numbers are.'

'I beat you one time,' said George complacently, still gazing up at the ceiling. 'I took you for thirty-eight cents one time.' He had a deep voice to begin with, and when he was supine the voice was even deeper.

'Thirty-eight cents,' said Phil, as though the figure were beneath contempt. He shook his head, and looked over at me.

'What about other papers?'

'What?'

'Newspapers, newspapers. This thing, the *Beacon*, it's the only local paper?'

'I think so.'

'What about others? You know, from towns around here. What is there, there's a Watertown or something around here, isn't there?'

'I think so.'

'So do they sell their papers in Wittburg?'

'I don't know. I'm sorry, I never paid any attention.'

Phil shrugged. He did it all the time. 'So I'll find out. Listen, I got a deck of cards, you want to play gin? Penny a point.'

'Sure. Why not?'

'Thirty-eight cents,' said George dreamily.

'I was setting you up,' Phil told him. 'I'll be right back.' He went out. A minute later he came back with the cards, and we both sat on my bed, cross-legged.

When two strangers first play gin, they always discover they know different rules, and the first thing they have to do is decide what rules to use. For instance, I always played that the dealer was dealt ten cards and the other player eleven, no card was turned over to start the discard, and the other player discarded on his first turn without drawing. Phil had always played that both players got ten cards and the top card of the stack was turned over to start the discard. After a while we got squared away, using some of the rules he knew and some of the rules I knew, and then we played. Phil kept score, with triple-scoring and boxes, and in no time at all I owed him three dollars and forty-two cents. He was one of those people who can remember every single card in the discard pile and which player got rid of it. At one point I said, 'I don't think I want to play you pinochle.'

He grinned reminiscently and said, 'Yeah. That's the game.'

After a while, George grunted loudly and got to his feet. 'Eleven o'clock,' he announced. 'When they coming back?'

'When they get here,' said Phil. He had just grinned, and was shuffling.

Eleven o'clock. Where was Gar? 'Hold it a minute,' I said. 'I've got to make a phone call.'

'I'm gettin' stiff,' George complained. He stood in the middle of the room and waved his arms around, a serious expression on his face.

I left the unit and walked down to the motel office, where there was a pay phone. Just as importantly, there was a phone book. Jeffers, Gar 121 7th Street . . . 4-8629.

The phone was answered on the second ring. A male voice said, 'Hello?'

'Hello? Gar?'

There was the slightest of pauses, and then the voice said, 'He can't come to the phone right now. Who's calling, please?'

But I'd recognized the voice. I held my breath, as though exhalation would give my identity away, and shakily replaced the receiver. What had gone wrong?

283

Back out in the sunshine, I stood in confusion a minute before the office, blinking and wondering what to do. I very nearly went back to Phil and George, to ask them for help, but I remembered in time that Fletcher didn't want me mixing into this business any more, and he'd surely told George to keep an eye on me and see that I stayed out of trouble.

The Ford was in front of the unit, and the key was in my pocket. I was frightened, because I knew by now my own inadequacies. What could I do to help? Nothing. Still, Gar had come to me, and he and I had chosen to be partners of sorts, and I owed him at least my presence.

I ran across to the Ford, climbed in, started the engine, and backed around to face the road. I'd half-expected Phil and George to come barrelling out when they heard the car start – I might even, in a part of me, have hoped they'd stop me, so I could have my gesture and eat it too – but the door remained stubbornly closed. I shifted into first and drove out onto the highway and headed toward town.

On the telephone, the voice of Jerry.

16

If I had learned nothing else in Wittburg, I had learned a sort of elemental caution, the caution of the sneak thief and the petty criminal. I hadn't yet learned enough caution to keep me from trying to help a friend, but I did at least know enough now not to go to him directly.

Jerry was at Gar's house, but that didn't mean that I wasn't still being followed, by Ben or another of Captain Willick's bully boys. My journey northward through Wittburg was circuitous, with much doubling back and random turnings, and my eye was on the rear-view mirror more than on the street ahead. But I couldn't find a follower.

I emerged on the hillside grid of the workers' Utopia at Sarah Street, three blocks west of Harpur Boulevard. In second gear, I drove up the hill to 7th Street, and came to a stop, prepared to turn left.

But just as I rolled to a stop at the intersection, the familiar blue Plymouth passed by on 7th Street, from my left to my right. I froze, hands clamped on the steering wheel, feet locked to the clutch and brake, and stared at them as they went by, but they didn't notice me. Whereas they crossed my vision directly, I was only at the periphery of their vision.

Jerry was driving, and Ben was in the front seat beside him. There was no one in the back seat. So at least they hadn't arrested Gar, they weren't dragging him down to their grim brick building for the kind of session they'd given me. But had they beaten him up? An old man like that – but I couldn't see those two having qualms about beating anyone.

I stayed where I was, the Ford poised at mid-hill, while a minute or two crept slowly by. I stayed there partially from caution, not wanting Jerry to notice me in his rear-view mirror, but even more than that I stayed there from confusion and fear. I was afraid of those two men. Mocking Jerry and sullen Ben; I didn't know which of them I feared more. I was afraid of them as a unit, a combination before which I was jelly, and defenceless.

At last, I forced myself to move again. For the first time in years I drove with conscious movement. As though I were a metal robot, of gears and chromium tubing, I lifted my right foot from the brake, moved it to the right, placed it on the accelerator. I angled my right foot down on the accelerator as I angled my left foot up from the clutch. The car moved forward, as sluggish as its driver, and my hands turned the wheel counterclockwise. I executed the turn with the halting precision of a learner taking his driver's test, and pushed the Ford slowly down the street.

121 was on the left. I parked across the way, and left the car. This section of the grid – like that surrounding the Hamilton house – was empty and quiet in the sunlight, as though it had been just yesterday abandoned. I left the car, looked up and down the empty street like a conspirator, and hurried across to 121.

Gar's house had no individuality. It was on the down-slope side of the street, like the Hamilton house, and could have been its twin. There was even the small rock garden in the steep angle of lawn down from the sidewalk to the house, though this garden was in somewhat worse repair. And the initial on this screen door was J.

I rang the bell, and waited, and then the door opened and a girl looked out at me.

In that first second I saw her, I thought Alice MacCann was seventeen years old. Then I looked again, through the screen door, and she was twenty-seven. Some women, slender and fine-boned, with a delicate carriage and pale thin hands, are deceptive that way. Their faces are tight-skinned, the pale flesh taut over prominent cheekbones and clean straight jaws and small temples, and they grow old without ever ceasing to look young. Lillian Gish is of that type. Every few years, too, an actress in her late twenties or early thirties makes a hit on Broadway playing a twelve-year-old girl – Julie Harris, for instance – and they are almost always of this slender fine-framed type.

286

True to the form, Alice MacCann had very large eyes, deep brown, and a short straight nose, flared like a thoroughbred. She gazed out at me reluctantly, with fragile solemnity, heightening yet further the impression of extreme youth. But she was garbed in a severe black dress, showing a wasp waist, tapered hips, and well-separated conical breasts.

After a moment of confusion – I'd been about to speak to a teenager, and then suddenly had to shift gears and speak to a woman – I managed to say, 'Is Mr Jeffers home? Gar? Is Gar home?'

Her voice was very soft, but surprisingly husky. She said, 'Are you Mr Standish?'

'Yes. Paul Standish, yes, that's right.'

'Come in.' She stepped back for me, and motioned me to precede her into the living room.

It was a less cluttered room than the one at the Hamilton house. The furniture seemed to be newer, and cleaner of line, and there were no doilies or overcrowded drum tables. Nor was there a television set. I turned in the middle of the room, which was empty when I came into it, and said, 'Is your grandfather home?' They hadn't taken him with them; I was thinking again that they'd beaten him, that he was now upstairs in bed, perhaps still unconscious.

But she didn't answer me at first. Instead, she said, 'Sit down. Please.'

I chose one of the armchairs, and she perched on the edge of the sofa, knees together and angled down and to the side, feet in black flats tucked close to the sofa. Her hands were cupped together in her lap. She looked at me solemnly, and said, 'My grandfather is dead, Mr Standish.'

'Dead!' I was suddenly on my feet, though I have no idea where I thought I was going. After Jerry and Ben?

'He was murdered,' she said. Her words and tone were flat, emotionless. Her brown eyes gazed at me solemnly. She was reporting a fact which she herself did not yet fully believe, which she was probably refusing to believe.

I should have had sense enough to realize that this outer

287

dispassionate calm was only a desperate attempt to keep herself from flying apart completely, I know that. But I was too caught up in my own worries, too involved in my own hellish maze, to be able to think quickly enough about anybody else. So I did the worst thing I could possibly do – I asked her how it had happened.

She was all right at first. 'I had to go to the store this morning,' she said. 'We were out of butter. Everybody has the morning off, you know, because of the funer— because of Chuck Hamilton. So I went to the store – about nine o'clock. I was gone about twenty minutes, and when I came back Grandpa wasn't downstairs. I called him and he didn't answer, so I went –'

She stopped and closed her eyes. Her hands now were clenched into fists in her lap, and she looked so rigid that I thought if she were pushed slightly she would fall off the sofa onto the floor without changing position.

Belatedly I realized what I'd done. I was still on my feet, and now I took a hesitant half-step toward her, my hands out, and said, 'You don't have to. I'm sorry, I shouldn't have –'

'It's all right.' Her eyes were still closed. 'It's all right, I'll tell you. I want to tell you.' I knew that she was making the fact real for herself by relating its details to me, and that now she'd started she couldn't stop.

She finally opened her eyes again, but didn't look at me. She looked beyond me, at the window, with its constricted view of the rock garden. 'I went upstairs,' she said. Her voice was still soft and flat and emotionless. 'He was lying on his bed. He'd been shot, and the gun was lying on the floor beside the bed. They think it was the same gun as the one that killed Mr Hamilton.'

'And it happened while you were out at the store?'

'Yes. He was alive when I left. We'd been talking about you. He was alive, and he kidded me about letting the butter run out, and then I went away to – I went out to the store and – he was alive when I –'

'Wait. Wait!' I hurried across the room and went down on one knee and grabbed her hands. At the end there, her face had been virtually falling apart, the eyes getting wider and glassier, the mouth twisting around the words, and the words themselves had been jolting out of her in broken phrases, forced out, propelled by a kind of dulled hysteria. Her hands, when I clutched them, were cold and lifeless. 'Wait!' I cried, trying to stop her, stop the disjointed pulse of words, and she shuddered, coming to a stop, coming to silence, and slowly her eyes focused on me. And then she collapsed in tears.

I scrambled up onto the sofa next to her, wrapping my arms around her, and she clung to me as she sobbed. She wept brokenly and entirely, her whole body shaking and quivering. The sounds of her were ugly, and it was cruel that this slight body should ever have to be racked so. I grimaced in self-contempt, knowing my idiot question had brought this on. It was a moment she would have had to live through anyway, sooner or later, but still *I* had made it happen sooner.

I don't know how long it took her to exhaust herself, and she didn't stop until at last she was too worn to do anything but gasp for breath. I only know it seemed for ever that I held her tight, feeling the fragile bone structure and the tender flesh shaken and beaten, and I even had the wild fear that in the force of her grief she would break her body to pieces, her bones would snap under the strain.

But at last she lay against me, spent, quivering only slightly at each inhalation, and I took the chance of letting her go. But she didn't want to be let go. She clung to me even more fiercely, and so we sat together that way a while longer, till finally the tension drained out of her body and she released me. I got to my feet, one hand still supporting her, and then lifted her legs and stretched her out on the sofa. She suffered me to move her, as willingly as a child. Then I straightened, and looked at her.

Her face was puffed and red from weeping, but with still the delicate tracery beneath. Yet, she looked more her age now. And, in some strange way, sensually attractive. Not with a good sensuality: erotic imaginings rose in me, veneered by only a sham tenderness.

I was constantly guilty with her, first for tactless stupidity, now for sweaty imaginings. I wanted to make amends, to do something for her, I wasn't sure what. I said, 'Do you want some coffee?'

'Nothing,' she whispered. 'Please.' She turned her face away, pressed it to the back of the sofa.

I looked around, distraught. 'I'll come back later,' I said. 'Tomorrow, or some other time.'

'No.' The whisper was so faint I could barely hear it. 'Please stay.'

So I stayed. I retreated to the armchair on the other side of the room, and sat there watching her. She lay unmoving, her hands folded together on her waist, her head turned so the face was away from me. Her hair was a deep black, and soft-looking, and now rumpled and disarranged.

In the silence, I could think about what she'd told me. Gar was dead, murdered, shot. I remembered Captain Willick's phrase: *shot to death*. Now, a second time, it had happened. A living human being was now decaying vegetable. Shot to death.

By the same man, surely, and with the same gun. But this time he'd left the gun, after first being careful to wipe it clean. Could he wipe his hands clean as readily? Whatever he touched from now on, this unknown man, wouldn't he leave a smear, a slime, an invisible film of blood behind? Where he trod in the world from now on, wouldn't the mark of his foot be bloody?

I remembered *The Picture of Dorian Gray*; every man had a painting like that, down inside him. There would be no mark on the murderer, not on the outside. He would have to be found some other way.

Why had he killed Gar? Because Gar, like Charles Hamilton, had become a danger to him. Both had contacted men from the union, the one with knowledge that could harm the murderer, the other with awareness of that knowledge. Gar had started along the same trail that had led Charles Hamilton to his discovery and his death. It had led Gar to death, too.

Then another thought occurred to me. Twenty-five men had signed their names to the second letter Hamilton had sent to the union, and now two of those men were dead. Were more of them

290

to die? Still, the murderer this time had left the gun, as though to announce that now he was finished, that he had done all he considered necessary.

What were Ben and Jerry thinking now? What was their Captain Willick thinking? Walter had still been imprisoned by them when Gar was being murdered, and I had two witnesses to bolster my own alibi. Their play-acting at their jobs, their sham and their misuse of their authority, had resulted in more than the inconveniencing of two men from Washington, it had resulted in a second murder. Though I knew full well no legal responsibility could be held against them, I knew just as well that they were accessories to that second murder. In being more concerned about pleasing Mr Fleisch than looking for a murderer, they had left that murderer free to kill again. I wondered if self-defensive, hypocritical Captain Willick was thinking about that now, realizing his own guilt. I hoped so.

The time stretched by, expanding slowly, but still the girl on the sofa didn't move. After a while I looked around the room, noticing again the clean simplicity of the furnishings, and judging that the granddaughter had probably selected everything. Gar hadn't been the kind of man to worry about his surroundings.

There was a clock on one table, a glass face edged in gold and with gold hands. It read ten minutes to twelve, and when I saw it I remembered with a start that Phil and George didn't have any idea where I was. They were probably convinced by now that I'd been kidnapped. Since I wasn't doing any good here, I ought to get back to them.

I got to my feet. 'Excuse me,' I said. 'Miss –' I didn't yet know her name.

'Alice MacCann,' she said, lifeless voice muffled by the back of the sofa against which her face was still pressed.

'Miss MacCann. I really ought to get back to the motel. My friends will be worried about me.'

'Yes.' She sat up, all at once, smoothly, and turned to face me. 'Thank you,' she said.

'For what? All I did was make you cry.'

'You sat with me. Thank you.'

291

'I'll come back later on. Whatever you say. We can talk.'

'This evening. There are things I want to tell you.'

'All right.' I stifled a smile of elation at that – had Gar found out something, and had he told his granddaughter? But I had sense enough not to push it. 'I'll be going now,' I said.

Though I didn't expect her to, she got to her feet and came with me to the door. She opened it and glanced out, then suddenly closed it again. 'They're coming back,' she whispered, looking startled.

'Who?' I thought immediately of Jerry and Ben.

But she said, 'The neighbours. They're coming back from the funeral.' Her mouth twisted a little on that last word. 'They shouldn't see you here, someone will tell the police.'

That was true, and she was right. I didn't want the police to know I was 'interfering' again. 'I'd better wait,' I said.

'Till one o'clock,' she said. 'They only got half a day off.' She looked past me, at the stairs. 'They'll be getting another half-day off,' she said. 'Won't that make them happy?'

I touched her arm, because I didn't know what to say.

'I'm sorry,' she said, and the large brown eyes refocused on me. 'I shouldn't blame them, it wasn't them. I have some iced tea made, would you like some?'

I was going to refuse, but then I thought it would be better if she were allowed to do something, so I said, 'Thank you, I would. Oh, and can I use your phone? 1 want to call my friends at the motel.'

'Of course. It's in the kitchen.'

I followed her down the hall to the kitchen, where the window overlooked a view of the city, squatting below us at the foot of the hill, nursing its sores. There was a cream-coloured telephone on the wall beside the window, and as I made the call Alice opened the refrigerator and got out the pitcher of tea and a tray of ice cubes.

I asked the woman who answered in the motel office if I could please speak to anyone in Unit 5. She agreed reluctantly, and told me to hold on. While I waited, I watched Alice. She worked at the sink, breaking loose the reluctant ice cubes and dropping

292

them into two glasses. Then she took time out to rinse her face with double handfuls of cold water, and dry it by rubbing briskly with a hand towel. When she was done with that, her face still had more colour than the delicacy of its structure called for, but now the colour was healthy-looking and not the angry puffy red that follows weeping. Then she went back to preparing the tea.

About that time, a voice came on the line, saying hello. I turned quickly to the phone, saying, 'Hello. This is Paul Standish.'

'Well, Paul! Where the devil are you boy?'

I recognized the voice instantly. 'Walter! You're free!'

'Good old Fletcher,' he said. 'Read lawbooks at them till they all went to sleep, and then we just tiptoed out.'

I was practically laughing aloud, I was so pleased to hear his voice and know he was released at last. I was grinning so hard my cheeks hurt and I could just barely pronounce words. 'By golly, I'm glad!' I said. 'I've been running around like a chicken with its head cut off.'

'To coin a phrase,' he said, and laughed. 'I know, Fletcher's been telling me all about it. He wants me to send you back to Washington, air express.'

'Listen, Walter –'

'I know, I know,' he said. 'I told him I'd rather you stay, since you were here from the beginning. You'd probably like to see how the mighty look when they're fallen.'

'You said it.'

'So Fletcher said all right, if I'd guarantee you'd keep yourself out of trouble.' He paused, and then said, 'Now, I don't know what to say. Here you are, you've gone running off again. George is all embarrassed.'

'I'm not in any trouble,' I told him, 'and I'll be back a little after one o'clock. Oh, and there's one thing more. Some news. There's been –' Then I stopped, remembering Alice's presence behind me. I turned and looked at her helplessly.

She gave me a smile, wan but reassuring. 'It's all right,' she said.

Still, I stumbled along as I told Walter what had happened.

'There's been a second murder,' I said. 'One of the men who signed that letter of Hamilton's.'

Walter interrupted me before I got any further, asking question after question. I answered them all as best I could – and as briefly as I could, because it wasn't a good subject for discussion, with the dead man's granddaughter standing behind me – and finally, when Walter's questions had run out and he was totally filled in on what I'd been doing of late, I reiterated my promise to be back at the motel a little after one, and hung up.

Alice said, 'Here's your tea.'

'Thank you.'

'I didn't put anything in it. Do you want sugar, or lemon?'

'No, this is fine.'

'Shall we talk in the living room?' She was composed now, having drained the emotion out all at once.

'Yes,' I said. 'That would be fine.'

We went back to the living room and sat down.

17

'I don't think I want to talk about anything – serious yet,' she said. 'Do you mind?'

'Of course not.' I was in the armchair again, she once more on the sofa, though this time she was in a more relaxed and comfortable-looking position. 'Whatever you want.'

'That cry did me good,' she said, half apologetically. 'I think I'll be all right now. But I think I'd just like to talk about – *things*, inconsequential things, for a while. Until I'm sure the crying won't start again.'

'At your service,' I said.

'I can help you. But we'll talk about that later. The newspaper said you were from Washington?'

It was a rather leaden-footed change of subject, but I went along with it. 'Not exactly,' I said. 'I'd been there all of two days before coming here. I'd just been hired by the union.'

'I've never been to Washington,' she said. 'I've never been anywhere. Do you know the city I'd *really* like to see?'

'New York,' I guessed.

She laughed, lightly. 'No, I have seen New York. It was –' Then she stopped, in mid-sentence, and started to cloud up again, distracted, eyes sliding away from me, face working.

I could guess she'd visited New York with her grandfather, and the memory at this moment was a little too acute. Quickly, I said, 'What then? London?'

'No.' She forced herself back to the present with an obvious effort of will. 'No, Los Angeles. I think that must be fascinating, everything so different. Even the weather. And restaurants shaped like hats and birds. And the people are different, too. Did you go to college?'

'I still do.'

'You do?'

'Six months in college, six months working. It's the system they have there.'

'I never heard of that. I wanted to go to college, but I couldn't. We couldn't afford it. I could have gone to Potsdam State Teacher's College or something like that, and lived at home, and driven to school every morning, but that wouldn't have been the same thing, would it?'

'No, I don't suppose so.'

'I wanted to go to UCLA. I still have the catalogue they sent me. They have a huge campus, and it's summer all year round. I'd like to go to Bermuda sometime. And Havana. Do you think we'll ever be friendly with Cuba again?'

I grinned. 'I wouldn't be surprised, the way things shift around. Twenty years from now, Cuba and Russia will be our allies again, and England will be our enemy again. International friendships keep shifting round. If you wait long enough, you can go anywhere, or be barred anywhere.'

'I've never been anywhere,' she said. 'My parents went to Montreal on their honeymoon. Have you ever been there?'

'Yes. Have you ever been to Buffalo?'

'A few times, why?'

'Montreal is like Buffalo, except the bars stay open all night. And on the Rue St Denis, there's a restaurant called Corso's that serves the best pizza in the world.'

Her eyes shone, and she leaned forward, fascinated. 'Really? What else? It can't be like Buffalo, not really.'

'Not really,' I admitted. I felt a little foolish, impersonating a world traveller this way, but it was clearly doing her good to chat about faraway places. 'Along the Rue St Denis, late at night,' I said, 'the taxis zigzag back and forth from one side of the street to the other, looking for fares. Right from one kerb to the other. They pass each other that way, going in opposite directions, and sometimes it looks as though they're all going to pile up in the middle.'

'You're making that up!' She was delighted.

'No, I'm not. In Montreal, they have a different idea about automobiles from us down here. I think they look on them as being kind of sewing machines that move. I knew a guy once – in college – who swears he was driving on the Jacques Cartier

296

bridge, on the far right-hand lane – and the bridge is eight lanes wide – and he got involved in a head-on collision.'

'Now I know you're making it up'

'Cross my heart and –' I stopped that one in time, and hurried on. 'The other driver only spoke French,' I said hurriedly, 'so my friend never did find out what he was doing way over on the wrong side of the bridge.'

'Where else have you been?' she demanded.

'I've been to the Azores,' I said.

'*Really?*'

'Really. It was terrible. It's Portuguese, you know.'

'How did you get there?'

'The Army sent me. I was only there three months. Some guys have to spend a whole year there. It's just a fuelling stop for planes coming back from Europe, that's all. The nearest land is twenty-one hundred miles away, and *that's* Spain.'

'Were you in Spain?'

I laughed, shaking my head. 'No, I told you, it was over two thousand miles away.'

'Oh. I'm sorry.' She suddenly seemed timid, and very young. Only fifteen now, or even younger.

I suddenly remembered my first meeting with Walter, when I too had had years stripped away from me, and felt ashamed of myself. 'I've been to St Louis,' I said. 'I don't know if that counts as a glamour spot or not, but I've been there.'

That restored her good humour, and she said, 'Were you ever in Los Angeles?'

'No. St Louis is the farthest west I've ever been.'

'Oh, I'd *love* to go there,' she said. 'I so wanted to go to UCLA. And see the Pacific Queen, and maybe fly to Hawaii some day. Where are you going to live?'

'What?'

'When you get out of college. Where are you going to live then?'

'I don't know. In New York for a while, I guess. I want to get my master's at NYU. After that, wherever I get a job.'

'But some big city,' she said, forcefully. 'Not a place like Wittburg.'

297

I smiled. 'No, not a place like Wittburg. There aren't many openings in a town like this for an economist.'

She cocked her head to one side and studied me. 'You don't look like an economist,' she said.

'I'm not one yet,' I reminded her. 'What do I look like?'

She thought it over carefully, and said, 'A teacher. A very idealistic young teacher who wants all his students to love learning.'

'Like in books, huh?' I said, grinning at her.

'Do you think you'll be a teacher?'

'I don't know, maybe. I'll try for a job in private industry first, though.'

'What if you became a troubleshooter for an oil company or something?' she said. Her eyes were shining again, and her hands were clasped in front of her. 'You'd travel all over, to Saudi Arabia and Venezuela and the South Seas –'

'Do they have oil in the South Seas?'

'Well, North Africa, then. And I'll be your secretary, and travel everywhere with you.'

'It's a deal,' I said.

She sipped some iced tea, and then sat gazing into the glass. 'I wonder how you become an airline stewardess,' she said. 'Do you know how?'

'No, I don't.'

'I've seen ads in magazines for stewardess schools,' she said. 'Correspondence schools. But I suppose they're all just confidence games, aren't they?'

'I think they probably are, yes.'

'If I was a stewardess,' she said, 'I'd have my apartment in Los Angeles. And maybe I could even go to UCLA part time. I'm only twenty-seven, that's not too old for college.'

'Of course not. Look at me.'

She got to her feet suddenly and, not looking at me, said, 'Would you like to hear some music?'

'Sure, fine.'

There was a radio-phonograph console against the wall to the left. She started it cooking, and then brought out a stack of records from the storage shelf underneath. It was all dance music, and all fifteen or twenty years old, but re-releases on LP. There was a lot of Miller, and some early Miller-influenced Kenton of the Balboa Beach days, and some Ralph Flanagan, and even a Ray McKinley. The most recent album she had was a re-release of Sauter-Finegan's first album, from 1952.

Miller started, smooth as margarine, and she turned the volume down to where we could talk over it if we wanted to. But she didn't talk, or go back and sit down on the sofa. She stood awhile, listening to the music, standing in front of the console with her back to me. Her head was bowed, and she was either listening intently or very deep in thought.

She stayed that way through 'Pavane', and then turned my way at last, but still not looking at me. 'I never learned to dance,' she said. 'I wish I could dance.' She spoke so very low, and not looking at me at all, that I wasn't sure whether or not I was supposed to have heard it.

But I was. When I made no response, she looked at me directly, and said, 'Will you teach me?'

'I'm not very good,' I said. It was half a lie. I'm a perfectly competent, if uninspired, social dancer. But the situation was suddenly making me feel uncomfortable. It finally occurred to me to wonder just how far off the rails this girl had been knocked by her grandfather's death.

'Please,' she said. 'I wish you would.'

'All right,' I said, reluctantly. I got to my feet and, to the sterile precision of 'Sunrise Serenade', proceeded to show her the basic steps.

It didn't take me long to find out she'd been lying more completely than I. She knew how to dance. She probably could dance better than I could, but she was deliberately hesitant, to maintain the fiction. Before 'Sunrise Serenade' had mathematically computed its coda, she had folded into my arms, and we were moving easily together, as though we'd been partners for years.

There comes a time when examination must cease. Her grandfather was four hours dead, I myself was up to my neck in murder and intrigue, but she wanted me to kiss her, and I did.

She held herself against me in a way to let me know she wanted my hands on her body, and I put my hands on her body. Why did she want me to pick her up, child-light, and carry her upstairs to her bed? I didn't know why, and I didn't care why. I was beyond questioning, beyond understanding that what we were doing, in these circumstances, was grotesque. I did pick her up, and she was child-light, and I did carry her upstairs to bed.

She spoke only once. Her face was nuzzled against my throat as I carried her, and as I reached the top step she murmured, 'To the right.' Thus avoiding the possibility that I might blunder with her into the room where her grandfather had been slain.

Far away downstairs, in another world that wasn't real either, the bands still softly played. Freed of our clothes, Alice Mac-Cann and I lay stretched out side by side on her bed. She had shaved herself, reinforcing again the child-image in her, and startling me very nearly into conscious reflection. But then she pressed my head to her hard little breasts, and contorted her belly beneath my palm, and when I rolled onto her, her luminous brown eyes were squeezed shut, her lips were parted slightly, and she moaned only once. After that, the beast with two backs was busy, but silent.

18

I dozed awhile, and I guess she did, too. When I opened my eyes again, in the cool dimness of her bedroom, the alarm clock facing me on the night table read twenty minutes past two, and Alice was standing at the window. The window was open a few inches at the bottom, and a slight breeze ruffled the lace curtains. She had donned a white terry-cloth robe and stood with her arms folded, three-quarters turned away from me, gazing out the window and down upon Wittburg. She was in silhouette, and I couldn't see the expression on her face.

I stirred in the bed, and she heard me, and turned. 'Are you awake?'

'Yes.' I looked down at my naked self, and sat up.

She came over and sat down on the bed in front of me, her lips curved in a sad and wistful smile. 'Paul,' she said, but not calling me or speaking to me at all, only tasting the sound of the name in her mouth. She reached out and rested her hand lightly on my knee. Watching the hand, and my knee, she said, softly, 'Do you love me?'

'I don't know.' It was the truth – I was too bewildered now to know anything – and I blurted it out without thought.

But she approved of the answer. She smiled more, and nodded. 'And I don't know if I love you,' she said. 'But I hope I do. Or will. And that you will, too.'

I fumbled for an answer, but couldn't find any. Clarity was returning to me, and I was becoming dismayed.

She went on, without any word from me. 'What a terror I was in high school,' she said, still in the same soft wistful voice. 'If a boy so much as touched my breast, I clawed him to ribbons.' She looked at me, and smiled, and shook her head. 'Still, I wasn't a virgin,' she said. 'You know that.'

I nodded.

'I'm twenty-seven,' she said. 'The fire's been banked in me for fifteen years. And how was I to know you'd come along? I was never promiscuous, Paul. I thought I would marry him.'

'It's all right,' I said. It seemed required of me to say that.

'Would you rather I told you about him? Or would you rather I wouldn't?'

'I'd rather you wouldn't,' I said.

'He didn't exist,' she said. 'You erased him. From this moment on, he never existed.'

I didn't want to talk about it. I didn't even want to think about it. Who was this woman? I didn't know her and she didn't know me, and in less than three hours she'd built a towering love affair over us, we were star-crossed lovers. She was crazy, that's all, she was out of her mind.

I caught myself up on that. Alice MacCann was a fragile and delicate girl who had suddenly seen murder, who had suddenly had her family torn from her – for her parents were dead, and her grandfather was her only real family, the only one who had lived with her here in this house – and if she was out of her mind right now, it was from grief. Alone in the house, suddenly alone, emotionally racked, and then all at once I had come along. I had been kind and sympathetic, I had held her while she wept out the first raw jolt of grief, and in desperation she had turned to me. She hadn't wanted to be alone, to be without love or compassion or human company, and so she had turned to me. I've read where people just rescued from what had seemed certain death – miners saved after a cave-in, miraculous survivors of plane crashes, condemned men reprieved minutes before the scheduled execution – very often feel a sudden overwhelming sexual desire, as though only in this act can they truly affirm the fact of their continued existence. It had probably been something like that with Alice, added to the sudden loss and the sudden solitude, enforcing it with the desire to affirm that *she* was still alive, *she* had not been stopped and turned to clay.

Brutal? Unfeeling? No, inevitable. In the sight of death, our first thought must always be of our own continued existence; only later can we afford sympathy or grief for him whose existence has ended. Besides which, such promptings and urges would hardly have formed part of her conscious thinking.

No, *Alice* was not to be blamed. Her emotions had been ripped to pieces, and she had striven, without conscious plan or design, to somehow make them whole again. But what about me? What was my excuse?

I needed one, I'll say that much.

Well, to begin with, I am weak. I had not seduced her, she had seduced me, and I am devilishly easy to seduce. If the girl is under emotional strain, and a man with any decency in him at all would forbear, I saw now that I would become aware of my duty only afterwards. Before and during, I hadn't been thinking at all.

Additionally, in my own defence, there's the fact that I too had been involved in something of an emotional hurricane for the last couple of days. Not with the suddenness or force of the hurricane that had hit Alice, but still I had been driven to the ragged edge.

Excuses, excuses. But, God help me, I've got to be able to forgive myself, haven't I? It would be impossible to live if we couldn't forgive ourselves. I don't believe that I was any less than any other man in my frantic search, as I sat there on Alice Mac-Cann's bed, for extenuating circumstances.

All right, I think of duty only afterwards. And I knew my duty now. It would be very easy at this point for Alice, emotionally jangled already, suddenly to make a complete aboutface and begin to loathe herself for what she had done, to the point where *she* wouldn't be able to forgive herself. Sooner or later, she was going to look at this afternoon with clarity, and say to herself, 'I went to bed with a stranger, four hours after my grandfather was murdered.' I had to soften that moment for her, if I could.

So I said nothing to destroy the fiction she'd built up around us. Instead, I answered her by saying, 'You tell me nothing about your yesterdays, and I'll tell you nothing about mine. All right?'

She smiled, pleased. 'We're brand-new,' she said, and clasped my hand in both of hers.

'Hello, Alice,' I said.

'Hello, Paul.' She smiled again, getting more radiant by the second, the shy wistfulness fading slowly. She got to her feet, still holding my hand, and said, 'Are you hungry?'

'I'm starved.'

'I'll make you lunch.'

'All right, I'll – Oh, my God, Walter!'

'What?' Her eyes widened in alarm.

'I told them I'd be back a little after one.' I pulled my hand free and jumped up from the bed and started scrabbling around on the floor for my clothes. 'They're probably going out of their minds.'

'Call them again, Paul. Don't go yet.'

'I told them I'd be back. I told them.'

'Paul, wait. I told you I could help you. Call and say you'll be late, and we'll talk while we're having lunch.'

That stopped me. 'Help me? How?'

'I know what Chuck Hamilton found out,' she said.

'You do? What – he told you?'

She shook her head. 'I told him,' she said.

19

My second call to Walter was less pleasant than the first. A touch of steel came into his voice when he recognized me, and though he didn't say it in so many words, I got the idea that Fletcher and the others considered me Walter's responsibility, and were beginning to wonder why in the world Walter had ever hired me.

I made excuses, I'm not sure what. I'm sure only that I told him no part of the truth. I didn't tell him where I was, I didn't tell him what I'd been up to recently, and I didn't tell him I was currently following a trail to Charles Hamilton's secret. He might like to hear the secret, once I had it and was safely back in the motel, but for now he wouldn't have liked hearing that I was still intent on butting my nose in. I promised to be back soon, and hung up.

Alice had made a salad, because by now it was once again a very hot day, the hottest since I'd come to Wittburg. There was white bread, too, and butter and cheese spread and bologna. And more iced tea.

Alice talked to me, while we ate. 'Chuck came to me about a week and a half ago, and showed me the letter he got from Mr Freedman, in Washington. He knew I worked in the bookkeeping department, and he said if there was anything illegal or, or anything like that going on, that would help the union, it might be in the bookkeeping department. So he asked me to help him, and I said I would.'

She paused to eat salad. I waited, watching her.

'I have a key to the office,' she said, 'and I know the combination to the safe. Chuck and I went in there in the evenings, after work, and we went through the books. There wasn't anybody around but old Abner Christo, the night watchman, and we made him think we were' – she blushed faintly, and her eyes skidded away from mine – 'were using the office for something

305

else. That way, he wouldn't say anything to anybody, about us being there.'

The recountal of this subterfuge seemed to upset her, and for a minute she devoted her attention to eating, her eyes fixed firmly on the plate. I drank iced tea, and finished my sandwich, and waited. She was calm now, and relatively self-possessed, but I didn't know how secure her grip actually was. If she was made upset by admitting a fictional adultery, the grip couldn't be very secure at all. So I didn't push her to go on with the story, even though I was pretty anxious to hear the punch line.

After a minute, she raised her eyes to mine again, and went on. 'We spent a week at it,' she said. 'Chuck wasn't really much help; he didn't know that much about bookkeeping. But we kept at it, and finally we did find something wrong.'

'Ah!'

'Yes. To tell you the truth, Paul, I'm not a really accomplished accountant either, so I don't fully understand just what was being done, but I do know that money was being sidetracked out of the business. It was complicated, but we could follow it at least part of the way.'

She put her hands flat on the table, palms down, one on either side of the plate. 'There are basically two kinds of expenses in the factory,' she said. She waggled the fingers of her left hand. 'Employees' salaries, and contributions to the Unemployment Insurance fund, and health and accident insurance premiums, and things like that. Things connected with the employees.' She waggled the fingers of her right hand. 'And there are the costs for raw materials, and shipping costs, and heat and electricity for the plant buildings, and things like that.' She lifted her hands from the table and pressed the palms together over her plate. 'But at the top of the accounting system,' she said, 'all the expenses come together. They're all linked. As you work down through the system, they separate out into expenses for this and expenses for that. Do you see the way it works?'

'More or less,' I said. As an Eco major, I'd taken more than my share of math courses, but accountancy was far from my strong suit. My main concern, in the field of economics, had always been at a more ethereal level.

306

'The way the money's been taken out,' she said, 'involves both kinds of expenses, and that's why it's so hard to follow it through the books. To begin with, on the raw-materials side, false vouchers are made out, for companies we actually do business with, and false check numbers are created – there's a whole false-check series in the books now – for make-believe checks to pay for these vouchers. But these checks would have to be made out to the *companies*, and so they'd be too hard to cash, so there aren't any checks made out at all. This part is just to explain where the money went.'

I nodded. 'But the money really went over to the other side, is that it?'

'That's right. Various employees, on the other side, are credited with mythical overtime, and checks are actually made out to them, with all the proper deductions and everything. But when you get about halfway through the books, those checks just disappear, like a river going underground. I'm not sure myself how it happens; the books keep balancing all along the way. But the checks disappear; the amounts are justified some way or other, and from there on, the books are accurate except for the embezzlement. But you see, on one side there's too much money, because of bills that were supposed to have been paid and weren't, and on the other side there's too little money, because of checks that have been written with incomplete recording. But when it all gets to the top' – she clasped her palms together again – 'it all cancels out. Everything works out even.'

'My God, that sounds complicated,' I said. 'Why not just stick with the phoney overtime checks? Why play around with vouchers and all that?'

'Because the overtime checks have to disappear from the books before they reach the point where they're joined to the worker's actual wages. Otherwise, his annual income figures and tax deductions wouldn't square with his own accounts.'

'Uh. And he can't just stick with the vouchers, because those checks are made out to company names. All right, I see it. But how does he cash the overtime checks?'

'I don't know. I suppose he has bank accounts in other cities, and just endorses and deposits them by mail.'

'I suppose so. Something like that, anyway. How much has he taken?'

'I don't know how long it's been going on. It averages two or three thousand dollars a month.'

'Nice work if you can get it. All right, who is he?'

She shook her head. 'That's what I don't know. There are three people who could do it, and I don't know which one it is.'

'Oh.' That brought me down to earth again. I'd thought it was all finished, and it wasn't.

'There's Mr Petersen,' she said, 'the head of the department. And Mr Koll, the chief accountant. And Mrs Fieldstone, Mr Petersen's secretary.'

'His secretary?'

'Mr Petersen believes in delegating responsibility,' she said. 'Mrs Fieldstone does more of his work than he does. So those are the three people who'd be able to get at the books and the files and the check-writing equipment.'

'All right, it's one of them. Any guesses?'

She thought it over. When she frowned in concentration that way, she looked very young and very appealing and very defenceless.

Defenceless. Mr Petersen or Mr Koll or Mrs Fieldstone. One of those three had been stealing money from the McIntyre Company. Charles Hamilton had found out about it and had been murdered. Gar Jeffers had found out about it, and had been murdered. And Alice MacCann found out about it.

I didn't tell her then, but all at once it occurred to me just how lucky she'd been to run out of butter this morning. The murderer had come here to silence them both. It had to be that way. They both had the dangerous knowledge. And the murderer couldn't have known that Gar would be alone in the house. He had come here to kill, and must have expected to find both Gar and Alice at home. But Alice had gone out to the store, and that was the only reason she was still alive.

Not the only reason. The killer had surely waited around for Alice to come home. Not in the house, that would have been too dangerous, but somewhere nearby. And then Alice had come

308

home, but had immediately called for the police. And after the police had left, I had arrived.

Was he still out there, waiting, cursing me, watching my car still parked across the way. If I had waited, fifteen minutes more, before coming up here, I would never have met Alice MacCann in life. If I had left at one o'clock, as I'd planned, I would never have seen her again.

The knowledge of just how close we had come to never meeting, to never knowing one another, shook me and made me regard this slender girl with sad tenderness. How nearly we had missed one another!

She looked at me oddly. 'What is it?' she asked me.

'What's what?'

'Why were you looking at me like that? So sad.'

'Nothing. I was thinking.' She could hear about how close it had been some other time. 'Well?' I asked her, wrenching the subject away again. 'Any guesses about which one it is?'

She shook her head. 'I can't see any of them doing anything like that,' she said. 'I know it has to be one of them, but I just can't – Mr Petersen is very lazy, and he complains all the time, but still, he's been working here for nearly twenty-five years. I just can't see any of them doing it.'

'All right. Let me think a minute.'

I finished the iced tea, and lit a cigarette. Alice brought me an ashtray and watched me, while I tried to figure out what to do next.

I knew as much as Charles Hamilton had known. Now, what was I going to do with that knowledge? Should I bring it – and Alice – straight to Walter now?

No. They were mad at me, and in no mood to listen to me. I'd have trouble enough convincing them to let me stay on in Wittburg, without bringing them hearsay evidence of embezzling. And even if they believed me, what then? They weren't the police; they had neither the duty nor the authority to start searching for the guilty one. Their concern here was to see to it the workers got a chance at the election that at least some of them desired. All else was incidental. Fletcher had made that clear: finish the unionizing first, and then let the new local bring pressure to bear, to force the police to get to work on the murder of Charles Hamilton.

But couldn't they use this information? Of course they could, and that must be why Fleisch was so worried. He must suspect – would he know for sure? That seemed doubtful – but he must at least suspect the presence of a skeleton somewhere in the closet. He wasn't the owner of this plant, after all, he was only the manager. And if there was sudden labour trouble, or that skeleton should get out of the closet – or both – he would be manager here no longer, and he would have a black mark on his record that would be no help to him when he went looking for another job. Fleisch was perched uncomfortably in his managerial chair at the moment, and was doing everything he could think of to keep anybody from rocking the boat.

Oh, God help us, block that metaphor!

But, wait a second. Why would Fleisch have to be involved in this embezzlement thing at all? He would certainly have more sense than to be a party to it, and if he suspected any such thing he'd be sure to call for an audit at once, to minimize whatever scandal might emerge. I disliked Fleisch, and so I was too willing to find him skulking under every rock. Leave Fleisch out of this. He was worried because labour trouble would finish him here, and that was all.

But that meant he'd had nothing to do with either of the murders. I didn't like that idea – I'd seen him as the evil genius behind everything crooked in this town for too long, and had liked the picture too well, to want to give it up now – but it was inescapable. The murderer was also the embezzler. If nothing else was really clear, that much definitely was.

Damn it, I had knowledge! What was I going to do with it? There was no sense going to Captain Willick with it; he wouldn't listen to any bad news I might bring him about the McIntyre plant. And at this point there was no sense going to Walter and Fletcher with it either.

But *they* could use it, if they would. What if they were to go to Fleisch, and tell him they had evidence of embezzling going on at his plant? And what if they were to offer him a deal? Either he could co-operate, set up the election and abide by its results, and be allowed therefore to handle the embezzler with a minimum of publicity and fuss, or he could continue to obstruct the union, and have the embezzlement bomb go off with a roar that would be heard even on the soft Southern sands where the current brood of McIntyres wiled away their profits. What if they were to give him the choice?

I knew what. He'd stall for time before making his decision, have a quick audit done on the books, and clean things up himself before the union could make the bomb go off.

If he had the books.

'Hey!' I said.

Alice looked across the table at me, bewildered. 'What?'

'Listen,' I said. 'Can you still get into the bookkeeping offices?'

'Sure.'

'And you can still get at the books?'

She nodded.

'Okay. *Okay.* I want you to take me there tonight, will you?'

'Well – all right, Paul, if you want.'

'I want. What time?'

'You'll come here?'

'Right.'

'Nine o'clock?'

'Nine o'clock it is.' I pushed back from the table and got to my feet. 'I've got to get back to the motel,' I told her, 'before I get fired. Is there anybody you can stay with today?'

'Stay with? Why should I stay with anybody?'

So I had to tell her now. I said, as gently as I could, 'Alice, two men have been killed for knowing what you know. The murderer couldn't have known you weren't going to be home when he got here this morning. He came here to get you, too.'

Her face paled even more, and she said, 'Oh,' in a faint lost voice.

'So you'll need someone with you today.'

'Yes. I can go next door. I can stay with Mrs Kemmler.'

'All right. I'll pick you up there tonight, at nine.'

'No!' She seemed flustered, and looked around helplessly before saying, 'I'd rather not, not yet, I don't want – I'll come back here. I'll be here when you come.'

She was already beginning to be ashamed of what we'd done. I said, 'All right. But be sure it's me before you open the door.'

'I will.'

'I've got to go now.'

She walked me to the front door, and suddenly folded into my arms again, clasping me close, and I could feel her trembling. She whispered something, but her face was pressed to my chest, muffling the words, and I couldn't make out what she'd said. I held her awkwardly, and said, 'I'll be back. Tonight.'

'Yes.'

I left, and went out to the car. The street was deserted again. I looked both ways, wondering if the killer were still lurking nearby, waiting for Alice to be alone, but I saw no one. I got into the Ford and made a U-turn, and headed back down the hill into town.

The thoughts were rushing and scrambling through my head, bumping into one another; I couldn't concentrate at all. I finally switched the radio on, to distract me so I could drive, and found a Watertown station playing old Glenn Miller arrangements by the new Ray McKinley band. The cool dim living room came back into my thoughts, and the steep staircase, and the cool dim bedroom, and Alice upon the white sheet. I was going to change the station, but then the Kingston Trio came on, so I left it alone.

Three o'clock happened while I was still driving along, and with three o'clock came the news. After the crisis here and the crisis there, the announcer said that one particular crisis had worsened, so maybe Sondra Fleisch was a better journalist than I'd thought – but after the mess the world was in had been recorded, the announcer turned to local news, and told me that a long-time employee of the McIntyre Shoe Company, one Gar Jeffers, had been murdered in his home this morning. He had been shot to death. In a clumsy attempt to make the crime seem a suicide, the murderer had closed Gar Jeffers' dead fingers around the gun, to leave his fingerprints. But there were no other older prints; the gun had been wiped off before being placed in Gar's hand.

20

I parked in front of the unit I would be sharing once again with Walter, and went on inside.

They were all in there, waiting for me. Walter was lying on his own bed, George was on mine. Fletcher was seated with grim patience in the easy chair, and Mr Clement sat knees together in the wooden chair in the corner, while Phil Katz was prowling around the room.

They all turned to look at me as I came in. Fletcher said, 'Where've you been?'

'At Gar Jeffers' house,' I said.

Fletcher glanced at Walter, and then back at me. 'You're a damn fool, Standish,' he said.

'Yes, sir.'

Walter sat up and looked at me. He was still bruised and battered, but he had fresh clothes on and had apparently taken a shower. He shook his head and said, 'I don't know what to do with you, Paul. You've been acting like a kid.'

'I was trying to help,' I said.

'I know that.' Walter shrugged and looked over at Fletcher. 'Paul and I had a rough time up here, Ralph,' he said. 'Things were pretty frantic for a while. I don't really blame Paul for getting shook up.'

'Nor do I,' said Fletcher. His words were gritty, and full of the same grim patience as his posture in the chair. 'I understand the situation here,' he said, 'and I don't blame this young man at all for being upset and using bad judgement. What I *do* blame him for is his refusal to concentrate on his job.' He turned to me. 'You are an employee,' he told me, 'of the American Alliance of Machinists and Skilled Trades. As such, you are a part of a team which has come to this city for one purpose, and one purpose only, to wit: to create a local of our union in the McIntyre Shoe

Company plant. But you have chosen to ignore this purpose. You have chosen, instead, to become an amateur detective. I will remind you one last time that your job is *not* to track down murderers. There are hundreds of thousands of better-qualified men for that job.'

Angry answers burned in me, but I kept them to myself, and said, 'Yes, sir.'

Fletcher fumbled in his pockets, and produced a pipe and a tobacco pouch. 'I can understand,' he said, 'that when Walter was in custody, you conceived the notion that you should free him by tracking down the actual murderer of Mr Hamilton. A beautifully romantic idea, to be found frequently in the type of novel on which my wife squanders her time. Be that as it may, it is an idea I can understand, though I cannot approve it. But you see Walter is here now, free and exonerated. Only stubbornness can keep you on your search.'

'Yes, sir,' I said.

Walter said, 'Ralph wants to send you back to Washington, Paul, but I'm against it. I brought you here to show you how an organizer works, and up to now there's been damn little organizing to watch. I'd like to have you stick around. But you could put me in a rough spot, Paul, if you go wandering off on your own again.'

'I can see that,' I said.

'Paul, will you give me your promise you'll leave these murders alone from now on?'

'I promise,' I said. 'I'll work only for the union from now on, only to get the local here. Mr Fletcher's right, you're free now and that's that.'

But even while I was delivering these half-truths, I was wondering why I shouldn't simply tell them the way I felt. Gar Jeffers had come to me for help, and in the very short time I'd known him he had become my friend, and now he was dead. Gar's granddaughter, Alice, was in danger from the same man who had killed Gar and, although my feelings for Alice were a little too complex yet for me to be able to state them clearly, I did know the sum of it, that I wanted to protect her, I wanted to keep her from being hurt.

315

Why not tell them this? I can't forget the murderer, because he killed a man who was my friend and is endangering a girl I feel very close to. And while I know I don't have the knowledge or the training to track him down myself, I have a plan that should wind up with Fleisch putting his tame police force to work *really* to look for the killer. And, as an incidental, this plan will also put the union in a very strong bargaining position with Fleisch.

It would have been so much easier if I could tell them the truth. But they didn't trust me, they didn't trust my competence or my judgement. And if I told them that I was still primarily concerned with the murders rather than the creation of the local, they would send me back to Washington. So I had to lie, and smile, and convince them that I would be a good boy from now on.

They accepted it. Fletcher, looking less grim, settled back more comfortably in his chair, and said, 'I'm glad to hear that, Paul, and I hope you mean it.'

'I'm sure he does, Ralph,' said Walter. He grinned at me and got to his feet and said, 'Well, Paul, you learning much about economics?'

'I'm learning,' I told him, smiling back at him.

'Right.' He made a half-turn, to face all of us at once, and immediately the businessman's façade snapped into place. 'It's time we all got to work,' he said. 'We've been delayed, but we can make up for it. Ralph, you want to go to City Hall, check the local laws on assembly, pamphlet distribution, and so on. Phil, you and I will go to Watertown now, place our newspaper advertising, and see what kind of sympathy we'll get in the local press. Paul, find us a printer in town here to make us up a batch of pamphlets and throwaways.' He winked and grinned, the phoney wink and false grin of the businessman, and said, 'The union trades with local business, of course. George, you go along with Paul and make sure he doesn't get lost again. Right?'

'Right,' said George. He gazed at me and nodded solemnly, and I realized it had been a great embarrassment to him this morning when I'd suddenly gone running off. So it might be

316

more difficult than I'd thought to get away this evening, unless I could lull George into a false sense of security. I smiled reassuringly at him, and he smiled reluctantly back.

We all got ready to leave. Walter and Phil were using the car Fletcher had rented, while Fletcher would travel by cab, and George and I would take the Ford. Mr Clement, almost invisible in his corner, would stay at the motel and mind the store.

On his way out, Walter stopped beside me and the businessman mask slipped as he whacked me heartily on the shoulder and said, 'Now you'll see the way it's done, Paul! Now you'll see organization.'

'Fine,' I said.

21

I let my fingers do the walking through the yellow pages, and copied down the addresses of Wittburg's seven printers. Then I gathered up the samples of the two pamphlets and three throwaways, and George and I went out to the Ford.

As we headed up Harpur Boulevard, George said to me, 'Mr Fletcher was real mad at you, little friend. You know how I can tell?'

'How?'

'Up here on the head.' He tapped two thick forefingers against his temples. 'When Mr Fletcher is real mad, he gets white up here.'

'I could tell anyway,' I said.

'Let me tell you something,' he said. 'A good word. You been going around like Batman, you know what I mean? Catchin' the crooks and avenging justice and all that. But that ain't the way to be. You watch out for *you*, that's what you do. You take care of your own job and your own family and your own self, and you just forget everything else. That's the way to be.'

'I suppose so,' I lied.

'You know,' he said, 'I got to thinking about Batman one time, and he ain't doing any good. Like, say one time he catches this jewel robber, him and Robin. And they turn him over to the cops, like they do. So this jewel robber, first thing, he calls a lawyer. And the lawyer comes in and says. "What you guys doing with my client?" And the cops say, "He was caught robbing jewels." And the lawyer says, "You got any proof? You got any witnesses?" And the cops say, "These two guys that caught him, that's all. They said they was out wandering around and they caught this client of yours here robbing jewels." And the lawyer says, "Who are these two guys? Are they prepared to testify?" And the cops say, "It's a couple guys with masks on, they call

318

themselves Batman and Robin." And the lawyer says, "Hold on a minute. You got these two guys with masks on, and they come in and accuse my client of robbing jewels, and these two guys don't give you their right names, and they go wandering around in the middle of the night." And the jewel robber says, "Yeah, and they wear funny suits, like a couple of nuts, and they got this souped-up customized car." And the lawyer turns to the assistant DA, and he says, "You sure you want to go to court with this? You sure you want to put these two kooks on the stand?" And the assistant DA says, "The hell with it." And the jewel robber walks out of the precinct, and that's it.'

George, one way and another, had an astonishing gift of mimicry. When he was talking as the lawyer, he did a very good imitation of Fletcher's impatient perfectionist. The cop talked the way gorillas would talk, if gorillas talked, and the jewel robber sounded like Arnold Stang. I was laughing aloud by the time the jewel robber walked out of the precinct, and George was grinning at me like a big friendly Saint Bernard. He said, 'You see what I mean, little friend?'

I had to admit I saw what he meant.

I had to admit I was going out on a limb, and I had to admit I was going around like Batman (or Philo Vance, depending), and I had to admit I hadn't done anybody any good so far. But I also had to admit that I was stubborn, and I was still angry and upset at the local imitation of a police force, and I was still determined to do what I could to help and protect Alice MacCann. So whatever I had to admit, and however many well-meaning people proved I should quit, I wasn't going to quit. I was damned if I was going to quit.

And then I wondered what the murderer would think if he knew of my fiery resolve. He'd probably laugh for a week. And he might even be right.

I had worn myself into a blue funk by the time we reached the first print shop. Whatever confidence I had in myself had vanished. Only blunt childish stubbornness kept me from throwing in the towel.

George and I walked into the print shop, and found a cluttered roll-top desk, and sitting behind it a genteel lady with lace cuffs and a pince-nez. I told her we wanted to order a printing job done, and she called to a man named Harry, who came out to us, ink-stained and greasy-shirted, from the noisy back room. 'We need a relatively fast job,' I told him. 'We'd like a thousand of each of these.' And I handed over the pamphlets – which were simply four-page affairs, made by doubling a sheet of eight-by-ten paper – and the throwaways.

'I'm not sure I could match the paper,' he said. He was a mild-mannered, pleasant-faced man, with stubby hands.

'That doesn't matter,' I told him.

'Well, I think I could do you a job,' he said. He glanced then at one of the throwaways, and read it slowly, moving his lips. He frowned, and looked through the other material, and then looked back at me regretfully, and shook his head. 'I'm sorry,' he said. 'This is a tougher job than I thought. I don't have the proper founts and –'

'That doesn't matter,' I said. 'We don't have to match it exactly.'

But he shook his head again, and said, 'I'm really sorry. I'd like the job, I could use it, but I just don't think I'd be able to handle it. I don't want to take on any job unless I can do a good job of it. You understand.'

Well, if he didn't think he could do it, that's all there was to be said. I thanked him, and gathered up the samples, and George and I went back out to the car.

At the second place, the man seemed interested, but when he read one of the throwaways he said, 'No,' and pushed everything back across the counter.

I said, 'What?'

'I don't want to get involved,' he said.

'Involved in what?'

'The answer is no,' he said, and turned around and walked away from the counter.

In the third place, we hit another man who didn't have the right founts or the right paper, and who was convinced he wouldn't be able to do the kind of job we wanted. By then, I was beginning to get the idea. I'd believed the first man, and the knowledge that I'd believed him angered and embarrassed me. I stalked out of the third shop while the mealy-mouthed owner was still apologizing, and George came along after me.

We stood on the sidewalk, in the late afternoon sun. 'Well, George,' I said, 'it looks like we're getting the runaround.'

George nodded ponderously. 'Nobody wants to get the shoe company mad at them.'

'That about sums it up.'

'Maybe we ought to go to Watertown,' he said.

'No. Walter said we support local business, and by God we support local business. Where's a phone?'

'Now, little friend,' said George worriedly, 'you aren't going to start no trouble, are you?'

'Not me, George,' I said. 'I'm cured. There's a drugstore down there. Come on.'

George trailed me, not happy, and in the drugstore I looked up the number of the Wittburg *Beacon*. I left the phone-booth door open, both to get some air and to let George hear what I was going to say, and dialled the *Beacon*'s number. When a female voice answered, I asked for Sondra Fleisch. George stirred at that, and looked more worried than ever, but he didn't try to stop me.

She was in the building, and eventually got on the line. 'Hello, there,' I said. 'This is sneering, defiant Paul Standish.'

'How nice,' she said. 'I see you got your voice back.'

'That's right.'

'What a pity.'

'Sure. How would you like to do me a favour?'

'A *what*?'

'I'm trying to get some stuff printed up, and the local printers are scared to take the job. Now, I could just as easy go to Watertown and have it done, right?'

'But you want the *Beacon* to loan you its presses for a while.'

'Not quite. One of the guys I talked to, one of the printers, he seemed like a nice guy, and he looked like he could use the job. I'd like you to come on down and tell him it's okay, he won't have his shop wrecked or anything if he prints this stuff up for us. We'd get it done anyway, in Watertown, so you don't have anything to gain by refusing. Will you do it?'

There was a kind of stunned pause, and then, in a surprisingly low voice, she said, 'People like you just don't happen. You like this print-shop man, and you want him to get the job. You're an actual shining prince, aren't you? You're a God damn *saint*, aren't you?'

'Not quite a saint,' I said.

'Oh, I wish you were a bastard,' she said. 'I want to hate you, I really and truly do. Say something so I can get mad at you again.'

'I promise I will. Right after you talk to the printer.'

'Are you sure you just aren't trying to make me ashamed of myself?'

'Definitely not. I guarantee it.'

'. . . All right. Where is this print shop?'

'It's the Bizzy Art, on –'

'Oh, that one. I know it. All right, I'll be there in fifteen minutes.'

'Fine. Thanks, Sondra.'

She hung up without answering.

George was looking at me oddly as we went back to the car. I grinned at him, and punched his arm, and said, 'Well, what do you think of Batman now?'

'You ain't Batman,' he said. 'Robin, maybe, but you ain't Batman.'

322

22

We parked in front of the Bizzy Art Printing Company shop, and waited in the car. After a couple minutes, I saw Sondra coming down the block, and I climbed out of the Ford. George came along with me, and we met Sondra in front of the plate-glass window with *Bizzy Art* curving across its dusty face.

Sondra looked blankly at George. 'This is George,' I said. 'The union sent him along with me, in case the local police decide to exceed their instructions any more.'

'So now you have a bodyguard,' she said.

'That's the way life goes in Wittburg.'

I held the door, and Sondra, looking thoughtful, went on inside. I followed her, and George came third.

The lady with the lace cuffs and the pince-nez looked up at our entrance. 'I'd like to talk to Harry again, please,' I said.

She looked doubtful, and a little scared. 'He told you we couldn't do that job,' she said.

'I know. But I'd like to talk to him anyway.'

She debated, and then got to her feet. She wasn't just going to call Harry this time; she was going back to forewarn him.

He came through the doorway, looking very reluctant. He frowned when he saw Sondra, then came on to the counter and said, 'Well?'

'This is Sondra Fleisch,' I said. 'You've probably heard of her.'

He nodded cautiously.

Sondra said, 'My father wouldn't mind if you printed those things for the union. I guarantee it.' He still looked doubtful. 'Well . . .'

I said, 'You don't believe she is Miss Fleisch?'

'Oh, yes,' he said. 'I've seen her picture in the paper.'

For some reason, that made Sondra blush. Using her job on the paper to con me hadn't bothered her, but using her influence to get her picture in the paper made her blush.

She said, 'In fact, I'm sure my father would be upset if word got around that these people couldn't even get their posters printed in our town. After all, this is a democracy.'

'Well . . . All right, Miss Fleisch, if you say so.'

'I say so,' she said.

He nodded. 'All right, then,' he said to me. 'I'll do it.'

'I want to be sure of something, though,' I said. 'You told me you didn't have the right founts. Do you?'

He looked uncomfortable. 'I think we could, uh, find some, uh . . .'

'Sure. But you also said you didn't think you'd be able to do a job that would satisfy us. Now, do you think maybe you could satisfy us, after all?'

'I . . . uh, I think I could, yes.'

'Thanks a lot.' I turned to George. 'Isn't he a mealy-mouthed bastard, though?'

George looked just as confused as everybody else, so I turned instead to Sondra. 'I promised you,' I reminded her, 'I'd say something to let you be mad at me again, right after you did me the favour, right?'

She didn't answer. She watched me warily.

'When I first got to this town,' I told her, 'I was kind of stupid. I was so stupid I let you use me for your yellow journalism. But I learn fast, Sondra. I'm a real quick study. This cheap bastard here, this Harry here, told me a bunch of cheap cowardly lies, and I believed him. Just like you told me a bunch of cheap cowardly lies and I believed you. I told you I liked this Harry, but I'm afraid that was a cheap cowardly lie. You see how quick I learn? I wanted to be able to come back in here and listen to Harry tell me he was a cheap cowardly liar. That's why I called you up, and that's why you're down here. You see what a fast study I am? Now *I'm* using *you*.'

I turned to the door, saying, 'Come on, George, let's go to Watertown and get this stuff printed up.'

23

We got back from Watertown a little after six. Walter and Phil Katz were already back at the motel, playing gin, and Phil seemed to be winning heavily. George watched Phil deal out a new hand, and then nodded sagely and said, 'Thirty-eight cents.'

'Yah,' said Phil. That one loss in his past bothered him more than he wanted to admit, and George's needling was more to the point than I'd at first thought.

His comment made, George stretched out on my bed, composed his arms at his sides, and gazed sleepy-eyed and smiling at the ceiling. Any time George was at rest, it seemed, he was supine.

Walter looked at the cards he'd been dealt, shook his head, and said, 'Last hand, Phil.' He looked up at me, saying, 'You eat yet?'

'On the way back.'

'We'll go have a beer.'

'Fine.'

Phil won handily, collected forty-seven points from Walter's hand, and Walter reached for his wallet. He handed three singles to Phil, got some coins back, and said, 'We'll be back in a little while.'

'Alcohol,' said George dreamily, 'ain't good for the system.'

We went outside, and Walter told me to drive. 'Not into town,' he said. 'The other way. I saw a place about a mile south of here, looked pretty good.'

'Check.'

We were both silent on the way, both, I suppose, lost in our own thoughts. The bar was a rambling yellow-brick building, with blacktopped parking area across the front. A neon sign suspended from a pole stuck to the front of the building over the door read: *Tango Inn*. There were two Plymouths, a Chevrolet, a Volkswagen Microbus and an elderly Packard parked in front. We left the Ford with them, and went inside.

The main room was a large square, with a horseshoe-shaped bar jutting out from the left and filling up most of the space. There were small tables along the front wall, and a broad doorway in the back wall showed an unlit second room, lined with tables. A shuffleboard flanked this doorway on one side, and stacked beer cases flanked it on the other.

There were no women in the room. Six or seven men in work clothes sat here and there at the bar, and four more men, younger than the rest, were playing shuffleboard. The bartender was very short, somewhat stocky, and totally bald. His head gleamed amber in the indirect lighting.

Walter led the way all around the horseshoe to the far corner, where we'd have semi-privacy. The beer cases were behind us, the wall was to our right, and the nearest other customer was four stools to our left.

We ordered Budweiser. The bartender brought them, took Walter's money, and went back to his conversation around on the other side of the horseshoe. Walter drank some beer, nodded, smiled, and said, 'Well? You want to tell me about it?'

'What? Tell you about what?' To my own ear, I sounded guilty as hell.

He smiled some more, and shook his head, and patted me on the back. 'Paul,' he said, 'you're a good guy. I'm glad Dr Reedman sent you.'

'You are?'

'Did you ever think of staying with the union?'

I hadn't, and the question was totally unexpected, so I didn't say anything at all.

'You'd be a good man for it,' he said. 'You're intelligent, and you're resourceful, and you've got a good honest face.'

'Well,' I said.

He jabbed me with his elbow and laughed out loud. 'It isn't always like Wittburg, Paul,' he said. 'Usually, it's a lot better.'

'I'm sure of it.'

'You ought to think it over,' he said.

'Well, I've still got my degree to get.'

'Oh, sure. I didn't mean quit school. You need a college education, Paul. If you're going to get anywhere in this world today, you've got to have that diploma.'

'That's the way I figure it.'

He turned serious. Not the businessman façade, simply earnestness. 'You're an economist,' he said. 'Or, you will be. Now, you'll want to make a decent living, why not? Not a million dollars, but a comfortable wage. So teaching and the government are out; with both of those you make peanuts. Now, that leaves industry and unions. Unions hire a lot of economists, Paul, and pay them damn good salaries.'

'I wanted to go on for a master's,' I said.

'Well, of course. You can't be an economist with a lousy B.A. But the union's got a programme for that. You hire on when you graduate from Monequois. You sign a contract with the union. Then the union pays for the rest of your schooling, and you get on-the-job training during school vacations. When you've got the M.A., it's possible you can get the union to go along with you for the doctorate. That depends on your school record, and what the union thinks your potential is. In any case, you finish school with a job waiting for you, in an organization where there's plenty of room for advancement. This isn't the Miners, Paul, this is the Machinists. We're one of the few unions around that can expect to *grow* with automation. You ought to think it over.'

'I will,' I said, and meant it. The schooling assistance sounded good, and the union looked as though it might be a more exciting outfit to work for than anyone else I'd had in mind. And the point about automation was a good one; it *was* important to pick an outfit that would be expanding in the future, and not simply holding its own. It was important if you wanted to move up the rungs, anyway.

He nodded, satisfied. Then conversation waited while we ordered two more beers. They came, I paid this time – over Walter's protests – and when the bartender left again, Walter said, 'Now, about your more immediate plans.' He was grinning when he said it, and looking humorously sly.

327

Once again, I took a vain stab at appearing innocent. 'Such as?'

'That's what I want to know.' He leaned closer, smiling, and said, 'You can kid old Fletcher, Paul. He's a humourless self-satisfied clown. But you can't kid me. I know you, Paul, and you don't give up.'

I busied myself pouring more beer from bottle to glass.

'If you didn't have some scheme in that head of yours,' he said, 'you'd have told Fletcher to go to hell for himself. But you've got an idea, and you want to be left alone to try it. Right?'

'Aw, now, Walter –'

He laughed out loud again, and jabbed my arm. 'Oh, those great big innocent eyes!'

'It's the glasses,' I said, trying vainly to change the subject. 'They make my eyes look bigger.' I took them off and said, 'See?'

But he refused to be side-tracked. 'I can help you, Paul,' he said. 'Whatever it is, you're going to have to spring it on Fletcher sooner or later. That's why I wanted to know if you'd thought about making a career of the union. If you're going to stay with us, you don't want a man like Fletcher down on you.'

I studied my beer and thought that over. As usual, Walter was right.

'I can help soften the blow with Fletcher,' he said. 'And maybe I could help with the scheme, too. Besides, if we're going to work together, we ought to trust each other. And you'd like to talk it over with somebody, wouldn't you?'

I would. I'd been thinking that all day long, wishing I could tell them all the truth. And now, it seemed, I had the chance. Walter had seen through my apologies and pledges, and had said nothing to Fletcher. I *could* trust him.

'All right,' I said.

'Good. Hold on, let's get another beer.'

We got another beer, and I told him the story, everything except the details of my stay with Alice. He nodded from time to time, and grinned, and seemed pleased all the way through. When I finished, explaining that the scheme, if it worked, would serve a dual purpose, forcing Fleisch into line the way the union

328

wanted and also forcing the police to go out and find the murderer the way I wanted, he laughed out loud, shook his head, and said, 'The union can't afford to pass you up, Paul! The way you operate, you could start a local in Congress!'

Then we had another round, before he said any more. The bartender was getting more displeased every time we called him away from his conversation, and he tapped his foot impatiently this time while Walter and I argued about who would pay. Walter finally won, and the bartender went away.

Walter turned back to me. 'To begin with,' he said, 'it's illegal. It could backfire, Paul. If you were caught, the union couldn't very well admit it had anything to do with your going there.'

'I'm not asking the union to back me,' I said. 'I wasn't going to say anything about it at all.'

'I know. I just wanted to get that on the record. All right, it's illegal. And one more thing, it isn't the kind of scheme the union would normally consider. We work through legal and honest methods, Paul. We have an unusual situation here, and you want to do something as a private individual, so that's something else again. But I don't want you to think that the union normally engages in illegal activity of any kind at all.'

'I didn't think that,' I told him. 'I know better.'

'I know you do. As I say, I just want to get these facts on the record. So. Now that I've told you your scheme is illegal and against union policy, I've gotten all that out of the way.' He winked. 'Mr Clement will love to see those books, Paul,' he said.

'I should go ahead with it, then?'

He cocked his head, and grinned at me. 'Are you asking me as a representative of the Machinists?'

I laughed, shaking my head. 'I don't think I better.'

'You're right. Okay. Now, when we go back, you follow my lead, all right? We'll have to let Fletcher know ahead of time, but let me do the talking, and don't be surprised at anything I might say. Believe me, I know how to handle Fletcher. Okay?'

'Fine,' I said.

'Good. Now, let's have another beer.'

'I'll be right back.'

I found the men's room off in a corner of the rear dining-room area, and when I came back, Walter was looking pleased and conspiratorial. Low-voiced, he said, 'You see those four fellas down to our left?'

'Yes?'

'I've been listening to them. They work in the shoe plant, and they've been talking about the union. Three of them want a local of the Machinists, and they want it bad. And the fourth one said a local will be just as bad as the company union, so the hell with it.'

'Three to one,' I said. 'That's good odds.'

He shook his head, grinning hugely. 'Better than that,' he said. 'Four to nothing. One of them finally told him the local couldn't possibly be any worse than the company union, so it was at least worth a try, and he agreed. Four to nothing, Paul. *Those* are good odds.'

'So all we have to do is get a hands-off from Fleisch.'

'That's all. Drink your beer. You play shuffleboard?'

So we had two more beers, and Walter beat me at shuffle-board, and then we went back to the motel.

24

We left the Tango Inn at eight o'clock, and Walter drove us back to the motel. I asked him to; I was feeling the beer a little bit. We'd each had seven or eight bottles of the stuff.

George didn't seem to have moved. He was still lying on my bed, arms straight out at his sides, smiling dreamily at the ceiling. Phil was gone, and Mr Clement was nowhere in sight, but Fletcher had come back to the room's easy chair. He was reading a black-bound book when we came in, but looked up from it at our entrance, nodded, and stowed the book away in the briefcase beside the chair. 'No particular legal problems,' he said. 'We'll need a permit and to pay for the presence of a fire marshal, if we have any indoor rallies. Other than that, we have nothing to worry about.'

'That's okay,' said Walter, sounding pleased. 'What was their attitude?'

Fletcher smiled icily, and without humour. 'Distant, when I told them my affiliation. But properly helpful when I let them know I would brook no prejudiced behaviour.'

'That's the boy, Ralph,' said Walter. 'They don't stay on their high horse long when you're around.'

'I know the law,' said Fletcher. 'That is my job.'

'And you're good at it, too, Ralph.' Walter fought his necktie off, and draped it on the bedpost. He winked at me as I went by him, heading for the wooden chair near the bathroom door, and said, 'Oh, by the way, Ralph, I have news.'

'News?'

I sat down, at the fringe of the group, and watched to see how Walter would handle it.

'Something Paul found out today,' Walter said. 'The same thing that Charles Hamilton found out, and the same thing that old man what's-his-name found out.'

Fletcher leaned forward, interested in spite of himself.

Walter smiled and nodded, prolonging Fletcher's suspense. Then he said. 'There's a sticky finger in the McIntyre till, Ralph. Somebody's been doing bad things to the books.'

'Not Fleisch?'

'Oh, no. He doesn't even know about it. But Hamilton and old what's-his-name's granddaughter went poking through the books and found it. That's what Hamilton was going to give us. I suppose he figured we could use it if we got into a fight with Fleisch.'

Fletcher frowned. 'I don't see how,' he said. 'If Fleisch has nothing to do with it.'

Walter grinned, and raised one finger for attention. 'That's the beauty of it, Ralph,' he said. 'Fleisch isn't the *owner* of the McIntyre plant, he's just the *manager*. When we come in, there's indications of labour trouble, and already Fleisch is worried, and already the owners are saying to themselves, "Maybe we need a new manager." So what if all of a sudden a scandal breaks? Embezzlement going on under Fleisch's nose!' He turned to me. 'How much you say it was?'

'Two or three thousand a month.'

'How's that, Ralph? Are the owners going to get themselves a new manager, or aren't they?'

'I see,' said Fletcher. He rubbed a knuckle thoughtfully along the line of his jaw. 'It could be leverage,' he said. 'I see what you mean.'

'We want to do this right, Ralph,' Walter told him. 'If we just go to Fleisch and tell him there's an embezzler in the plant, he'll run a quick audit, very quietly grab the embezzler, and our leverage is gone.'

'A point,' admitted Fletcher.

'I was thinking about it on the way back,' said Walter. He turned to me again, so his profile was to Fletcher, and winked the eye Fletcher couldn't see. 'Paul,' he said, 'this girl, what's-his-name's granddaughter. You said she can get at the books?'

'That's right,' I said.

'Could she get at them tonight?'

'Sure,' I said.

332

'Um,' said Fletcher. 'What do you have in mind, Walter?'

Walter's head inclined back toward Fletcher. 'We hold the books for ransom,' he said.

Fletcher reared back, startled. 'You mean, *steal* them?'

'Borrow them.'

'Ridiculous,' said Fletcher. 'I thought you had more sense than that, Walter.'

'I thought you had more imagination than that, Ralph. What happens if we steal them?'

'Fleisch phones the police,' said Fletcher, promptly.

'And compounds the scandal? He wants the embezzlement kept *quiet*, Ralph.'

'Um,' said Fletcher. He thought some more, pondering the idea.

'We put Albert to work on them,' said Walter. 'By morning, he'll have the evidence ready to turn over to Fleisch, along with the books, in return for certain considerations.'

'It's a drastic move,' said Fletcher, but I could see he was being swayed.

'It's a drastic situation,' Walter told him.

'Um. I'd have to check with Washington, Walter, you know that.'

'I'll make the call, Ralph,' said Walter.

'No need for that.' Fletcher was on his feet.

'I'll go along,' said Walter, rising beside him.

'Very well.'

They went out, and I sat there and lit a cigarette. Walter had surprised me, claiming the idea as his own, but I'd seen right away what he had in mind. Fletcher would be more likely to think seriously about an idea from Walter than from me. It hardly mattered whose idea it was to begin with, just so it worked.

George turned his head slowly on my pillow, and smiled dreamily at me. 'Fletcher would of stole the credit,' he said.

'Oh?'

'Sure. That's how come Walter went along. These career boys!' He shook his head fondly, and went back to gazing at the ceiling again.

It was a warm night, and there wasn't enough air circulating through the room. I was still feeling those beers. I lit a cigarette and promised myself to stop for coffee on the way to meet Alice.

Fletcher and Walter came back, finally, and Walter nodded at me, smiling hugely. 'They went for it, Paul,' he said. 'What do you think, boy? You want to be a burglar?'

'Just one moment, Walter,' said Fletcher. 'Standish seems hardly the man for the job.'

'Oh, come on, Ralph, give the boy some credit. Besides, he's the one the granddaughter knows. I don't think she'd cooperate with any of the rest of us. What do you think, Paul?'

'I'm sure she wouldn't,' I said.

'You see?'

Fletcher saw, but was displeased. 'George at least should go along,' he said.

I shook my head. 'No, sir. Alice will help me, but she'd back out if there was anybody else along.'

'That's another point,' said Fletcher. 'How do you know this girl will agree to help us?'

I was about to say she'd agreed already, but Walter got in first, saying, 'Paul can talk her into it. Can't you, Paul? She and Paul have a sort of – understanding.' And he winked.

I hadn't told him anything about what had happened between Alice and me, or even hinted, and this unexpected direct hit rattled me. I felt the blood rushing to my face, betraying my embarrassment, and stumbled around in an unsuccessful attempt to say something coherent.

'I see,' said Fletcher, studying me.

I saw Walter quickly cover his surprised realization that he'd hit a bull's-eye he hadn't known existed, and then he said, 'Paul, you just tell her how it'll be helping avenge her grandfather's death, and all that. Okay?'

'All right,' I said, low-voiced and still embarrassed. And the beer wasn't helping me get my control back.

Walter plopped down onto his bed again, and said, 'Why not go now?'

'Now?' Fletcher frowned at both of us. 'Shouldn't you wait till later?'

'Why?' Walter asked him. 'Stroke of midnight and all that? They'll be much less conspicuous going into the plant at nine in the evening than at midnight. Right, Paul?'

'Right.'

'Right,' said Walter, airily. Still airily, he said, 'You can take the car, Junior. But don't be out all hours.'

'Yes, sir,' I said, grinning back at him. Walter had handled it beautifully, far better than I could have done, and I was grateful to him.

'And no necking,' he said, and laughed when I started to blush all over again.

I grabbed the car keys and hurried on out.

25

Even though I stopped at the City Line Diner for two hamburgers and three cups of coffee, I got to Alice's house early, at quarter to nine. I was regretting not having found out on which side lived the neighbour with whom Alice was staying, when I noticed the living-room light was on in Alice's house. I went down the stairs and rang the bell.

Alice opened the door almost at once, and smiled through the screen at me. 'You're early,' she said. 'Come on in.'

'You shouldn't open the door that way,' I told her. 'How did you know who it was?'

'Oh! I forgot.' She looked more embarrassed than frightened. 'I'm not used to hiding out,' she said.

I know how she felt. She wasn't the only one who'd suddenly been thrown into a world she hadn't been trained for. I said, 'All right, never mind. But you at least should have been next door.'

'I just this minute came back,' she said. 'To get ready for you. I was just going to get dressed.'

She was wearing a man's white shirt and faded blue jeans, which emphasized the contradictory slimness and provocativeness of her body. I said, 'What's wrong with what you've got on?'

'Silly. I couldn't let anybody see me like this. Anybody but you, darling. I'll have to get into a black dress.' Her mouth suddenly twisted, and she said, 'Listen to me. I sound *happy* about it.'

'Relax, Alice,' I said. 'You're alive and you're healthy and you're young. I know you loved your grandfather, and I know how much grief you feel that he's dead. But don't tie yourself into knots trying to keep a glum frown on your face all the time. It wouldn't be natural, and you'll just get yourself all upset again.'

'You're good for me, Paul,' she said. She rested a hand on my arm, then turned away and headed for the stairs. 'I'll be right back down,' she said. 'Play some records, if you want.'

I didn't play any records. I sat in the living room and read last week's issue of the *Saturday Evening Post*. It had been a long time since I'd seen the *Post*. They'd changed the cover logo, and they'd changed the format inside, making the layout and illustrations all *Playboy*-flashy, but they hadn't changed the content of the magazine at all. It was still fine-ground corn, and the stories were still about slim blonde girls in red bathing suits. I have a two-part question I'd like Hooper or Elmo Roper or one of those pollsters to ask Americans sometime: (A) Did you ever read a Clarence Budington Kelland serial all the way through? (B) If so, did you understand it?

Alice came back down in a black dress, with a fitted bodice and pleated flaring skirt. She looked like Leslie Caron, Audrey Hepburn, Mitzi Gaynor. She looked like all the girls who ever danced beneath the Eiffel Tower with Gene Kelly. Her lipstick was dark, her eyes darker. She hooked her hand in the crook of my arm, and smiled up at me, and we went out of the house to the car.

It was like taking a girl friend out to a movie. I wished I *was* taking Alice MacCann out to a movie. I tried to make believe that was all it was, a date, the two of us going out for a good time together. But the make-believe kept falling apart, and I gave it up.

She directed me through town to the plant building containing the bookkeeping offices. In the huge parking lot, there was only emptiness and a tiny Metropolitan, green and white. 'That's Abner's car,' said Alice.

'Abner?'

'The night watchman. Don't worry, he won't bother us.'

'If you say so.'

I left the Ford up close to the building, in the shadow, and we went around to a small side entrance. Alice produced a key, and unlocked the door, and we went in.

There was a metal stairwell on our left, leading down to blackness, up to blackness punctuated by reflections of a small weaving light. 'That's Abner,' Alice whispered. 'That's his flashlight.' Then she laughed, a little nervously, and said, in a normal tone, 'I don't know why I'm whispering.' She went over to the stairs and called, 'Abner! Abner?'

A heavy tread sounded above us, and the reflected light grew stronger. A voice called down, 'Who's there?'

'It's me, Alice. I'm not alone.' She reached out and took my hand and pressed it. 'We'll be in the office a little while,' she called.

'All right,' shouted the voice, and the heavy footsteps receded again, the flickering light grew fainter.

'This way,' Alice told me. Still holding my hand, she led me through a pair of doors from the stairwell to a long hall. Far down to the right I could see the glass of the main doors. We turned to the left and walked down the hall, Alice's heels clacking hollowly on the composition flooring. There was practically no light, only that which seeped in through the front doors far behind us. And when we turned a corner, even that light was gone. But Alice seemed to know exactly where she was going.

We stopped, finally, and she let go my hand to fumble with the keys. I heard the sound of the key going into the lock, and the click of its turning, and then the door opened. There were windows along a wall to the left, overlooking a side street. The street lights there shone wan afterthoughts of light into the office. I could make out two rows of desks in a long room, and filing cabinets along the wall opposite the windows.

Alice led the way down between the rows of desks. At the far end, wood and frosted-glass partitions rose to a foot from the ceiling. Alice unlocked another door here, and we went into a smaller office, with only one desk, and that one about twice as large as the desks outside. Light gleamed pale through the single wide window, and aside from the desk I could make out a leather couch along one wall, another filing cabinet, and a squat safe.

Alice said, 'Light a match, will you, Paul?' She knelt before the safe.

I lit a match, and watched her slim fingers turn the combination dial. Then she twisted the lever downward, and it clicked. She waited, twisted it farther, and it clicked again. Then she pulled the door open.

338

The first match burned down. I shook it out, threw it on the floor, and lit another. Alice pulled a large heavy ledger book from the safe, and then another, and a third, and a fourth. 'We'll need all of these,' she said. 'There. That's it.' She closed the safe again, and spun the dial.

We both straightened. 'They look heavy,' I said. The second match burned low, and I shook it out. I was reaching for a third match when she came against me and kissed me.

I am not a phlegmatic man. My reaction to sexual invitation is, I think, normally hearty. On the other hand, I don't suffer from satyriasis, either. But there was something about Alice that caught me where I lived. My reaction to her invariably was immediate, unthinking, and total. Within seconds, we were on the couch.

While there was still some clothing between us, I did manage one sobering thought. 'Pregnant,' I whispered. 'What if I make you pregnant?'

'I've taken care of that,' she whispered back. 'Don't worry, Paul, I've taken care of that. Dear Paul. Come, Paul. This leather is cold. Warm me, Paul.'

Does it spur any man on, to hear a woman softly speak his name? The sound of my own name, spoken in hot sweet urgency, with Alice's breath on my ear, left no questions and no doubts.

We left twenty minutes later, me carrying the four very heavy ledger books. There was no sign of Abner.

26

Mr Clement was delighted by the books. For the first time, I saw actual vitality in that man's face. He and Alice sat side by side at a card table in the unit he shared with Mr Fletcher, and together they went over the books, while the rest of us hung around in the background, watching.

Mr Clement was having a lovely time. He shook his head, and chuckled, and made little admiring sounds. Alice led him through the labyrinth of the books, and they flashed back and forth, from this ledger to that ledger to the other ledger, the four books all spread open, filling the entire surface of the card table and hanging over the edges. And in those places where the embezzler's river had gone underground and Alice hadn't been able to follow the progression of the sidetracked money for a while, Mr Clement leaned close and traced rows of figures with a rigid finger, concentration bowing his back and freezing his features, till he would cry, 'Ah *hah!*' and point a triumphant finger, and say, 'There it is!' and explain rapid-fire to Alice, who sometimes would nod in agreement and other times merely nod in bewilderment.

'Grand,' muttered Mr Clement, and, 'Lovely.' He was a professional, lost in admiration of the work of another professional, seeing nuances and inspired creativity that a layman could never really appreciate.

It went on and on, and the rest of us began to get tired. Even Alice, who was interested in this sort of thing, began to show signs of weariness. But Mr Clement was having the time of his life. George was the first to give up. He mumbled something about eight hours of sleep every night and went off next door to his bed. Phil Katz, who didn't see how this new development applied to his own particular specialty, followed soon after. Fletcher announced that he proposed to take a nap, as we would all have to be alert in the morning, and stretched out, fully clothed and proper and unwrinkled, on his bed. His eyes closed. His face slowly relaxed into sleep, but he still looked like a perfectionist forced to live in an incompetent world.

Walter and I kept the vigil honest, but even Walter, eventually, began to yawn hugely and stretch his arms out. 'This is enough for me,' he said. 'Nice to have met you, Alice. See you in the morning.

Alice looked up. 'What time is it?'

Walter checked his watch. 'Two-thirty.'

'Oh, good heavens!' She jumped to her feet. 'I've got to get home.'

Mr Clement, impervious to us all, kept right on mumbling and chuckling his way through the books. We finally got his attention, and told him we were leaving. 'Yes, yes,' he said. 'I'll have it written up in the morning.' And he dove back into the ledgers.

Walter and Alice and I went outside, into the darkness. It had cooled off nicely, and we paused to light a round of cigarettes. Then Walter said, 'As we promised, Miss MacCann, Fleisch will never find out exactly how we got the books. We'll keep your name out of it completely.'

'Thank you,' she said. 'It was awfully nice to meet you, Mr Killy.'

'Likewise, Miss MacCann.'

They shook hands, and Walter went on into our unit. Alice and I got back into the Ford, and I drove her home.

On the way, she said, 'They're nice people, aren't they?'

'Sure,' I said. I was too tired to be much good at conversation.

'They've all got a *purpose*,' she said. 'They're dedicated. I bet that Mr Clement won't sleep at all tonight.'

'No bet,' I said.

She turned to me, her eyes glowing in the light from the dash. 'Paul,' she said, 'I've done you all a favour tonight, haven't I?'

'You sure have. A big favour.'

'Will you do me a big favour back?'

'If I can.'

'Take me back to Washington with you.'

341

I stared at her. 'What?'

'Look at the road, she said. 'Let's not have an accident.'

I looked at the road.

'I want the union to give me a job,' she said. 'I can type sixty-five words a minute, I can take dictation at ninety, and I can keep financial records. When all of you go back to Washington, I want to go with you.'

My feelings at that moment were too complex to be given in a single simple word or phrase. Alice wanted to come back to Washington with us, and I knew that that meant she would be available for me for the next six months. The prospect was pleasing. At the same time, it suddenly was brought home to me that Alice might very well be thinking of something a lot more permanent than a six-month affair. And the prospect of permanence of any kind, at least at this stage of my life, was far from pleasing. Besides, I hardly knew the girl. That may sound either ridiculous or callous, considering, but it is nevertheless the truth. I knew we were good bedmates. That, essentially, was all I knew, and it was hardly a broad enough foundation for marriage.

Marriage. Good God, I hardly knew her! I did, I hardly knew her!

'Well –' I said. 'Well. I'll talk to Walter in the morning.' And Mr Clement isn't the only one who'll stay awake all night.

'Thank you, Paul,' she said. She smiled, and snuggled close to me, and I drove one-handed.

When I stopped in front of her house, she said, 'Do you want to come in for a little while?'

'I better not,' I said. 'I ought to get back. We've all got a busy day tomorrow.'

'All right,' she said. She leaned close and kissed me, her tongue flickering out. 'Come see me when you can.'

'I will,' I promised, and already I was regretting having refused to go inside with her now.

She got out of the car, though, before I could change my mind. She waved at me, and started across the street, and I called out, 'Hey, Alice!'

She came back to the car.

'We've been forgetting,' I said. 'He may be in there.'

'Who? Oh.' She looked across the street at the house. 'You mean the murderer.'

'Yes.'

'I'll go next door. I can sleep on the sofa.'

'Look. Go in your own house, and then around the back way. So in case he's watching, he won't know where you've gone.'

'All right.'

I got out of the car after all. 'I better go with you, just in case he's in there.'

'Yes. Do.'

We searched the house, but it was empty except for ourselves. Alice began to think sexually again, but by this time I actually was too exhausted to follow my inclinations. We turned off the lights, and I watched as she crept out the back door and across the lawn to the right. 'You go on now,' she whispered back to me. 'I'll be all right, I really will.'

'I'll wait till your neighbour lets you in.'

'You will *not*! What would they think?'

I gave in, and closed the back door and went on through the dark house and out the front way and across the street to the car. I sat behind the wheel and lit a cigarette and yawned and drove back to the motel.

Walter was in bed, and the lights were out. I thought he was asleep, so I undressed in the dark, but as I was getting into bed he said, soft-voiced. 'That's quite a dish you've got there, Paul, that Alice MacCann.'

'I know,' I said.

'I didn't expect you back here tonight.'

'Walter, for Pete's sake, her grandfather *died* this morning.'

He chuckled. 'Paul, sweetie,' he said, 'you've got all the marks of a boy who's been breaking his fast.'

'Good night, Walter,' I said. I was angry, and let it show.

He was instantly contrite. He sat up, over there in the other bed, and said, 'Paul, I'm sorry. I was kidding you. Okay?'

'Okay,' I said, grumpily.

'She looks like a very nice girl,' he said. 'I mean that sincerely, Paul.'

'She wants to come back to Washington with us,' I said. It just popped out, without my intending to say it.

'She wants to do what?'

'She wants the union to give her a job. In return for her getting the books. She can type, and take dictation, and keep financial records.'

'How about a job with the local here, once we get it going?'

'No, she said she wanted to come back to Washington with us. She wants to get out of Wittburg.'

'I don't blame her. Okay, sure. Tell her she's on the payroll. I can hire her on as our field secretary now, and when we get back to the city she can go into the steno pool. Okay?'

'Okay,' I said, a little dazed. It was all decided. I didn't have to stay awake all night worrying after all. But I did, anyway.

I awoke late, to find myself alone in the room. I didn't know exactly what time it was, but the sun was high and my stomach was empty, so I thought it must be around eleven o'clock. I wandered around, washing and dressing, with a wan kind of empty feeling, mopish and wistful. I couldn't figure out at first what was wrong with me, what this feeling reminded me of, and then at last I got it. It was end-of-the-semester blues. I was breaking-up-that-old-gang-of-mine lonesome.

Once, during my stint in the Army, I was given temporary duty, a special assignment to a normally empty Army camp near Cincinnati, Ohio. Our particular numbered Army Corps was preparing its budget submission for the Congressional Armed Forces Appropriations Committee for two fiscal years hence. We made up maps of all the posts in the Corps, we had lists of all buildings on each post, and all equipment in each building, and value of this and value of that. And we had our requests for new buildings and new equipment, and eight- or ten-page justifications for every request. Lists were adjusted and justifications were rejected and rewritten, maps were found faulty and redrawn, columns of figures were added and added again, and we had ten days to finish the job. There were about forty of us, officers and enlisted men, working twelve and fourteen hours a day. In my own group, from St Louis, there were two captains, a bird colonel, a Specialist 3, and two PFC typists. I was one of the PFC typists. We lived an odd life in those ten days, disjointed and crowded and filled with a sort of jerry-built camaraderie. There was so much work to be done, and so many other things to think about, that Army rank and protocol seemed to fade into the background. Only three buildings had been opened for us, so officers and enlisted men lived unusually close together, working together and eating together and – on Sundays, our one day off

– going into town and getting half-smashed together. There's an awful lot of talk about teamwork today in government and in big corporations, but mostly it's just talk, mostly it's just a way of sugar-coating authority. During those ten days at that condemned and abandoned Army post, we forty actually did become a *team*, in the true sense of the word. And on the last day, I think we all felt a little forlorn and wistful and empty, at having to break up the team and go back to the regulated abstractions of reality. The bird colonel was no longer the man who had introduced me to Cardinal Puff, a drinking game guaranteed to leave the neophyte a sodden mess under the table. And I, to him, was no longer the youngster who had taught him one riotous lunch-time the words to 'The Bastard King of England'. The protocols were back, the herd defences were up again; I was a PFC, and he was a colonel, leaving neither of us with any more individuality than a vacuum tube. I think that's the acid test of a true team: it accentuates individuality.

At any rate, I suppose this sad empty feeling is common in such situations. Whenever men have worked together with such intensity and single-mindedness on a particular job, the completion of the job and the dispersal of the team is a sad thing. And it was this kind of sadness and loneliness and forlorn emptiness that was plaguing me this morning, though there was no sense in it. The team had been created, perhaps, but far too recently to have yet become welded into the kind of group I mean. Besides, the job wasn't ending. It was, in fact, barely beginning. So why the blues? Walter wasn't around – I supposed he was off with Fletcher and Mr Clement to see Fleisch – but so what? There was no sensible reason for the blues, which I told myself, but I had them anyway. I washed my face with cold water, twice, and I still had them. So I got dressed and went next door.

Phil was sitting yogi-legged on one bed, playing solitaire. George, of course, was supine on the other, studying the ceiling. They both looked over at me when I came in, and Phil said, 'Sleeping Beauty.'

'You were supposed to come in and kiss me,' I told him. 'What time is it?'

'Eleven-twenty.'

'The others gone off to see Fleisch?'

'Yowzah.'

George reared up and gazed at me. 'You hungry?'

'Starved.'

'Let's go eat.' George heaved himself up off the bed, shook his shoulders a little, and said to Phil, 'What about you?'

'I'll hold the fort,' Phil told him. 'Three meals a day's enough for me.'

'Huh,' said George. 'You're skinny.'

'Huh,' said Phil. 'You ain't.'

We went outside. The Ford was gone, and George handed me the keys to Fletcher's rented car, a new Chevvy. 'You drive, little friend,' he said. 'I got no licence any more.'

'All right.' We got into the Chevvy and I backed around and headed for the City Line Diner. 'What happened to your licence?'

'They took it away.' He smiled as he said it.

'What for?'

'I tried to run over this guy. I missed him, but a cop seen me on the sidewalk, and they got me for reckless driving and resisting an officer and a couple other things. So they took away the licence.'

'You tried to run him over?' I wasn't sure whether George was kidding me or not. His huge face was creased in the same dreamy smile he always wore.

'I didn't see the cop,' he explained. He shifted around, looking out the side window. 'I like this town,' he said. 'I'd like to live in a little town some day.'

'I suppose it's all right,' I said.

He looked at me again, with that sleepy big-dog smile. 'Not you,' he said. 'Not you, little friend. You're a big-city boy. You gonna stick with the union?'

'I'm not sure.'

'You'll do good,' he said. 'Whatcha gonna do to Killy?'

'Walter?' I took time out to pull into the parking lot next to the diner. 'Nothing,' I said. 'What are you talking about?'

347

'I figured you'd do him like you did that girl yesterday,' he said.

'Sondra? What for?'

'Yeah, that chick at the printer's.'

'George, I don't know what you're talking about.'

He shrugged, and got out of the car. 'I been wrong before,' he said. 'Let's eat, little friend.'

We ate, and George told me about his experiences as a sparring partner for heavyweight contenders. He'd never been a sparring partner for a champion, only for contenders. I asked him once or twice what he'd been talking about there in the car, but he slid away from the questions, acting big and dumb and friendly and full of anecdotes. He did a Yiddish fight manager from Detroit in a three-way argument with a Negro sparring partner from Louisiana and an Italian gambler from the Bronx that was really pretty funny. But he didn't answer the questions.

When we got back to the motel, Walter was there, looking like a Marlboro ad. He wore a dark grey suit and an expensive white shirt with button-down collar and a thin black tie. The slender suit and slender tie detracted from his halfback's physique, making him look narrower, but still healthy and well-physiqued. He sat in the easy chair, relaxed and smiling. His suit jacket was open, his legs were stretched out in front of him with the ankles crossed, and his right elbow was on the chair-arm as he held a cigarette in the air. The Marlboro ad, complete, except that he smoked Newports.

'Hiya, Paul,' he said, smiling. 'You're a heavy sleeper.'

'How'd it go?' I asked him.

'Like a breeze" he said. 'Like a charm. When you get an idea, Paul, it's a dilly.'

George made a comment about his digestive processes, and lay down on the nearest bed.

I said, 'He gave in, huh?'

'Sure he did. Fletcher played him like a piano. Fleisch bluffed this way and bluffed that way, and Fletcher knocked him down at every turn.'

I sat on the other bed, cross-legged, the way Phil played solitaire. 'Tell me about it,' I said.

348

He was glad to. He had, I was sure, just been sitting here waiting for me to get back so he *could* tell me about it. That was a part of Walter's charm – his natural charm, I mean, not the painfully false charm that went with his conception of a business-man – the fact that his enthusiasms were essentially childlike. He didn't hop around in his enthusiasm to tell me the story, the way a child would, but that was only the external, anyway. His *desire*, if not its expression, was simple and uncomplicated and child-like.

Walter was full of contradictions like that. No, that's wrong. It wasn't that Walter was full of contradictions, it was that my view of him was full of contradictions. I saw him as a big healthy boy, as a child, and at the same time he made *me* feel like an even younger child in his presence. And though I looked up to him and considered him more capable and knowledgeable than I, at the same time I felt – this is a strange word, and not quite accurate, but it's the closest I can come to the feeling – I felt somehow more *sophisticated* than Walter. These contradictions were not in him – he was not an obscure or heavily complex personality, by any means – but in me, in my view of him, and my recognition of that fact was itself one of the contradictions.

At any rate, he told me the story.

'We went in,' he said, 'Fletcher and Clement and me, and right off the bat Fleisch was full of bluster. He thought we wanted to make a deal of some kind, without any ace in the hole, and he wanted to be on top of the bargaining right from the beginning. Well, Fletcher let him go on for a minute or two and then he said, "That's not exactly why we're here." And he told him about the embezzlement. It's a hefty chunk of money, by the way. Clement worked it out last night. The thing's been going on for a year and a half, and the guy's pulled down about forty-five thousand so far.'

'Son of a gun,' I said.

'Yeah, isn't it? Anyway, Fleisch got rattled for a minute, because he didn't know anything about any embezzlement, and then he started to pull the stall bit, all about how he'd look into it and see if there was any truth in the charges, and if there was, he'd get in touch with us and we could talk it over some more. Fletcher'd already mentioned the McIntyres, just kind of casually, saying we thought it was better to tell Fleisch about the embezzling than go to the owners. So Fleisch knew the score, and, just the way we figured, he tried to stall us off while he cleaned it up quick and quiet all by himself.

'So then Fletcher told him we had the books.' Walter grinned at the memory of that, and leaned over to get rid of his cigarette in the ashtray on the writing table. 'He hollered like a virgin,' he said. '"I'll have you people put in jail for theft! You stole those books!"' He didn't have George's flair for mimicry, but I got the idea. 'So Fletcher picked up the phone on his desk and said, "Mr Fleisch wants to call the police. Put the call through at once, please." Then he turned to me and said, "Walter, you better go call Bobby McIntyre, after all." And then he handed the phone to Fleisch. So I started for the door, and Fleisch shouted into the phone, "Cancel that call!" And he hollered at me to stay where I was.'

'Who's Bobby McIntyre?'

'Who knows? One of the owners.' He lit himself a fresh cigarette, and went on. 'So Fleisch blustered awhile about how we couldn't threaten him, and Fletcher just sat there and waited. And when Fleisch slowed down a little, Fletcher handed him Clement's facts and figures, and then we started to deal.'

'What kind of guarantees do we get?' I asked. I didn't trust Fleisch an inch.

'The best,' he said. 'This afternoon, the *Beacon* runs a signed letter from Fleisch himself. In it, he comes out in favour of the workers deciding in an election whether to stick with the company union or form a local of the Machinists. Phil is down there now, getting the wording right.'

'So we're in,' I said.

'Like Flynn.' He grinned some more and uncrossed his ankles, and recrossed them the other way. 'I told you you'd see organizing at its sweetest and easiest,' he said. 'It took a while, but that's exactly what you're going to see. We've started to move, Paul, and from now on it's smooth sailing all the way.'

'Where are the books now?' I asked. It had occurred to me that Fleisch wasn't above promising the moon and then sending Jerry and Ben and a few more boys out to the motel to grab the books.

But the others had thought of that, too. 'In Watertown,' said Walter. 'Clement's got them there, for safekeeping. When the *Beacon* comes out this afternoon, and we see everything's all right, we call Clement and he comes back with the books and turns them over to Fleisch.'

'Fine. So what do we do now?'

'Now?' He grinned and stretched, straining his arms up over his head and bunching the shoulders of his jacket. When he lowered his arms, his shirt was tire-mounded around his waist. 'Now,' he said, 'we relax. Tomorrow, we go rent us a store front, and meet with the officials of the company union to set up the date and details of the election, and start putting our posters up, and hire kids to hand around our pamphlets, and do a half a dozen others things. But today we relax. I personally am just going to sit here and take it easy. You can go see your girl if you want.'

My girl. For God's sake, Alice! I hadn't consciously thought of her once since waking up. Now, how the hell had I managed that?

'Take the car,' said Walter. 'We won't be needing it today.'

How was she. Was she all right? Was she still staying with the neighbour, or had that carefree inacceptance of personal danger been at work again and was she alone in her own home?'

'Thanks for the use of the car,' I said. 'I'll see you later.'

I headed for the door, and behind me Walter commented to George, 'In a hurry, isn't he?'

'Always on the go,' said George, dreamily.

I went out and got into the Chevvy – the Ford was gone, apparently off in Watertown with Mr Clement – and headed toward town.

Along the way, I gnawed at the improbability of my having forgotten Alice. No, I hadn't actually *forgotten* her, I just hadn't thought of her. That was ridiculous.

I remembered, too, the blue funk I'd been in when I'd

awakened, and which still hadn't entirely left me. Could Alice be the cause of it? I'd analysed the depression as being the kind that comes with a change in one's way of life. Was Alice going to change my way of life?

I tried the neighbour's house first, on the off-chance that Alice had begun to act sensibly about the danger she was in. Going down the steps to the front door, I tried to remember the neighbour's name – Alice had mentioned it once – Mrs Kremmel? Mrs Kremmler? Something like that. But I couldn't remember exactly what, and the name slots were blank by doorbell and mailbox, so I'd have to get along without. I rang the bell.

A very short, very heavy woman came to the door. Cool foul air drifted out past her. She had thick black eyebrows and she peered at me from under them, not trusting me at all. I said, 'Excuse me. Is Alice MacCann here?'

'Wrong house,' she said. 'Next door.'

I was going to explain, but she shut the door before I could say a word. Nice neighbour. I could see why Alice preferred to stay home, despite the danger.

Despite the danger? Going up the steps and along the narrow sidewalk and down the steps next door, I re-examined that thought. Was Alice staying home *despite* the danger, or merely in ignorance of the danger? Somewhere in the town of Wittburg there was a man – or a woman, but it was easier to think of him as a man – who had committed murder twice. If there was to be a third victim – and what was there yet to stop or deter the killer? nothing – the third victim would be Alice. She, too, had the knowledge of his guilt. He couldn't know yet that the knowledge had now spread to too many people for his methods. He could no longer kill as a practical answer to his problems. The time had come, though he couldn't know it yet, for him to flee.

But he must still think that murder was the answer. Charles Hamilton had learned the truth, and had talked coyly and knowingly, and the talk had filtered its way to the embezzler, and Charles Hamilton had died. From that point, there were two possible paths: either the killer learned that Hamilton had been helped by Alice, and supposed that Gar Jeffers had been told the secret by Alice, or the killer learned that Hamilton had talked to Gar, and had supposed that Gar and Alice would compare notes. Either path led to the same conclusion: in the killer's mind, both Gar and Alice must die. Gar was dead. Alice must be next.

But she didn't really believe it. Like me, she was untrained for the life of the hunted. I had not believed the enormity of the potential when I'd been stuck away in police headquarters, not even when it was happening to me, Alice now, in her own home and her own town, could not believe at the emotional level that she had become a hunted creature.

Well, I hadn't believed it, either, not really. I had been after her to protect herself, but it had been a kind of theoretical fussing, like a mother putting overshoes on a child when the morning sky is grey.

All at once, on the quiet sun-bright street, I believed it. Finally and suddenly, I had managed to convince myself. It had been insanity to let Alice come back here, imbecility. We should have gotten her a room at the motel, George should be guarding her night and day, her location should be kept a secret from everyone. You can't beat a loaded gun by sneering at it and calling it melodramatic. The gun's unanswerable argument is to kill you.

I ran the last part, bounding down the steps two at a time. My thumb was white and flattened and straining, pressed against the doorbell.

She was at home. She was alive. She had at least caution enough to peek through a living-room window at me before opening the door.

If I had been the killer, would I have fired through the window?

When the door came open, I bounded in like a hunted deer, and slammed the door shut. Alice stared at me, the colour draining from her face. 'What is it? Paul, what's the matter?'

'You've got to get out of here,' I said. 'Right now. Pack a suitcase and let's get going.'

She looked past me at the door, wide-eyed. 'What's out there, Paul?'

'Nothing. I don't know what. Maybe anything.'

'Well . . . what's got you so upset?'

'I've been thinking. I talked myself into it. Come on.'

'Paul, wait.'

I had her arm, and was propelling her toward the stairs. 'It's a miracle you're alive this long.'

'Paul, *please*. Wait now.'

I waited, but still burning with impatience, and too caught up in a belated sense of urgency to pay full attention to her.

'I'm safe here, Paul,' she said. She took my hand in both of hers, and pressed it. 'I really am. And you're frightened for me, aren't you?'

'Of course I'm frightened for you!'

'But I'm safest right here, Paul,' she said reasonably. 'He doesn't dare come back here. How does he know the house isn't watched by a whole cordon of policemen? I'm here like the goat staked out for the lion, so he doesn't dare do a thing. If you take me away some place else, and try to guard me, it'll just make things worse. He'll follow, and he'll know where I am. And he'll see the guards, and know who they are and how many they are and where they are, and he'll be able to plan. This way, he can't plan because he can't see the defences. Don't you see that?'

'But there *aren't* any defences!'

'But *he* doesn't know that. All he knows is he can't find them.'

At the moment, that was too subtle for me, and I wondered if it wasn't too subtle for the killer as well. He hadn't acted so far like a particularly subtle man. He had murdered once in a crowded parking lot, and the second time he had come straight to his victim's home. He was subtle with figures, with groups and bunchings of money, but as a killer he was anything but subtle.

Before I could try to express this, though, she went on: 'Besides, pretty soon he won't be thinking about trying to silence me any more. There won't be any point to it any more. Not after you talk to Mr Fleisch and give him the books.'

'They've already talked to Fleisch,' I said.

'Well! See?'

355

'But he doesn't *know* that yet. Fleisch won't get the books till after the *Beacon* comes out today.'

'Then you can still protect me till then.'

'Fat lot of protection I'll be.'

'Don't sell yourself short, Paul.' She touched her fingers to my face, and her eyes were warm and gentle. 'Come into the living room. Tell me all about the meeting with Mr Fleisch.'

'I wasn't there,' I said, allowing her to change the subject and to lead me into the living room. 'I got it second-hand.'

'Tell me, anyway.'

We sat on the sofa, and I repeated what Walter had told me, and she was pleased. She was sure Fleisch had capitulated without reservations. There had been a feeling at the plant for some time that Fleisch was insecurely fixed in his job. There had been a tight lid at the plant, as though Fleisch were frightened the McIntyres in their faraway resorts would hear something that would make them decide to find a new manager. So she was sure that Fleisch had truly given in, and would avoid trouble. And she was just as sure that Fleisch was this very minute writing a long letter to the owners, trying to claim the change in union as his own idea and finding justifications for it from the management point of view.

I supposed she was right. I also supposed, when I thought about it, that she was right about being safest here in her own home. Gradually, the panic urgency that had struck me outside faded away, and when, our conversation finished, Alice put on the records again and suggested we dance, I was pleased to agree, knowing that once again the dancing was only the prelude.

We left the house together at four o'clock and drove down into town, and picked up a copy of the *Beacon*. On the way back, she read the item to me. It was a front-page box headed, AN OPEN LETTER TO MCINTYRE EMPLOYEES. Alice read:

'Well over two thousand years ago, Heraclitus, the Greek philosopher, wrote, "There is nothing permanent except change." The world is constantly changing, and we ourselves are constantly changing. At the same time, it is true that we all try to keep to what we have and what we know, because it is never possible to tell if a particular change will be for the better or for the worse.

'We in the business of manufacturing and selling footwear of all kinds to the great American public are well aware of the constant nature of change. Fashions change, styles change, prices change, the needs of our customers change. If we are not capable of seeing the changes and willing to accept the changes, we will soon go bankrupt. Change is a way of life with us, and all we ever demand of change is that it give us some assurance that it will carry us forward rather than backward.

'In recent months, there have been growing signs of a desire for a particular change among the employees of the McIntyre Shoe Company, in reference to the kind of union representation and bargaining agent they believe best suited to their needs. Over thirty years ago, in the black year of 1931, when the jobless filled the nation and breadlines were the order of the day, the late William F. McIntyre, the respected and beloved founder of McIntyre Shoes, created the McIntyre Workers' Association, to speak with management on behalf of the workers. The MWA has a proud and enviable record over these thirty years. Memorial Hospital, McIntyre Park, low-cost housing, these and other improvements were made possible by the joint co-operation of "Bill" McIntyre and the MWA.

'No one can say that the MWA has not done a superlative job, and is not continuing to do a superlative job. But times change, the world changes, and for new problems there must be new answers.

'We live today in the era of the national union. Workers today are represented not only in their own plants, but throughout all the plants in their industry, and by lobbies in Washington itself. A number of McIntyre employees believe that the time has come to join this trend toward centralization of union power, and have requested that the entire body of employees be allowed to vote their choice, whether to remain with the MWA or to join a national union. Such a vote was made once before, nine years ago, and the overwhelming majority of the workers at that time chose to remain loyal to MWA. But nothing is permanent except change, and nine years is a long time.

'We feel that there is a certain degree of loss in the transfer of bargaining power from a local union to a national union. The close personal knowledge and respect between the officials of management and the officials of the union is lost. The particular and personal interest of the union for the workers of a single plant is lost. That there are advantages to place against these losses we do not deny. Whether the advantages

357

are more important than the losses it is up to the workers themselves to decide.

'We are in favour of an election. The Company will supply voting materials and a location for the voting at its own expense, and will grant its employees a half-day off for the election. In order to give both the MWA and the national union currently contesting it time to fully present their arguments to the workers, the Company proposes that this election be held three weeks from today, Friday, July 12th, the afternoon of which day the plant will be closed for the election.

'Regardless of the outcome of the election, the Company is certain that union negotiations in the future will be as pleasant, as productive, and as mutually satisfying as they have always been in the past. Since union representation is a concern solely of the employees of the Company, and not the concern of Company management, we intend no recommendations or statements of personal choice. The choice is up to *you*, the workers.

Jacob M. Fleisch,
General Manager'

I had her read it to me twice, the second time looking for implications and hidden reservations, but the thing seemed straightforward enough. Fleisch was prepared, with this letter, for either side winning the election. If the Machinists won, the letter could prove that it had been his idea, that he had 'recommended' change. If the company union won, the letter could provide plenty of proof that Fleisch had favoured the company union all along. Fleisch, according to the evidence of the letter, was resigned to the election and now was bending his energies to survive it unscathed.

I wondered if this letter had actually been written by Fleisch himself, or if it was another example of Sondra's talents. It had the same occasional shaky understanding of sentence structure, and it seemed a little pompous to be Fleisch. Slightly pompous, slightly devious, and slightly awkward in the writing; it sounded like Sondra, at that.

'Well,' said Alice, after the second reading, 'it looks like we've won.'

'This round,' I said. 'We're not finished yet.'

'But at least I don't have to play heroine-in-danger any more.

358

Mr Fleisch must have the books by now, and the killer must know there's no point trying to keep me quiet any more.'

She was right. We went back to the house, and Alice made us highballs, and I sat in the living room and kicked off my shoes and really relaxed, for what seemed like the first time in years.

After a while, she started the record player.

29

The next week was full and busy. We had a store front on Harpur Boulevard now, and my first job was to help convert it to a campaign headquarters. The shop had most recently been a barbershop, though it had been stripped of equipment when the last proprietor had left. The lower half of the walls was lined with a plastic covering in a pale green tile design, and the original plaster of the upper walls was painted a slightly darker shade of green. Earlier squares of grey paint showed where the mirrors and cabinets had been taken down, and capped water pipes jutted up from the floor along the left-hand wall, where the sinks had been. The floor was covered with cream-shade linoleum with a black fleck design, and four circular cutouts to the wood beneath showed where the barber chairs had stood. Four fluorescent lights spaced around the ceiling formed a square.

We had some money to spend on the place, but not very much. We were, after all, expecting to occupy the store for only three weeks. Nevertheless, there was a question of prestige, so the place had to look fairly decent.

Walter put me in charge of the refurbishing, and gave me George as assistant. We began by cutting the linoleum floor covering into strips, ripping it up, and throwing it away. It had not been glued down, but had – properly – been laid over a layer of old newspapers, three or four sheets thick. We threw out the linoleum and the newspapers – they were twelve years old, and I dawdled too much time away seated on the floor, caught in the fascination of reading yesteryear's headlines – and then we rented a buffer and cleaned and waxed the floor. It was a beat-up old wooden floor, with wide dirt-filled separations between the slats, but any wood floor with a polish on it, no matter how old or beat-up, still has more dignity than linoleum. Besides, a new floor covering would have been more expense than the union was willing to pay.

There was nothing we could do with the fake tile. It had been glued to the wall, and would bring half the plaster with it if we tried to rip it off. A coat of paint over tile, even fake tile, is the cheapest-looking thing in all the world, even cheaper-looking than tile itself, so we just ignored it, and painted the upper walls a pale cream colour to take attention away from the tile. Alice helped us with the painting. She had quit McIntyre, and was now our secretary-receptionist. And paint-roller-operator.

Next came the furnishings. George and I took the Ford and went to Watertown, where there was more variety and so more chance to find what we were looking for. An office-furniture dealer in Watertown supplied us with an ancient wooden railing, to use as a partition, plus three wooden desks with chairs and two wooden filing cabinets, all second-hand. The other two desks we found in a store in Wittburg.

We placed the furniture so as to hide what we hadn't been able to improve. The store was twelve feet wide and thirty feet deep. Eight feet in from the door we put the railing across. It was too wide, and George sawed it down to fit. In front of the railing, on the right, was Alice's desk, with a telephone. Directly opposite her, beyond the entrance, was a sagging green sofa we'd found in a used-furniture store and which made that area our waiting room. The sofa also hid one set of water pipes and some of the green tile. An outsize four-colour union poster – a brawny worker of the socialist mural type, clutching tools in his mighty hands and gazing resolutely forward, while smaller people representing Family, Neighbours, Government, and Industry stood behind him, watching him respectfully, with appropriately crude slogans above and below – filled a lot of wall behind Alice, hiding some more of the green tile.

Beyond the railing, the other four desks stood under the four fluorescent lights, the desks on the left placed so as to hide the other water pipes. Tan drapery material stretched across the width of the store behind the desks cut the length to twenty-two feet and hid the rear wall, which had resisted our efforts to prettify it.

The four desks were like so: Left front, Phil Katz. Right front (closest to Alice), me. Left rear, Mr Clement. Right rear, Walter. George didn't have a desk. He found a cot somewhere and put it behind the drapery, and spent most of his time back there on it, not quite asleep and not quite awake. Mr Fletcher, having found us a local lawyer to handle whatever problems might come up, had gone back to Washington.

Walter rented the store the same Friday that Fleisch capitulated, and we worked that weekend and Monday getting it fixed up and furnished. Tuesday, it opened. The plate-glass windows were full of posters, more posters were scattered around the walls inside, and a banner over the store front announced: HEAD-QUARTERS, WORKERS FOR AAMST.

On Tuesday, Walter gave me a new job. I was to hire school-boys to distribute pamphlets and put up posters. I was to keep them supplied, see they did their job, and keep the books on how much they were paid. It was undemanding work, leaving me plenty of time to enjoy my new return to calm and peace of mind, and I enjoyed it.

On Thursday, Edward Petersen, head of the bookkeeping department at McIntyre, was arrested for embezzlement and murder. I read about it in that afternoon's *Beacon*, under Sondra Fleisch's byline. They had caught him in a simple and undramatic manner. He had been trapped by cancelled checks. A comprehensive audit of the entire financial system at McIntyre had revealed that a number of cancelled checks were missing. These, of course, were the ones Petersen had made out for himself, the fake overtime checks. He had destroyed them as they had come back, cancelled, because an investigation, if begun, could use these checks to trace the banks where Petersen had been cashing the money. But the audit had come too suddenly, with no warning. The investigators had simply waited, watching every day's mail, and Thursday morning three of the false checks had come back, cancelled by three widely separated banks along the Eastern Seaboard, one in New York City, one in Columbia, South Carolina, and one in New Haven, Connecticut. A quick check of the three banks had revealed that in one of them, the one in New York, a new account had just been opened by Edward Petersen, using a check against the embezzler's account. Petersen, it was thought, had suspected that the end was near, and had started moving his funds to where he could get at them more quickly. Ironically, the three checks that had caught him had been prepared the day before Alice and I had stolen the books.

The three accounts had proved disappointing from a money point of view. Among them, they accounted for less than fifteen hundred of the over forty-five thousand dollars stolen in the last year and a half. But the police, Sondra assured us, were confident of tracing the rest of the money shortly. Petersen had been taken into custody.

That day, Thursday, I was out of the office most of the day, checking up on the high-schoolers who were doing the distributing for me. It hadn't been so long since I was a high-schooler myself, and I understood the temptation to drop a wad of pamphlets down a sewer, announce that the distribution had been made, collect the pay, and go to a movie. So I spent most of the day prowling around town, making sure the boys were doing the job.

When I got back to the store, at twenty to five, Alice had already gone on home. That surprised me doubly. In the first place, she was supposed to work till five. In the second place, I'd been going home with her after work all week. She'd been cooking dinner for me, and then we'd spend the evening together.

Phil was out somewhere, as usual, and so was Walter. Mr Clement sat birdlike at his desk, writing. It seemed he wrote minute mysteries for crossword-puzzle magazines, in his spare time, and since Fleisch's capitulation Mr Clement had had nothing but spare time. He used the nom de plume Felix Lane, which was supposed to mean something to mystery fans, and his minute mysteries, while diabolically clever, struck me as totally unreadable. He wrote a precise barren English, any sentence of which could have been used as an example in a grammar book, and the total effect of which was utter tedium. He wrote his little vignettes in pencil, printing rather than writing, and sent them off when finished to some woman in Washington who typed them for him.

I interrupted him to ask where Alice was, and he told me she'd left about twenty minutes before, and that Walter had driven her home. Since she should be home by now, I went back to her desk and used her phone to call. As I was dialling, George came lumbering out from behind the drapery and stood watching me, not saying anything.

She answered on the second ring. 'I've got a terrible headache, Paul,' she said. 'It's been drilling into me all day, so Walter finally drove me home.'

'I'll come on out,' I said.

'No, not tonight. I'm sorry, Paul, but I just feel miserable. I'm going straight to bed.'

'Oh. Well, I'll see you tomorrow then.'

'All right.'

'I hope you feel better tomorrow.'

'I'm sure I will.'

'Did you see where they got Petersen?'

'Yes, I saw it in the paper. That's good, isn't it?'

'It sure is. I'll see you tomorrow.'

'All right, Paul.'

I hung up and looked back toward the drapery, but George had retired again. I wondered what he'd been thinking just then, watching me. He had some kind of idea or theory about me, and he was watching me to see if he was right. I wished I knew what the idea was.

I left the office and went back to the motel. Walter wasn't there. I hadn't been spending my evenings in the motel myself, so I had no idea what Walter did with his free time. I grabbed a paperback book and read awhile, but felt at loose ends. I went out after a while and had dinner, and then went to a bar and drank beer and got into a discussion about unions with some of the other people there. They knew I was one of the men from the Machinists, and they were full of questions, most of which I couldn't answer. When I got back to the motel at midnight, about half in the bag, Walter was still out. I went to bed and fell into uneasy sleep, and heard Walter when he came in around two o'clock.

I was very tired and slightly hung over Friday morning. I had

364

to be at the office at nine o'clock, to hand out the day's quota of pamphlets, but after that I didn't really have to be there till late afternoon, when the boys would report back for their day's pay, so by quarter to ten I was back at the motel and sound asleep again. I'd managed to ask Alice if her headache was gone, and understand her when she said yes it was, but that was about the extent of the conversation I was capable of.

I slept four more hours, getting up just before two in the afternoon. The room was hot and stuffy, and so was my head, this time from too much sleep, particularly in bad air and at the wrong time of day. I took a cold shower, and went to the City Line Diner, where I finished off steak and salad and French fries and coffee and ice cream and coffee. Feeling more sensible, I went back to the office.

Once again, only Mr Clement was there, printing away laboriously with a number 2 pencil. When I got his attention, he told me Walter had gone off to confer with officials of the MWA, in re details of the election and of the change-over should the Machinists win, and had taken Alice with him to take notes. I sat around feeling glum, took care of my boys as they straggled in, and listened to Phil Katz complain, when he came back from an irritating interview with a television station manager in a town some distance away. It wasn't Watertown, it was some place else, thirty-some miles from Wittburg, but the station was a principal supplier of Wittburg's television viewing, and Phil had wanted to arrange time for speech-making by both MWA officials and Machinists. The station manager had contended that Wittburg was merely a village on the fringe of their area, containing something like seven per cent of their total audience, and he could hardly see any justification for turning over valuable air time under the circumstances. Phil was irritated beyond measure, and his ill humour perversely improved my own disposition somewhat.

George came wandering out from behind the draperies just after five o'clock, and he and Phil suggested I have dinner with them. Mr Clement intended to stay awhile; he was still working on his latest minute mystery. I said I would stay, too; I was waiting for Alice.

They looked at each other, and Phil said, 'Forget it, Paul. Those conferences with the party in power, they last for ever. They're liable to be at it till nine, ten o'clock.'

'Oh. Okay, then, I'll come along.'

There are two Chinamen in every city and town in the United States, at least two. If a town has a population of at least a thousand, two of that thousand will be Chinese. One of the Chinamen will run a laundry, and the other Chinaman will run a restaurant.

In Wittburg, it was called the Lotus Leaf. It was a small place, only eight or ten tables, occupying a second-floor over a men's clothing store on Harpur Boulevard. I assume the employees of the place were the family of the man who owned it. The owner sat behind the cash register next to the door, a small round sprightly man with practically no hair, just wispy white eyebrows and a fringe of mist around his ears. Two young men were the waiters – apparently the owner's sons – and through the kitchen door I caught a glimpse of the cook, a stout elderly woman who was probably the owner's wife.

I have always found the popular superstition that Chinese food leaves one hungry again an hour after eating to be false. It isn't the food that disappears shortly after the meal, it's the names. Except for egg drop soup and egg rolls, I have no idea what anything I ate was called. It was good, but anonymous, at least for me.

After dinner, Phil suggested we all repair to a bar nearby, where there were dart boards, and where George would drink orange soda, but I said, 'Not for me, thanks. Maybe Alice is home by now.'

They looked at each other again, and Phil said, 'You going out to her place?'

'Sure,' I said.

'Listen, she probably isn't back yet. I tell you about these conferences. Come on along for a while, and you can go up there later.'

'No, I'd rather go now.'

'What if she isn't home?'

'I'll wait for her.'

'Go ahead, Phil,' said George. He was watching me again, in that interested way.

Phil took a deep breath, and looked past my ear, and said, 'I wouldn't go out there if I was you, Paul.'

'Why not?'

He stalled long enough to light a cigarette, and then inhaled deeply again and said, 'Ah, what the hell. It's not up to me to cover. Walter's with her, that's what I mean.'

By then, of course, I should have guessed half a dozen times. But I hadn't. The idea hadn't even entered my mind. Not about either of them. My only fear with Alice was that she might want to cling too close. And Walter – Walter was married.

I still refused to believe it. I had to hear it all, the hard way. I said, 'So what? They went to the conference, so what?'

'I don't mean the conference,' Phil said. 'I mean Walter's got her now. I mean he took her away from you.'

'Yesterday,' said George. 'While you was out of the office.'

'Oh,' I said.

'Forget it,' Phil told me. 'She's just a piece of tail.'

'But she –'

'I could of had her, too,' Phil told me. He was being purposefully brutal, in a medicinal sort of way. 'I probably still could. But I keep away from that kind.'

'That kind?' Was I so dense? I'd met tramps before – there's always a few on any college campus, and my years in military uniform had been conducive to a study of the type – and I'd simply assumed that I could recognize one when I saw her. Was Alice like that? Was I only one in an endless string?

I remembered what she'd told me about going to the plant with Hamilton, those nights she was going over the books, how she'd justified their presence to the night watchman by making believe they were having an illicit affair. And I remembered that the watchman hadn't bothered to come down and see who was with her the time she'd taken me to the plant, though Hamilton was dead then. But the watchman had assumed that I was just another of Alice MacCann's boy friends. I wondered how often she'd used the leather sofa in that office. She couldn't be serviced at home, not while her grandfather was alive.

All the emotion had been within my own head. I had seen her the way I wanted to see her, excusing and ignoring and justifying all the signs. And that headache yesterday. 'It's been driving into me all day,' she'd said. 'I'm going straight to bed.' I could visualize Walter, cracking up on the other side of the room, trying to keep from laughing out loud.

Oh, the dirty *bitch*!

Phil said, 'Don't go up there, Paul. Take my advice. You take a swing at Walter and he'll tromp you. I'm telling you for your own good.'

He was right. I wasn't even to have the satisfaction of beating up my successor. Not that there would be much satisfaction in it, anyway. *She* was the tramp. *She* was the one who deserved the beating.

'Come on along with us,' Phil said again. 'We'll get stinko, and George can carry us home.'

'All right,' I said.

We left the restaurant and went around the corner to the side-street bar with the dartboards. I didn't feel like getting stinko. I nursed my beer, and while George and Phil talked together I tried to plot my revenge.

I had to *do* something. Alice couldn't be allowed to get away with it. She had made a fool of me – worse, she had allowed me to make a fool of myself – and it would gnaw at me until I evened the score.

George was watching me again, in his patient interested way, as though he expected me to do something very enlightening any minute. I'd noticed it before, and it had been bothering me – as his cryptic comments about Walter in the diner that time had been bothering me – and now, in my nervous angry state, it irritated me beyond standing. When Phil finally went away to the head, I said, 'All right, George. What is it?'

He looked mildly surprised. 'What's what, little friend?'

'What are you waiting for?'

He shrugged, and drank some of his orange soda. 'Nothing special,' he said.

'You've been staring at me, George. What do you want? What are you waiting to see?'

He seemed to think it over, fiddling with the half-empty glass of orange soda, and finally nodded. 'Sure,' he said. He turned to face me, and said, 'Like I told you once before, you're one of the bright boys. You figure to stick with the union and make vice-president some day. You're a lot like Killy, but younger.'

'Like *Walter*?'

'Well, sure,' he said, as though it should have been obvious. 'All you bright boys are the same. Everybody figures what you really want, all you bright boys, is to get ahead, but that ain't it. You want to get even, that's what you want.'

'You aren't making any sense, George.'

'Like with that girl reporter,' he said. 'She was one up on you, so you got even. And like when Walter swiped your idea about the books. You'd got him in dutch with Fletcher, being away all that time and everything, and he was just getting even. A lot of people would figure he swiped the credit so he'd be a big man with the union, but that isn't why. He did it to get even.'

'No, you're wrong. I don't like Walter any more than you do, but –'

'Who says I don't like Walter?' He seemed genuinely shocked. 'I like all you bright boys,' he said. 'I like you fine.'

'The point is,' I said grimly, 'Walter let Fletcher think it was his idea because he knew Fletcher was mad at me and wouldn't pay any attention to any idea that came from me.'

'Fletcher?' George grinned and shook his head. 'Fletcher's mad at everybody,' he said. 'All the time. He don't care where the ideas come from. If they're any good, he'll use them. You know that yourself.'

He was right. Fletcher might consider me the worst cretin alive, but if I came up with a useful idea, he'd accept it without a second thought. He was a perfectionist, and perfectionists don't care about people, only about results.

'And like when Killy wanted to go along with Fletcher when he called Washington,' George said. 'Killy was afraid Fletcher'd steal the credit from him, so he was getting even right away,

369

keeping Fletcher in line. Fletcher don't care about credit.' He drained the rest of the orange soda, and signalled for another. 'All you bright boys,' he said. 'You keep pushing, you keep on going up, you stab each other in the back, and people say, 'That guy, he'll do anything to get ahead.'' But that isn't it, is it, little friend? You people, you'll do anything to get *even*. And that's what keeps you pushing on up.'

'You're talking about Walter,' I said. 'Not about me.'

'You're younger, that's all.' He grinned amiably at me. 'That's why I been watching you. I never seen one so early before.'

That was ridiculous. I'm not like Walter. I never saw myself as one of those smooth devious characters, scaling the mountain of success with pitons hammered into the backs of their associates. I've never been clever enough, for one thing. And I've never had that much ambition, for another. It isn't success I want, it never has been. All I've ever wanted is peace and quiet, to be left alone to live my life, not bothering anyone else and with no one else bothering me.

If I get angered at being made a fool of, as Walter made a fool of me, as Alice made a fool of me, does that make me a Walter? Is it so unusual to be angry when you realize you've been played for a fool? George was clever about some things – he'd understood Walter's stealing of my idea, which I hadn't – but he fell victim to the easy generality.

'Just one thing, little friend,' he said. 'I told you, I like you. You're gonna want to get even with Killy now, and then he's gonna want to get even with you again, and then you'll have to get even with him again, and that's the way it goes. But he's been around longer than you. You want to be careful before you start anything.'

Phil came back then, and we did no more talking. I drank more steadily after that, and lost a few dart games – but didn't feel as though I had to get even with the people who won, so the hell with George's ideas – and when we left I was more than half drunk for the second night in a row. Well, I could sleep late tomorrow, so it didn't matter so much.

Phil drove, and I stretched out on the back seat. Phil switched the car radio on, and we listened to music. Then the one o'clock news came on, and the newscaster told us that Edward Petersen had not murdered Charles Hamilton. Edward Petersen had a rock-solid alibi for the time of Charles Hamilton's death. Petersen was still being held for the embezzlement, but the search for the killer of Charles Hamilton and Gar Jeffers had begun again. An arrest was expected shortly.

I was barely half awake on the back seat of the Ford. The news didn't interest me very much.

30

I woke up at 3:00 a.m., knowing who had killed Charles Hamilton and Gar Jeffers. I had a blinding headache, but I was wide awake and my mind was functioning with almost startling clarity, as though I'd been fed some sort of stimulating drug. I looked at my knowledge, and turned it over and over, and looked at it from every side, and knew it was the truth. And then I lit a cigarette, noticing that Walter's bed was still empty – tomorrow wasn't a workday, so he'd be spending the full night with her – and decided what to do with my knowledge. And when I had decided, I got out of bed and put on all clean clothes, and took the car keys from the dresser where Phil had left them, and went out to the car.

It was a clear night, and cool. The streets were empty. Harpur Boulevard stretched straight before me, flanked by solitary street lights and occasional distant bits of red neon, lit through the night in the windows of liquor stores and dry cleaners. I drove to police headquarters and parked illegally out front, and went inside to talk to the man on the desk.

'I want to talk to Captain Willick,' I said.

'Not here,' he said. He'd been reading a paperback, and considered me a minor interruption.

'My name's Paul Standish,' I told him. 'You call Captain Willick at home, and tell him I know who killed Hamilton and Jeffers.'

He frowned at me. 'Are you kidding? It's after three o'clock in the morning.'

'The killer may not be here tomorrow,' I said. That wasn't true, but I wanted Willick now. It was some small satisfaction to be able to roust Willick out of bed in the middle of the night, when he could have no complaint. I really was handing him a killer.

The desk man and I argued about it some more; neither of us getting anywhere, and then he used the phone and in a minute Jerry came wandering out to see me. The mocking smile was on his face, as usual, and he said, 'You just couldn't stay away, huh, Paul?'

'I want to see Willick.'

'Aw, now, Paul, you don't really want to wake the captain up in the middle of the night, do you?'

'I hope you're the one who booked Petersen,' I told him.

The smile faded, and he looked puzzled. 'Why?'

'Then you'll be the one he'll sue for false arrest.'

In a distracted way, he said, 'He can't sue me. He'd have to sue the city.'

'Then the city wouldn't like you very much.'

He shook his head impatiently. 'Come on now, Paul. You got some information or haven't you?'

'I'll tell Willick.'

'But you do know who killed Hamilton?'

'And Jeffers.'

'How come you didn't come forward with this information before?'

'I didn't have it before. I didn't have it till I knew Petersen had been framed.'

He considered, studying me, gnawing on his lower lip. Then he said, 'Take a seat over there. I'll be back in a little while.'

He went away, and I took a seat over there, and the desk man went back to his paperback book. I waited twenty minutes, and then Captain Willick came through the front door. He glowered at me, and said, 'This better be good. Come on.'

I came on. We went up to his office. Jerry was already there, with another plainclothesman I hadn't seen before. Willick sat down, and said, 'All right, I'm here. Let's have it.'

There was a chair, brown leather, facing the desk. I settled into it without being invited, and said, 'Who could have doctored the books? Give me the names.'

'Why?'

'I want to see if your list is complete.'

He grimaced, and said, 'Edward Petersen. Julius Koll. Mrs Alberta Fieldstone.'

'And one more,' I said. 'Alice MacCann.'

He frowned, and looked up at Jerry. Jerry was already looking defensive. He said, 'She works there, that's all.'

'She has keys to let her into the building and the bookkeeping offices at night, and she knows the combination to the safe. She helped me steal the books.'

They hadn't heard about the stealing of the books. Fleisch had kept quiet about that. I told them about it, and Willick nodded, looking grim, and said, 'All right. She could get at the books.'

'Wait a second,' said Jerry. 'She's the old guy's granddaughter. She's Jeffers' granddaughter.'

'That's right,' I said. 'She'd been embezzling for about a year and a half. She wants to get away from Wittburg, see the big cities, the big time. She was having an affair with Hamilton –'

'He was married,' said Willick.

'He was an ass man from way back, Captain,' said Jerry.

I nodded. 'His wife as much as told us that. Walter and me, when we went to see her the first time.'

Willick's fingertips rapped rhythmically against the desk top. 'All right,' he said. 'She's the granddaughter of one of the murdered men, and she was having an affair with the other. What else?'

'She was getting ready to leave,' I said. 'And she figured Hamilton would go with her. She told him all about the money she'd stolen, and figured he'd run away with her to help her spend it. But he was sceptical, so she took him to the bookkeeping office and showed him the books, showed him just how she'd done it. You can check with the night watchman there, Abner. He saw them go in together, at night.'

'If she planned to run away with him,' said Willick, 'why'd she kill him?'

'Because Hamilton didn't want to go. He played around, but he planned to stick with his wife. And he also planned to make an in for himself with the new local that was going to be started here by tipping Alice's embezzlement to us. He figured we could

374

use it as a bargaining weapon with Fleisch, which we did. But he wasn't clever enough, and Alice discovered somehow what he planned to do. So she shot him. If you check that gun you found, I bet you'll find it belonged to Gar Jeffers. She wiped it, and killed Hamilton.'

'Wait a second,' said Willick. 'That was *Jeffers'* gun?'

'Where else was she going to get one? Jeffers told me he once had a brother who was a policeman. Maybe it was the brother's gun. Would you have any records like that, showing the serial number or something of Jeffers' brother's gun?'

Willick pointed at the other plainclothesman and said, 'Find out. Quick.' The plainclothesman left, and Willick turned back to me. 'All right. Next.'

'Next, her grandfather. He came and talked to me that night, after your boys beat me up.' Willick winced at that, but said nothing. 'He was a friend of Hamilton's, and he knew that Hamilton had planned to turn some sort of scandal information over to the Machinists. I promised to help him try to find out what that information was. When he got home that night, he talked to Alice, asking her to help him find out if the information was in the bookkeeping department. He said something wrong, maybe, or maybe she slipped somewhere, or maybe he just noticed his own gun had been fired recently. I don't know which it was, you'll have to ask Alice. At any rate, she shot him, too. Then in the morning she went out to the store and came back and made believe she'd just found him dead.'

Willick thought it over. His fingers rapped and rapped against the desk top. He shook his head, and sighed, and said, 'You got any proof of all this, Standish?'

'Somebody framed Petersen. The day after Hamilton was killed, Alice made up three phoney overtime checks and sent them out to the three smallest accounts she had, so she wouldn't be losing much of the money. Then she faked Petersen's signature – that wouldn't have been hard to do, not with all the examples of it she could find around his office – and started an account in Petersen's name, switching money over from one of the overtime accounts. She did that the day *after* Hamilton was

375

killed. With murder having been committed, would any embezzler in his right mind keep on with business as usual, and even leave a clear link with an account in his own name?'

'I'm already convinced Petersen was framed,' Willick told me. 'That's what convinced me to come down here so late. But Koll could have done it just as easy as this girl. Or Mrs Fieldstone could have done it.'

'Alice has a thing about Los Angeles,' I said. 'That's where she wants to go, more than any place else in the world. I imagine you'll find most of the stolen money in accounts in Los Angeles banks.'

'You still aren't giving me proof,' he said.

I tried to think of something that would convince him. The fact that Alice had never been frightened enough for her own safety after her grandfather had been killed. The ease with which she had gone on being the tramp she'd always been. Her unusual skill at ferreting out the embezzler's methods in the books, even though it had taken a trained and inspired accountant, Mr Clement, all night to work his way through the tangle.

I explained these things to him, talking and talking, but I was beginning to realize I didn't have the kind of absolute proof he wanted. If I could convince him to make the arrest, she'd break down and tell the truth quickly enough, but first I had to convince him to make the arrest.

In the end, I didn't. It was the plainclothesman, coming back with the news that my guess had been right. Owen Jeffers' gun and badge had been turned over to his next of kin, his brother Gar, at the time of his death. The serial numbers matched. It was the proof Willick had needed.

It was nearly four o'clock by now, and time was running out, but there was still one more thing to set up, if I was going to get Walter cold. As Willick was getting to his feet behind the desk, I said, 'Captain, will you do me a favour?'

'What is it?'

'I got into a fight with Sondra Fleisch,' I said, 'and now I'm sorry for some of the things I said to her. I'd like to make it up to her, by calling her and telling her you're about to make the arrest.'

'Go ahead.'

'But that's just the point. She's still mad at me. She probably wouldn't even believe me. Would you call her?'

He shrugged. 'All right,' he said, and reached for his phone.

'And tell her to bring a photographer along.'

Willick made the call, and when it was finished, I said, 'By the way, the reason I didn't want to wait till morning. Walter Killy has been seeing a lot of Alice lately, and tonight he didn't come back to the motel. Alice has been looking for a man to run off with, and I wasn't sure but –'

Willick was already out the door.

31

They were in bed when we got there, but not asleep. There was a second-floor light on – her bedroom, I remembered – and when no one answered the doorbell, Willick figured they were packing or something, maybe slipping out the back door this very minute, so they broke the door down and stormed upstairs, and broke in upon the two of them in sweet oblivion.

I'm glad I didn't go up with Willick and Jerry and the other two. Sexual humiliation is always a very uncomfortable thing to be near. But I stayed outside on the sidewalk, while Willick and the others barged in, for reasons other than the humane. I was waiting for Sondra. She showed up just after the scream sounded from the second floor. The Thunderbird I'd seen in front of the Fleisch house now came whipping down the road and dug into a jolting stop in front of me. Sondra popped out on one side, and a pale-haired acne-troubled young man carrying a Speed Graphic climbed out on the other.

I ran over to Sondra, looking terrified and humble. 'Please, Sondra,' I pleaded, 'don't take pictures! Walter Killy's in there, don't take his picture!' Knowing then she would.

She swept by me without a word. She and the photographer went down the concrete steps and through the doorway and past the hinge-sprung door, and out of sight.

I went over to one of the two police cars we'd all come in. The driver was sitting there like a hypnotic subject, hands on the wheel, eyes on the road, cigarette in the corner of his mouth. I got his attention, told him Willick could find me back at the motel if he needed me any more, and left.

It was a longish walk back to police headquarters, but I didn't mind it. The night was cool and pleasant. Most of my headache had gone away, and for some reason I felt as though I'd had a full night's sleep instead of just two hours.

Willick and the others got back to headquarters before I did. In fact, the three cars – Sondra's Thunderbird grimly trailing the two official cars – passed me two blocks from headquarters. I kept walking, got to the Ford in my own time, and drove it back to the motel. I had to call Fletcher, but first I had to get rid of Phil.

Walter would no longer be running the operation up here, not after I called Fletcher. But who would be put in temporary charge? Not George, certainly. Not Mr Clement, just as certainly. It was between Phil and me, and Phil would be their first choice. But if I showed I was on the ball, and I put Phil to work so he wasn't available for instructions, then that left me.

When I got to the motel, I woke George and Phil and told them what had happened, and that a *Beacon* photographer had probably taken Walter's picture with Alice. I told Phil he ought to get right down to the *Beacon* office and see what he could do to soften the blow. George just sat up in bed and watched me. Phil, looking worried and irritated, dressed and hurried off to see what he could salvage. I told George I'd be right back, and drove down to the City Line Diner, where I had a cup of coffee, got a lot of change, and went to the phone booth.

It took me for ever to get Fletcher. First, I had to call the Machinists building, and got hung up a while with a night watchman or somebody. Eventually I convinced him to give me Fletcher's home phone number. He lived in Bethesda, outside the city.

It was by now nearly four-thirty in the morning. I called Bethesda, Fletcher's number, and listened to the sound of the ringing. On the ninth ring, Fletcher's voice, irritable and sleep-drugged, said 'Wh' is it?'

'This is Paul Standish, Mr Fletcher. I'm sorry to wake you up like this, but something's come up, pretty important.'

'All right.' The sleep was already leaving his voice. 'Get to it.'

'Alice MacCann has been arrested for the murders, Mr Fletcher.' I automatically paused there, to allow for his excited reaction.

What he said was, 'Uh huh. Did she do it?' I'd never heard him say 'Uh huh' in person, but over the telephone it was practically his entire conversation.

'It looks that way,' I said. 'But the thing is, Walter was with her when they arrested her.'

'Killy?'

'Yes, sir. They were in bed together. Now, the police are holding them both.'

'Uh huh,' he said. It was a sour sound.

'There was a photographer there,' I said. 'I sent Phil down to the *Beacon* to try to put the lid on.'

'Uh huh. What's your number there?'

'5-0404.'

'I'll call you back.'

'All right.'

I went back to the counter, and told the man on duty I was expecting a long-distance call on his pay phone. He said sure, and I ordered another cup of coffee.

The call came at five after five. Fletcher was brisk. 'For the time being,' he said, 'you take charge up there. If Killy is released, tell him he's relieved of duty there and he's to stay in the motel until I arrive. For everything else, carry on as though nothing had happened. If it's absolutely necessary to make a statement to the press, say the Machinists is conducting its own investigation into any possible wrongdoing on the part of its representatives. I'll get up there as quickly as I can.'

'Thank you,' I said.

'That was fast work on your part, Paul,' he said.

'Thank you,' I said again.

I went back to the motel, and told George what Fletcher had said. He smiled and watched me. Then I said, 'I think Walter's going to be mad when he gets back here. I've got to tell him he's not running the show any more, and that he's got to stay here in the motel until Fletcher arrives. I don't know what kind of temper Walter has –'

'Mean,' said George.

'Well, he won't try to take his mad out on you, because you're bigger than he is. But I'm smaller than him, and besides I'm the one who has to give him the bad news. I'd like you to be with me, and make sure he doesn't do anything to get himself in worse trouble.'

George grinned in great enjoyment. 'I sure will, little friend,' he said. 'Don't you worry about a thing.'

George really did like me, in his own off-beat way. His pleasure was genuine. I amused him by being an interesting phenomenon to watch, and that made me his friend. And I also suspected that as long as he called me 'little friend' it would mean he still liked me, but that if he ever should call me by my name, or by some other nickname, it would be time to watch out.

I remembered he always spoke of Walter as 'Killy.' I wondered if George had ever had a nickname for Walter, and what had happened between them to end it.

George and I went next door to my room, and waited for Walter.

32

Walter showed up at quarter to nine. He looked haggard and tense, his suit was wrinkled, and he was puffy-eyed from lack of sleep. He started to tell us what had happened, and that we ought to call Washington right away, and I interrupted, saying, 'I already called, Walter. I knew about it right when it happened, so I called Fletcher, like last time.'

'Good,' he said. He sank into the easy chair, relieved but bushed. 'Where's Phil?' he asked. 'They got pictures of me; they tried to get me involved with the little bitch. Phil's got to get the lid on.'

'I already sent him.'

He focused on me, slowly. '*You* sent him?'

'That's right.'

'What – Did Fletcher tell you?'

'Not exactly. Fletcher checked with somebody else in Washington, and then he told me I was to take over here until he could get here. And that you were supposed to stay right here in the motel.'

'You're taking over?' His expression was changing, he was looking sullen and angry, but then he glanced at George, and his expression became wary. 'What if I tell you to go to hell, Paul?' he asked me. 'What if I go down to the office and run things just like usual?'

I shrugged. 'I'm sorry, Walter, but if Fletcher asked me about it I'd have to tell him the truth.'

'You rotten little bastard.' He said it quietly, almost unemotionally.

George stretched hugely, and yawned, and said to me, 'Okay if I go get some breakfast, little friend?'

'Sure,' I said. 'Have Clement drive you.'

'Okay, little friend.' He looked briefly at Walter, and smiled his dreamy interested smile, and left.

Walter and I sat in silence awhile, and then he lumbered to his feet and went away into the bathroom. I heard the shower running. I picked up the book I'd been reading, lit a cigarette, and settled down to wait. I still didn't feel tired.

When Walter came back, nude except for a white towel around his middle, he looked in better shape. The puffiness and uncertainty were gone from his face. He looked at me, lying on my bed, and said, 'I'll ride through this one, Standish. I want you to know that. I'll get chewed by Fletcher and a couple other people for endangering the union's standing in the community, and that'll be it. I'll keep my job, and you'll still be working for me.'

'I don't think so,' I said. 'Phil will do a good job of keeping things relatively quiet, under my direction. I'll handle things well here, and Fletcher will take you back to Washington with him, but he'll leave me here in charge, because I'm doing the job. Fletcher doesn't care about people, only about results. You'll keep your job, Walter, but I won't be working for you. I'll be working for me.'

'You'll be coming back to Washington in two weeks,' he said. 'I'll have almost six months to even the score. I just want you to know where you stand, Standish.'

'Stand Standish?' I grinned at him. 'The score *is* even, Walter. You stole an idea from me, and you stole a girl from me. Now we're even.'

'I don't figure it that way,' he said.

'I didn't think you would.'

He stood glowering at me, his hands on his hips, his face thrust forward, the whole stance somehow very familiar. Then I realized why. I'd never seen it from this close before, but I had seen it, a number of times. From the stands, during a football game, when a particularly vicious player is finally caught on a personal foul, clipping or unnecessary roughness or something like that, and the player stands just that way, glaring at the referee. It isn't outraged innocence, it's outraged omnipotence. This shouldn't have happened to *him*.

So there's the other side of the club-car football hero.

After a minute, he said, 'Don't think you're riding so easy,

Standish. You played around with that little bitch yourself. She could implicate you, too, you know.'

'I don't think so,' I said. 'I think she'll be too busy proving she didn't kill anybody.'

'You mean *trying* to prove,' he said.

'No, proving. The note exists. Unless she destroyed it, and I don't think she's that stupid.'

His face looked absolutely blank. In the silence, I could hear my own breathing and the passage of cars outside and the weight of the sun on the motel roof.

He said, 'How did you know about that?'

'About the note? In it, Gar Jeffers admits killing Hamilton and states he's taking his own life. That's the story she's telling, isn't it?'

'How did you know, Standish? Where did you hear it?'

'I didn't hear it. It's the truth.'

'But –'

'I talked Willick into thinking her guilty. She is, in a moral sense. She was playing around with Hamilton. They were both involved in the embezzlement, although she did all the actual work of it. But when they got enough – fifty thousand, I suppose, or maybe a hundred thousand – they were going to take off together. Gar found out what was going on, and he blamed Hamilton. I don't know if he knew about the embezzlement, or just about the affair. Whichever it was, he tried to stop it. I suppose he talked to both of them, and Hamilton told him to mind his own business, and I guess Alice went into her act, playing Trilby to Hamilton's Svengali, getting the blame off herself onto Hamilton, being sure her grandfather was still sympathetic toward her and wouldn't blow any whistles. But Gar couldn't stand it. Alice was all the family he had, and Hamilton was a bum who'd been cheating on his wife for years. So when Gar couldn't take it any more, he dragged out his brother's gun and took it to work with him in his lunch bucket. He tried one last time to talk Hamilton into leaving Alice alone, and Hamilton told him to go to hell again, and Gar shot him.

'I suppose Gar expected to be picked up right then. He shot

384

Hamilton in the parking lot, with a hundred witnesses around. Alice would have picked a quieter spot. I suppose he hadn't really thought beyond shooting Hamilton. Just shoot him, and then wait for them to come get him and take him away. But they didn't come to get him. Everybody milled around, and nobody even looked twice at Gar. He was an old guy, and a friend of Hamilton's, and he had every right to be in the parking lot, and nobody thought for a minute he'd had anything to do with Hamilton's death.

'So that gave him a chance to think about what would happen next. If he gave himself up, or if he were caught, the whole truth would come out, and Alice would be neck-deep in scandal. So he got away from there and decided to keep quiet. But you and I were picked up and slapped around, and he figured that was his fault, too. He saw his guilt spreading out all the time, including more and more things. He wanted to confess and get it over with, but he couldn't because of Alice. That's why he came to me. He couldn't go to the police, so he came to me, hoping I'd somehow figure out the truth and take over the job of exposing him. He couldn't do it himself, but he had to have it done.'

I shrugged. 'I guess I didn't impress him very much. He went home that night and thought it over and decided there was only one way out. He'd said something to me about having lived a long life already, and now he figured it was time to end it. He couldn't admit his guilt. The law was working overtime not looking for the killer. I had proved a dud. So he got out the gun again and shot himself. There's no other reason for the gun still to be in the room with him. Then Alice came along and read the note he'd left, and knew she couldn't show it to the authorities, because it told too much about her. I suppose she's claiming Hamilton forced her to do the embezzling?'

'Yes.' He seemed dazed. Then he shook his head, rousing himself, and said, 'But why'd Hamilton write to us? If he was going to take off anyway, with Alice and the money, why start a big fuss about the union?'

'I don't know. I can make a guess. He was a guy who'd lived through twenty years of nothing working out the way he wanted it. I suppose he never really believed this setup with Alice would work out either. It sounded good, running off with a good-looking girl and a lot of money, but maybe it sounded *too* good. It couldn't really happen, not to Charlie Hamilton. Chuck Hamilton. He was like a man who sells fallout shelters with twenty-year mortgages. He's preparing for something he doesn't really believe in. So all the time he was figuring to run off next month or next year, he was still living his ordinary life and making plans for that ordinary life for next month and next year. And maybe, if the thing fell apart, he figured he could sell out Alice and get himself a cushy berth with the union. Alice had done all the embezzling herself. There wouldn't have been anything but her word that he'd been involved, and who would have believed her if he'd been the guy who turned her in?'

Walter said, 'So she didn't kill anybody. And you knew it all along.'

I shrugged.

He said, 'But why make up that other story and sell it to Willick?'

'I owed Willick a pratfall. He's taking it now. Sooner or later, he's going to listen to Alice, and he's going to send somebody to look where she says she hid the note, and it's going to be there. Then he's going to know he just took a pratfall, and he's going to know I did it, and there isn't going to be a thing he can do about it.'

'And you wanted to make sure it was a noisy arrest,' he said. 'You knew I was with her. You wanted to make sure there'd be photographers.'

There was nothing to say to that. I yawned and stretched, suddenly very tired. I was way behind on my sleep, and I wanted to be fresh and alert when Fletcher got here. I put down my book and took off my glasses and scrunched lower in the bed, resting my head on the pillow. 'Don't go running off anywhere, Walter,' I said. 'You'll just get yourself in trouble with Fletcher.'

He didn't answer me, but I knew he'd stay put. Right now, he was too dazed to think very clearly. By tonight, when Fletcher arrived, Walter would be his old self again, smiling and cheerful, apologetic to Fletcher about the business with Alice, but making a locker-room joke out of it, and watching for his chance to stick the piton in my back. That was all right. By tonight, I'd be on the ball again myself.

Drifting down into sleep, I thought of George, and saw his big heavy face, saw the interested eyes and the sleepy smile and the slow big body, and I thought I could hear George chuckle and say to me, *Little friend, you are Killy.*

That was a strange thought. I took it with me down into sleep.

I am Killy.

ALLISON & BUSBY CRIME

Jo Bannister
A Bleeding of Innocents

Simon Beckett
Fine Lines

Denise Danks
Frame Grabber
Wink a Hopeful Eye

John Dunning
Booked to Die

Chester Himes
All Shot Up
The Big Gold Dream
Cotton Comes to Harlem
The Heat's On
A Rage in Harlem

Russell James
Slaughter Music

H. R. F. Keating
A Remarkable Case of Burglary

Ted Lewis
Get Carter
GBH
Jack Carter's Law
Jack Carter and the Mafia Pigeon

Ross Macdonald
The Barbarous Coast
The Blue Hammer
The Far Side of the Dollar
Find A Victim
The Galton Case
The Goodbye Look
Meet Me at the Morgue
The Ivory Grin
The Moving Target
The Way Some People Die
The Wycherly Woman
The Zebra-Striped Hearse
The Underground Man
The Lew Archer Omnibus Vol 1
The Lew Archer Omnibus Vol 2

Margaret Millar
Ask for Me Tomorrow
Mermaid
Rose's Last Summer
Banshee
The Murder of Miranda

Richard Stark
Deadly Edge
The Green Eagle Score
The Handle
Point Blank
The Rare Coin Score
Slayground
The Sour Lemon Score

Donald Thomas
Dancing in the Dark

Marilyn Wallace (ed.)
Sisters in Crime

I. K. Watson
Manor

Donald Westlake
Good Behaviour
Sacred Monster
The Mercenaries
Trust Me On This